THE
PRAGUE
REPRISAL

This book is a work of fiction. Names, characters, places and incidents are the product of the author's imagination or are used for fictitious purposes. Any resemblance to actual events, locales, or persons, living or dead, is coincidental.
Copyright © 2022

All rights reserved. In accordance with the U.S. Copyright Act of 1976, the scanning, uploading, and electronic sharing of any part of this book without the permission of the publisher constitute unlawful piracy and theft of the author's intellectual property. If you would like to use material from the book (other than for review purposes), prior written permission must be obtained by contacting the publisher at robertushybooks@gmail.com. Thank you for your support of the authors' rights.

First Edition: April 2022
10 9 8 7 6 5 4 3 2 1

ISBN 9798440963498

www.robertushy.com

ALSO BY ROBERT USHY

The Ivory Betrayal
Protecting The Pride
The Zodiac Connection

THE *PRAGUE REPRISAL*

Created and Written by Robert Ushy

Experience Life. Live Life. Love Your Life.

Taking a journey into yourself is how we learn about what we love and who we are. Once you discover that true identity, embrace it. You will find that the sun shines brighter, colors are more fruitful, and that even time slows so we can enjoy our surroundings. Appreciation for others begins with appreciation for ourselves. Smile at yourself in the mirror, a puddle, or window reflection every day. I guarantee it will always make you feel better.

PROLOGUE

A late afternoon setting sun signified the turn of the day into another early evening over the city of Prague in November, but the flaming ball seemed destined to stray a little longer before dipping behind Petrin Hill. The last golden rays would be used to highlight the picturesque ninth century Prague Castle, holding it as the perfect backdrop for the enamored couple ambling across the middle of Charles Bridge.

It had been a perfect day the woman thought to herself while fixing the wool knit cap, and her dark auburn red hair that swayed more towards the brown end of the color dye spectrum. Her boyfriend only smiled as he waited while holding the extended arm of the selfie stick to work the phone's camera feature.

Smiling together, another beautiful photo for their journey. An iconic baroque statue of a patron saint on one side of them, and the majestic castle alive as the framework behind. Again, pleased with the turnout, she inhaled a deep breath of the clean crisp fall air and accepted the natural splendour of where they were standing.

Charles Bridge was still full of tourists, but unlike in the middle of the summer months, you could move around freely. She spun. Closing her eyes and slowly twirling around twice. Freedom was all she could feel. A slight giggle followed assuming she must look like a young school girl on a playground.

A local busker's talented accordion interrupted her blissful daydream as she sensed his approach. The tempo was slow, romantic, and as she opened her eyes, her chest erupted with elation. She almost cried instantly. Her boyfriend had slipped onto one knee and was holding a small red velvet box in his outstretched gloved hands. Finding his piercing blue eyes, she wanted to scream at the top of her lungs, but found no words. The perfect day was concluding as he was about to propose.

The soft tempo of the music was drawing a crowd of onlookers as excitement was growing. Murmuring to keep the moment intimate, the gathering's anticipation peaked with the kneeling man beginning to speak.

"Sophia Marie—" He began.

"*sawf tahtariq li'anana sanaeish 'iilaa al'abad!*" Screaming interrupted the music as another man ran up to the group of people that had surrounded the couple in their moment of personal paradise. Yelling it again, he raised his hands, jacket fell open and panic erupted.

Chaos and shrieking replaced the soft tones of the street musician's keys when the crowd saw the explosives wrapped around the man's torso, but they did not detonate. There was a malfunction and now the suicide bomber was panicked. He screamed a third time while furiously punching at the button on his handheld device.

The piercing blue eyes from the fiancée-to-be with the chiseled jawline turned from adoration into one of an apology. He did not hesitate. When the explosion did not occur, he sprang from the cobblestoned archway, taking two steps before launching himself into the body of the terrorist. Catching the man flush in the stomach, the two were propelled up and over the heavy stone railing towards, and then down to the cold Vlatava River below.

Sophia ran to the ledge, unable to yell, scream, anything that would produce a sound. Her throat closed, cutting off the intake of oxygen and strangling herself from somewhere within her heart.

Now only a step from edge, she was determined to use one of the patron statues as her own launching point and dive in after the man she loved, but that would never happen. Reaching out, she was hit by the shock waves, tossed in the air and thrown back across the celebrated bridge as it exploded from below.

Stones and history were cascaded across a now darkening sky with the sun shielded itself from the carnage. The large explosion had blown a massive hole in the midst of Charles Bridge, but could've been catastrophic if it had happened when the attacker had first attempted to detonate.

Sophia's ears rang with a dense whine. She tried to stand, but fell, her eyesight blurred between reality and complete darkness while her equilibrium was impossible to balance. The bomb had rocked her, but not killed her, at least not physically.

Small particles of stone continued to slowly rain down as smoke and dust gently dissipated. Crawling, she found herself on the opposite side of the bridge. At the base of the Statue of St. John of Nepomuk, Sophia felt something soft. It was small and rounded, but not a rock or stone.

Her hands were cut and scraped, eyesight fuzzy, but she knew what it was. The little red velvet box which was holding her engagement ring. Through the blood and tears, Sophia found her voice and screamed before curling into the fetal position. Wailing as the terror subsided, she passed out still clutching the small red velvet box tightly.

PART I

Chapter ONE

"Rock! Rock!" Sneakers squeaked as the six men hustled back and forth on half of the green and grey Flex Court. A weekly pickup basketball game, the friends and acquaintances gathered under the lights on the famed courts of the Goodman League in southeast Washington, D.C.

"Yeah Dame! All the way." The square-jawed man in navy shorts with a small white bison head on the right thigh spun away from a block and slipped a bounce pass to his current teammate streaking towards the hoop.

It was the third week of August, nearly ten o'clock at night, humid, but still some of the nation's capital's best seasonal temperatures were approaching as the month of September drew nearer. During the primary summer months of June and July, the metal pulpits of supporter's stands along the courts would be filled with local residents hooting and cheering while the league's commissioner entertained them with commentary and play-by-play. New stars and heroes were born every summer as one of the premier summer basketball leagues in all of the United States continued attracting some of the very best athletes from high school, college, streetball and even the odd appearance from NBA stars past or present.

"Post it Mike." Another quick instruction to the man defending their opponent just outside the key. "Pressure. Make him chuck! Bro's ice tonight." With that encouragement, the bigger man closed his defensive stance onto the attacker, forcing him to shoot prematurely. "I got glass." The biggest voice on the court called again before the ball was out of the shooter's hand. "Yeah bro, great D!"

Even with the organized league finished for another summer, the lights shone brightly with four separate half court games in action while night ascended on the recreation center of Barry Farms. Demolition and construction sites still surrounded and projected above as the neighborhood's skyline and backdrop, with the city poised to redevelop the urban housing project, but all at a standstill as years of changes were pending while the local district continued fighting to increase their Historical Landmark status and improve the number of affordable homes to be constructed.

"Flat out! Make noise!" The court general barked to his teammates while directing their movements with his left hand.

"You all talk bro." The larger defender swiped at the ball, but his hand was swatted away. "Drive on me. Try it." A faked stutter step didn't affect the ball controller, and he met eyes with his opponent who laughed while quickly wiping the sweat from his brow and pulling back on his cluster of dreadlocked hair.

"Hope your girl ain't here to see this." Winking at the man, the square-jawed offender dribbled twice before stepping out to his right, exploding back left while driving the ball between the man's legs, whirling around him and finishing with a perfectly placed finger roll lay-up after completing a three hundred and sixty degree rotation in mid-air.

The arrogant defender lunged at the first movement from the ball handler and knew he was caught. Trying to reverse his course, then stop the ball from passing under his legs, instead the man knees buckled, crashed into one another and forced him to sprawl onto the court face first before rolling over to see the winning bucket drop through the netting with the shooter only looking at him instead, and smiling.

Whistling, cawing, and a few cursed laden calls of appreciation echoed following the six men leaving the court from the few observers they had watching their game. "Shit bro!" The larger dreaded man grabbed his opponent from behind, sucking his head under his arm and tightening around the neck with the crutch of his elbow joint. "You done did me dirty." Still laughing, he released his friend.

"No, no, no Mac. That wasn't dirty. That was just plain *nas-ty!*" The teammate referred to as *Dame*, Reggie Lillard chided back as the two teams reached their bags, towels and replenishing drinks.

"C'mon man. You should know better than to challenge your boy." Another of the players added. "Didn't he constantly whoop ya ass in college too." Another chorus of laughter erupted between gulps.

"You should really know by now that *DHL* always delivers." A fourth member spoke up, this time one of the dreadlocked man's current teammates referencing the shooter's collegiate All-American nickname.

"Alright. Enough fun with Mac," A quick pause from *DHL* as he purposely overreacted by looking around and pretending to scan the faux crowd. ", unless of course Tanya's here somewhere?" Another burst came the group with even Mac having to laugh this time before throwing his towel at his friend.

The men continued reminiscing through the night's game, their plays and misplays before slowly departing from one another. Hugs were exchanged amongst friends, and as Reggie embraced the shooting hero he whispered to him. "I put a USB into your bag earlier. Photos from my phone that I took a few days ago. He's into something big this time."

"Thanks Dame." It was a short hushed reply, but also sincere and purposely kept private to ensure nothing seemed different from any other of the men's weekly farewells. He knew Reggie was referring to his own boss, Texas Senator John Ryan Paxton. Lillard was a staff assistant, one of many, and it was doubtful that the Senator even remembered his name, but to him, his friend was immensely valuable. In Washington, political capital was gold, but as a journalist covering the men and women in power, those relationships with staffers, janitors, and security guards were worth even more than that. Those who sat in the upper thresholds of D.C. often forgot about who truly had the power to take it away from them if they ever chose to do so.

Excitement mounted in his stomach as he wanted to race home, find the small digital device and plug it into his laptop, but he knew he had to continue the same routine as he always did. Nothing different from any other Monday night pickup game, you never knew who was watching from the shadows.

"*Der-ian* Haynes." A deep graveled voice dragged out the syllables of his first name while calling to him as he reached the open gates of Barry Farms Recreation Center. "DHL, the *legend* of Howard University lives and breathes on a basketball court again." The old man drew out his vowels with an accent crossed between Mid-Atlantic America and New York City. He chuckled as his hand was extended.

"Evening, sir." Haynes accepted the man's outstretched hand and jested back. "Just fooling around a little with some friends." A quick flash of his college days filled his thoughts. As an All-American Sophomore he led Howard University to their first ever NCAA Tournament victory. The fourteenth seeded Bison were thrust on the back of his fifty-two point performance, toppling the heavily favored Duke Blue Devils and garnering him legendary status among the alumni. *DHL* was born.

"That was more than fooling around out there son." The grizzled man laughed again. "That was the dominance that I remember seeing from a young man destined to be a star in the NBA."

"Thank you, sir." It was all Derian could think to say. The highs of being a collegiate superstar were immediately met the following season by devastation. Four games into his junior season, catastrophe struck. A home game against rival Hampton University, he was driving to the basket, went up for a finger roll, but then landed awkwardly. Knee twisting on impact, combined with his leg seizing like cement into the court, three of his four ligaments were torn in his left knee instantly and then followed up with a broken kneecap when he crashed hard into the backboard stanchion.

"Tough break what happened," The silver haired black man grumbled softly. ", but it looks like you're moving around pretty good out there nowadays." Adding more jovially with his eyes drifting towards the lighted courts where another group of men had taken their place on the open half-court.

Nodding respectfully, Haynes responded. "It felt good today. I must've loosened up properly."

"That's the key." Another laugh and cough from the man before he became more direct. "Listen, I don't want to keep ya, but I run one of the best teams here in the Goodman League every summer, and if we added you to it, it could open some exposure, maybe get ya back on some NBA team's radars seeing ya play like that."

Returning the good-humored attitude, Derian tried to be direct with his recruiter, but didn't want to offend the man. "Thank you again, but I'm a journalist now." A quick look back towards the lit courts as other men darted back and forth. "I just play for fun every now and then."

"Okay son, I'll respect that." Another deep inhale of humid air after a second brief collection of coughs. "Washington Post, right?"

"That's correct." Haynes hesitating when he spoke this time. Carefully looking over the old stranger one more time as he felt his heart beat extra and pulse quicken. Was there something more behind this not-so chance encounter, or was his mind over-reacting to his anticipation. He gripped the shoulder strap of his knapsack a little tighter knowing the USB was hidden somewhere inside.

"You do good work there. You're honest, just like your mother was." The man's reference snapped Derian's mind back to the present and away from the shadowed conspiracies it was beginning to head towards.

"Did you know my mother?" A simple question that was truly asked.

"No, nothing like that." A rumbled clearing of his throat. "I just like honesty in the media when it comes to politics, and she seemed genuine." Smiling again, he chuckled to himself. "I also like to see strong black folk make that white country club squirm when they get caught red-handed." Haynes couldn't help but laugh at the statement. The grizzled man tried to stand a little more upright as he offered his hand once again. "I hope you change your mind about playing son, you still have a lot left out there. If you do, just ask anybody around here for Doc and they'll get you in contact with me.

"Thank you again." Derian accepted the man's hand one last time. "I honestly am happy with just playing pickup, but will keep you in mind." The two men parted.

Reaching his road bike, Haynes looked back towards the courts. Against the backdrop of the night, he could see the old man's shadow gingerly hobbling towards the active games, probably checking out more possible players. He was truly flattered by the recruitment, but also sincere in his feelings about not playing professionally anymore.

Determination and anger consumed him after the major injury. Anger first, fueled by the continued questions not of him playing again, but if he could ever even walk properly. Once his mother felt that enough time had passed for his self-pity and dwelling, she helped turn that negative energy into positive anger. Determination.

Using her connections in the government, she was able to get him into Walter Reed National Military Medical Center. He wasn't admitted as a patient or receiving care, but was able to visit, speak with doctors and other military personnel recovering themselves. Many of his visits were with soldiers that had lost limbs or battled with trauma or stress disorders, but also he saw how much heart they continued to fight with to get back into their units or general day-to-day life.

Derian's focus changed into coming back even stronger, better, and to put himself back onto that stage he desired. He was nearly there when it all crashed back down once again. A medical red-shirt designation allowed him an extra year of college to recoup, recover, and then return as a senior student the following year, but tragedy struck one more time.

One late July evening, he had just finished a ten mile run and was expecting his mother to return home from work, but was instead met by two police officers at his front door. A three car accident on the Anacostia Freeway had claimed his mother's life. The strongest person he had ever known, the one who believed in him the most, was gone, and so was his desire to continue to fight and get back on a basketball court.

The loud rattling of a backboard and jeering from a powerful dunk returned Haynes to his present situation. Thinking of that day brought a pit back to his stomach, but no tears. He had used all of those up years ago.

    The pit of dread changed to excitement as he remembered the USB that was hidden amongst his things in the backpack still slung over his right shoulder. Reggie believed that it contained something big, something compelling enough for him to risk being caught taking pictures of, or sneaking out of a sitting Senator's office. Derian was definitely intrigued. He finished unlocking the latch securing his hybrid bicycle, connected his helmet and raced home.

Chapter TWO

A gentle hand on her shoulder was followed by the simple request to return her seat back into the upright position. It was a pleasant appeal and smile from the flight attendant, but the actual reality of landing soon back in Prague brought more feelings of anxiety and uneasiness.

Her hairstyle had changed from a long, dark auburn red to a short, wavy blond sitting just below the ears, and her plane ticket read, Rachel Stackwell, but the last time she was in the medieval city of Prague, she was Sophia Warner.

The lush greens and browns of forests and fields below transformed into the cascade of orange roofs, a staple of the majestic city, and then back to the deep greens as the large airplane banked away from the urban cluster for a southwesterly arrival into Václav Havel Airport. A low rumbling signified that the landing gear was extending and Rachel, Sophia, felt her stomach knot once more.

Looking down at her bare hands, she closed her eyes. They did not quiver any more. It had been nine years since that day on the Charles Bridge, nine years since terror had struck her directly when her lover, the man she never got the chance to answer, to officially become her fiancée, heroically sacrificed himself for what could have been an even larger, more devastating and tragic attack.

Sophia had been temporarily assigned to the American embassy in Morocco as a translator and interpreter when she met Sean Trevelyan, a U.S. diplomat's aide who had eager aspirations of his own, but still relatively new to the Foreign Service lifestyle. He was fit, had a full head of dirty blonde hair and a tightly trimmed beard that sat barely above what was considered facial hair, but still enough to add character to his face. Through his professional, yet rugged looks, it was his piercing blue eyes that first caught her attention. They were determined, yet soft and compassionate, and she couldn't ever remember meeting anybody with such quietness in their eyes.

Sophia was trying to find a free minute to speak with the American ambassador, Sean's boss, but was directed to him instead. Their meeting was simply happenstance, completely unexpected for her, but one that she later believed to be a fateful one.

Her career involved much more travel around Europe, the Middle East and back to North America, but they found time for each other when they could.

Meeting in Paris, Rome, Cairo, anywhere that could be considered a central meeting place, thus allowing time together. Their fling turned into months of finding reasons to see one another, and then an additional year of actively scheduling their lives around the other's to ensure much longer bouts within the same city so they could actually *be* together. Prague had been a celebration. Prague had been perfect. *Had been.*

Another drop in altitude resulted in her stomach fluttering again. Opening her eyes, Rachel tightened her jaw. She could feel a tear forming in the corner of her right eye, but she would not allow it. One last thought of Sean's soft, caring blue eyes, but that was all she would permit of herself. Focusing instead on the walls that she had built up strong in order to keep those feelings away over the past number of years. She knew she was stronger than this.

The rear wheels touched lightly, followed by the nose and the plane was parallel on the runway. Rachel decided to slowly disembark the plane, not out of procrastination or fear of in fact being on the ground, but simply because she truly had no idea where she was going. She had been to Prague more than once before, but never in the international airport. The train systems connecting Europe were superb, fast and reliable. In fact, it was her desired way to travel. Slower than an airplane, and sometimes considerably more hectic with station changes and waiting times, but much of the countryside across the many nations were a soothing backdrop to just relax against and watch peacefully go by. Following the herd towards the baggage carousel was her plan, and then she would find her way to customs and certainly a row of waiting taxis outside.

Her phone buzzed once, twice, and then a third time as reception was located and missing emails and messages poured in from students and colleagues. After Sean, she had left her job, retreated away from society and essentially disappeared for a long while. When she did decide to re-emerge, she nestled into the college town of Madison, Wisconsin, was hired as a professor at the University of Wisconsin-Madison's Linguist and International Divisions where her skills only helped their already exceptional foreign language department continue to be one of the country's most prominent.

Rachel was fluent in nine base languages, formidable in another dozen or so and even passable with some rudimentary dialects if it was needed. She specialized in Middle Eastern tongues, but the major languages of German, French, Spanish, Mandarin and Russian as well. Lately, she had been exploring the Old Church Slavonic while attempting to have it added to the specialized language course programs that her university offered. In fact, that was the only part that excited her about this trip back to Prague.

Skimming over the messages from a couple of her summer students, her eyes focused on the one from her colleague, her friend Iris. An Englishwoman teaching at a British prep school in London. They met two years ago at the International Languages and Linguistics Conference in Lisbon. It was Rachel's first time attending the annual event and one in which she grew to eagerly anticipate each announcement for its next location. *Let me know when you land! Can't wait to see you again!!* The messages were short and made Rachel smile again. Last year, they explored and feasted in Paris. Keeping in touch throughout the year via emails, messages, and video calls, but they only had the opportunity to spend time in one another's company this one week per year. It was nice to have somebody that she truly felt was a friend.

Iris was also a language enthusiast, but was more fascinated and focused with the history of it in different cultures. Through her friend's interests, it also peaked Rachel's own as the more they spoke and she learned about the fellow linguist. This tempered curiosity grew more and more once the conference hosting committee revealed Prague as the next destination for their summit.

The medieval language was often considered a *dead* language by scholars, but the history of it thrilled Iris, which as she explained it to Rachel, also excited her. Deciding to dig deeper into the dialect that represented some of the oldest text in Slavic spoken accounts, she found that it was currently being examined and taught at other universities like Yale, Columbia, Chicago, Georgia and Toronto. Then, after reaching out to these communities provided her a framework to set conditions for her own school to feasibly follow as well. The possibility of adding it to their curriculum grew after her last meeting with the Vice-Provost who found merit with her request, and hoped to speak again after her seminar.

Rachel understood people, she had been trained to do so, and figured that using the heightened status of the other schools could push her proposal to be one that the man had wanted to pursue, but now she had to stamp the final seal of approval by proving first-hand experience. The opportunity excited her, but potentially even more for Iris once she told her about the school seriously considering her request.

Upon exiting, the airport attendant directed Rachel to a hired car instead of the row of waiting taxis. The car was nicer, a black Skoda Superb and the driver wore black dress pants, a white button down shirt, and had a jacket in his trunk which he would normally wear, but the warmth of the August afternoon made that unbearable.

Rachel's message to Iris was returned almost immediately. Her friend had been already touring the stunning city, sightseeing with their regular mutual conference acquaintances, and they insisted on meeting up with her. Sitting back in the car, she reluctantly agreed. Knowing she couldn't hide away the whole trip, she was already arriving on a date later than many of the other participants. The conference was designed for linguists and professors around the world to come together, share their knowledge, experiences and drive the importance of learning languages of the past and present for their students and those of the next generations. Between announced speakers, workshops and forums, there was always time allotted to explore the chosen city, visit its new cultures, and simply become the everyday tourist.

This particular year, Iris had organized a small group to arrive even a few days earlier to really find time to immense themselves into the majestic city of Prague. Rachel had made an excuse, claiming she couldn't join them, the summer workload needed some extra attention. In truth, it stemmed from a feeling that she couldn't ever remember having, fear.

Astronomical Clock. 1 hour? Staring at the bright screen, she didn't reply. She knew she had to. She was actually back in the city now and couldn't ignore that reality any longer. The three dot icon signifying another message was incoming popped up below the last message, there was another incoming. Iris was anxious. Her message simply had four question marks this time. Rachel responded.

Pushing the meet back closer to two hours, she agreed, feeling it would take her longer to get there. The hotel chosen for the summit was attached to the Prague Progress Centre. Bordering the undefined municipalities of *Prague 4* and *Prague 2*, the convention setting was perfectly designed for large gatherings and functions with bars, restaurants, a local brewery, and a world renowned five-story hotel all within walking distance to a secure train station.

Settling into her room, it was obvious that the American hotel chain tried to keep a simple semblance of its international aspect while integrating the Czech charms and nuances. The room was unexpectedly large, a full desk and two chairs, but the bed was the typical European style with two twin sized ones pushed together. A small bathroom, bidet included, and although modern looking, the artwork and color pattern was definitely chosen to stay with the local expression.

Within the hour, Rachel found herself reinvigorated and heading for the underground train station. The uneasiness returned to her stomach, but she was uncertain if it was a nervous feeling of heading into the heart of her past, or a genuine excitement for seeing the one person she actually felt to be her friend.

The train ride was quick, less than ten minutes to Národní Museum and emblematical Wenceslas Square. Not a square in the traditional meaning, the illustrious gathering ground is actually a long street renowned for shopping, dining and a favorite of tourists. The wide expanse stretches nearly two miles long, consists of one-way traffic lanes separated by a large pedestrian plaza and greenspace between them.

Currently it was busy. A burgundy and yellow open-topped, double-decker sightseeing bus had broken down a block from the street's apex, and the flock of tourists patiently waited for a replacement while snapping photos and breaking off towards the small shops and eateries. Combined with the regular stream of visitors, travelers and locals, the vendors, street performers and promoters were kept busy.

Rachel kept her pace, politely declined the three separate invitations for free entrance, and, or drinks from the men attempting to attract patrons to one of the local gentleman's clubs, and quickly found herself at the base of Wenceslas Square. Notably known as a meeting point in Prague, the large open piazza was not accessible for regular traffic. Delivery vans and trucks slowly weaved through the thralls of people, but it was commonly a pedestrian center.

Stackwell stopped, closed her eyes and felt the sun on her skin. A deep breath to expel any last thoughts of doubt, but instead, another staple of the historical city grabbed her attention. The mouth-watering aroma of the local cuisine. She loved the traditional foods, but this scent was her favorite. Spying the wooden street hut, she couldn't resist.

The *Trdelník* warmed her hand through the paper napkin. Picking at the coated pastry, Rachel surrendered to a genuine moment of happiness. The round, hollowed dough was just baked over hot coals, then rolled in a blend of sugar, cinnamon and crushed nuts. Many people preferred to have the soft snack dipped in chocolate, but she did not. She preferred the natural flavor of the coating and sweet dough.

The sugary covering was melting in her mouth with each bite. From here, the cobblestoned streets narrowed, twisted and turned into a mosaic of confusion if you didn't know where you were going. Tourists used paper maps and phone applications, while others just followed one another simply knowing the general direction that they were headed, but Stackwell did not need any of that. She knew the Astronomical Clock was a five minute walk north.

Already in the heart of *Prague 1*, this time, Rachel understood what that feeling was currently gripping her stomach once again. Slowly taking another bite of the warm pastry, she smiled to herself. Anticipation. She was back within the allure of the medieval sanctuary of Old Town Prague.

Chapter THREE

The labyrinth of streets and alleyways tapered even tighter with the stone buildings looming over the ever-growing throng of tourists clogging the cobblestones. Boutiques covering a vast array of shopping essentials from expensive jewelry, glass and crystal ware to cut-rate trinkets and souvenirs filled the open doors from the ground floor businesses.

Rachel was thankful for her outfit choice. A simple pair of jean shorts and stretchy white three quarter length crew t-shirt. The material was breathable in the warm air, but mostly she was glad she chose to wear her favorite pair of comfortable sneakers. Charcoal in color, they were soft, slipped on with faux laces simply for fashion, but perfect for walking long distances.

As she tried skirting around a mature couple carefully examining the advertised drink specials of a local pub, she was cut off by two younger girls darting past her. She stumbled, apologized for the misstep and felt her stomach knot again.

While the shadows of the late afternoon created a constricting tunnel on her current flat-stoned street, she knew the end was just ahead. Breaking the darkened shades encompassing the maze was the brightness of the sun once again. It was the opening where her winding branch joined the mouth of the immense courtyard in Old Town Square.

Closing her eyes, inhaling deeply and then releasing a long controlled breath allowed Rachel to feel the perspiration building on her forehead, control the mounting anxiety from within, ease the tension that was tightening in her throat, and stop the tremors that had begun in her hands. Repeating the process two more times permitted balance to return to her body and mind. She stepped through the veiled alleyway and back into the warmth of the afternoon sun.

Old Town Square was considered the heart of Prague. A complex string of connected medieval buildings encircling a massive courtyard. Baroque and gothic architecture highlighted the centuries old structures that now housed museums, pubs and extravagant restaurants.

Passing the large sunshade of a hotel's patio, Rachel spotted the dueling spires of the inspiring *Church of Mother of God before Týn*, or Týn Church. Across the open space from the eminent church was

Orloj, Prague's iconic Astronomical Clock and the Jan Hus Memorial resting between.

The last time she was here, it was late November, the celebrated Christmas Market was just beginning. Bright red canopies protected vendors and their goods while the colorful lights of a sixty-foot symmetrical spruce tree captivated the scene perfectly. Less tourists visited in the cooler offseason, but the annual month long marketplace was certainly a desired destination for all Christmas lovers. *This is simply magical.* She remembered saying to Sean when they first arrived into the plaza.

Currently, the courtyard was chaotic. No vendors or tree, but instead, filled with tourists and street performers ranging from musicians, mimes and magicians, but also the flamboyantly painted human statues all coveting the *koruna české* that the international onlookers were willing to dole out. The largest gathering was huddled in front of a man that was draped in flashy purple robes and appeared to be floating in midair while an oversized golden lamp rested below him. The observers were impressed by the feat, and the children astonished to see the genie emerging from his bottle.

It brought a genuine smile back to Rachel's face momentarily. Her favorite part about travelling and visiting different cities and cultures was listening to the multitude of languages spoken with people dashing around. The excitement in their voices about seeing new places with their majestic sights, but also sometimes even the confusion, annoyance and anger in tones. It all brought out energy, and she could hear distinct nuances in each of the tongues.

The sharp distinction of an irritated command caught her attention. Two men spoke an interwoven cross of Kabardian and its more westerly sister dialect of Adyghe. Commonly known as Circassian, the language is remote, and generally spoken only by those local to southwestern Russia, and some in Syria, Jordan and Turkey. Stackwell listened.

The men were certainly from the Greater Middle East region, darker skinned than most Russians, and had thick, well maintained beards. Stepping closer, Rachel confirmed them to be Turkish as she could see the tattoos on both of the men's right hands, a filled in star and crescent moon. She remembered the training from her past, to be able to spot any distinguishing markings and connect them to groups, factions or terrorist organizations was standard protocol for officials working in some dangerous countries. These tattoos were not from any of the ones that she could remember, but they were definitely symbols for somebody, she was sure of that.

Rachel followed their line of sight and was disgusted. The men spoke crassly, were arguing about looks, legs and shapes of women's bodies. Currently their gaze had fallen upon the two young girls that had run past and cut her off earlier. Neither were more than sixteen years old. She now wished that she hadn't heard their vulgarity.

"Rachel!" Hearing her name called out, and then a second time, her focus changed towards where it was coming from. Iris was standing, waving her hands emphatically above the crowd to catch her attention.

Waving back, Stackwell smiled towards her friend that had broken away from her associates and half jogged, half walked towards her while carefully avoiding the zigzagging crowds. "Oh my God, it's *so* good to see you!" The British woman threw her arms around her American friend, hugging her tightly. Rachel's inner turmoil almost immediately melted away. It felt good to be around a friend again.

Iris was nearly six full inches shorter than Rachel, had shoulder length dark hair, and considered herself to be *healthily plump*. It was the Englishwoman's way of admitting to be overweight, but she would always laugh when she said it, as she was completely happy in her own skin. Rachel admired her friend for accepting herself, even found it comforting compared to the strict workout regimen she kept. Old habits die hard she would often tell herself.

"You made it just in time." Iris was beginning to speed talk with her genuine excitement taking over. "We already got the tickets, and were just waiting for you before heading to the top of the Clock Tower. This place is *so* amazing, so beautiful, I can't wait to show you some of the history I've already seen." Guiding her American friend by the hand back to the other members of her party, Iris barely paused for a breath. "You remember Guillaume and Helena right? They were with us last year in Paris." Finally stopping for air, a concerned look crossed her face. "I'm sorry darling, I'm rambling. How was your trip?"

Rachel grinned, then laughed and hugged her friend again. "I'm excited to see you too. It was good, and it actually seemed shorter than I thought it would." She could feel the dread creeping back in, but kept it stifled with a broad smile as they approached their colleagues who waited patiently in a long line to enter the Prague Orloj. Rachel first greeted Guillaume, a Frenchman and then Helena, a Dane with the adorable French reception, *la bise*, the traditional two-cheek kiss.

The Prague Astronomical Clock is seen by many as the crowning jewel in the tourist industry for the medieval city. Attached to the Old Town Hall since the fifteenth century, the monument has three main components that make up the spectacle. The lower part has a calendar dial displaying time in three different ways with the heart being the sun going around a circle of twelve zodiac medallions.

The upper part of the renowned golden clock is an astrolabe, displaying the current positioning of the sun, moon, and other celestial objects. The third feature of the tower acts almost like an hourly show for the patrons watching below. Twelve wooden apostles appear in the windows, conduct a *walk*, as a skeleton and other sculptures ring bells to signify their appearance.

A soft tempo beat from three musicians echoed from across the open courtyard as Rachel continued to feel that aching knot in her stomach lessen. Speaking with her conference friends allowed her mind to wander from the thoughts of her past and focus on the topics for the current conversation. The line to enter the illustrious clock tower was moving fairly quickly as she explained her campaign of the Old Church Slavonic language into a desired curriculum to the Danish woman she vaguely remembered.

Helena was a professor from Aalborg University's Department of Culture and Learning in the Humanities Faculty, and a prime example of how the conference wasn't only designed for those specifically in the fields of languages. It was a beneficial seminar for teachers and learners from across the world to come together and develop one another's knowledge from other cultures as well.

In her early sixties, Helena was a widow after losing her husband to cancer three years ago, but after attending last year's forum, vowed not to miss another. She didn't entirely understand all the information being exchanged in the seminars, but had met new people that also enjoyed the company of others from so many backgrounds and cultures. It was an easy decision to allow the annual conference to double as her yearly vacation. Her late husband had always wanted to travel the world with her, take her to see many places, but once he became terminal, that could no longer be a possibility. He had made her promise to use her time to adventure for both of them. She fiddled with her wedding ring, while smiling to herself as the American rehashed a prior conversation with her boss back home.

Rachel could tell that Helena's mind was thinking about something else, but she continued anyway. The woman seemed happy in her own thoughts and she didn't want to break them. "Bringing back the history, and the origins of the Slavic language to my class—"

Stackwell stopped mid-sentence. It was not the light honking from a white delivery van's horn that distracted her, but the driver himself. He barked. The man's tone was deep, loud and rasping orders while his free hand had intended commands with pointed directions. The booming voice mirrored the distinct language of the two crass men earlier in the day.

Rachel's eyes fixated on the sturdy hand holding the steering wheel. A solid star and crescent moon tattoo were inked in the skin webbing of the thumb and first finger. "Hurry! Get them!" Commanding again, Rachel looked away from the driver's hand and towards the words that she understood.

Locking eyes with the man, she could see malice. There was also recognition. The driver knew that she could understand what he was saying. "Take them now!" Panic was in his voice. "Grab the girls!" The van lurched forward.

The last sentence froze Stackwell in place. Whipping her head towards the driver's commands, she saw the two men from earlier react immediately. They ran directly towards their unsuspecting targets, the two pubescent girls that they were crassly ogling when she overheard them.

Rachel did not hesitate. "Get the police!" Speaking firmly to Helena, she was calm, but her eyes told a different story. Fire raged as she knew what was coming. Pushing her way free from the unfettered line awaiting entry, jumping over a tired young boy squatting on the slightly elevated sidewalk edge, she sprinted towards the two attackers.

The young blonde girl screamed when she was first assaulted from behind. Two burly arms grabbed her around her waist, lifted her from the ground before tossing her through the air into the back of a small white van whose side door was slid open. Landing with a loud *thud*, she bounced once, hit her head against the back frame and skinned both her knees on the grooves of the metal cab base.

The second teen, a strawberry blonde with more of an orange tinge in her hair and frailer skin tone reacted quicker to her attacker. This man was shorter than the first, and didn't possess the same upper body physique. As he tried lifting his target, she squirmed, kicked out and the man ended up tearing her summer dress, knocking her to the ground, but not actually getting a firm grip on the girl. He needed a second attempt.

Screaming as tears streamed down her face, the crowd of onlookers were immobile. Two separate parents quickly gripped their children tightly, while others were stale with disregard, fear or in awe of an elaborate skit. The two men ignored it all.

Bending over to seize the shrieking girl, the shorter attacker's hands were unsure where to grab when she began defensively kicking out. One of her sandals had already fallen off and the second whizzed by the man's head with her first jolt. The larger of the men hesitated between helping his ally, or ensure his victim stayed where she was. He lunged towards the second girl on the ground.

Cursing at his partner to control her feet, the brawnier man firmly gripped the teen's arms, causing the screams of fear and panic to turn into ones of pain instead. The second assailant measured the thrashing, found an opening and clutched the girl's legs. Together the two men lifted their prey and carried her towards the waiting van.

Backpedaling, the bigger man checked over his shoulder momentarily for the van's distance, and was jerked forwards. The balance between the bodyweight carried was disturbed. The other end was dropped. Twisting again, the teen was free.

Horror was held in the crowd of tourist's eyes, but none moved. These men, kidnappers, had done this before, they seemed organized in their attack, but today would be different. Rachel sprinted from the line, judged her distance and picked her own target. The shorter of the two men.

They carried their second victim towards the waiting van while the driver screamed more orders in a guttural combination of tongues. Mainly cursive slangs. Stackwell knew she could reach them first.

Three strides, two strides, one more and she leapt. Rachel aimed high with her spear-like tackle. Launching herself above the waist height that the man lugged the teen, and driving herself into his right shoulder and bicep. She only had to knock the man off balance enough to force him to drop his end.

She was successful. The smaller man was not expecting the challenge, spiraling around his back, dropping the girl and landing on the ground. It was just the beginning. Rachel steadied herself on one knee, fire raged inside, but she was calm in her body language. Narrowing her focus, her pupils dilated when she saw her prey begin to stir.

Pouncing at the movement, she sprang like a jungle cat hunting from the bush. Landing perfectly on her left knee, Rachel swung her right leg across, kicking forward and planting the top of her foot squarely on the grounded man's exposed Adam's apple. A loud crack was followed with a gasp of expunged air. Her damage had been done. The man writhed on the ground, easily a fracture in the larynx or trachea cartilage, but for the moment he would live.

"*Aptal sürtük!*" The second attacker, the larger, brawnier of the two men roared at Rachel in Turkish this time. She imagined that it was his native language. *"Öleceksin!"* The man spat while withdrawing a knife from a sheath behind his back.

The blade was thick, dark stainless steel, almost black, but uncleansed. Rachel focused on the grooved teeth that tapered to the point, then noticed the reddish brown of the ridged handle firmly griped in the man's hand. It was a Katran, a soldier's knife, a Russian soldier's weapon to be precise. These men were certainly supplied by somebody else.

The man lunged towards her. Stackwell recoiled, blocking his advance. She had close combat training, and could tell that the man did not. He would be a brawler. He would assume that he had the upper hand because he was bigger, stronger and possessed a weapon. She knew he was wrong. It brought a sneered smile to her face.

Another stab attempt from the knife wielding man and Rachel countered. Side stepping the aggressive attack, she landed a right fist into his serratus anterior, a tender muscle below his shoulder and armpit, then followed with a left into his neck. The latter, a jugular strike, wobbled the big man's equilibrium, but the first didn't make him lose grip of the blade as she had hoped.

Cursing again during his bout, the man learned, used his larger frame to cut off Rachel's maneuver and changed the blade's trajectory to a horizontal path. This time, the sharp blade found skin. Piercing her forearm, slicing a thin stroke from wrist nearly to elbow, but only drawing surface blood.

The two were once again across from one another in a standoff. He laughed. Rachel cursed herself, but refused to look at the wound. Instead, it was her turn to be the aggressor. A quick stutter step grabbed the man's attention, stabbing wildly again, but missing and leaving his body open for assault.

The American propelled forward, got inside his bulky arms and exploded with a fury of body punches. Two rapid ones to stun the man, a direct palm based upper cut jarring his head, and finally a pinpoint elbow driving him backwards into the body of the white van between the sliding and driver's door. Repeating her offense, Rachel had gained the advantage. Using the solid backing of the vehicle strengthened the rate of her assault and the man dropped the Russian made blade.

The driver tried to interfere, but Stackwell used her left foot to kick the door closed as it opened, slamming it onto an outstretched arm. It was his turn to scream out when the pressure was applied, but nowhere near as bad as was expected.

Even though he was unsuccessful, the driver did gain valuable seconds for his partner, and it was enough for him to fight back. Rachel felt the hulking arms wrap around her tightly and begin to squeeze. Both of her arms were pinned to her side as the stronger man constricted his grip.

Kicking out with knees found thigh occasionally, but the pressure mounted, and her chest convulsed without new air entering. Rachel could feel an itchy tingling forming in her toes as she was losing her senses. Swinging her head to the side only blurred her vision more. She needed to break free from his massive bear hug.

Desperation had set in. Rocking backwards, Stackwell flung her head forwards, crashing her forehead into whatever part of the man's skull she could find. She felt his grip loosen a bit. A second bash staggered him enough to free her right arm. There was no hesitation.

Plunging her fingers into her attacker's eyes, the man squealed. His grip loosened even more, but not enough for her to be set entirely free. Now thrashing, he began to ragdoll her in an attempt to relinquish the gouging. It did not work. Spinning around instead, the man began hammering both of them into the body of the van.

Rachel crashed hard into the metal frame, first body, then hitting the back of her head against the roof. Two more times forced her to stop the pressure she was exuding on the man's eyes, but his grip had also loosened enough that she could breathe again.

A direct kick to the big man's groin doubled him over while he used his hands to reach for, and protect his bleeding eyes. Rachel was free. Raising her hand for another striking blow was too much. Instead, she fell. Her head spinning wildly.

She heard loud bleating of a whistle blowing and then a siren, but she did not know if it was real, or the just ringing in her head. Trying to stand, Rachel fell again. Her eyes straining for focus, but only saw bright flashes, dark spots and clouded movements.

Her left arm streaked with blood while forehead, nose and chest either were splattered or soaked in crimson as well.

Arms reached for her and she tried to swing out again, but this time couldn't. Her body was ravaged, exhausted with trauma. One more moment of clarity allowed her to see the white van pulling away with the brawny man in the back. The arms around her were soft, cradling her, not attacking her.

It was Iris. She was crying as she held her bloodied friend. "The girls?" Rachel tried to speak, but only found a hoarse whisper. "Are the girls okay?"

No words came from Iris. Through the tears, she only nodded and helped turn Rachel's head to the left. There was sunlight bouncing off the cobblestone road in front of her. When she focused though, a sharp pain would shoot through her head, but it was worth it to see the two young girls holding one another and crying. Iris found enough courage to praise her friend. "They're safe."

Chapter *FOUR*

Crossing the Frederick Douglass Memorial Bridge over the Anacostia River, Derian lightly squinted from the bright lights still shining from Nationals Park as he could hear the crowd cheering while switching lanes. The baseball game must have gone into extra innings. A quick maneuver with his bike around a stalled row of cabs allowed him to find a quiet side road and be home in a matter of minutes.

   A short street with a row of old brick townhouses lining either side dating back to the 1960s welcomed him. The common homes all looked the same on the darkened street where the streetlights were shadowed by the elder oak trees, but that did not bother Derian. He had ideal neighbors and found a great place to live. An impeccable little hamlet southwest of the gestating thralls of the Nation's Capital city.

   Relaxing evenings along the Southwest Waterfront Park, a comforting meal from one of the local restaurants or simply the picturesque sunsets over the Washington Channel were all considered normalcies for the local residents, and ways to escape the vigor of the demanding state district, but not tonight. Haynes was eager to plunge right back into the deepest foil of the political jungle if he needed to do so.

Deserae Haynes, his mother, had been a highly respected journalist, starting as a freelance reporter, but with her compelling writing and fact-based storytelling, quickly found herself onto the main pages of the Chicago Tribune. A few years after debuting with the national newspaper, they offered her a position with the Washington outlet, and press accommodations to cover the prestigious White House.

At the time, Derian didn't understand why they were moving, but he was young, and abided with the rules his mother had set. As he grew older, he began to understand the strength that she had within her, to first accept the position, and then also to thrive in it. A single black mother in Washington, D.C., surrounded by the history of a primarily old, white male culture wielding uncontained power, was a recipe for her failure.

Haynes fired up his home computer, the core processor was faster than his laptop and he glanced over at the framed photograph of him and his mother. She turned failure into success he thought.

Deserae's compassion, listening ability and compelling nature allowed others to confide in her, feel comfortable around her and believe in her, even when others tried to make her seem incompetent or a creationist. She would not relent on a story when she had the facts, and soon found herself not only asking hard questions on the White House Press floor, but also on national television and in private interviews.

Remembering his mother brought a smile of pride to his face. He knew the fame did not drive her, it was simply telling truth to the people when those they elected to speak for them did not. It had defined her not only as a journalist, but as a person. It was that pride in which he found the desire and courage to follow in her path and forgo that of sport. A doorbell like sound effect from the mainframe indicated that the USB drive was connected and ready for access. It was the moment of truth for his heightened excitement.

Derian's journey into the journalistic world had not been as easily defined as his mother's. The last name garnered him opportunities to meet people, but at first, he found himself driven more for that one significant story to make his statement. It failed. He was too eager, pressured sources too hard and found himself writing slanted and biased pieces, as opposed to being subjective, delving deeper into facts and delivering quantity or quality. As his foundation for achievement dried up, so did his self-love, expectations and growth of his flaws.

Clearing his mind, Haynes focused on the files in front of him. There were six in total, each a *JPG* photo transferred from Reggie's phone. Quickly operating his wireless mouse, he opened the first file. It was a copy of an email taken from another computer screen. The combination of the phone's camera and screens pixels degraded the still, but adjusting the *zoom* feature made viewing the contents possible. The correspondence was between Texas Senator John Ryan Paxton and three other men. Opening another window on his desktop allowed him the chance to search the names of the other participants.

Mentally and emotionally Derian had found new levels of self-pity. Believing his major injury could be the worst he could feel, but back then his mother would never let him give up on himself. Once again, he had found his courage through her. Deciding to step away from the brashness of the Washington political scene, Haynes pleaded for the correspondent position in the Middle East as another war continued to rage.

He didn't get the station, but instead was allowed to go as part of the filming crew. An opportunity probably only given to stop his endless pestering, but once the team actually landed in Damascus, everything changed again. The fighting in Northern Syria escalated more quickly than anybody had anticipated, spread rapidly and found the capital city like the turn of a key.

Derian's team fled immediately, but he was determined to stay. Finding safety in an American coalition controlled militarized zone, he began reporting stories from those involved on the front lines. Personal stories about firsthand experiences, following it up by training with the soldiers and eventually being allowed to venture outside the protected camp and joining the units on their patrols. His experiences were harrowing at times, but compelling, truthful and hard-hitting for those at home sitting on their recliners watching their nightly news channels.

The apex to his time as a war correspondent came when he was specifically requested for an interview by the man in charge of the rebellion prompting another country civil war. It was strongly objected to by the American and coalition commanders both on the ground and from oceans away, but Derian insisted.

The man was seen as zealot, a radical that would surely use the meeting as an opportunity to capture the *Westerner* that was increasingly drawing attention to human interest stories in the country as opposed to strictly the wanton acts of violence and battles for territory.

Neither were entirely true. Haynes did find the man to be fundamentally opposed to foreigners, deep-seated against those who he felt were trying to steal his country and religion away, but he was also not a crazy bloodthirsty abhorrent like many reports were substantiating.

The interview lasted nearly four hours, a meal shared between the men, and he was allowed to leave completely unharmed. In fact, Derian felt that his debriefing back within the compound with the military commanders was much more hostile than his conversation with the so-called radical. The direction that he was *told* to report was in line with everything else the military leaders were driving forth. When he wouldn't, didn't in fact, he was promptly escorted to the next military flight headed back to the United States. This was where Haynes found himself again. He found what drove his mother to be so determined to report hard truths, upset the old, white patriarchy that wanted their constituents to be hand fed slanted media stories.

All three names that Haynes searched were prominently featured with articles written about them. The first two men were Presidents and CEOs of the two largest oil and gas companies in the United States, while the third was Mason Williams, the current Secretary for the Department of Energy.

Williams had been newly appointed to the position less than eight months ago by the President himself, and as Derian searched further, found that the man was essentially completely unqualified for the job. Reading two separate articles from colleagues whom he respected brought about the picture of a man who failed an attempt to run for Governor of Oklahoma, but was rewarded the position because he was a dedicated proponent and wealthy backer for the man holding the American Presidency. One final quick search on the man and he discovered that he was also the brother-in-law to Senator Paxton.

The other five files were more of the same. Photographs taken from the email strain between the four men. Assurances were made between the government men and the businessmen to ensure that their companies would be protected. *I have personally spoken to the President himself about the matter, and he wants to assure you that YOU come first as long as HE comes first with your endorsements. America was built on oil and natural gas and will always be.* The sentence from the Secretary followed concerns from the billion dollar companies that the United States would concede to mounting pressures from other countries to look at more environmentally friendly sources of energy.

Derian opened the next image and continued reading. Another agreement from the Senator to ensure the government would put pressure on their main rivals in the renewable energy sectors. *I see no problems with us cutting off their funding, disparaging them through the media and turning the American people on their own. It's been done before, we'll do it again!*

Checking the clock icon on his monitor, Derian quickly gathered the two small notebooks he had been scribbling in. It was nearly one in the morning, he had been rereading, making notes, collecting thoughts while searching information for over two hours, but he needed more. He needed access to the archives at the Washington Post. Tapping the name in his phone that he hoped would help him, he waited for the man to pick up.

The fourteen hour flight time from Syria back to the United States allowed Derian plenty of opportunity to reflect on what he wanted in this career. He was being sent home as a punishment for breaking with the narrative that the government wanted featured. His last segment portrayed a side of humanity towards the radicals, and without openly questioning any motives, subtly asked why the coalition was even there. He knew the military flight would land at Andrews Air Base where he would be met once again by men in both suits and in uniforms sporting colorful decorations with the intention of holding his career hostage. If he recanted, repositioned his chronicles to a way that they approved, he would be free to report the story, but if he chose to stay the course, they could bury him. They would label him a traitor.

There was no correct choice. The easy decision was to fall in line with the directed stance, but he knew it wasn't entirely true. On the other hand, he could stay rebellious like many thought was easy behind their social media walls, but that had tangible consequences in the real world. Back and forth, his mind turned until he remembered something his mother had said to him when he was young. He had snuck down and saw her watching television, on it, a man yelled towards the viewers, spoke harshly and negatively about her directly. He cried.

Surprised by the sobbing, his mother quickly switched off the spewing head to comfort him. She said that it was alright and that the man was only seeking fame. She explained that not all reporters were dedicated to explaining facts and truths, that some merely spoke to one side of a story in an effort to benefit themselves. He remembered her laughing even and saying that sometimes these people didn't even believe it, but knew it would help them.

The part that he held on to was when she told him that she knew her job was important because there was a difference in the way people thought, sometimes just as plain as good versus evil, but either way they both needed somebody who cared enough to show them the truth.

Disembarking the plane that day, Derian felt in line with his mother, he walked directly past the men he knew would be waiting, continued with his original report, and found himself stuck as a newspaper stringer, freelancing, and as a social media writer hunting for clicks and likes ever since. The consequences were real, he had been essentially blackballed by the patriarchy of Washington politics, but he believed his mother would have been proud. Firstly of his choices to ensure the integrity of his journalism, but secondly, and mainly because he continued to fight.

Depending on late night commutes and how much he skirted the traffic laws, Derian knew he could speed bike to Franklin Square in about twenty minutes. A promise of two ice level tickets for an upcoming Capital's game this season was the only promise necessary for his contact to allow him into the Post's archives section for the night. Haynes teased a *Breaking Story* on his social media timeline, grabbed his helmet and flew out the door.

The art of reporting, feature articles and journalism had changed since when his mother had thrived. After Haynes was ostracized from the political scene, Kim Rawlings, his boss at the Washington Post kept him tightly protected. She believed in his strengths to see the humane aspect to covering stories, found herself compelled to his reports from Damascus, and appreciated the changes he was making towards becoming a hard-hitting reporter. She had respected his mother and saw that he had the potential to become just like her.

Derian had developed into an important part of the online media presence that the Post was changing focus towards. The importance of a physical newspaper was still prominent for some, but as the generations grew, that was waning. Blogs, Facebook, Twitter and more online destinations were the norm for people to receive their news nowadays. You could get information immediately, from all over the world, and from multiple sources. The days gone by of dictating propaganda to the masses was over, but it also brought new and sometimes more challenging issues.

Personal safety had grown as a concern amongst journalists with so many readers now able to make comments, or threats, all with courage found by hiding behind the anonymity of their phones or computers. Headline stories were broken in real time now, there was no waiting for the six o'clock news to report the exploding events of the day. With these new generational challenges brought the need for those who could react laterally, but also still had the personality to be listened to and followed simply by their way with words. Derian Haynes was one of those people and why Rawlings found him to be so valuable.

"*Bir şeyler yapmalıyız, usta!*" The bearded man cried out to his commander next to him. Panic was overtaking his nerves as he watched the attack below happening. "We must do *something*, master!" He begged the tanned man standing next to him.

The planned operation was falling apart. The van had moved into position, one girl was already inside, but the second had been stopped by a tourist, or resident. A woman had attacked one of *their* men, knocked him to the ground and already kicked him in the head. The bearded man, Burak Demir, was the *white* man's second in command, usually the man holding lead and over watch, but this time his boss accompanied them. Demir scrambled to find the sniper rifle that he carried just in case there were complications.

He settled the gun's stand on the old wooden sill of the hotel window, but was stopped from proceeding by a gentle touch from the man next to him. "Wait." The man's voice was soft, controlled and he even smiled callously. "I want to see how this plays out." Burak obeyed.

Lucas Viale, entitled *Zafar*, by the men who worked for him studied the movements of the woman in the courtyard below. Selecting the room with a square vantage point for his men's assault, the planned ambush had been organized perfectly. The extraction should have been over in a matter of seconds, fear gripping the bystanders, but also not truly understanding what they had actually seen. They had done it many times before.

They had never been interrupted by an outsider before either, but she moved fluidly and it aroused him. Without remorse, she seemed to have kicked the head of one of his men clean off, but that was an exaggeration. Viale's stoic eyes were gleaming with excitement as she pummeled at the bigger man. Finding himself almost cheering for her as one would a cage match fighter or boxer, he wet his lips anticipating more damage from the prevailing woman.

Teatro, the bigger of his men, gained the upper hand again with his powerful arms and Lucas felt a slight disappointment grow within. A short termed grimace appeared on his face as he watched her being slammed repeatedly into the metal frame of the van, but that was quickly replaced again by a smile. Growing wider as she fought back once more. Two head butts, hands and fingers extorting Teatro's face, and the blood. Viale's eyes opened sinisterly, craving for more.

Demir exclaimed again for him to *do* something as police whistles and sirens were becoming louder with each passing second. Whipping his head towards his second-in-command, *Zafar* smiled wildly before nodding. Kneeling and positioning himself behind the scope of the long range rifle in the window, Viale concentrated on the magnified images of targets below.

The operation was over, they had failed. The two girls had escaped, Teatro absconding into the back of the fleeing van, and the woman who interfered now being cared for by another bystander. He studied her bloodied face, laughed to himself and accepted her obstruction. Exhaling as he tugged on the trigger, he fired one shot.

The muted shot found its mark. Still grasping at his throat, the smaller of the two attacker's head whipped back as he attempted to stand. More screaming erupted from the onlooker's as the man's body lay sprawled half on the street with his blood staining the cobblestones red.

"Pack it up." Viale calmly issued an order to a perplexed Demir. "We'll need to get out of here before the police start searching for the shooter." Pausing, he finished his thought before the concerned man was able to even ask. "They failed. There has to be consequences for failure. Besides, there will be plenty more targets." The soft, nonchalant attitude of *Zafar* had returned. One last glimpse of the woman and he left the room.

Chapter FIVE

Derian's head sprang upwards. Unsure if he was awaken by the alarm buzzing on his cellular phone or from the heavy door of the archives room closing, but either way his short-lived power nap was over. It was now exactly *6:15* in the morning and he last remembered still working just after five. An hour of sleep was more than enough he thought he'd get, but was thankful for the recharge.

His research began with an introduction into Senator Jon Ryan Paxton, when and how he was elected into office, and his stances on political positions. The man was truly diligent to his party. Outspoken against the opposition in every arena, and would always have something to say if you put a camera and microphone in front of him.

The one change that Haynes found over the past few years from sifting through the sitting Senator's viewpoints and beliefs was how they changed towards the current President, Alan Wakefield. Originally toying with the idea of running against the man, Paxton was intolerant towards the man's condescending demeanour and felt that it wasn't appropriate for politicians, but that changed once the now current Commander-in-Chief had won his party's seat to challenge for the Presidency.

Paxton's tone went from a straightforward speaking Texan that was tutorially debateable, but open-minded, to one of absolute rederick and finding advantageous viewpoints to echo the political spectre that his party's new leader was brandishing. Through Derian's research, he also found that with this new attitude, brought a larger base following of the man, and much more division back in his home state, especially between voters.

In the past year, Paxton had suspended various funding programs aimed at helping immigrants and the poverty-stricken, championed bills and policies to benefit the wealthy and upper class, and helped reconstruct county lines for elections to favor candidates that he endorsed. Through the collection of articles, the one that caught Haynes's attention the most when pieced together with his other information was the growth of the big oil companies in comparison to similar potential resources. Derian focused on these details because of the screenshots he possessed of the emails. Money in the oil industry was nothing new, but when compared to the current struggles that the alternative energy programs were having, it painted a broader picture.

Quickly tidying the table he was using as a desk, collecting his shoulder bag, Haynes headed for the door. He knew he had to hurry. His story was getting bigger, but the only way his story would ever see the pages of print or screens of readers, he needed some more proof. Concrete evidence that he could tie them together before using the copied electronic transcripts as his final nail. An overly early morning call, apology and favor request were granted by one his sources. An Independent party commissioner from the Federal Elections Commission office would meet him in the food court of Union Station with a complete printout of donors, and to whom their monies were allocated over the past two years.

The line waiting in front of the new fruit juicery was more than double the symbolic coffee shop across the aisle in the basement of Union Station. People were once again focused on attempts to become healthier, but Derian also laughed to himself imaging what they then actually ate for lunch.

He was early, rested against the backside of the escalators across from his meeting point, and could tell when the latest string of trains pulled into the renowned station. A new mass of pedestrian traffic hurried down the moving staircase, fluttering into the line of their choosing all while faces were buried into the screens of handheld tablets or phones. There was no stutter stepping or crashing into one another, this was normal, it was routine for masses.

Spotting his contact, Vanessa Franklin, Haynes timed his gait to fall in line with hers and reach the queue of the coffee shop together, him directly behind her. They did not acknowledge one other the entire time, and the only contact they had was when Vanessa placed her tan leather messenger bag down to pay, and *forgot* to pick it back up. Calling out to her, Derian scooped it up, handed it back to her and with a slight of hand removed the light brown folder from the hidden side pocket while she thanked him profusely.

There were official channels that he could have entered to obtain the publicly accessible information, but it could take time, alert potential members, and he knew there was also some information that never did find its way into the *official* reports that were released. Performing their subtle clandestine dance, he was feeling more optimistic that Vanessa was able to see through his candid request and give him access to that *un*classified data as well.

Finding a corner bakery a couple blocks away on D Street, Derian pored over the file of pages that were supplied to him. Vanessa must have suspected, or maybe was hoping, what direction he was heading with his request as she had supplied only the donations and figures corresponding to the large companies, independents and Super PACs. It was detailed, at least as much as the Federal Elections Committee had been given, and broke down to whom each contribution amount was distributed in both the Republican and Democratic parties. There were also pages specifically focusing on the *Dark Money* of politics and investigations that the Elections Committee had been conducting in secret. Vanessa had come through on an even larger scale than he could've ever thought.

Skimming through the breakdowns, Haynes's eyes searched meticulously for one name, he found it. Jon Ryan Paxton. The Senator's receivable campaign funds had grown close to a half million dollars, nearly ten times the amount from the previous year when compared against one another. A low whistle and chuckle followed as Derian thought that they weren't even trying to hide it anymore, blatant bribery was being committed if anybody bothered to even check and hold the politicians accountable anymore.

His story was beginning to take shape now and he had to put the man on the hot seat to see his genuine reaction. Another quick social media tease on his timeline to ensure his followers were paying attention, and a simple message to Reggie. *Where is he?*

The sleek Gulfstream G650 maintained a cruising altitude of just over forty-one thousand feet, leveling off at a height that the pilots found to be the smoothest and comfortable for passengers in the cabin. There were seven in total, but the private jet's captain truly only cared about the opinion of one of them.

Lucas Viale sipped his whiskey with one hand, while the other skimmed across a touch pad on his laptop. He was scouring the spreadsheets that contained detailed information of his *inventory*. He cursed under his breath.

"The drugs seem to be wearing off, *Zafar*." Burak Demir interrupted his boss's thought process. "Should we increase their dosage?"

Arising from his seat, Viale strode over to where the *passengers* had been settled. Each girl drugged into submission and belted into a soft leather seat. They were all blonde, ranged from in ages around sixteen, but none of them were older than eighteen. One taken from Vienna, another from Bratislava, and the final two from the Czech cities of Prague and Brno.

All four girls sat upright in their seats, sedated, while connected to a makeshift intravenous administering system. An original shot of Ketamine Hydrochloride was used to render them unconsciousness, but to ensure their stability during the trip, a balanced distribution of Propofol was used. It was the safest way to transport his passengers to their new homes.

He was no monster. It was a thought that Lucas often had to himself when seeing reports about sex slaves and human trafficking operations broken and displayed for the world to loath. Drugging and beating women, boys and children was repulsive. The use of opioids, methamphetamines and heroine to addict and control their victims was for the uneducated. It was the means for the scum that prostituted their wares for the cheapest of wages. No, he was not like those animals at all. Viale prided himself in supplying beautiful, healthy fares who were not worn out, trashy whores abused and dependent on drugs or broken psychologically.

Two of his peaceful passengers began to stir restlessly. "Yes, increase the drip rate for these two by one, and monitor the others," Zafar checked his watch. ", but make sure it is only one. Just keep them blissfully *asleep*." He was direct with his man. "We'll be landing in under two hours and the Sheikh will want them to be able to walk on their own when he takes them."

Demir nodded to the command and reiterated one of his own towards the man who drove the van. The order had been for six young blonde teenage girls, preferably Eastern European in descent, and all with particular features and body sizes. Normally, the two squandered girls could easily have been replaced with others, but this order had been an urgent one, needing to be completed within three days and he had run out of time.

Viale cursed himself again. He did not have any other girls already waiting that matched this particular request. He never failed an order, which was why he was the best, and why he would personally make it up to his royal client. The replacements would come with no cost and would be special. It would be a personal promise to the Sheikh that he could fulfill within a week.

Lucas Viale, presumably a European because of his tanned white skin, rigid square jaw and full lips. He kept his light brown hair short, styled, and a bristle of facial hair parallel to designer stubble. He knew he was handsome, confident and mysterious. Prizing in the fact that nobody knew whom he truly was, or where he came from. Feigning various accents to different clients to discredit rumors or debate towards his origin, and seemingly appearing overnight, the man was the most prominent supplier on black market. Primarily staying away from drugs and weapons, to avoid the major international intelligence agencies and other warlords, the man revolutionized the human and sex trafficking industries into personal shopping experiences for those who could afford his services.

    The traits that people actually did know about him was that he thrived on the power of his reputation. His ego craved recognition of being the best. He loved to spend money on the finest clothes, food and alcohol. Many assuredly proclaimed him a monster who enabled such perversion amongst gluttonous men and women, but he did not care. He did not like to think about what was going to happen to his victims once he completed his transaction, instead, he only cared to think about what his money would do for him. Ambition was his mistress, his addiction and vice that drove him to this world. *Fuck it*, he would tell himself, it was his life and he *had* to enjoy all the very best that it could offer. He was a cold and ferocious man.

    A light buzzing from the plane's satellite phone drew his attention back to the table with his portable computer. Only one person was capable of contacting him on the phone, Cullen Verger. The billionaire business magnate and high-tech entrepreneur was also the only man that Viale would allow to dictate orders to him since the man did own the island where his base of operations was housed after all.

The buzzing continued, but Lucas stopped himself from advancing towards the device. He scowled. Whatever Verger wanted could wait, he needed have his plan ready for the Sheikh when they landed. The order was for six girls, not the four that were currently narcotized en route. Failure was not acceptable, however not being prepared to rectify the situation would be even worse. He had a self-duty find the perfect replacements to complete the transaction.

Striding to the cockpit first, Viale instructed the pilots to tell Mr. Verger that he was resting if he contacted the plane directly. Now, settled back with his laptop, the trafficking expert logged into one of his imitation social media accounts. Connecting it with another specialized program he paid to have created, he began searching for the optimal *gifts* for his client.

The sun shone brightly without a cloud in the sky to protect the Nation's Capital from another searing August day. Finding a slice of shade on the steps of the Capitol Building, Derian waited for the break in the assembly and for Senator Jon Ryan Paxton. Feeling his phone vibrate once signaled that the man was on his way.

The iconic white Capitol Building is legendary with politics in the United States. Recognizable for the massive dome atop the country's House of Representatives, the home of Congress has famously hosted Presidential inaugurations, outdoor concerts to celebrate the Memorial and Independence Day holidays, and funerals or memorials to past leaders. The fabled monument also has a notorious past with historical scenes of burnings, bombings, and even an insurrection led by the charge of a petulant former American President.

Derian felt the sweat on his back as he gazed across the wide courtyard and onto the lush grounds. Inhaling deeply, he readied himself for what could be the second biggest story of his young career depending on the reaction he could prompt from the Senator. The sound of murmuring and clattering voices drew him from his tranquility and he jogged determinedly up the steps between him and the exiting flock.

"Senator Paxton!" Haynes calling out loudly, repeating himself two more times before the stout man turned his head towards the recognition. "Senator Paxton, Derian Haynes with the Washington Post, look—"

"Sorry, I don't have time for reporters." Paxton snarled back with a derogatory smile.

"Senator Paxton, I'm looking for a quote about a story that we're running tomorrow." Haynes followed after the Texan, continuing through the man's dismissal attitude. "Regarding your campaign funds tied directly to Polygon Oil and America's Petroleum Corporation, and why they've increased tenfold after Mason Williams, your *brother-in-law*, was named as the Secretary of Energy."

Paxton's pace down the steps grew as he tried to increase the gap while continuing to disparage the reporter hounding him. "Lies. Baseless fabrications. I'm not surprised that the Post wants to keep spreading fake news."

"We at Polygon can concur with ACP's notion that it would be extremely lucrative for all parties involved if your administration looked upon us favorably." Haynes stopped chasing the Senator down the historic stairs of the Capitol Building. Speaking loudly, he quoted one of the emails from the strain that he had memorized.

Paxton froze immediately hearing the words. "What did you say?" Turning abruptly, the man held a sneer on his round face. Jon Ryan Paxton was not tall, or fat, just viewed as a normal body shape for a sixty-eight year old man. Clean shaven with a full head of hair, distinguished and salt-and-pepper throughout, even though lately it was becoming closer to the more saline color. The man was always dressed splendidly, full suit, and looked like he came out of the men's pages of a 1960s catalog.

Derian held firm. He did not know the Senator personally, but the prominent feature of the man was his ability to spin the narratives on negative press. Many of his colleagues had been tongue twisted when attempting to question some of the newest policies implemented in Paxton's home state, only to have the story turn into a beneficial outlook when it should have been the opposite. He continued with the same decibel. *"I have personally spoken to the President himself about the matter, and he wants to assure you that YOU come first as long as HE comes first with your endorsements."*

"Where did you get—" Paxton exploded both in tone and back up the steps towards the questioning reporter, but caught himself. Still ascending, he motioned for his staff to keep going without him until he was next to Haynes. Focusing on the reporter's eyes, Senator Paxton now spoke low, gruffly, but controllably. "What do you think you have there, son?"

"I know that I have bunch of emails that show collusion," Annoyed at the final reference to Paxton's statement. ", but I also know that is just the opening story to my many, *many* others." Haynes emphasized the latter to draw out the man's ire.

"You have obtained, *illegally*, I might add, private correspondence between two business associates." The snarl in his voice was deep this time. "One of them being the United States government."

"Would that mean, you're saying that the American government, and not just yourself is colluding with the largest oil companies? To what end?" Haynes felt he was leading with too much arrogance too early and wanted to ease back, but he was caught first.

"Don't be so smug you little shit." Paxton rasped just over a whisper. "All that you *think* that you have is conjecture, and words taken out of context." The Texan did not let the reporter rebuff before continuing. "Obviously obtained illegally, so if even one word is written, I will have the State police track you down and bury in a hole below the shittiest jail I can find in Texas." The man's eyes were afire.

"No comment, then." Derian scribbled in his notepad, but also kept his voice low so the two of them were the only ones that could hear each other. "What is the President getting in return for the *favors* that he is providing these oil companies Mr. Senator?" Quizzically placing his pen to his lips, he pondered again. "What exactly are the favors that the companies are getting from our administration anyway? I suppose if all I'm getting from you is, *no comment*, I guess I'll go ask the President himself during his next briefing." A subtle threat for the government man.

"You're not *listening* son." Paxton inched up, closing the small gap between them to almost nil. Haynes was taller, but that did not stop the older Senator from bulldogging his antagonist. "There is no victory for you here." Paxton's face crinkled as he snarled steadily. "Your *fabricated*, hit piece, because that's what it is, would last what, one day? Maybe two? And at that time, you'd either have been arrested, fired, or maybe situated with new surroundings." Trailing off into more of an undertone than an actual sentence. "There is no Arlington for the media."

Haynes wanted to retort, but found himself gasping for words. He had been in more tenuous of situations before, but wasn't expecting one to be while on the grounds of an American landmark. "Was that a threat Mr. Senator?" It was all he could muster up to say.

The stout Texan did not reply immediately, stepped back and winked with a wry smile. "Haynes you said, right?" Turning away and descending back towards the arriving Town Car, Paxton's voice elevated. "As in the same Syrian correspondent, Derian Haynes who already turned his back once on his government? Yeah, I'm sure your story will do just fine." A sarcastic drawl was volleyed back his way, but left the reporter still inaudible to respond.

"Damnit!" Derian cursed himself as he watched the Senator climb into the back of a black Lincoln Sedan. Part of him wishing he was recording the conversation, but another part of him wishing he had found something to say, yell, hell even curse the man, but he had found no witted response, just silence. Closing his eyes, he exhaled and remembered his mother saying that adding fuel to a burning fire never allowed it to simmer. She was right, he needed to regroup. He knew there was a story here, but also just blew his element of surprise.

Pulling out onto Independence Avenue, the shiny black Lincoln Town Car reversed its course and headed back away from the heart of Washington D.C. Jon Ryan Paxton sat alone in the back, barked for the driver to return to the office instead of their intended destination and elevated the window panel between them, allowing him privacy.

Finding his small phone, he scrolled for the name he wanted and tapped the screen. "Yes, it's me. We might have a problem." Speaking carefully, he explained the confrontation that he just had on the Capitol staircase.

"How did this reporter get our emails?" The powerful voice boomed at the Senator. "Weren't they all government protected? Didn't you delete them?"

"Yes! Of course I did. I don't know how he got the emails, but he has them somewhere."

"Then get them back." A slight hesitation between each of the words to highlight their importance. "I don't care what it takes." The voice paused before continuing. "Did you say that he was going to ask *me* about them as well?"

"Um, yes Mr. President. He did mention—" Paxton stuttered and swallowed before continuing. "He did mention something about confronting you about his suspicions."

"That stupid fucking sonovabitch!" American President Alan Wakefield roared. "If he asks me those goddamned questions in front television cameras then more than just one two-bit hack reporter will start an investigation."

"Yes sir." The Texan hesitated, but wasn't sure how to continue.

"Make this bullshit go away Jon." Wakefield was seething. "This problem started in your fucking house, you resolve it. I won't go down for this incompetence." Direct and stern. "This falls on you and your family, either squash this story or eliminate the source of it."

"Yes, Mr. President." Another nervous reply, but it was too late, the connection had already been severed. Paxton exhaled, he was sweating and hands shaking. He knew that Wakefield was serious. If he didn't put an end to the story, the President would make sure it was *he* who would face the firing squad from the press, and he would face it alone. It was an unwavering order from his Commander-in-chief.

Chapter SIX

"Rawlings wants to see you," A welcoming, but inquisitive warning from the security door man, and one of Derian's pickup basketball teammates when he walked back through the main entrance of the Washington Post. ", and she seems pissed man." The taller man added in a hushed voice as if he didn't want anybody else in the lobby to hear him.

"Ah, dammit." Haynes stopped and looked back towards the doors. "Any chance you could say that you didn't see me." A troublesome grin was now etched across his face.

"Sorry bro, but if she checks the feed and sees us talking." He paused to point towards the cameras overlooking the foyer. "You do know that'll she'll fire me, kill me, and then fire me again." The man laughed lightly in an attempt to ease his own tensions. "Nah, for real, you know I'm mad afraid of her." A serious look was now in his eyes.

"You're good Kev." Haynes sighed before laughing too. "She'd just hunt me down in my bed tonight if I skipped out on her all day anyways." He decided to take the stairs as it would prolong his stay of execution.

Derian was in a state of flux. He wasn't sure how to proceed with his story, or if he should even. On his way back to the newspaper headquarters, he caught a glimpse of a guided tour and was randomly drawn in by listening to the group's leader churn out facts and anecdotes about the city. It was cathartic for his mind, and without noticing, he had walked a couple blocks passed the Post. They were now approaching the White House.

Breaking away from small crowd he had fallen in line with, he casually strolled around the great American landmark. Becoming late-afternoon, the sun was still relentless, but as he stood on the oversized walkway between Lafayette Park and the Presidential manor, he took in the sights around him. Tourists still flocked to see the house of nobility, even if it had been tarnished in the past.

The images of cameras still strapped around necks mixed with cellular phones, tablets and selfie sticks made him realize people still cared. When he found himself facing the historic views of the South Lawn and the Ellipse, Derian spied a rambunctious group of children obviously on a summer day trip all huddle up against the thick black bars. Their chaperones spoke thoughtfully and meaningfully, but the biggest takeaway was that the children were listening.

The house itself was a beacon, just like the towering obelisk of the Washington Monument across the President's Park. They were the constants that the American people could look to for leadership. The men and women inhabiting them came and went, but there was always hope for the next incoming wave to be better. Derian needed to have that same belief. He headed back to the newspaper, he wanted to continue to search through the archives to see if there was anything that he might have missed earlier.

"I'm surprised you didn't try to slip out the back without coming to see me." Kim Rawlings spoke firmly as she stood from her chair behind her large wooden desk. The Chief Editor at the renowned newspaper was in her late sixties, but never seemed ready to retire. Her husband had passed four years previous, and she was determined to keep leading the press towards future generations.

"I honestly did think about it, but figured you'd just hunt me down anywhere that I went." Haynes tried to smile and ease any punishment he might face from his boss. The top floor office was hot and he wasn't sure if his sweat was because of the temperature or his anxiety. He knew that he shouldn't have been down in the archives and hoped the security who let him in wasn't in any kind of trouble either.

"Bollocks." Rawlings scoffed. Originally from England, her accent was only mild unless she was upset. "I would've just waited for you until you got home." Her temper leveled as she tried to apply her own joke to the situation. "I'm too old to chase you all over the city, but be sure that I still would've caught you."

"I believe you." Haynes spoke humbly. "Listen Kim, I truly am sorry for being here overnight—"

"Pish posh, I don't care about that." Rawlings snapped her hand and wrist showing she was concerned about something else. "Hell, I wish more of our people here would actually *use* them and do some research before turning in some of the drivel we put out as columns." Her attention was focused solely on him. "No. I want to know what you're digging into."

"I'm not actually sure, it might be nothing." Derian lied. The beads of sweat were growing, but still he wasn't sure if he should let her in to the story just yet."

"Nothing?" A rebuff. "I don't think *nothing* involves accosting a sitting Senator on the steps of the Capitol Building."

"Are you kidding me?" A miniature outburst was followed by a composed question. "Did that asshole actually make a complaint?"

"No." A determined statement followed. "A much bigger asshole did."

"The." Derian paused between words. "President?"

"Not directly," Rawlings came out from behind her desk. ", but his pit-bull Chief of Staff wanted to know everything that we were working on and for it to be turned over to them for *National Security*." This time the editor muttered. "Such a lame and bullshit excuse."

A breath of silence filled the hot, stuffy room. Both parties just looked at one another. Rawlings with questioning eyes, waiting for a response, and Derian's hesitancy in pushing a story that he wasn't entirely sure about. "Well? Let's have it." Rawlings spoke first.

Derian reiterated everything he had discovered for his boss. Deciding that he needed to trust her and hope she could help him in facing the direction of the story. Explaining that he had received trusted inside information and about the photos on the USB, to the printouts from the Federal Elections Committee, and the meeting with Paxton, he left nothing out except the actual names of his sources. Rawlings would never ask, she was a veteran of exposé articles.

Interrupting only periodically to clarify some facts, the head of the Washington Post listened intently. The heat of the room seamed to disappear with even more divulgence into a potential breaking story, and when Haynes finished, she only picked up her phone and spoke quickly to the voice on the other end.

"What do you think? Is this something that we should go after?" Derian was generally interested to know his boss's opinion.

Checking her watch. "It's a quarter past four now, you have a five-thirty flight out of Reagan."

"Wait. What?" Haynes was confused as his boss scrambled around her desktop looking for something. "Where am I going?"

"Wisconsin. Madison to be exact." She emptied the contents of her top drawer onto the blotter. "There you are you little bugger." Whispering to herself as she scooped up and handed a lanyard to the confused journalist frozen in her office. "Take this down to Harvey and get him to put your photo in it. It's an official press pass to get you in anywhere."

"Why am I going to Madison Kim?" Haynes took the cotton woven necklace and saw the brimming smile from the woman across from him.

"You are going there, because that is where the President will be tonight." Her tone was resolute. "After he gives his speech, basically a political rally, he plans on doing a small town hall type of meeting, and I want you there to ask him precisely about what you found."

"Are you serious? Is that a good idea?"

"Absolutely." Rawlings felt the adrenaline of another political scandal happening and her paper as the one to expose it. "If your questions for Paxton has riled up the President enough to sick his lapdog on me, then I have to believe that you struck some sort of a nerve. A nerve that needs to be puckered to see if we draw some blood."

Still somewhat awestruck, Derian didn't know what to say. He wasn't expecting this type of reaction from Rawlings. She was sending him out like an investigative reporter, and purposely looking to pick a fight with the American President.

"Don't just stand there." The editor winked and smiled again at the man she was glad she shielded those years ago. "Get going. You have a plane to catch."

The changes in weather and climate patterns brought another unusually hot day to the Latvian resort town of Jūrmala. Unhindered by a single cloud in the sky, the scorching sun beat down on the crowded stretch of tourists, locals and day-goers escaping the city life of Riga, thirty minutes away.

Nearing mid-afternoon, the over twenty miles of beaches were brimming with excitement. Two National Parks, and Dzintari Forest Park beckoned for those looking to find shelter under the trees, while the small and great boardwalks boasted opportunity to lavish in both sun and shade.

Basketball and World Championship beach volleyball courts were full with participants and observers, but the busiest attraction was Līvu Akvaparks, one of Northern Europe's largest waterparks that included indoor and outdoor complexes.

White quartz sand splashed between the toes of the young blonde girl as she carried her sandals in one hand, and cellular phone in the other. She laughed at the comment her sister next to her joked about the boys who had just attempted to get them to join them in the cool shallow waters.

Both girls wore matching woven cover-up dresses, sunglasses and foldable straw beach hats. As they walked through the sand, many second looks and stolen glances were made towards the stunning duo. In fact, other than the different colored tankinis under their dresses, they appeared to be indistinguishable. The scans would be correct. They were identical twins.

Shielding the screen from the sun, one teen checked her phone again and pointed towards the cordoned off section with tarped cabanas and flush red beach chairs with matching umbrellas. The private area was for one of the exclusive resorts and reserved for its wealthy clientele. The sisters knew they could not gain entrance, but they were hoping to get a glimpse of one of their favorite Hollywood movie stars.

They had been following a social media account for the starlet. The actress had made reference to a holiday in Latvia, geotags marking *Jūrmala Beach*, and the most recent posted photograph seemed to match the surroundings of this particular hotel's private expanse.

"There she is!" It was supposed to be a whisper, but the excitement had overtaken the younger girl.

"Oh my God!" Her twin sister responded immediately. "Mom is never gonna believe that we found her!" The girls had begged their parents to bring the family out for the day once they discovered that the celebrity was less than an hour away from their home. At first reluctant, their parents agreed that the family could spend the day at the beach, but warned them not to be disappointed if their idol was not actually even present or available.

"May I help you girls?" A soft, sultry voice interrupted their excitement and hugging of one another.

"We're sorry."

"You *really* are here." The sisters took turns speaking over one another.

"You are her, right? You're—"

The bronze skinned woman quickly placed a finger to her lips and made *shh* sound with her thick lips. The teen girls obliged. It was their secret. Behind her sunglass hidden eyes, she carefully scanned her surroundings. Motioning for them to join her in the private cabana while she slipped into a turquoise mesh cover up. The girls quietly nodded, stepped over the low hanging white chain entered the tented shelter.

Poles and chains were simply a decorative fence line, didn't truly act as a security measure and the bearded man overseeing the hotel's *private* area was simply a member of guest services and not security. It was generally acknowledged to be exclusively for the resort guests and the passersby accepted the small area as it was. The bearded man did approach the private cabana though to ensure his guests were not being disturbed.

Dressed completely in white, the man's English was choppy, but still passable. "Everything okay here *abla*?" He asked politely, but stern and loudly.

"Cheers *dahling*." The Hollywood starlet waved nonchalantly at the servant. "These are friends of mine." The woman acted the part of a diva. "They've stopped by for a drink, could you bring us some of that *fabulous* rose mezzer, um, meh-zer—"

"Rose Mežezers." The man interrupted calmly.

"Yes, a chilled bottle, *lūdzu*." Turning haughtily, she faced the teens who were silent and nervous in the presence of their beloved star. She sensed a newfound nervousness between the two. "Don't worry, it's not alcoholic. Sparkling water with cranberry and rhubarb juices." She smiled widely to try and comfort the young girls who were still sixteen. "I discovered it the other day in the city. It was so refreshing and delicious," Sitting back into a half erect fold down chair, she continued. ", especially on such a hot day like today."

It had been less than half of an hour before the *celebrity* motioned for the bearded man to once again return to her cabana. After bringing the bottle, she insisted he take a photo of the three *friends* with both of the girl's cellular phones. This time, she motioned for him because it was to finish the mission.

"We are ready." She now spoke directly into a small handheld radio. Gone was the sultry, flamboyant pedigree, and replaced with a hard, determined poise.

"That was well done." Another calm and callus voice emerged from under an umbrella shielded chair. "It was almost like you actually were *her*." Lucas Viale sneered as he checked the breathing of the two unconscious teens.

"Pretending to be a rich American snob." The woman laughed. "That's too easy."

"Two minutes, *Zafar*." The all-white clad Burak Demir reported as he reached the cabana, still scanning the waters of the Gulf of Riga.

The buzzing of an engine could be heard and Viale made his orders with his fingers. He and Demir each snatched a sleeping teen, threw them over their shoulders and sprinted to the open waters. The woman, scrolled through messages on the girl's phones, sent the pictures to their mother's and included a message. *We found her! OMG mama, sooo cool! Be back in a bit. Love you!*

It was a typical message that the teen had messaged in the past. It would be the last one she would send. Joining the men, the *starlet* tossed both phones into the water as she climbed aboard the waiting Zodiac.

The combat rubber boat's engine erupted from idle and roared away. Viale's piercing eyes studied the open beach. A couple leisurely sauntered without regard to their escape. An unexpected watercraft interrupted the dozen or so swimmers, but none seemed to object either. He knew the beach had no cameras. He smiled to himself, it was a perfect extraction.

Checking his watch, Viale mentally timed his next hour. The Zodiac would meet up with his yacht in ten minutes, once aboard, he would once again ensure the two teen's health from the drug they used, and then contact the Sheikh. His order would be fulfilled. The Middle Eastern Royal had requested six blonde teens, but when he only delivered four, he had promised the man, two more of the finest, *purest*.

The algorithm that his people created, sifted through all social media accounts, hunting for posts, pictures and comments that focused on any key words that they entered. He had found what he was looking for. European twin sisters, blonde, sixteen and virginal. It would certainly be to the Sheikh's liking.

Delving into the two girl's private media accounts, a plan was made. Using a formula to mirror their favorite actress's account, he created the posts that she was in their home town, and where she'd be. He knew it would be too tempting for the naïve girls. The task had been completed and now he could wipe all existence of that account completely.

Then he could rest. Exhaustion was setting in and he nearly fell asleep two, maybe even three times while waiting on his own beach chair. Viale's plans had all been put together and executed within just over thirty hours, and he had not slept a single one of them. Refusing the Sheikh's hospitality was made because he hadn't finished the job, but also because he knew he needed to act quickly. He would not refuse the man's generosities this time.

Lucas Viale smirked to himself this time when he looked down upon the two young girls as the boat bounced and dipped in the blue waters. He truly was the best. His *merchandise* was always intact and unharmed, but the American in Prague had nearly ruptured his reputation. Her interference had cost him the life of one of his men, replaceable of course, but it also meant he would have to stay out of Eastern Europe awhile because the police and Interpol would certainly increase their presence.

It wouldn't last though, it never did. They would crackdown on some small trafficking groups, the ones selling whores and drug addicts, look good to local media outlets, and maybe even *save* a few girls. It would all be grand posturing, but they would lose interest within a couple weeks. Their simple standard operating procedures, and one that even helped him by cleaning out some of the drivel and clusters interrupting his potential business dealings.

Viale even laughed aloud to himself about it. He was over-tired. His thoughts drifted back to the American woman. Why was she even there? *She* had to intervene? And, now he couldn't get *her* out of his mind.

Chapter SEVEN

Sweat glistened on her skin as she turned right, off the short gravel path and back onto the cement of Edgewood Drive. Rachel was pushing herself for tonight's run, and was beginning to feel the pressures she was placing on her body. It had only been a few days since she woke up in a hospital bed in Prague, head and arm wrapped tightly, while a constant aching sensation was burrowing between her temples. She had had a concussion before and knew this one was minor compared to that one many years ago.

Iris was with her, still shocked by the ordeal, but thankful her friend was alive. The doctors wanted Rachel to rest for a day or two so they could monitor the symptoms, but when Iris stated that the *policie* and news reporters wanted to question her, she knew she could not stay. The police she could handle, but she did not want the public attention. Iris playfully called her an *American Heroine* and *Wonder Woman* because that was what the media was already heralding her as, but it only annoyed the constant throbbing behind her eyes.

That first night, Stackwell slipped out of her room, stole clothing and headed directly for the train station. An eleven o'clock night train would get her across the border into Poland by morning, and then an early afternoon flight should be available back to the United States. On the train, she found what she needed for the international flight. She needed another change of clothes, preferably a long sleeved shirt to cover the bandages protecting the large wound on her arm, and most importantly, a piece of carry-on luggage.

Rachel knew she looked out of place as a traveller and could sense the eyes of security and staff following her, but that nagging feeling was growing, pitting in her stomach and causing the light throbbing in her head to spiral and churn into sensations of anxiety, dread and that she was being tracked. She had found herself sitting alone in a dark, cold corner of Wrocław Nicolaus Copernicus Airport, constantly checking and rechecking for faces that were not following her. She was crying, and sweating for no reason. Her head was not right. Paranoia was beginning to set in.

That was two days ago. Tonight, instead of choosing the more basic six mile circuit trail, Stackwell forced herself to run it twice, and was beginning to feel the consequences of that decision. Even the constant pulse thumping music in her

AirPods was no longer masking the sensations she once again was feeling. Twice on the first loop, Rachel slowed to study other runners she thought were watching her.

Listening intently again to the beat. She hated the loud, percussive electronic vibes of the *EDM* genre of music, but if enforced discipline on herself like she had been taught. *Find one discomfort to combat your other discomforts.* It was a training technique that she actually believed helped to trick the mind.

She had removed the wrapping on her forearm before leaving the house and the long slice stung with her perspiration meeting the healing wound. It wasn't painful, but as her body began to revolt against the length of the workout, minor disputes became major focal points for her thoughts. Rachel concentrated on the beat of the wordless song and the environment directly in front of each landing foot.

The skies had grown dark as the late afternoon circuit drew into early evening, but even more so under the heavy hanging trees lining the street. Dull street lamps were alive, bringing what light they could muster to the life below, yet eventually night would win back its throne. Stackwell turned left onto Munroe Street and tried for one last push of energy, but found her legs rebel. Slowing to a walking pace, she conceited that she had pushed passed maximum training levels and allowed herself to give in to her overstressed system. Making the full twelve miles was optimistic, but falling just short was still satisfying.

Removing the small buds from her ears, Rachel was first surprised, but then thankful for the silence around her. The street was quiet. Odd she thought, but then remembered why when she saw the advertising signs plastered on a local storefront window. The President of the United States was in Madison tonight, and hosting a political address or something at the stadium. She was not politically aware, nor cared, not anymore.

Restaurants, cafés, and retail stores were all unusually closed. The lumber store, local florist and even the post office all also had their lights turned out and signs in the door. The town was certainly clamouring for the party choices and turnout was surely going to be as expected. A light rumbling overhead made Rachel smile to herself as she passed the only person on either side of the street. The old woman wearing a Presidential hat scowled at her from the bench she sat on at the bus stop.

Thunderstorms had been predicted for the majority of the day, holding off so far, but with a thick cloud cover moving across the sky quickly, combined the low guttural calling, Rachel sensed they would arrive tonight. She glanced back towards where the elderly woman was seated.

There was something about the woman that didn't feel right. Was the glare simply disapproval towards a woman wearing only her sports bra and compression leggings in public, the fact that she obviously wasn't going to be partaking in tonight's political event, or not even directed *at* her, but because of the ominous incoming weather. A second glimpse was interrupted by the arrival of a transit bus, and the woman sluggishly rose and boarded.

Rachel was once again alone on the street. The hot day had turned into a warm night, but she shivered as the bus pulled away. Learning to trust her senses had made her very good once, but she didn't know what they were trying to tell her now, or if she could even trust them. Her paranoia was still real. Crossing the street, she would take the shortcut through the cemetery back home and hopefully beat the fast approaching thunderstorm.

The scene around Camp Randall Stadium was a spectacle in itself as Derian pulled up in a cab. Almost circus-like he thought to himself. The large college football stadium was home to the University of Wisconsin Badgers, a perennial sport juggernaut in college athletics, but tonight was apparently hosting a *town hall* address from the President of the United States.

Using his phone to capture the images of the surrounding chaos, Haynes could only whisper to himself. Lights flashed, both police, fire truck and personal ones from supporters. Horns blared from cars and air compressed canisters, but the political debates were already raging in the streets even though it wasn't an election year.

The state of Wisconsin, and the city of Madison precisely was extremely motivated by political beliefs. The state could potentially flip-flop every four years, and the citizens there were always proud to show you whom they supported.

The threats of thunderstorms had held stagnant throughout the day, maintaining a look of coming to life at any moment, but still hesitant, as if they were afraid to damper the festivities. Heading towards the media entrance, Derian passed another thriving horde. Currently civil, yet still separated by a line of cautious police officers in body armor. While one side chanted, and sang affirmative and optimistically, their opposites countered by ringing out damaging and negative slogans about the keynote speaker tonight.

The flight out of Reagan International Airport was delayed twenty-five minutes, but the pilot made up the flight time in the air. Upon landing, Derian flicked his phone back out of Airplane mode and was instantly bombarded with messages, all from Rawlings.

A string of one sentence texts instructing him where to enter, and specifically with whom to speak once he arrived. Kim had been able to work her magic and ensure that he was one of the selected and pre-determined reporters that the President would call upon during the question forum after the *rally*. He would've loved to know how she was able to make this all possible in a matter of hours, but he knew better than to ask.

Once inside the massive stadium, Derian could see the stage set up in the north end zone, facing the rounded corner stands which cut the eighty-thousand seat capacity into less than a quarter, thus allowing it to give the impression of a full and sold out backdrop for the many intentionally placed cameras.

The press pass he had been given was prominently displayed around his neck to avoid interrogation from the extra abundance of security parading the grounds, and after asking multiple harried staffers, Haynes was directed towards the portly woman in whom he was searching on behalf of his editor.

The rumbling in the clouds overhead was increasing, and the evening skies had turned black just as easily as if somebody had turned off a light switch. The deluge that had been threatening was nearly ready to show itself, Rachel could smell the rain in the stiffening air.

Quickening her pace through the southeastern tip of local Forest Hill Cemetery, Stackwell hoped to beat a possible downpour with how hot the day had been. Skipping off the pathway, she carefully sidestepped the last few remaining grave plates and was about to exit through the thin bush line. She froze. A single car was creeping along Speedway Road, much slower than the posted speed limit, but what bothered her was that it was the same dark colored car, navy or black, she had seen on the opposite side of the cemetery moments ago.

Molding herself back into the bushes and pressing against a large round tree, Rachel squinted, narrowing her focus on the car's occupants. There were two, but she could only see shadows.

After passing a gas station and convenience store combination, the car sped up again and disappeared around the bend in the road. It was nothing. Rachel cursed herself under her breath. She was allowing her once trained senses to turn those instincts into hyperbole paranoia again.

Re-emerging from the shadows, Stackwell tried to run the across the quiet roadway, sprint the final few blocks before getting back home, but her legs objected. She had forced them to their limits earlier tonight and now they protested to more. A light jog was all that she could muster.

This time the reverberating above her had grown stronger, longer and echoed across the sky. The storm was about erupt. Rachel was only a block away and fantasized about relaxing in her bath while allowing her muscles to recuperate. She also couldn't wait to strip off her sweat soaked clothing as she could literally smell herself at the moment.

The rains had started. She could hear the large drops falling on the leaves above that protected her from the initial light droppings. The neighborhood was older, most of the houses built in the early or late 1940s, and the tall, dense trees that lined the street accentuated the date. They sheltered the homes, guarded them from the blistering sun in the summer and from the devastating winds and snow during the winter months.

Rachel had never regretted choosing this part of Madison to live. Originally built in 1942, the seven hundred square-foot Tudor style home was small, quaint as Rachel liked to describe it. Two bedrooms, although one was never used, a renovated bathroom, kitchen and an attached one car garage, which was also always empty. She had been drawn to the steeply pitched gable roof initially and found that it made the house appear larger than its single floor layout.

The home previously had one owner, an elderly woman who had survived her husband and had no children or family. When she passed, it had become property of the bank, and Rachel was able to transfer the paperwork easily.

The lot size wasn't extensive either, but her neighbors were also older, originals to those homes as well, but did keep tabs on the comings and goings in their surroundings. Jogging past the couple living next to her, Rachel waved and smiled to herself. The house was dark, but she knew they were watching out the windows.

The rains picked up their pace and began carving through the concentrated leaves. Rachel hopped the small curb, cut short onto her lawn and stopped her jog. Her house was dark too. She was sure that she left the brass lamp on next to the front window, she always left that light on, it was a habit.

She could feel the cool wetness on the back of her neck and forearms growing from the storm as an even louder roar resonated. Holding her place, she wasn't entirely in the open, but also found an obscure dark void as she knelt. The rains increased. Studying her home, Stackwell narrowed her focus back to the front window. The blinds were open, but a thin white sheath protected the privacy of inside. Did the veil move?

Fighting between trusting her instincts or the paranoia, Rachel ran low to the side of the house with the vacant garage. There were no windows here. Listening intently, she heard nothing except the sounds of rain beating down upon rooves and branches.

Inching around to the back, she peered through the side of the kitchen window. The roller blind was down and through the slits she watched for movement. There was none. Seconds turned into minutes, but still no shadows moved about in the darkness.

Carefully, still crouching, Rachel unlocked the back door. There was a small alcove, step up and then the kitchen. From here, she needed to move quickly. Closing her eyes, she visualized the house's layout and executed her plan.
Springing through the door, Stackwell made sure she had a foot fall on the raised step before launching herself into the kitchen and sliding her now drenched body across the Luxury Vinyl Tile flooring. Crashing into cupboards on the far side, she immediately

scrambled to her feet, grabbing two knives from the wood block on the countertop, and flung her body back across the room, opening the fridge door and setting it as a shield. Light filled the room, but there was no attack. The only sounds she heard were that of the glass bottles in the swaying refrigerator clanking together and the outside storm intensifying. Instincts or paranoia, Rachel still could not tell.

A standing ovation and chorus of cheers heralded Alan Wakefield as he completed his speech. The fifty-two year old man was the youngest to claim the title as President of the United States since Barack Obama. He was slender and fit, strong health and still possessed a full head of dirty blonde hair that was currently trending towards blonde with summer being the seasonal month.

Waving to the crowd, he was joined by the First Lady, Teresa Wakefield, who at ten years his junior was initially questioned by the doubters, but only proved to be a strength to his campaign when they undertook that challenge a couple years ago. Smiling and waving in unison, the raven haired stunning woman was joined by the President's Chief of Staff, the pit bull, Turner Jarvis.

Three extra tall padded wooden chairs followed the duo and all three organized themselves into a predesigned arc to appear welcoming and close knit for the chosen reporters to ask the already predisposed questions.

Derian was amused during the Presidential address, not so much by what the man was saying per se, but how the other members of the press core in attendance were reacting. Men and women scribbled furiously into notebooks with their own coded hand script, while others used recorders and cellular phones to ensure that they were able to catch every little word, stutter and breath. At one point he even found himself quietly shaking his head thinking about how the minutia of it all would be analyzed for days and weeks by whatever media outlet they all worked. It was the first time in a long time that he was actually glad to not have become that kind of journalist.

As the second of the selected members was finishing her question, he remembered the one that he was directed to ask. *The American government still hasn't truly addressed the state of medical care in our country. As a pressing topic during your campaign, you had promised to tackle the problem. When should we see that take place?* On the surface, it was truly a legitimate question, but Derian knew that it must've been planted to set up a talking point that the administration wanted to strive towards.

Looking up, he made eye contact with the President and the man gestured in his direction. It was his turn to pose his question. Butterflies filled his stomach and he swayed momentarily while standing to address the host. "Thank you Mr. President. Derian

Haynes, Washington Post." The time was now or never. Feeling the swell of courage enter his body, he wanted the basketball again, he wanted to be the court general once more. "I was looking for comment about the reports of collusion, bribery and excessive exchanges of quid pro quo between your current administration, Senator Paxton, his family, and the oil companies." Haynes held a firm stare back at Wakefield as he directed his question. Inhaling and exhaling somehow, he continued without needing a break. "Specifically, what exactly is the government providing Polygon and APC Oil for their monstrous donations both through the federal channels, and the enormous amounts that haven't properly been accounted?" The heightening in his voice turned the statement into a haughtily posed question.

A brief moment of staggering silence seized the night before rolling thunder interrupted the moment, followed by murmurs resounding around the *circus pit* of media performers. The President's eyes were momentarily set afire and bore into the ones of the young man across from him. "I would expect nothing less from the Washington Post." Wakefield snapped at Haynes without losing focus on his target. "Lies. Fabricated stories and fake news. That's all you ever publish about me." As impromptu as the question, so was the failed response. Smiling once again to the pandering crowd, Wakefield grabbed an unsuspecting Teresa by the elbow and both walked off, ending the scheduled format prematurely.

"What the fuck was that?" The President roared at his Chief of Staff as the two men were barely away from the main stage.

"That wasn't scheduled—." Turner Jarvis tried to respond.

"No shit!" Wakefield's ire had not diminished. "Get that little bastard back here before he slinks away into whatever fucking hole he just crawled out from." The President's order was answered instantly by the two Secret Service members he was staring a bullet through. Both men tore off down the makeshift hallway, heading towards the throngs of reporters that were still milling around hoping to delve deeper into this potentially growing story.

Word had spread quickly around press floor, and the masses wanted to know what Haynes was reporting. They wanted his scoop, his contacts and his sources. As he battled answering their questions with vague non-responses, the *mob* of his colleagues advanced on him until he was momentarily rescued by the two black-suited agents. The liberation was fleeting though as he was forcefully taken to the awaiting President. The whole ordeal had been accomplished in less than five minutes. Out of one fire and into another Haynes thought to himself.

Chapter EIGHT

Closing her eyes, Rachel allowed herself to sink under the warm water in the vintage cast iron Clawfoot tub before re-emerging and listening to the thunderstorm outside beat upon the roof above. It felt good to relax. The last hour was taxing to her head that was throbbing once again. She had allowed the paranoia to take control.

After assaulting her own kitchen, she went room-to-room, knives in hand, ready for a fight. None came. The lightbulb in the brass lamp that she was expecting to be on, had burned out, a simple explanation. Rain streaked as winds outside grew stronger, and with the increasing ferocity, so did the natural creaking and scrapings of a timeworn house. Every screech and groan from the windows, under the floors and between the walls were added as ingredients in her mind that *they* had come for her.

Rachel inhaled deeply. She had chosen not to turn on any lights, set up two aroma candles instead and unwind in a controllably designed darkness. It was working. The pounding to her temples was diminishing into a dull ache, the wailing from her quads and calves had been eliminated by the soothing warm water, and she no longer reeked of sweat and adrenaline. A calmness had returned, which brought a relaxed smile of contentedness.

Another loud crash of thunder shook the small house and was followed immediately by a flash of light. The storm was directly above, but Rachel would not allow the obsession of noises to get the better of her again. Deciding against powering each room full of light, Stackwell found a ceramic tray, an unused soap dish to be honest, set one of the round candles upon it and carried it to her bedroom. A quick change later and she was heading back down the hall towards the kitchen, allowing her mind to drift from the shadows that brought chaos to the rains that soothingly pummeling overhead.

An additional rumble and flash essentially on top of one another caused her peripheral vision to spring into the main room to her left. A moving shadow? No, Rachel would not allow her mind to go there again. Another deep breath and exhale. Serenity. She had leftovers and a protein shake in the refrigerator. The food would certainly revitalize her body and help bring stability back to the turmoil she continued to create in her mind.

Reaching for cool shaker, Rachel froze. Her senses picked up a smell, an aroma that was out of place. A light fragrance of lemon, but it was attempting to mask the pungency of body odor. Thunder clapped again. This time the guttural roar had moved further away and the accompanying lightning was delayed. Her instincts screamed. As she closed the appliance door, the lightning outside reached its apex.

The full body of the flash was blocked by a moving black mass. A large body ran towards her. This time, it was not the paranoia. Swinging the refrigerator door back open, it caught the attacker hard in the chest. Bottles and jars crashed together before shattering as the door was jarred from its hinges.

The body was large and his hands tore at the door as he cursed in Turkish. Rachel spun, pouncing across the room and finding herself at the counter and sink. She needed a weapon. A stainless steel spatula would suffice. Gripping it in her forward hand, she held it downward, set her balance and was prepared for blade combat.

Pitching the deterrent aside, another echoing crash broke the silence. Only deep breathing was resonating. Stepping closer, out of the shadows and into the aura of light that the candle resting on the kitchen island produced. It was the same sneer from Prague. He was seething, sweating, and Rachel could see the scars on his face that she had caused. The larger kidnapper whom she battled with once before. "This time, you die. *Orospu!*" The man's English was terrible, but he finished his sentence with his native tongue, drawing on the "*r*" to accentuate his cursive.

Rachel would not respond. Talking would waste seconds, cause one to lose focus, and right now she was focused on the man's untrained stance and the knife in his right hand. Undoubtedly it was the Katran he had previously.

Teatro lunged forward with his blade directed towards his target. Rachel swatted it away with the spatula. It was the same attack he started with in Prague. Uneducated and untrained. This time he followed it with his large left fist, but Stackwell ducked, driving her forearm under his, blocking and deflecting the stronger man's punch. Slapping the flat steel utensil against the Turk's face twisted it to the side and she stabbed the flat end into his throat.

Momentarily retreating, the larger man checked his throat and the stinging his face now felt. A small slice produced a thin trickle of blood on his neck. Switching the Russian blade to his other hand, he lunged.

Stackwell was a trained fighter, and prepared. The spatula once again deflected the uncleansed edge and she blocked his following flurry of punches with her forearms. She had survived his outburst and succeeded his attack by sliding back under his armpit. Rolling forward, Rachel added a somersault kick to stagger the man.

The maneuver did not land flush, but her foot still found its mark, glancing off the side of his neck, but shoulder taking the brunt of the assault. It was enough to open him up.

Teatro was knocked off balance. The soles of his shoes were slick, wet with spilled milk, water and juices that had broken on the floor. He slipped.

Stumbling forward, wheezing and defensively grabbing at his injury. Rachel did not relent. From behind, she hammered her foot, kicking at the fleshy back of his knee, toppling him before stomping hard on the outer side of his right knee. A loud pop was followed by intense screaming. Her pinpoint assault tore the man's anterior cruciate ligament.

Stackwell's eyes were afire. Her attacker was howling and writhing on her vinyl tiling, but that was not enough. Instincts and training had set in. Raising the spatula over her head, she crashed down hard twice, and then a third time onto the back of Teatro's skull. The fourth time broke the thin steel. Crimson red covered her hands, spreading to her face as she wiped at the sweat on her brow. Blood seeping from the larger man's skull now intertwined with the white of the spreading spilled milk.

Two gun shots rang into the kitchen through the doorway from the main room. There was a second attacker. Rachel immediately dropped behind the island for cover. The first bullet screamed through the room, shattering the back window, the second embedding into wall to the right of the sill, but only after grazing her already damaged arm.

Under normal circumstances, a private audience with the President of the United States was a journalist's dream scenario, but it didn't feel like one right now for Haynes. After shuttling him away from the mob of other reporters, the Secret Service agents physically manhandled him before tossing him to the ground at the feet of their Commander-in-Chief.

"Derian Haynes." The prestigious man in a charcoal Dolce & Gabbana suit began deliberately by first towering over his quarry, but also allowing him to slowly stand. "You are becoming quite a nuisance."

The younger black man could feel the power ploy. Thunder echoed overhead as the storm outside was in full effect. They were in a short corridor somewhere behind the main stage, shrouded with dim lighting and dark shadows. The President was joined by his Chief of Staff Turner Jarvis, and the two Secret Service agents that had originally grabbed him. All four kept a tight circle, and all were Caucasian, that fact did not escape Derian's sensitivity. He would not be intimidated. "Just looking for answers Mr. President." The statement was coy, but he still found himself being respectful to the leader of the free world.

"Answers?" Jarvis scoffed. "Your questions are bullshit and you know it."

Alan Wakefield held up his hand to silence his friend. "You are probing at questions that have no merit and do not need to be addressed."

"Then, would it be possible to have an *official* statement in regards to the quid pro quo dealings that appear to be happening with the oil companies, sir?" Adding the elevated *sir* at the end turned it into another question.

"There's nothing to find and you *know* it." Direct and with fire in the man's eyes once again.

"I have personally spoken to the President himself about the matter, and he wants to assure you—"

"Hearsay." Wakefield immediately shut down the reporter who began quoting the emails he had in his possession. "Rumor and fake news."

"I got that line from Senator Paxton already." Haynes shot back, but subtly and without elevating his voice.

"Nobody wants to hear from you, you little shit!" Turner Jarvis stepped forward into the face of the journalist. The main aide was shorter than Derian and had to push off his toes to reach eye level.

"You're a nobody Mr. Haynes." The President continued without interfering with Jarvis's verbal assault. "The people don't want to hear about your make believe stories and concocted forged emails. You won't last two days in a news cycle."

"Then, *no comment* is your official answer I suppose." A slightly smug response as Derian was beginning to fight back. "The American people want to know that they can trust the man that they elected. They want to believe that their President has honor, ownership and integrity." Haynes continued his speech. "That he believes not only in the constitution, but in adapting, improving and amending as our ways of life advance, and cultivate. You know, *of the people, by the people, for the people.*"

Wakefield laughed. "Spewing Lincoln at me." The President's demeanor changed instantly, becoming fierce and menacing. "Listen to me closely one time you fucking lightweight. The American people don't give a damn about what I do or don't do as long food and gas prices are low, taxes are affordable and they get entertaining television." He was seething. "The only time we even talk about the goddamned Constitution anymore is when some idiot with a gun goes off, or when people like *you* want to attack me. *Freedom of the press*, freedom of this, freedom of that, nobody fucking cares unless it benefits them. People don't care what you have to say."

Derian wanted to lash out the ignorance of the man, but was lost for words himself. "Then I suppose we can let the people decide what's important." It was a weak response, but all he felt he could provide.

"No. You won't write anything about the matter *at all*." It was a veiled threat. Simple and direct. "I am the President of the United States and you have already been a traitor to this this country once before." Wakefield could see the confusion come across the reporter's face. "Sure the administration back then might've let you off with a slap on the wrist, but *believe* me, I will not!"

"I was upholding my journalistic integrity." Haynes retorted.

"You broke the commands of your superiors, thus committing treason."

"I was not an enlisted soldier. I do not follow orders from colonels, or generals, or—"

"Or Presidents?" Wakefield interrupted. "You will follow mine. This, I will promise you. If not, I will see you placed in Leavenworth. I don't care if you're not military personnel, I am the President of the United States and can do whatever the hell I like."

"You said that already too." Haynes muttered under his breath. "There is no legal precedent that would ever allow that to happen." Derian wanted to continue the fight, but was once again grabbed from behind by the two larger agents.

"Get rid of him, we're done here." Wakefield stepped forward one last time to whisper directly to Haynes. "This is over, or you are over. I will simply make you vanish and your life, your mother's legacy, it'll all disappear too." A slight hiss on the final warning as he shoved the restrained man.

"Do you think he got the message?" Turner Jarvis posed the question to the President as the armored limousine, *Cadillac One*, sped along U.S. Highway 151 towards Dane County Regional Airport.

"He better." Wakefield derided. "The last thing we need is for a goddamn hack reporter, hell he's not even that much, to shit in my pool." Jarvis snickered at the comparison.

"Do you think he actually could?" The First Lady chimed in as she turned away from the window. The rains were slowing, but still very much present in the skies above. "I mean, do you actually believe that he has enough that the people would even care?"

"The people wouldn't understand spit from rain." Smiling at his wife. "No. The general public probably could care less, but the House Ethics Committee would, and that could cause problems going forward."

"Not if we limit their powers, essentially disband them." The pit-bull in Jarvis had excitement in his eyes. He had wanted to remove the governing body for years.

"We can't do that Turner. That's an even bigger shitstorm to worry about."

"Then we need to create a new narrative." Theresa Wakefield stated softly. "A new story, bigger than anything that this journalist could even try to reveal."

"Another war in the Middle East?" The Chief of Staff threw out the most obvious answer to all Presidential concerns and scandals.

"No, something closer to home." The First Lady smiled devilishly to her husband. "Something that could pull at the hearts of people instead of their brains."

"You have an idea." The President knew that he loved the way his wife's mind worked.

"I do." Another glance out the reinforced window to her right. "Cullen has an associate on his island that specializes in breaking family's hearts." Theresa saw that her husband wasn't entirely sure where her train of thought was heading. "Well, Senator Paxton has a fifteen year old granddaughter.

I'm sure it would make a much more interesting story if she *disappeared*."

"There would be an outcry of support and compassion towards him instead of outrage." Alan Wakefield's voice trailed off as he thought about the idea even more.

"Plus," Theresa crooned her head and patted her husband on the chest. ", who knows, there might even be the prospects of combating the human trafficking issues in America and gain more voters." Now smiling at one another, there was an opportunity that both the President and Jarvis liked equally.

The second intruder fired three more times at the wooden island Rachel was using as cover. Five in total she thought, but did not know how many bullets were available. She knew she had to move. With the door torn away from the refrigerator, the light was filling the kitchen, thus her shadow displayed on the cupboards behind her.

The gunman knew exactly where she was, and certainly only hesitating because he was uncertain about his teammate's status. He was dead. Face down on her vinyl floor, surrounded by the coagulating of his own blood and milk.

Rachel's eyes darted around, searching for another weapon. Broken bottles and jars would not help, and the already used stainless steel spatula was useless. The Katran! It had to be on the ground somewhere. Stackwell now had purpose for her hunt.

It *was* there. Inches in front of the dead man's limp arm and hand, but also laying in the open. Two more shots. Wood splintered to her right. One of the bullets either perfectly hit the corner, or it went through the essentially hollow kitchen island. Regardless, the killer was getting more aggressive and she could not wait any longer.

In one swift motion, Stackwell set into a crouch, launching herself across the wet-stained flooring and towards the darkened alcove of the rear entrance. The liquids helped with the slide, but she could also feel the pricks of broken glass tearing at her skin through her t-shirt.

Another two shots followed her into the shadows, but neither found their mark. Crumpling into a ball after falling down the one step, Rachel rolled over. The gunman was sprinting towards her. The rear door sat directly behind her, but she would not flee. Rachel bit her bottom lip and gripped the handle of the Russian knife tightly, as her eyes narrowed on yet another target.

The second attacker's attention was momentarily displaced when he saw the lifeless body of his comrade, and it was all the American woman needed. Springing from the shadows, Rachel caught the advancing gunman in the body with a spear attack. Her forward momentum instantly meeting with his deescalating one and he was driven backwards hard.

Their bodies met with a crashing thud, stunning both with the man then releasing the grip of the pistol. Rachel was expecting the impact and hers held firm around the Katran. Swinging out, she found flesh on the man's chest, but he was more skilled in combat than his larger companion. Spinning away from the knife attack, it ripped through his skin, but also forced his attacker to lose a firm grip. Bleeding, he pulled the blade from his body, tossed it to the ground and stood facing Stackwell.

He was only a little taller than her, stood in a fighter's stance and even switched his feet twice. The man had some skill, which brought a smile of delight to Rachel as she recognized his face as well. It was the driver from the van in Prague. She attacked.

A leaping left forward kick was followed by a right roundhouse, he blocked both. Returning with a punch to her stomach and raised kick that caught her in the right shoulder. Staggered, but not hurt.

A side chop towards his throat was tossed away by blocking forearms creating a cross shield and he kicked again at her stomach, driving her back and toppling her this time. The man sneered, mocking her to attack again.

A deep breath. Right punch. Blocked. Left punch. Blocking again, he returned with a sweep kick which she jumped over and then drove her foot sideways into his solar plexus. The driver gasped as he regained his footing. Stackwell now snarled and was her turn to beckon him to attack with her fingers.

He obliged. A quick right hand was knocked away and she returned a left fist to his face. He stopped the right, then caught her in the side with a swing kick. Another left foot from Rachel made contact. The man punched back, landing a fist of his own to her right cheek.

There was no relenting now. Punching his wounded chest, she found a brief opening. Grabbing both his shoulders, pulling him forwards and driving two swift knees into his bent over upper body. He took both firm shots. Shoving her away, before swinging a right foot. It missed over her head as she ducked. Both kicked out with their right feet, neutralizing one another.

Rachel didn't rest. A sweep kick took the legs out from under her assailant, and she followed it with a heel stomp to his chest. He rolled backwards and she hit the floor instead. Following it immediately with another stomp. This time the man grabbed her calf, spun her to the ground while twisting himself up into an attack position. Another crass smile allowed her time to get back up.

Both combatants were breathing heavy, but neither would relinquish. Rachel lunged to her right and caught the man leaning. He went to block, but she jumped, attacked with spinning heel kick. He wavered. A small opening and Stackwell didn't hesitate. A firm right, spinning into a solid left forearm shot and then rotating back into another jumping spin kick. All three were direct hits. The last whipped the driver's head up while he spit blood and teeth.

It only enraged him more. Screaming, he propelled himself at her, but she caught him. Jumping up, she landed on the back of his neck, cradling his head behind her right knee. Somersaulting, and tightening her grip. Both rotated over each other before finding their feet. Rachel kicked out. The fuming Turk caught her foot, lifted her onto his shoulders, twisted around and flung her in the air across the room.

Rachel crashed hard into the wooden cabinets, bounced off the countertop and fell to the floor. She was groggy and the man did not yield. Picking her up and tossing back across to the other side and into the broken refrigerator.

Kicking her twice in the side brought instant pain, but also determination. The American broke the third onslaught, grabbing and twisting the man's foot and ankle. The pain forced him to retreat and she found the opportunity to rise. It was Stackwell that was now incensed.

Jolting towards him, she kicked the gunman in the chest, a second time and blocked his punches. He spun and elbowed her in the back. She didn't feel it. She still had his other hand and bent his wrist under and backwards. Tendons popped. Flinging her body around his like a spider, Rachel rolled the driver to the ground, gripping his neck and began pummeling knees into the side of his skull.

Her fuming desire for victory burned hotly. Climbing onto his back, Stackwell dug her grip around the flesh of his neck and began choking the man. When he tried to straighten, she wrapped her legs around his torso and squeezed even tighter. Choking and cutting off all air and circulation to the man. He began to lose consciousness. It was only seconds now before he was out. The brawl was over.

"Don't move!" The order was shouted loudly as one, and then a second flashlight was shone on her face, and in her eyes. "Don't move lady! I don't know what's going on here, but it's over." Two policemen approached cautiously. The man yelling at her spoke into the radio on his shoulder.

Rachel spit blood and surveyed her surroundings. The kitchen now looked like a war zone. The floor stained red, one dead body and her covered with blood. The officers were still approaching slowly.

Below her, Rachel could hear the man beginning to wheeze. The driver from Prague was regaining consciousness. Her eyes blazed again. "Ma'am, I'm going to approach and help you off the ground, okay?" The stout officer was still in the doorframe to enter the destroyed kitchen, but did not advance.

Rachel could taste iron on her lips from the blood, but didn't know whose it was. Staring blankly at the policeman, she tried to stand, but only felt the grip of the man below her around her ankle. Reacting immediately, Stackwell reached back, grabbed a half shattered wine bottle and plunged the jagged end into the man's thigh, then immediately sprang back, driving it twice more into his chest before one final time into a still smirking face.

Both police officers shouted for to her to stop. Guns were drawn, but did not fire. More blood and the stench of death filled the room as the lifeless man's body released its fluid. Rachel did not take her eyes off the Turk below her as she slowly placed her hands in the air. Dripping crimson, the palms slowly turned towards the bright flashlights, and she arose again.

Rachel was calm. She had physical pain, but the throbbing in her head was completely gone. Smiling to herself as she approached the police, she could see more flashing lights through the front window. She was content. There was no paranoia. It had always been her instincts.

Chapter NINE

Willful disruption of state government processes. Derian scoffed to himself as he read the half-filled out police report still on the desk in front of him. The President was flexing that power he possessed by having the Secret Service escort and march him into the nearest police station for detention.

They did not choose the on campus station across the parking lot from Camp Randall Stadium, but the newly established Midtown District. The Commander-in-Chief wanted Haynes paraded into a precinct where everybody could see the journalist's consequences, especially any other reporters looking to join his crusade of questioning.

Twice, he had already asked the officer entering the information into a computer if he could remove the handcuffs, and twice he received merely a snarl and uttered threats to remain quiet. That was easily an hour ago, but now he was sitting alone. It wasn't the actual fact about being handcuffed that was causing the discomfort, but it was the angle that they had seated him while being chained to the desk.

Derian was sure that the officer would've preferred to see him placed in one of the holding cells in the basement, but that was not physically possible. The night had quickly turned into chaos at the Midtown District. As the weather flared fiercely above the town, so did the temperatures between the pro and against rally goers. Three fights had broken out, one after the other outside the stadium. Rains poured down, separating some brawlers, but not enough. Jail cells across the city were now filling, but the central Midtown station was taking the brunt of the detainees. Any overflow of sober or less violent arrestees had been locked in offices or conference rooms, but the chanting and yelling still echoed in the corridors while officers ran frantic in all directions and shouted back-and-forth.

"We're not usually this much a circus in Madison." An older black man spoke softly to Derian. "It's usually pretty quiet and peaceful." Sipping a steaming mug, he gazed across the calamity before continuing softly. "We get the odd break and enter, but mainly graffiti complaints." The man must've shaved his head a day or so ago, as the gray stubble was beginning to grow back in. "I'm Chief Xavier Sampson. Let me get those for you." An exhale of exhaustion came from the head policeman as he leaned over to open the shackles restraining Haynes to the desk.

"Thank you, Chief." Skepticism was still in his voice. "Does this mean I'm free to go?" Haynes rubbed his wrists.

"Not yet son." The elder answered the reporter, sighing as he sat on the edge of the desk across from him, placing and offering a cold soda can for him to drink. "The agents that brought you in were dead set on seeing you charged and paraded right back out of the building before taken to county, but things are a little messy around here right now," Sampson chuckled to himself. ", as you can see."

"And yet, you're uncuffing me?" Derian's hesitancy in his question was equally matched by the look in his eyes. "Aren't you afraid I might sneak out?"

"Heck no." Genuine laughter came from the Chief of police. "I've read up on you, watched the interaction from earlier this evening between you and the President, and I can see when a bully is trying to flex his muscle." Another shorter laugh this time. "No, the President is trying to once again trample on the media for speaking up against him, and unlike him, I actually fought in a war for this country, so having certain freedoms means something to me." Leaning in closer, Sampson winked before fruitfully adding. "Plus, I never voted for the man." He laughed again, before his face lost its darkened hue. Sampson's mouth gaped open and he rushed towards the entrance.

Haynes was turned away, in the opposite direction, but spun in his seat to follow the panicked look of the police Chief. Two more officers were escorting a shorter individual. A police blanket wrapping them and covering their head, but their hands were protruding forwards, handcuffed together and stained red.

As the individual was walked past where he sat, Derian could see the face of a woman under the hood that the blanket created. Her eyes were set forward, did not change their focus, and seemed dead. Sliding himself closer, Haynes was intrigued by the situation.

"What's going on Parker?" Sampson spoke to his officer as he sat the woman down.

"It was awful Chief. I've never seen anything like it before in my life. I'm still not entirely sure—" The officer was still shaken when he thought about what he arrived on scene to find. Genuine concern was in his voice. "We were responding to a call about shots fired." Parker began slowly, deliberate in his recollecting the events leading up to his discovery. "A neighbor called 911, they heard what sounded like loud crashing, a fight possibly, but then gunshots, next door to them." Looking towards the woman seated in the chair across from them, he continued. "The only thing was that the caller claimed that her neighbor lived alone so it wasn't a domestic thing." Pausing to find air, Parker was preparing himself for the details. "When we arrived, we could tell the front door had been broken, handle removed, so we, um, entered." Another pause, deep swallowing in his throat as he remembered the graphic scene.

As the woman was seated, the blanket fell open and Sampson noticed the stained blood covering her hands and body. He was shocked silent.

"Upon entry, we could see signs of a disturbance and hear what sounded definitely like a fight." Meeting eyes with his partner, they both were grim. "We moved from the main sitting room into the kitchen where it looked like a warzone. One deceased male, face down, plus one more, um, injured male with her, set female sitting atop of him." The officer was trying to be professional in his details.

"So is she the victim of a break in gone wrong, or the assailant?" Sampson still hadn't taken his eyes from her as she appeared to be traumatized and unmoving.

"Records state that she is the home owner, Rachel Stackwell, a resident here in Madison." Parker was deliberate in his speech as he was trying to forget about the next part of his evening. "Possibly victim yes, but when asked if she was okay and instructed her to slowly move towards us." Another gulp of air. "She scooped up a broken bottle, stabbed the man repeatedly in the body before plunging it, into his, his, face."

Sampson's eyes immediately shot back towards his officers and could see in theirs that it was a horrific act. Scenes that he knew soldiers had witnessed, but not cops in a small town. "Has she said anything? Who the men were, or what was going on in *her* house?"

"Nothing Chief." Parker retorted. "She hasn't a said a word. She's barely moved."

"Alright, keep her here, away from the rest of this mess tonight." The office they were in was currently vacant, a retired detective's post hadn't been filled yet and situated in a quieter corner of the chaos in the building. "Get Grace from CSI up here and have her process Ms. Stackwell. Let me know when she's done so we can get a couple officer's to escort her to the bathroom and showers to clean up."

"Sir?" Parker was still concerned. "About the man she *killed*?"

"Let's find out who they were first, and what the hell they were doing there. We're going to treat her as the victim here until we know more." Sampson looked down at the woman who still hadn't moved. "Keep the cuffs on, lock the door and we'll post Jenkins outside until we can figure this thing out."

"Chief?" Another man rushed into the room, interrupting him as he was about to continue. "You have a call in your office."

"Take a message Will."

"No, sir, you *need* to take this call." The uniformed man was direct and insistent. He stepped closer and half-whispered to his commanding officer. "It's somebody from the government, the CIA." Nodding towards the static woman in the chair. "It's about *her*."

Derian Haynes carefully slipped into the barren office behind the exiting officers, looked at the woman seated under the hooded blanket and warily sat down across from her. He had been watching through the window, but also standing close enough to the cracked open door to overhear the conversations between the policemen. Placing the still cold can on the empty wood desk next to her, he deliberately opened the tab slowly, allowing a long release of fizzy carbonation to consume the silence in the room. "Do you want my soda? They gave it to me right before you came in so it'll still be cold."

There was no response from the woman. Haynes continued. "It'll help restore the sugars back into your body and allow you to think a little more clearly," His voice changed from soft to one with some firmness behind it. ", because I know you were listening to everything they were saying." Pausing for a reaction.

The woman's stateless gaze moved from the floor and slowly met his. Her eyes were fierce and penetrating. Derian had a chill run up his spine as he instantly felt fear of the woman whom had already killed two men tonight. "I've been watching your eyes." Haynes continued guardedly. "Your focus has been seemingly away from them, but you were listening to every word those officers were saying. A person's eyes narrow or flare when they are concentrating, yet trying to look or be inattentive." It was basic cognitive psychology, but also a useful tool to remember as a journalist when interviewing subjects that had things to hide. He waited again for a response. The woman simply reached for the can without removing stare she bore into him.

"Who are you?" Rachel asked quietly, but directly to the man seated across from her. "You're not a cop or a shrink?" He was right, she had been listening to everything that was being said to and about her. Time was now of the essence, she could not simply stay seated until they were ready to release her. There was also no need to speak to the police, she already knew why the men were in her home, but she didn't know whom they *worked* for. Local law enforcement would not be able to help with that.

"How do you know that?" The man's response was hesitant, he wasn't actually expecting her to answer him.

"You don't talk like one." He was also right about the soda. It was cold. The condensation on the can nearly causing it to slip right out of her fingers, but Rachel readjusted the grip of her hand. She drank the cool lemon-lime flavored liquid. "You aren't determined to have an answer immediately, you want some sort of connection, but it also isn't on a personal level." Another large gulp of the sugary beverage. "That rules out both." Offering up a wry smile, Stackwell concluded. "Plus, you keep rubbing your wrists. I'm guessing you recently were wearing these as well." Rachel held her hands forward and shook the loose handcuffs that had once connected her hands together while the remaining soda fizzed once more from the aggravation.

"I'm a reporter." Haynes replied to keep the conversation going, but couldn't help staring at the fact that she had already slipped out of her restraints. "Washington Post."

"That would actually make sense." Rachel remembered her minor dealings with journalists covering the Middle East. "What brings you to Madison, Mr. Washington Post?"

"The President actually." There was a distaste behind the reporter's words.

"You're not a fan I assume." It wasn't a question, just a presumption as Rachel continued the conversation while her attention was through the blinds and across the building.

"He had me arrested for asking a hard question." Haynes refocused, he didn't want to talk about himself. "So what actually happened to you?" He was undeviating. "Two men break into your home and both end up dead?"

Stackwell's focus immediately shot to the man asking the question. "What do you know about it?" Her own query was sharp and hissed. Was he part of the men as well? Her instincts said no, but the paranoia screamed yes.

"Only what I heard the officers talking about." There was defensiveness in the reporter's voice now. "I was more interested in how—"

"Sorry Mr. Washington Post, but your interview will have to wait." Rachel's words trailed off at the end as her attention was drawn back towards the movement through the windows behind the man across from her. From her vantage point, she could see into the Chief's office and that phone call he *had* to take was over. Time was up, she couldn't wait any longer. Rachel sprang from her seat, directly pointed for the journalist to stay put and headed for the door.

"There's at least one officer outside by now." Haynes called out. "Maybe two, or three even." Stackwell froze as she was reaching for the office door. She had assumed one man to the left, but he was right, there could be more than just one. "I could check for you." She heard him finish his thought as she looked at him from the corners of her eyes. A shrewd smile came across her lips.

Derrick Cross rubbed his eyes as he sat back in his firm high-back desk chair and watched his people work below through the clear reinforced glass. He was exhausted and bored at the same time. Officially designated as *Retired*, the United States Air Force Colonel was now in charge of a specialized operations department of the Central Intelligence Agency.

Situated in an unassuming wing of the Pentagon, Cross's team worked in a large windowless room, rows of computers, desks and people vertically lined like a movie theater all facing a massive wall screen. Currently they had no active operations, and the screen was half dark while the lit parts were active camera feeds from major cities across the world. He held no title, his people no positions, and there was no designated name for his division. It simply did not *officially* exist.

A flashing red light above the only entrance to the room caught his attention. A request to enter the private crisis suite was being initiated. Cross checked the camera outside the door and tapped a button sequence on his keyboard to unlock the bolted double doors.

Determined to meet his visitors on the main concourse, Cross jogged from out behind his desk to the walkway above his people. He arrived just as the first figure entered the unlit office. "Madam Deputy Director, what can I attest to this visit? I have no active missions that should concern you."

Virginia Bennett was the Deputy Director of CIA Operations. The former case officer had a diluted past within the Agency, but was known as a dedicated task manager when she was a Station Chief in Islamabad, Moscow, London and Rome. Still attractive in her early fifties, the woman was a recipient of the prestigious Intelligence Star, but also ruthless if you opposed her. That was not a side of the woman that Derrick wanted to test, since if there was anybody that could be considered as *his* boss, it would be her.

"Who the hell is Rachel Stackwell?" The CIA woman was direct and to the point.

"I, don't know." Her explosion caught Cross off-guard and he stammered momentarily.

"I'm not in the mood for your bullshit Cross." Bennett continued fiercely. "I've got Senator Duvall busting my ass to find this woman and when I did, all my systems shut down and security clearances blocked, by authority of *you*."

Cross wanted to object, but he truly didn't know who the name was. His eyes wandered to the Deputy Director's aide that was standing behind her. Chelsea Williamson, a smart and pretty former member of his team that was hand selected to be the right hand of Virginia Bennett, but he didn't see her now as more than a glorified secretary. Eyes determined to tell him something important, she was nodding slowly at the man she still was loyal to, encouraging him to act on the information.

It was one of Cross's hidden secrets. His section may not exist on paperwork, but with his unlimited budget, it allowed him access to unrestricted funds to privatize his own faithful army of spies within the Washington elite. He knew more about secret deals and clandestine alliances than probably the President himself. As he thought he should.

The nod was also a warning to be careful as to what he said next. "Why is Senator Duvall looking for this woman? Rachel Stackwell?" Cross was carefully deflecting. "Who is she to the Chairman of the Senate Intelligence Committee?"

"She's the American hero that disappeared from a Prague hospital last week after stopping an abduction." Bennett's voice was contentious. "You *must* know who *that* is."

"I remember hearing about it, but it's not any operation of mine." Cross raised his voice at the end to accentuate that he wasn't involved.

"I *know* that you're not," Another patronizing remark. ", but the Senator wants to do some grand ceremony to recognize this woman's bravery."

"So a fucking PR stunt."

"She disappeared from Hospital Na Bulovce before the local police could question her," Bennett ignored the comment and half-smiled to show that she agreed. ", but Chelsea was able to track her down and back here in the United States."

"She was always one of *my* best." A wry, conceited smile and statement.

"May I?" The pretty blonde assistant held out thumb drive while motioning towards an empty computer station. Cross nodded and extended a welcoming jester. "We know that she was taken to and admitted with a concussion, right? So, figuring it wasn't an abduction of her own, and that if she was so determined to leave the hospital, I assumed she would head to the airport or the train stations." Chelsea began rambling as she pounded furiously at the keyboard. "Planes are faster, but train stations are easier to manipulate. Here." The woman transferred grainy footage to the main screen that towered in front of the room. "This is her here. Boarding a night train at Praha hlavní nádraží with a final destination being Wrocław, Poland. Now, there isn't any footage at all the stops so it took some time, but she does stay on the entire trip." Another even grainier video footage this time showed a figure moving on a busy platform and towards the exits.

"Do you know where she goes after this?" Cross was now intrigued. "More security cameras?" Chelsea only looked disparagingly at her former boss. Eye contact was made and he only knew better than to ask.

"She changed clothes on the train, but I was able to eventually find her again. Here. Local train to Wrocław Nicolaus Copernicus Airport. Purchased a one-way flight to Chicago with a two hour layover in Frankfurt, with her own passport and credit card." Williamson smiled widely this time.

"Okay, so what's the problem?" Derrick was confused as to why this woman would be flagged by his division.

"Rachel Stackwell doesn't exist." Bennett spat out again. "She disappears again in a goddamn Chicago restroom." The Deputy Director's voice was growing and so was her temper. "There are one hundred and seventy-two Rachel Stackwell's in the United States, and she is *not* any of them!" Bennett collected herself. "Tell me how this is possible Cross. Explain to me how this woman has a valid passport and credit cards, but does not have a driver's license, social security number or pays taxes. Hell, she doesn't even have a social media account anywhere."

"You just described millions of Americans." Cross shot back. "How should I know her from any of them?"

"Because she's been flagged by your goddamned little secret treehouse here!" Bennett fumed again.

"Derrick, you *need* to see this." Chelsea interrupted the war of words. Partly because the other members of the room had turned their attention towards them, but mostly to protect him from overstepping his bounds. She knew her former boss, and he believed that he was untouchable. He was not.

"What?" Spitting out the retort while still glaring at Virginia Bennett, Cross's eyes widened in shock. The anger and fire inside of him immediately drained when the passport photo of Rachel Stackwell was displayed on the main screen. "Holy shit." He whispered to himself.

"You do *know* her." The disdain had not left Bennett's voice yet.

Cross ignored her. "Send everything you have to the main database." His first order was for Chelsea, and he followed it by addressing the rest of his team below. "Alright people, we're back on. You all know the target. Exploration and pursuit. Chelsea's going to drop a bunch of files into the queue, I want them all dissected down to every pixel. Get me everything! If you find something you don't like or something that's distinct, send it back here. Chelsea is at station twelve, she'll highlight it."

"Derrick? What are you doing? *Who* is Rachel Stackwell?" It was Bennett's turn to be confused.

"You were right. She doesn't exist." His statement was simple. "It's a legend." There was anger in his face again, but this time it was not directed at anybody in particular. "It's just not a legend created by us. It must be one of her own."

"A legend? For whom? Who is she?"

"She's one of ours. She *was* one of mine." Cross corrected himself.

"One of your, what?" The Deputy Director had a stern tone to her question, but it was also laden with confusion and hesitancy.

"You do remember exactly what we do here right Virginia?" The man was a combination of condescension and panic.

"Black Ops. You're a special activities division."

"Exactly. We do the work that needs to get done, but nobody wants on their ledger."

"Are you saying there's more to your work here than I know about?" Bennett dove deeper.

"Jesus Christ Virginia. You can't be that naïve? You've seen movies, you know *specialized* people are needed." Cross didn't have time to explain his true operations to the woman that went before congress every year to fund his team. "Well sometimes those movies come true. She's our Jason Bourne, our James Bond. Only thing is that this is real life, so real bullshit happens."

"What the hell does that mean Cross? The Deputy Director railed again. "She went missing? Amnesia?"

"No, not exactly. That's Sophia Warner. Designation, *beyond salvage*." Sighing as he said her name and looking at the towering screen in front of him.

"Cross. Enough games. Who the hell is that woman?"

"She *was* one of the best." Trailing off before refocusing, Derrick turned towards the government woman. "The bombing of Charles Bridge in Prague, nearly, um, ten years ago."

"She was responsible?"

"Hell no!" Cross recomposed himself after the brief outburst. "No, she was *on* the bridge." Chelsea directed her boss to the screen as she brought up the files. "She survived, but her lover was killed."

"But, we do know whom was responsible, do we not?" Bennett asked softly.

"Yes, and we took them out," Cross nodded for Chelsea to access another digital page. ", but it didn't stop her. She believed that her own evidence uncovered that the Russians were initially responsible for funding the terrorist group, and she sought her own justice."

A new photo emerged. "Pavel Taratukhin." Bennett was barely audible, but also unsure of the meaning for the connection. "The Russian President's son's assassination?"

131

"Unsanctioned." Cross was resolute. "Still, it was her."

"Making her a trained rogue assass—"

"*Beyond salvage* is the term we use here." A quick correction.

"Meaning what exactly Derrick?"

"Meaning," A slight pause before meeting eyes with the Deputy Director. ", meaning that we put her down the first chance we get."

"I got something!" A man's voice bellowed across the active crisis center.

"Where?" Cross pounced at the announcement. "Send it here."

"Madison, Wisconsin." The bald man continued. "A home belonging to a Rachel Stackwell had a possible burglary, but the intruders were killed instead."

"How plausible is this one?

"The woman was taken into custody, but this Rachel Stackwell is supposed to be over ninety years old according to state records."

Derrick Cross stared at the black and white photo of Sophie Warner on the screen in front of him. The red stamp across it designating her status grabbed his attention firmly as he ran the prospects of this finally being her. He cursed. "It's her. Send a team there. Now!"

"She's at the Midtown District in Madison." The bald technician called over again as he worked his touch screen monitor.

"Get me whoever's in charge of that police station on the phone right now!" Cross exclaimed. "I don't care if they have to put the entire department on her, they can't let her leave." He had finally found her.

"Where did she go?" Xavier Sampson barked with panic in his voice. The man from the CIA had given direct orders to place her in the most secure cell he had until their agents had arrived, but now she was gone.

Rushing immediately from his office with the closest officers he could find, Sampson's anxiety flared when he noticed that the two men placed outside the office were gone. Instead of finding his catatonic victim sitting shackled in the chair he left her in, he saw his men sprawled on the floor, unconscious, and the journalist from Washington handcuffed in her place.

"Don't know." Haynes responded to the ordered question before smiling to himself. "Said she had somewhere to be." Four more policemen filled the room behind their Chief, checking on the fallen comrades. Derian raised his bound hands as high as he could. "Little help here please."

Sampson wanted to curse at the man, but restrained his temper, he had bigger problems if Rachel Stackwell, or Sophia Warner, or whatever her name was, wasn't in his custody when the government agents arrived. "Get him outta here,"

Yelling now at nobody in particular in the room. ", and put him in *my* office. I want to have a word with Mr. Haynes before he leaves."

"She also drank my soda." Derian reached for and shook the open can to prove that it was empty." The frazzled Chief of police only scowled at the cynical comment. His eyes bore through Haynes momentarily before turning and heading for the door. Calling again for his men to follow, he added more once out in the hall. "Good luck finding her. I'll be waiting for you." Haynes called back as one remaining officer approached him with a key to the handcuffs that bound him. As he was released, he smiled while rubbing his wrists again and thinking about what the woman had noticed earlier about him. He found humor in the moment, and this time he couldn't help but laugh when he cooed again towards the frantic officers. "And don't forget my soda!"

PART II

Chapter TEN

Excitement mounted in the crowd as the young speedster collected the black frozen puck onto his stick and with an explosive stride split the two defensemen while entering into the offensive zone. Flying by the larger men, he was now set one-on-one with the veteran goaltender, there would be no chance for the padded guardian.

The seventeen year old was already a superstar in the hockey world and was being compared to two of the greatest goal scorers of all time. Wayne Gretzky was the first name branded, but he preferred the comparison to his personal idol, fellow countryman Alex Ovechkin. Unlike either, he was going to be the first player chosen during the upcoming summer's National Hockey League's Entry Draft.

Three more elegant strides. Dipping his back shoulder, adding in a sudden stutter with his trailing skate while gliding across the glistening ice forced his opponent to make a decision, and he knew he had the man beat. The goaltender reacted to the fake, lunged to his right, but was now caught. Doing the splits while sliding, the protector tried to recover, but the agile young forward was too quick.

Standing and screaming in unison the capacity crowd filling the Ice Palace roared as the frozen black puck met the mesh netting, bulging it outwards and a loud horn blared while the flashing red siren of the light beaconed, signifying a goal had been scored. The home fans were ecstatic. Many waving towels, signs, singing the local goal hymn or simply banging their palms on the clear Plexiglas separating the athletes from the purchased seats. It was their young hero's second goal already tonight and it was still the first period. Anticipation would now course through the elated fans every time he touched the puck for that memorable hat trick celebration.

Above the festivities on the ice and in the lower stands, the party in the owner's suite erupted as well. It was January 7th in Moscow, Christmas Day, and a national holiday. Because the Russian Orthodox uses the Julian calendar as opposed to the Gregorian one, the fêted date falls into the first week of the New Year as well as the prominent one at the end of December.

Tonight, the owner of the renowned CSKA Moscow hockey team had exalted guests, the Russian President and his eldest son. Mikhail Taratukhin had been hand selected by the preceding President to replace him, and as many past elections in the country's notorious history, was rumored to have been rigged to ensure his successful nomination.

He was nearing sixty-three years of age and had held his position of power for almost a decade. The essential *appointment* to Presidency was his first official sitting in the political world, but he had become a favorite within the United Russia party for his years of military service and ascension to Marshal of the Russian Federation.

Taratukhin's selection was at first seen as a curious one too, but it was made because of his stark differences to most Generals from the Russian military ranks. The man was prototypically strict and harsh, but also possessed a humane side that was a welcomed one from the people he now presided. The Russian Federation also wanted desperately to be back on the world stage with the other prominent powerful countries and he fit the mold that could help put them there. A staunch military man who spoke elegantly, precisely and with compassion. He was an easy choice for confirmation by the rest of his party.

Although, even with Mikhail's reign, the levels of corruption within the government itself had not diminished. It was now simply a way of life in Moscow. This was evident most notably by and through his eldest son Pavel. The Taratukhin heir was twenty-five, and lived the life of an oligarch.

Pavel graduated from Secondary General Education at the top of his class, was enrolled at Moscow State Institute of International Relations,

Harvard of Russia, for three years, but found that his last name and father's position of power allowed him exceptionally more influence and authority than he had earned.

Originally partnering himself with two of Russia's rival criminal organizations, Pavel brought peace through the naturalization of wealth. Rumors swirled about how much hands-on presence the President himself actually had, but none could question that the in-state violence between the warring syndicates had declined.

With the dwindling hostilities also brought new found wealth and business opportunities. The days of the Russian mafia were stronger than ever, and potentially even more dangerous as it was infused with political prowess and strengthened with legitimacy. The old *rules* of the Russian hierarchy seemed to be back under the watchful eye of Pavel Taratukhin. It was a simple message, do not challenge the state and leave visiting foreigners alone. If these guidelines were followed, the government would allow you to do your own business how you wanted, and even help you set up connections with whomever you needed.

The father and son duo were orchestrating a new world in the *Motherland*, but one that did not reduce the wealth of its truly most powerful. Tonight, they celebrated a tradition that they had for all of the years that Pavel could remember. Even as a young boy, he could recall spending Christmas night at a hockey game with his father. He didn't ever remember missing one. Most years, especially as a child, they would sit in the secondary seats, high above it all, but as his father's position advanced, so did the vantage point for the on ice action.

As the prominent hockey scorer below celebrated with his teammates, Mikhail broke away from their host to revel the moment with his son. Regardless of politics, religion or business, this had always been *their* night and tonight would be no different. Pavel could feel himself being that little boy once again sitting in the hard wooden seats high above the ice.

Patience was a skill for a trained sniper. Across from the owner's suite in the Ice Palace was a row of small connected rooms held firmly in place by heavy metal beams and scaffolding. At one time, they were used as a press box for reporters, television commentary teams and scratched players to sit in expensive suits. After the hockey arena's renovation, the boxes were painted black, kept dark and unused on most nights.

Tonight, after the President's security team swept through them, the figure descended from above and into one of the vacant shadowed rooms. For almost two days, the figure waited to descend. Two days without food or water, controlling one's body and mind to stay alert, rested and mobile through stasis. Patience.

The two days passed easily as the sniper would have waited as long as needed to feel this moment. Another loud horn blew. Lights flashed and screaming and cheering erupted from everybody below once more. It was time and the figure didn't hesitate.

A delicate tap of the trigger and the long range rifle spat forward. From this distance, it was impossible for the trained professional to miss, but wanting to feel the agony in the eyes of the target was paramount. Escape was not necessarily the objective, pain and anguish was.

Pavel Taratukhin threw his arms up and screamed as the young Russian phenom netted his third goal of the night. Jubilance exploded from the spectators in the crowd and in the owner's suite as once more the senior Taratukhin reached out to embrace his son.

The moment of bliss instantly turned into one of horror. During the hug, Mikhail felt his son's grip disappear and body go limp. Trying to hold himself up, he couldn't and fell to the floor with the dead weight of his son crashing down atop of him. Two women screamed. Shouting immediately followed from the armed security forces as President Mikhail Taratukhin wailed while clutching Pavel's body. One hole was perfectly placed in the middle of the boy's forehead, and a slow trickle of blood began to ooze out.

Through the scope, the figure had been focused solely on the face of the distraught President once the man understood the reality of the situation.

A wry smile crept across the face of the trained killer. The father was heartbroken. Escape would now be considered.

It would not take the personal security, mainly FSB trained agents long to distinguish from where the shot had come, and the shooter knew that the arena would be in full lockdown in less than five minutes.

Exiting the tiny dark press box, the killer turned right and headed away from the main artery of walkways. Within seconds, the farthest door would fly open with Russian agents flooding the old rooms. It was no longer an option. Instead, the blackened figure sprinted towards a thin metal catwalk. Shouting began in their wake as the predicted private security emerged even quicker than anticipated.

Barely wide enough for a person to carefully walk on, the figure raced diagonally over the thin beams like a dancer hurrying across the performance floor. Two shots ricocheted loudly off the support pole to the right. The President's son's killer had been spotted.

Scampering over another hollow opening high above the arena, the fleeing figure re-evaluated the new plan and understood that they would not make the paneled door at the far end. Another barrage of piercing bullets echoed and froze the alerted crowd sitting over twenty feet below. Two more shots, one missing by millimeters and chaos erupted from the spectators who now fully realized the noises were gunshots.

Death was certainly imminent keeping on this path as the agent's marksmanship steadied. This new planned escape was also no longer viable and the figure instead launched themselves from the beam. An eight foot gap separated the rafters as the mid-air flight was unforeseen. Stunning the gunmen momentarily too, and causing them to hold their breath in awe. Catching a cross section bar with both hands, swinging twice, then flipping over to another strut like a child on a school's set of monkey bars, the killer created some distance.

One more aerial maneuver and the sniper used their momentum to swing out over the evading spectators before spreading their arms out wide, and swan diving into the chaos below. The volley of gunfire stayed silent. Partly because the agents didn't want to shoot into the crowd, but also mainly due to the pure wonder they were still in from watching the performance executed by their target.

Plunging onto a group of bodies in the crowd, the darkened figure landed hard, crushing three or four people as they hit, rolled and fell to the ground, but all were alive. The sniper laughed internally about the feat while looking up from the ground into the beams high above, but also did not wait for the surrounding mob to understand the situation. Shouting in Russian, the killer fled down the nearest arena tunnel.

Ripping off the black skull tight cap, the figure shook loose her long dark auburn red hair before unzipping the black tactical jacket and throwing both into the nearest trash can. Sophia pushed her hair up and back, allowing it flow over the white, red and blue CSKA hockey jersey she now exposed.

The scents of cooking popcorn and hotdogs held the air, but also the traditional aroma of Elesh caught her senses. Chaos ensued over the tasty fragrances. Quickly sidestepping one small group, she joined a larger one heading in the opposite direction. She needed to put as much distance as she could between herself and any of the fans that might have seen her remove her previous outer shell. The running from the crowds had been slowed as they neared a blocked entrance.

"*blayd'.*" Sophia cursed to herself. Russian *politsiya* and special agents, undoubtedly more FSB had already began taking over the exits. She was confident that nobody knew whom to be looking for, but at the same time, she could not afford to be stuck inside while the Special Forces were called to vet each person individually.

That was it, she thought to herself. Nearing the front of the slow moving mob, another idea quickly formed. Studying the officers guarding her exit, they were pulling aside both men and women, but all were alone. A quick glance to her left and right, Sophia found a perfect duo. A father held his son's hand tightly. There was fear in the man's eyes. Perfect.

Sliding back and across to her right, she sidled next to the concerned man and took hold of his free hand. "*mne zhal'.*" Continuing in a fluent Russian accent. "I'm sorry. Do you know what's going on here? I, I keep hearing people say there was a shooting." Sophia feigned a panicked tone as the three of them approached a pair of *politsiya* that were vetting the still fleeing crowd.

"I don't know," The man was startled momentarily at the gripping of his hand, but his own shock diminished when he saw the anxiety in the beautiful woman's eyes next to him. ", but I'm sure everything will be okay." He gently squeezed her hand back.

Sophia smiled graciously, continuing the façade of fear and that the stranger was comforting her, but at the same time, she was watchful of the officers that they were approaching.

The elder of the two men had a scornful look on his face. Weathered and scarred from his years in the military before, the man sneered at the *family* that approached the exit blockade. The boy and his *mother* flanked the man, hands were clasped in attempts to stay close together and all three were wearing jerseys from his beloved hockey team. "*Idti!*" A hard look from the veteran, but he snarled out while flipping his head back in a gesture for them to leave.

The doors were held open as another throng of armed soldiers stormed into the arena. Sophia and her *family* carefully stepped back, allowing the young men to run passed before taking their turn to be escorted through the final set of double doors. Flashing red and blue lights filled the night's darkness while sirens wailed both in the distance and all around her. Once outside, the father, gripping his son's hand even tighter looked around for the woman who just moments ago was on the other side of them. She was no longer there. The boy tugged for his dad to leave and he obliged, but still kept glancing over his shoulder. The woman had vanished completely.

The fleeing fans splintered and ran in all directions. They were free. So was Sophia. Feeling the cold winter wind swirl and whip across her face, she had fulfilled *her* mission. Her personal crusade to avenge Sean's death had been completed. Expecting to scream in celebration, jump or dance, instead Sophia found herself still hollow. Trying to force a smile, she could not, instead only the frigid air brought notice to the icy tears that crept down her cheeks.

Chapter ELEVEN

Lifting the wrought iron latch and handle before heaving the large oak door, Rachel was met by the thick musky odor from inside the old redbrick church. She paused. Incense blended with beeswax candles, cleaning solution and decades old wood pews and supports. It was a powerful combination as the stale air was only circulated by two high ceiling fans.

The aroma brought her back to Winton Hills, a neighborhood in Cincinnati that she barely remembered as home. She was the only child to a single mother that tended a local bar and treated her abusive partner better than her own daughter. Rachel had good grades in her early high school years and was a notable athlete, but found herself desperately still trying to please an intolerable parent. Drugs and alcohol were not her vices as a teen, but fighting was. Twice, she had been removed from school by police for beating up another student, and twice her mother's boyfriend hit her when she returned home without a word raised by her true guardian. The man believed himself to be her custodian and demanded atonement, but when she refused, he tried to rape her, and that was his final act.

It was the first life she had taken and she had felt no remorse. Her mother cursed her, tried to defend the dead man, but Rachel would not listen. She ran. The police found her hiding in a church only lit by beeswax candles. It was the last night she had ever seen her mother. Angry and broken, the woman wanted the police to arrest her for murder, prosecute her as an adult and send her to jail for life. Swearing her own daughter's name as she left the precinct, there were no other family members or friends to help her that night. Knowing nobody to call or trust, prison was inevitable with her third violence connected arrest, but she would accept it. It did not matter anymore. Another revolution came a week later when a stern faced man in a dark suit was able to have her released. He claimed he was a lawyer, but Rachel quickly learned differently. The man was from the government. He promised her freedom, opportunities to see and experience places and things she never could from a shithole apartment in Cincinnati, but it was available for a price. The cost was allegiance.

One last look over her shoulder and Rachel was still satisfied it was safe to enter. The church rested perfectly in the middle of the city block, bordered by a small park and surrounded by taller walk-up apartments. The staunch Irish-American church was from a generation gone by, but it was still a staple of the neighborhood.

Clinton, Manhattan, west of Midtown, known for its all-embracing selection of businesses, bars and bodegas, but also for its gritty reputation. Hell's Kitchen was alive as the noon crowds approached the New York renowned delicatessen across the street.

Rachel had been patient, changing her observation point every hour since seven o'clock that morning. First finding a vacant apartment above the sandwich shop that faced the church, then the roof diagonally away, to the street corner, and lastly in the greenspace directly next to her target. Finally she felt safe to enter. The *Company* was not expecting her to ever return to their fabled black site.

Two days had passed since she fled the police station in Madison. Knowing that she could not return home, she went to the university instead. Showered at the school's gym to clean herself up, found a change of clothes that she kept in her office, and used some loose change to buy a small bag of chips and two candy bars from the vending machines in the main corridor of Van Hise Hall. She was never a fan of the local cafeteria, but how she wished it was open at that hour.

The thunderstorms that had echoed through the night were gone as she could see a seam of daylight beginning to force its way through the deep navy morning sky. The college town would soon be waking and undoubtedly her name would be bantered across campus while police officers searched and grilled her students and fellow faculty members. Rachel knew she needed to leave immediately. The appeal for the small quiet town would instantly blow up into a hunt, there was nothing left for her in Wisconsin.

  Less than a mile from her office was a used car dealership. The owner was generally fair with students that needed loaners or couldn't afford the costs of new models, but he also had limited stock. Leaving the four cars in the front showcase lot alone, Rachel scampered around back and found a silver Honda Civic with its rear door left unlocked. It was perfect. Using a broken shard of metal and a flathead screwdriver she found near the garage door, Rachel was able to start the car. One final stop three blocks over would be her last in Madison as she removed the license plate from another car that looked similar to the one she had just stolen. Finally, heading out of town for Beltline Highway and then the US-6 East, she had already decided New York would be her next stop.

  Carefully allowing the heavy door to close behind her, Rachel scanned over the nave of the timeworn church. It wasn't overly large, but could still pack in a crowd of the dedicated on Sunday mornings. Currently, nobody else was around. An air draft wheezed above her while she warily walked through the heart of the old building. Passing between the long sturdy pews, Rachel's eyes drifted from the large hanging cross in the sanctuary and apse towards a built-in confessional booth on the western wall to her left.

The creaking and groaning from the wooden floorboards silenced as she stopped her pace. Nine years ago was the last time she visited the booth, and she figured it was the last time she ever would. Inhaling the stouter fragrance of the incense, Rachel pushed forward and opened the delicate door.

"Good morning Father. Please forgive me, for it has been too long since my last confession." Rachel had waited until she heard the deep breathings of a man who in his younger years had smoked too many cigarettes. "I should come more often, but *time* is sometimes our worst enemy and biggest of sins." She continued the rehearsed dialogue.

"It's—" There was a pause from the other side. The screened man was taken aback by once again hearing the code he hadn't heard in many years. "It is alright my child, we all must find our own *time* to pray and honor the Lord."

The response was correct, but also Rachel could hear sadness in the old man's voice. "Yes Father, I should make more time in my daily life for penance and forgiveness." With her appropriate finishing of the coded message, a clasp snapped in the darkness and the booth's wall directly in front of her slid away. The blackness went deeper for a second, then three tiny orange lights blinked before holding steady and revealing a slim winding staircase.

Rachel entered the chasm, descending through two rotations of the slim pathway before the shadows opened into another room. Much larger than one could ever imagine, the walls were painted a crimson red which was deeper than the carpeting that matched. There were no paintings or pictures and a simple round wooden table with two brown stuffed leather chairs as the only furniture. Rachel's eyes were immediately drawn to the wall across the room, paneled into large squares, each with a glowing electronic keypad so a private entry number could be inputted. There were eight across and five reaching to the lowest one, forty in total, personal vaults in a way.

"I could not believe my ears when I heard your voice again, my child." Out of the darkness, the rugged old expression of the screened Father emerged. "It is good to see you again Sophia." Reaching out, a once stern faced *lawyer* hugged his favorite student.

Embracing the man, she could clearly hear his uneasy breathing. He had not aged well. Thin and frail now, his early years were catching up to him. "I honestly didn't think I would ever be coming back here." There was shame in her tone as she helped guide her fragile teacher to one of the bulky leather chairs.

"Neither did I." The man laughed hoarsely, but seemingly gleefully. "After Russia, the Company didn't want anything to do with you anymore. They designated you as *Beyond Salvage*, an enemy of the state that had gone rogue."

"They weren't wrong." Rachel replied. "They didn't send me on that mission, that one was personal and unsanctioned."

"But still needed to be done." A firm voice came from the Father across her. "You proved that the funding for that terrorist group was coming out of Russia, and we couldn't allow that to continue." A temper had returned to the old man. "Cross new that too." His voice was stern.

Rachel's mind wandered in the moment of silence. She had tracked down and killed all that helped set up or knew about the attack on Charles Bridge that day in Prague, but she had continued pressing for more. Her research had discovered hidden volumes of cash funneled from the Russian government to the leader of the newest organization taking shape in Syria, but there was no *actual* evidence to what those monies were used for or towards. At that time it didn't matter, she sought only vengeance for Sean's murder and wanted as much as possible.

Derrick Cross, the newly minted director of their clandestine program, *Red Shimmer*, wouldn't sign off, he was not prepared to take the United States to war with Russia over what he believed were bloodthirsty theories. Maybe he was right. Rachel remembered thinking those very words that night after killing Pavel Taratukhin. She did not feel any better and wondered if the Russian President should be her next target.

"Where have you been, my child?" The elder spoke, but Rachel had not heard him until he repeated the question seeing she was lost in her own memories.

"I—" Refocusing her eyes back onto her current situation. "I stayed there, in Moscow I mean, for two years, another in St. Petersburg, and then a couple more around Europe. Mainly the smaller towns in case anybody was looking for me still, but then I decided to come back to the US." Pausing again with a slight smile. "It just felt right."

"You found peace." The Father gently urged.

"Yes, probably, something like that." Rachel's brief happiness returned. "I even settled into one place, took a job as a university professor of languages, and—" The hollowness was gone, it no longer was able to control her. "And I *had* moved on from that part of my life."

"Yet you are here, now?" It was a posed question, but one from where a teacher would allow the student to find the answers themselves.

"*They* came for me." Sharp and without compassion.

"The Company found you?"

"No. Not the CIA. Somebody else." Rachel's eyes narrowed as she concentrated on the wall behind her teacher. The bright glow of the electronic keypad to her private safe was her focal point. "I was back in Prague, for work, and some men tried to take these young girls." The fierceness was growing inside her once more. "It was right in front of me. I couldn't let them do it, I just had to help." Rachel's tone was becoming deeper, raspier and the Priest leaned forward to take hold of her balled hands.

"So you stopped these men," It was a pacifying response. ", but it wasn't the end?" He continued holding her hands as they unclenched and her jaw softened.

"No." Rachel met eyes with the robed man directly in front of her. She had calmed. "I don't know who they are, but somehow they found me." The fire was still there. Rachel had remembered her training. She was fully in control of her emotions.

"And what are you going to do now my child?" True curiosity emerged.

Rachel's eyes were quiet, soft and pretty. "What I do best." Her lips parted into a tender smile as her cheekbones gently raised. "They came for me and missed. Now, I'm going for them." Her eyes flicked towards the wall again. "Is everything still in there as I left it?"

"Yes, my child. It has not been touched." One smile was met by another from a proud tutor. "Thank you, my child." One last forgiving squeeze of her hand was offered. The priest could see some confusion settle on to the face of his past pupil. He genuinely smiled from his heart. "I worried and prayed for you, for your soul, and I can see that you are where you need to be. Our Lord gives us personal scars and demons to battle, but now that I can see you again, I know that you have won yours." A tremble was in the old man's throat as he spoke before slowly rising, placing his frail hand on Rachel's head before blessing her. "I must warn you. Once you enter your code, you have no more than five minutes. The Company still hunts you and will know as soon as you initiate a sequence into that device." Pointing at the wall of vaults, but not truly understanding how they all worked with the quickly advancing new and superior technology.

Rachel was glad she came. There was initially concern as to what to expect. She didn't know if her mentor would accept her, or immediately alert the CIA, but after seeing the man, his frailty, his love, she was ready to become her old self once again. It was almost as if she was still seeking approval for the past individual choices. Somehow, she believed she had received exactly that from him. Another burden that gnawed on her was carefully released, and a new calmness took its place within. As she entered the first digit into the electronic lock, she started her mental clock.

Derian weaved through the puddles from the early morning shower as he peddled his customary route through the Nation's capital to work. His pace wasn't as sharp as usual, he was still tired and body cramped from spending over a day on a bus riding back from Madison, Wisconsin. It was Rawlings way of keeping him out of the media circus he started for a day or two, but also his punishment for missing his return flight after the arrest. Leaving at just before two in the morning, Haynes had a three hour trip to Chicago where he changed buses and then rode for another nineteen hours, fourteen painstaking stops before finally reaching Washington.

Getting home just over four hours ago, Derian was exhausted, but only due to inactivity and boredom. The Secret Service agents had confiscated his phone, so after using a landline at the police station, he had been without contacts. Once home, He immediately went to his computer and researched what he had missed over the past couple days. While it was booting back up, Derian's subconscious sightline caught the photo of him and his mother. Picking it up, he wondered to himself what she would do in his shoes. He knew she would disapprove of his tactics in Madison, she always sought the truth in politics, but also believed in being upfront with her delivery. *The world has changed so much since you were doing this.* Setting the frame back down, it was the phrase that he hoped she would understand. The home computer was ready. *He* was already trending out of the social media spotlight as another, much larger news story had cycled.

"The prodigal son returns!" Derian's friend, Kevin Porter bellowed as the journalist entered the staff entrance at the Washington Post. "Hat in hand and hoping mother doesn't chop it off." The security guard hooted with his ever present jovial tone.

"Ah shit! Rawlings didn't fire your ass yet?" Returning the ribbing, Haynes passed through the metal detector and half embraced the larger man.

"Nah, she's saving that for you my brother." Both men laughed together this time before he added in a much more thoughtful tone. "Good to see you D. They've been replaying your takedown of the President *all* over social media."

"I wouldn't exactly call it that, more like *I* got taken down." Haynes thanked his friend for the encouragement before heading to his boss's office. Once again, very appreciative that Xavier Sampson was the Chief of police at the Midtown District precinct. If it had been almost anybody else, he might still be sitting behind a set of bars or even just rereleased back into the hands of the Secret Service. Neither were circumstances that he wanted to think about. He definitely owed the man a phone call of gratitude.

Kim Rawlings was on the phone, but still motioned for Haynes to enter her office. It was morning, but the room was still hot and stuffy. Derian looked for the air conditioning, but realized that the old building didn't have a gauge in every room. There was a large fan though and he reached for the top button to activate it. "Don't touch that blasted thing." Rawlings called out before he could step a foot closer. "It only messes up my office and fills it with rubbish."

"How can you work in here?" Wiping an already perspiring forehead, Haynes muttered to himself, but the look the British woman returned was more of content than annoyance.

"I find it quite quaint and comfortable actually." She might have been sincere or prodding him, he wasn't sure. "Now sit." Although the firmness of the last sentence confirmed her seriousness.

"I am sorry once again for missing the flight and that whole arrest thing, but you did tell me to go there and *draw some blood*." He tried to imitate a hint of her accent.

"Oh don't start. Putting you on that bus was for your own good." Rawlings genuinely wasn't upset. "I needed you out of the spotlight for a couple days because we need the story to blow over."

"Blow over? No. No, I need to dive deeper into this. I still have some connections that I haven't even spoken to yet." Haynes was frantically trying to remember whom he might be able to use. "If, after one day, my digging has discovered enough to make the President scramble, then what am I going to find if I keep looking?"

"Derian. It has to end here."

"Bullshit!" Haynes was fuming. "Did they get to you too?"

"Oh bloody hell Derian!" Now Rawling's accent flared with her temper. "I'm pissed as much as you are about this, but we can't go after Senator Paxton again."

"But I haven't even started with him yet really." The journalist didn't have a plan, yet could sense one coming. "I understand this thing with Paxton's family makes it difficult, but I can dig into the brother-in-law, Mason Williams instead. I guarantee that if you give me a week that I will have much more, maybe even front page stories for a month."

"You're not listening Derian. We *can't* go after Paxton *or* his family." Rawlings was much calmer and composed as she contritely explained. "It would be a public relations nightmare for *us*, especially you, if we continue to investigate Paxton angle now." Checking her watch, she noted the time. "In just over an hour, the President will be hosting a press conference with the Senator. They will be addressing the kidnapping of his granddaughter two days ago."

Haynes froze as he actually pieced the events together for the first time since he read about the abduction. Compassion and confusion filled his face and mind. "That's the day after I spoke with him."

"Yes. It is." The newspaper senior editor sat down too. "The day after you spoke with him, and then pressed the President about a connection between them and corruption. We can't go after that story now, the outpouring of support for the Senator and his family has made him essentially untouchable." Rawlings was allowing the information to sink in. "You, *we*, would be cast out as pariahs into the street."

"We can sit on it, for a week, or a few even, maybe a month, until this cycles out," Haynes was borderline pleading now. ", but don't abandon it completely. You know it has teeth. Otherwise, you would've never sent me to Wisconsin to face the President in the first place."

"Bollocks." Rawlings quietly cursed herself. She knew he was right. She had sensed the enormity to the story before this new revelation. "Damn you." Exasperated, she caved. She could still hear the squirmy voice of the President's Chief of staff, Turner Jarvis, trying to issue her orders. "Alright. You can stay on the story, *but*." Pausing to reinforce her specific instructions. "But! It has to be entirely focused on Wakefield. You can follow your leads," That word was coming again. ", *but* the entire Paxton, Williams, whomever else in the family is off limits. You hear me Derian?"

"Yes ma'am." Excitement was building within him again.

"Repeat it back to me." Her accent flared once more, she was deadly serious.

"Senator Paxton, Mason Williams and their entire tree lineage is untouchable. Ignore all leads that include them."

"Now don't be an ass."

Haynes laughed as he had been toying with his boss. "No, I get it. I can note what I find, but can't be caught digging into their family."

"For now." Rawlings quietly added with a sly look.

"For now." The Washington Post reporter chuckled again. This time to himself, as he kept finding ways to see how remarkable a woman his boss was, no wonder she was such a highly regarded senior editor.

Chapter *TWELVE*

An early morning shower had already been pushed aside by the growing power of a creeping sun. It would be another warm day, but still shaded and cool, the beige chairs set on the lush green grass of the White House Rose Garden were beginning to fill. There were only thirty-eight of them, and the members of the media had been all hand selected by Turner Jarvis, the President's Chief of Staff himself. It was orchestrated as in intimate setting for a press conference, but there were also no questions to be asked afterwards, it was designed to honor and respect Senator Paxton's family.

Nearing eleven o'clock, the low murmurs were dwindling as the extra bodies of Secret Service agents began appearing. Confusion and rumor were the topic of late night and early morning reports when it was first announced that the President would be addressing the nation the following day.

The rumors ranged everywhere from the state of the President's health to another invasion and war in the Middle East, but the one that continued making its rounds was still highlighted by the confrontation the powerful man had with a Washington Post reporter. The video clip of Derian Haynes clashing with President Wakefield, and then what appeared to be the man running away was replayed over and over, some people adding sound effects and an overlapping of the Roadrunner and Wile E. Coyote.

Naturally, those closest to the President and his team disparaged the media outlet, its employee, and even subtly accused them of having knowledge, or showing some responsibility in the tragedy that had befallen the Texas Senator. The actions of attacking through social media had become a staple in American politics. Mostly because the companies responsible for monitoring their guidelines kept shifting their own parameters into what was considered *legal* or permissible. But, also because it allowed a voice to those who would never actually speak the words that they typed or posted. The cycle of politics in the world had become hijacked by the term *Keyboard Warriors*.

The invited men and women finished taking their seats and the cameramen focused on their task at hand. The White House Press Secretary was the first to appear at the podium set perfectly in line to display the impactful backdrop of the Oval Office and the West Wing of the stead. Typically optimistic, outfitted in lighter hues and colors and smiling, today the blond woman was stoic, wearing a black designer dress and somber.

Resigned in facts, the Press Secretary read over the police report from the kidnapping of Virginia Paxton, the granddaughter of the Senator. Including some of the harrowing particulars, but also skimming over the most graphic ones, the woman painted a perfect picture of the horrors that the family was facing.

In total, she spoke for almost ten minutes. Pausing timely for some details to sink in to the audience before thanking them and introducing the President of the United States and Senator John Paxton.

Emerging from a hidden path shrouded by the thick foliage, Rachel found herself back in the small neighborhood park next to the old church. She would have never have found that secondary exit even if she was trying she thought to herself with a smile when glancing back, and still truly not being able to see where she had just appeared from.

Adjusting her black backpack from one shoulder to the other, she stepped out of the greenspace and looked once more towards the deep redbrick outer shell of the church that she knew was much more. It would be the last time she would ever see the sanctuary. Scanning both directions of the one-way street in front of her, Stackwell started back south towards the bustle of New York City.

Horns honked, sirens wailed, while shouts, jackhammers and whining car brakes echoed through the tunneled streets, Rachel heard the sounds from the distance, but felt like they were all around her as she crossed Tenth Avenue heading towards Ninth, and eventually making her way into Times Square. She knew she could get lost in the crowds if she felt herself being followed. A plan was already forming, use the chaos of the metropolitan, the massive refuge of Central Park, then a cab to LaGuardia International Airport. It was the closest, and she could find multiple flights to anywhere across the Atlantic Ocean. Her eyes narrowed as she focused her mind on her new target, *targets*, she corrected herself. She was coming for them now.

It was still morning, but morning in New York City was not the same as anywhere else, it was always busy. Criticisms of the smells of sewer gases, carbon monoxide and general garbage were often described by visitors, but locals didn't recognize those aromas any longer. Instead, they focused on the fragrance that caught Rachel's attention at the moment, the smell of fresh bread and pastry.

Two screeching tires, followed by a long, loud car horn interrupted her internal planning and mild daydream of fresh baked goods. Stackwell's eyes immediately found the source of the disruption and the reason that it beaconed. Ahead of her, crossing through Ninth Avenue, two large black SUVs blew through a red light, racing towards her direction. The Priest was right, less than five minutes.

Rachel lowered her head, ducking it into her chest while carefully placing the second strap of her dark, undersized military backpack over her other shoulder and securing the front belt. Both vehicles sped by.

Another squeal. This time much more deafening. Both black Chevrolet Suburbans slammed on their brakes, she *had* been spotted. There was no hesitation. Rachel's head spun at the loud sound and knew they would come after her. She sprinted.

Racing South, Stackwell checked over her shoulder once to gauge the distance she had before refocusing on the path in front of her. The Company trucks were speeding in the other direction, but four men chased on foot. Her advantage was in all the thin one way streets and congested traffic that would keep the large SUVs in a circling pattern off every second street at best, but two of the suited men behind her were also gaining ground. Rachel pushed harder.

Left on Ninth. The sharp turn nearly was disastrous as a middle aged woman was exiting the local corner market at the same time. Rachel quickly contorted her body to slide past her as the woman cursed loudly at the near miss. Stackwell had to change her direction as two of the agents were much faster and nearly were on top of her, but slowed to avoid the crash themselves. Redbrick, Brownstone and white sandstone apartment buildings lined both sides of another westerly running numbered street.

Side-stepping and elderly man, crashing through a couple holding hands, and hurtling a small dog out for his daily walk, Rachel picked up her pace when she found a brief opening. "Shit!" She cursed internally, one of the black CIA trucks was on the street coming towards her.

A loud buzzing caught her attention, and she changed direction once more. Colliding through a collection of teens, Rachel raced through a playground basketball court, up a set of concrete steps and into a large four-story high school. Confusion set in. The halls were full of students, but the corridors ran in multiple directions. Rachel couldn't stay here, a building meant being trapped, she sprinted back up the nearest hallway, pushing and forcing her way past the bedlam of students heading to class.

Senator John Paxton began by thanking the American people for their thoughts and prayers in what he described as the worst heartbreak a family could go through. Repeatedly pausing and fighting back his own emotions, he pushed on. "It's difficult, but my family understands and appreciates the efforts, and hard work put forth by all the police officers, search team members and FBI agents who helped us in our pursuit of Ginny." Another pause and crack in the man's throat. This time he froze as an image of his granddaughter was flashed onto the standing electronic screen to his left.

As almost timed exactly, President Alan Wakefield stepped up and placed his arm around the man he was calling a great patriot and friend. "Teresa and I are so sorry for your family at this time, my friend."

This was his cue. Nodding and humbling himself to step back and away, Alan Wakefield now stood alone at the podium addressing his audience. "These are dark times in America." He began boasting. "One where our little girls, our daughters and granddaughters, are not entirely safe." Pandering for his own spotlight was always one of the elected man's strongest characteristics. "But we will not *let* that happen any longer!"

"Across the world we see human trafficking, sex trafficking, growing and almost becoming a business of its own." The President spoke with disdain in his voice. "We cannot allow these *monsters* to continue taking our children. No! It ends today." It was now time for him to be the politician. Feeling the pride in himself, he continued. "Last year in the United States alone, there were almost twenty thousand reports of child sex trafficking, from all states and cities, communities, suburban and rural, and targeting all ages from toddlers to teens." A gentle look towards Paxton when he said *teens*. "My administration will do something that no previous administration ever did. *I* will stand up to these predators that prey on *your* children and attack this global crisis head-on." Politically pandering and fearmongering for the camera. "I will be speaking to our National partners about assembling a task force, led by my administration and the United States to track, identify and hunt down every person and group responsible."

Speaking for another twenty minutes, President Alan Wakefield laid out more gruesome statistics, then his plans and what he was expecting from his Senate and the House voters to agree upon. Following that, he went on to what expectations were going to be from other governments across the world. What had begun as a press conference of honor had turned into a full blown political rally on the White House lawn. Subtle threats were made to the countries harboring criminals, and those whom were considered as *high value threats*. He did also adorn subtleties towards his opponents that would attempt to stifle his work. Finally, calling for unity in America, fighting a common foe that *every*body could battle, but yet, he did it with indirect threats. Wakefield had rehearsed his speech twice that morning. He knew what he was asking for was not truly what he wanted. It was merely the first step to setting himself on a much larger stage.

Bursting out a set of metal double doors, Rachel took a second to acclimate herself to where she actually was. One street over, but once again closer to

Ninth and where she began. She was fine with it. The agents had been slowed somewhere in the school behind her and this was an opening to gain some ground. She ran again.

A quick turn back onto an avenue, Stackwell zipped passed a Ramen kitchen, Indian takeout restaurant and a laundromat before slowing to join the small cluster of people passing through the crosswalk as the glowing indicator changed to signal that a red light was nearing.

It was a moment to recompose, but the moment was fleeting. A distinguished heavy revving of a powerful engine and Rachel spotted one of the Suburban vehicles. They marked her as well. Then the slower two of the four original pursuing agents. They must've circled back around instead of entering the school with their speedier teammates.

The foot traffic wasn't as dense on this stretch, allowing Stackwell to harness her speed on the pavement. The extra paces she forced her body through back in Madison were paying off now as her legs did not revolt. It could have been the training, but also could be the natural adrenaline created by being hunted for real.

Sprinting through another green light allowed her to continue, but it also gave the black SUV the opportunity. The next block was a vacant lot. Chain link fencing set up around the perimeter to keep unwanted people from using the grounds, but there had already been a hole cut in the metal meshing.

Zigzagging to first indicate a right turn, Rachel spun, dashing between two parked cars and running across the street narrowly missing an oncoming moving van. The driver bellowed his horn loudly, but she didn't even hear it. Ducking under the half pushed, half torn screening, Stackwell raced across the open lot diagonally.

The driver of the government truck spun his wheel hard to follow down the initial street, but quickly reacted to her change in pace as well. Crashing first through two more parked cars, then the flimsy chain link fence, the black beast roared through the uneven vacant grounds as well.

Rachel glanced back when she heard the metal sheath explode and cursed again. She was almost across the open lands, but wouldn't outrun the truck. Planting her left foot, she stuttered to the right hard, nearly falling as the dry dirt slid under her footing, but it did not give way. Running hard back in the opposite direction, she listened for her pursuer to do the same.

It came. The hard rustling of brakes being stomped upon, followed by another revving engine, then soft dirt and sand spinning into the air. Rachel whirled her head to see the driver change direction, and she repeated her maneuver once the truck neared once again.

The furthest point of the square plot of land was a tall wood fence, originally white in color, it had now been covered with sprayed graffiti art and a row of trees behind it. Stackwell aimed herself for that target. The Suburban was again slowed by changing direction and she knew the driver would not make the same mistake again.

Focusing directly on the wooden wall in front of her, Rachel pushed her legs are hard as she could, small clouds of dust shot up behind with each step removed. Ten feet away, the timing had to be perfect or she would never be able to make the climb. Five feet, two more steps.

Pushing hard with her left leg, Stackwell planted her right foot onto the wood fence as high as she could and propelled herself upwards, launching from the right, gripping the top of the planks before throwing her body up and over.

Immediate panic set in as the ground was not on the backside of the fence. Instead a fifteen foot drop onto stone and the metal tracks of the underground subway system. Rachel's hands thrashed out for protection.

Cadillac One, the American President's indestructible limousine pulled onto 15th Street NW and headed south. Senator John Paxton sat across from Alan Wakefield and the First Lady, Teresa Wakefield. The Texan Senator stared blankly out the window, he had no words for the moment.

"I think that went very well." The President spoke confidently.

"Yes, my dear." Teresa Wakefield was delighted. "I thought you were very good. The American people can easily see why they elected you. Your strength in troubling times and vision to fix the system. It is remarkable. Wouldn't you agree John?"

Paxton had barely been listening, his thoughts still on his fourteen year old granddaughter. "When can she come home?" Heartbroken, he spoke.

"I'm sorry John." It wasn't a remorseful tone, the Commander-in-Chief was reissuing orders. "Did I not make that clear earlier?" A rhetorical question. "She cannot come back, ever. It's the only way the people, hell, the world unites with me, with us."

"But she's just a kid!" The older man was pleading. "She's a little girl who doesn't—"

"She's collateral damage!" The President snapped back. "She's *your* collateral damage John. I had to clean up your mess. It was your emails that that reporter had, uh, *has*." His tone was becoming more condescending. "I can't just make a member of the press simply disappear." His eyes narrowed intently as he rasped. "There would be questions."

Paxton's teary eyes darted towards the First Lady for sympathy. "Don't look to me." Her tone was equally as cruel. "I was on that stage when *we* were ambushed with those accusations. All night long, rumors swirled about illegal activities and we could *never* be affiliated with that. Something had to be done."

"But she's just a little kid." Stammering again with the same defense was the only one had.

"Yes, the abduction of young granddaughter to a prominent American Senator by foreigners. Sold into the sordid world of sex trafficking. That's a scary tale to tell about protecting ourselves at home. The American people and mainstream media ate it up." The President looked towards his wife. "Just like you said they would." They shared a smile. "Instead of you becoming a treacherous villain, you are shown empathy, consideration and pity. You are a valuable piece of my administration again John. Now, we can actually *use* you."

Between his blood pressure raging and his eyes fighting back the tears, Paxton couldn't find any other words. He sat in silence until finally asking one last question. "Where is she at least?" It was uttered almost monotone.

"She will still live a good life, I'm not a monster John." The President spoke much more soothing this time. "I've sent her to Cullen's island." Once again the Texan's eyes shot instantly towards the man across from him. Panicked eyes. "Don't worry, he promises me she'll be treated properly, and who knows, might even end up running the place one day."

Grasping for the tree around her, and nothing at the same time, Rachel found a loose branch. A firm hold on the limb swung her into another chain link fence that was on the backside of the wooden one. She slammed hard into the meshing, expunging any air as she was holding her breath during the brief fall.

Stackwell could hear two agents on the other side of the thin wood paneling. Again, holding her breath as her hand agonizingly slid down the rough bark of the bulging limb. The men tried to jump and climb the vertical planks but quickly instead gave up and spoke into radios, phones or communication devices.

With one eye, she judged a calculated fall onto the tracks below, but that was immediately distinguished as the silver roof of a speeding subway began to zip by. Squeezing even tighter to her branch, Rachel gritted her teeth and clenched her jaw muscles. She knew she was actually less than five feet from her pursuers. They could easily keep her there until back up came or simply fire through the fences. She was trapped.

The dry limb bowed even further from her hanging weight. It could not hold much longer. The train was still below. Another joust and the branch snapped. Rachel threw both hands towards the metal meshing and gripped tightly while smashing into the preserved fencing, rattling loudly and expecting the men to hear the commotion.

Nothing. Instead, Rachel heard the distinct engine revving and tires spinning in the dry dirt. The agents were back in their vehicle and searching once more.

Using the individual openings of the chain links, Stackwell scaled sideways until she met an opening, pulling herself up and over, and back onto the streets of Hell's Kitchen. Her right hand ached from the battle with gravity and the tree branch. It did not bleed, but was raw to the touch. Picking up her pace, she debated entering the hotel across the street in an attempt to hideout, but decided against that strategy. She knew the numbers were against her right now, but certainly they would continue to decrease as time went on. No, she needed to keep running and get out of New York altogether.

She was heading west, away from the immense buildings and large crowds in the heart of the city. A tourist attraction sign indicating the Sea, Air and Space Museum was just ahead, which meant the Hudson River was near, and she could probably steal a boat somewhere along the docks.

Rachel's mind raced around a new plan while waiting for the crosswalk light to change at Eleventh Avenue. Two blocks until the river. A loud commotion to her left drew her attention. A woman had been knocked over. She was cursing feverishly towards the suited man who kept running past. It was one of the faster agents, his partner across the street, but also rushing in her direction.

Stackwell spun to go backwards, but spotted one of the black beasts creeping through the traffic and instead bolted out into the rushing cars on the avenue in front of her. Trying to cross, but instead driven further south, parallel to her goal of the river, but that too was now in jeopardy.

Horns blaring, Rachel sprinted between cars as another red light turned green and the traffic picked up. Eleventh Avenue was a one way street, but as she sprinted down the middle, it opened with a divider separating the turning lanes from the ones going forward. It gave her a straightaway.

It also gave the pursuing agents that same opportunity, and the closest one did not fail. His pace quickened, he was stronger and faster, and was nearly on top of her. Rachel could hear the man's foot falls increasing, growing louder and knew she couldn't out run him on a the flat roads.

Another intersection changed colors. The lead vehicle was a jeep, and it sprang forward anticipating the clearance. Rachel pushed herself hard, was almost in reach. She lunged. The dark green jeep sped ahead and Stackwell was able to leap, grab onto the spare tire sitting on the back tailgate and put distance between the men pursuing her.

The aching sensation was growing in her right hand once more as she gripped the rubber tire tightly with both hands. Two city blocks sped by as the traffic lights were timed to allow a steady flow, but she was not clear. The black government truck raced from behind, the faster agent holding onto the side and weaving through cars much faster than her driver was going.

Poking her head above the tire, Rachel could see that the next light had already turned amber, the driver would be forced to stop again. As they slowed, Stackwell leaped, kept her feet and sprinted past the forest green jeep, into the intersection, and weaved her way through an additional onslaught of encroaching cars and taxis.

Another course of horns and curses were met with even louder blasts of metal against metal when screeching brakes were eliminated by the rapid bodies of vehicles crashing into one another to avoid the fleeing woman.

Rachel's legs ached, hand throbbed and her lungs burned. She couldn't keep this pace, and she knew the agents wouldn't relent, and even grow in numbers and resources. Looking up, she recognized the area, she was now in the Hudson Yards, a new array of skyscrapers had been constructed since the last time she was here, and that gave her an idea. Dashing between the flock of tourists in the courtyard visiting the attraction known as The Vessel, Stackwell pushed past the stunned doorman and flew through the lobby to one of the massive new apartment buildings. Brief bouts of panic came across the residents as the current building's keeper fumbled for his phone to call the police.

Fifteen Hudson Yards is an eighty-eight story tall residential tower overlooking the southwest end of Manhattan Island and the Hudson River. The multi-block radius was transformed into a state-of-the-art housing and commercial development designed to bring both the upscale living and blue-collar workers together.

Rachel hammered on the button for the elevator doors to close. They obliged. The last thing she saw was two agents begin speaking with the man guarding the door. He would point out her direction and they would follow. The new elevator was rapid, not as fast as the high speed ones in Mumbai, but hopefully fast enough.

A quick glance up to the ascending metal box's camera and Stackwell turned away, squatted down and began fumbling with her backpack. The Priest was right, her pack had not been touched and was exactly as she left it. There was a chance to get through today after all. She needed only a few minutes, the pursuing team would report her location and somewhere another specialized agent would hack into the apartment complex's mainframe and take control of the elevator shafts. If that happened, she would be trapped, caught and arrested or killed. She was not sure what the orders would even be right now.

The elevator slowed, but they were not near the top floor yet. "Shit!" Hunched over, Rachel spun while cursing to herself, Beretta in hand and poised to fire. Two girls stepped forward, talking to one another, then screamed when they saw the black muzzle pointed towards them. They ran. "Sorry." Trying to call out as the young women fled, she punched the top button again.

Another agonizing minute later and the doors slowly opened to the roof deck, but it was not what she expected. A lavish sitting area for residents to enjoy the views and fresh air, but it was also built with the utmost of safety in mind. Shatterproof windows reaching at least another twenty-five feet in the air momentarily slashed her plan. She quickly searched for an alternative exit.

Sprinting across the sky top, she spotted a door, colorfully painted to match the surroundings, it was designed to disappear into the framework of the open space. A maintenance door. Trying the handle, it was locked.

A soft bell caught her attention as the second elevator arrived. Three men cautiously stepped out. Rachel recognized the two faster men from before, but not the third. Regardless, all three were there for her. She needed time.

Raising the Beretta, Stackwell fired twice. Purposely missing over the men's heads, and forcing them to dive for cover behind the rooftop's elegant furniture. More screams erupted from the three other resident's peacefully enjoying the morning sun. Rachel fired again. This time into the lock of the door.

There were no descending stairs, only another set going further up. Rachel smiled. Something was finally going her way she thought to herself while running upwards, at first skipping every second step, but found her legs too tired to keep up that pace. The three men had entered the stairwell, she could hear them running up behind her, but were two platforms behind.

Another door. Also locked. Firing two more shots down the small concrete shaft forced the CIA men to slow, press themselves against the walls and wait. One more shot ripped apart the weak door's deadbolt, and Rachel was free onto the complex's actual roof. She could hear the agents running again. Tossing the gun aside, she looked for something to block the broken door. There was nothing.

It didn't matter. Reaching over her shoulder, she found the soft meshing from her backpack that she had loosened in the elevator, and set herself at the farthest part of the roof. This had to work. The door opened once again and all three men appeared, weapons drawn, but they did not fire.

Rachel sprinted. The men were taken by surprise at her actions. Racing past them, Stackwell garnered everything her legs had left to offer, timing her steps perfectly and from the edge, launching herself from the peak of the eighty-eight story building.

Face down, Rachel counted one and threw the balled mesh from her hand up and back. The small white pilot chute caught the air immediately, streaming upwards and tearing another bundled parachute from the stitching in the top of the black backpack. The force jerked Stackwell, but considerably slowed her momentum as the canvas blossomed above her. Sailing across the Hudson River as tourist and commercial boats below skirted the waves, Rachel was trying to angle her descent into a safe landing point, but the small parachute was not designed for tactical insurgents, only a last ditch resort.

The wind began carrying her north. At first, she thought she wouldn't make it completely across, would have to drop into the river and swim the rest of the way, but with the push, there was also a brief uptake and Rachel found herself landing on the plight of grass between a public running track and football field.

Landing hard, rolling over twice and finally being able to untangle herself from the white canvas and strings. Rachel found the small blade in her pack and cut herself free. She wanted to just lay in the grass, enjoy the warmth of the sun and rest, recharge her battered body, but couldn't. All she did was buy herself time, hopefully enough of it to be able to once again distance herself from her previous CIA handlers.

Chapter THIRTEEN

The roaring sun sat at its peak arc for pelting the small southwesterly island in the archipelago known as the Maldives. Lucas Viale cursed the exuberant warmth, not for the actual temperatures resting in the mid-nineties, but for the raging waves of heat encasing the tarmac as he walked from his private jet's boarding stairs to the waiting black Land Rover.

The Maldives, a tourist's paradise. Islands in the Indian Ocean teeming with resorts and spas welcoming visitor's with the whitest of beaches and bluest of waters. Often described as the most romantic vacation place on earth, it was no different here on this particular island. At least for the average traveler blissfully engaging in the amenities supplied by the hotels owned by Cullen Verger. Lucas knew better.

The three connected resorts were only a portion of the island. The rest was the billionaire's sheltered recluse. What he considered his private home, but also where he hosted secluded parties and entertained only his wealthiest and most powerful of clients. On his island, *anything* was possible.

The isolated airstrip was east of Verger's sprawling mansion and only available to private aircraft that he allowed. The guests to the mogul's hotels were brought in by speed boat after landing at the international airport in Malé, and separated from his estate by dense mangrove forest. The threat of swampy sinkholes and snakes was always enough to keep interested tourists to stay close to their hotel and avoid the private other half of the island.

Viale readjusted his sunglasses as he climbed the stone pathway that led to the rear of the main house. He could hear music coming from within, a higher tempo dance and knew Verger was hosting. In truth, he had already known because of the tan and brown Gulfstream GIV sitting next to an open hangar at the airfield. Viale had no interest in seeing who was *visiting*.

"Lucas. You're back." Cullen Verger greeted him cordially with drink in hand as he entered the courtyard between the rear patio, outside bar and the swimming pool.

"Just long enough for the plane to refuel." He was direct. "I have to collect some *personal* information and meet a Sheikh." He knew the invite to stay and join the party was coming when he saw three young girls staggering into the house. All were naked and either drunk, high, or both.

"Feel free to join the party." Verger artfully referenced the attraction. "Just a couple of Hollywood guys from those huge super hero movies that keep making millions." The American born magnate jokingly added.

"No, I really need to take my meeting." Tactfully refusing his benefactor's offer. Viale had never partaken in Verger's affairs, he knew what the consequences were, and he had no interest in being held hostage to the man's *diplomacies*. He was about to head to his personal bungalow, but was stopped by another motion that caught his eye. Alyona. A beautiful blonde Russian girl waving to him.

He remembered first meeting her when he initially came to the island to discuss business with Verger many years ago. She was nineteen back then, one of Cullen's escorts, but now, at twenty-five the man's personal assistant, and considered a headmistress to the other girls who would never leave their new lives.

"Welcome back Mr. Lucas." An unmistakable Russian tongue, the shapely woman approached wearing a white bikini, heels, and smiling widely. Her striking green eyes always drew Lucas in, but today it was whom accompanied her that caught his attention. A shorter girl, young and wearing a coral dress cover-up. "This is Ginny." Alyona introduced the youth whose hand she was holding. "She's new here, but she can't wait to see how much *fun* we're going to have." The blonde fluctuated her voice in higher pitches to substantiate happiness to the teen. "Say hello to Mr. Lucas Ginny."

"He..llo, Mis..ter, Lu..cas." The girl was happy, smiling, but was obviously sedated to keep her blissful.

"Make sure she's comfortable," Cullen was addressing Alyona. ", and make sure you keep her away from *them* in there." An ominous warning about his guests and their private party. Another smile from the Russian beauty before she led Ginny away.

"Who is the new girl?" Viale inquired. "She looks young."

"Thirteen I think," A blithe response. ", but she's not here to be like the others." This time, Verger's tone seemed almost annoyed. "She's here as a favor for the President. Some Senator's granddaughter that he needed to disappear." A laugh replaced his carefree attitude, the man was clearly intoxicated as well. "So I said she could stay here."

"Thirteen. American." Viale sneered. "I could easily get you a pretty price by the end of the week for her." He liked when his champion financier spoke too much. Undoubtedly, the President of the United States would not have wanted anybody to know who the girl truly was. "I know a Prince or two that would certainly love to add her to his harem."

"No." A conservative pause as Verger was either thinking it over, or searching for more words in his state. "No, I can't. I promised nothing would happen to her. We'll just keep her on levels of depressants and MDMAs to keep her calm and happy until she's ready to live here on her own. You know, the usual treatment." This time he laughed callously.

Cullen's name was boasted from an open door and Lucas recognized the face of one of Hollywood's leading actors. "You should get back to your party." Viale mocked. "Your friends are starting to miss you."

Without another word, Verger spun on a heel, staggered once, and bolted for the door. Lucas whispered another curse at the man before heading in the opposite direction. He had planned on staying for a couple days, and even gave his team the time to return home, or go wherever they wanted, but now he would have to find somewhere to go too. Walking past another guest bungalow, he spotted Alyona with the girl, Ginny. They were relaxing on padded loungers, the Russian woman tanning and the American teen asleep, or dead, he couldn't tell. For now, he would not approach the subject again. Time would tell if the youth would submit and allow this to become her new home, but if she did not, he knew he could convince Cullen to allow him to sell her. This time he smiled to himself. A cute, virginal American teen born into a politically strong family with connections to the President of the United States directly was a payday that he could not allow to escape him. He would check on the girl's progress in a week.

Derrick Cross was anxious. Gripping the ends of the table he was leaning against, he gritted his teeth while intently staring at the large wall screen in the front of the room. Next to him, Chelsea Williamson whipped her fingers across her keyboard, occasionally skimming the touchpad to move the cursor.

The members of his task force had worked for nearly two straight days, and the only evidence of Rachel Stackwell, Sophia Warner, that they could find was a brief glimpse in a video surveillance camera near her office. They pieced her escape together, found various camera angles of her leaving the police station, but only a split second of her at the university. She obviously had already figured out where the cameras were placed.

Chelsea had been working the lead on a stolen car from a used sales lot, but no records of the license plate anywhere in Wisconsin or the surrounding states. She was in the process of expanding that search when another tech across the room had called out. He had movement in New York. A security code had been entered at the *Oasis*, an asset was retrieving their tools. Sophia Warner had surfaced.

The revelation set the room afire. Cross had immediately called for a React team, and cursed loudly when they said it would take eight to ten minutes to get there. They didn't have the time. Twice during the chase through Hell's Kitchen, he wanted to flood the city with more agents, but also knew he couldn't risk opening their operations up to the eyes of the public and media. Too many feet on the ground would eventually lead to somebody being noticed or saying the wrong thing.

Now, he was edgy. The bodycam from one of his agents was showing them poised behind a closed door. They were about to breach the roof of the massive structure in the Hudson Yards. Sophia was trapped, she had nowhere else to go, but that would only make her even more dangerous. The agents whispered to one another and used hand signals to organize their next assault.

The man wearing the camera pushed through the door first. Gun drawn, but he did not fire. Cross furrowed his brow. Chelsea's fingers stopped, only inhaling deeply and holding it. The operation room went dead silent as all watched their target streaking across the large screen before launching herself from the top of the building.

Shock hung in the air for what seemed like minutes, but by the time the pursuing agent had sprinted to the ledge, a combination of anger and relief had merged in the sighs and whispers. A small, white canvas popped on screen, the freefall was already over, and their target gliding through the air across a bluish gray streak of water ahead of her.

"Shoot her!" Cross yelled into his communications that connected him to the lead field agent. The footage showed the man respond without hesitation until he was to pull the trigger. "Fucking shoot her!" Another shouted order.

The man did not relinquish his weapon, but also did not fire. "Negative sir." Seemingly looking at more angles, this time he lowered the barrel. "No clear shot. Target is too far away."

"Goddammit!" Cross bellowed, but this time at nobody in particular.

"They can't be sure where the bullets will go if they miss." Chelsea was trying to calm her former boss.

"I know. Damn it!" Slamming his fist onto the desk made the computer hop briefly and the room return to a murmur. "Tell them to stay there. Watch where she lands and which direction she heads." Derrick knew there would be hell to pay if his agents fired openly. Even more so, if a stray bullet found its way into an American citizen, but he was still fuming that Warner had escaped, again.

"She's gonna want to put as much distance as she can between us." Williamson was speaking, but already working her magic with the computer. "She'll be close to Union City, closest bus terminal—"

"Newark Airport." Cross cut her off. "Shut it down. Redirect two teams there."

"It's one of the busiest airports on the east coast." Chelsea objected.

"I don't care if every New Yorker and their momma are trying to get on a fucking plane today. Shut. It. Down." The head of the clandestine unit was direct with his order. "No planes leave the ground until I say they do." When Williamson didn't react immediately, he continued. "If you're not gonna shut the airport down, get your *boss* on the line and have her do it. Hell, if the Deputy Director doesn't want to do it, tell her to get the goddamn President and I'll *make* him do it." Chelsea didn't answer. This time she turned back to her computer and began the operation of closing Newark International Airport.

Satisfied, Cross skipped across the room to another technician, the man who reported the code breach at the sanctuary. "Who do we have available?"

"Available?" The man asked back, but knew exactly what his boss was referring.

"Yes. Who's *available*?" Repeating himself with a sterner annotation.

The operator brought the screen up, then proceeded to remove profiles until two remained. "Crimson and Cordovan."

"Get them up."

"*Both* of them?" This was a genuine question as the rules of the *Red Shimmer* program stated that assets never worked together, and that only one would be assigned a particular target.

"Activate both assets." A direct command. "A target package like any other." Cross spoke calmly and with direction. "Send each one the same information. The file on Sophia Warner, *Cardinal*, beyond salvage, location, TBA." The technician entered the data into his computer and hesitated before sending. Looking first towards Chelsea who didn't believe the orders, then at his boss. Cross simply nodded slowly. He sent the new mission target.

"It is dependent on *us* to be the leaders that our people have asked us to be." Alan Wakefield sat confidently at his desk in the Oval Office addressing the faces on his computer screen. "We make up the largest contributions in NATO and *must* use that power to institute a new plan of attack. The time is now to fight back, as a unified front against the terrorists who threaten *all* of our children." Nods of agreement were returned by the Presidents from France, Italy and the German Federal Chancellor, while the Prime Ministers from Canada and United Kingdom sat stoic.

The secure Zoom call between the nations had been approaching two hours. Most world leaders were on board with an allied partnership, but were still hesitant to appoint an individual administrator, or even build a new committee.

"I agree Mr. President, these human trafficking gangs are becoming out of control and rivalling some of the principal syndicates, but what I do not see, is why the United States is in the best position to *lead* a new coalition." The Turkish President was angling for the position now. "If any of us, our countries, should take the command of a new commission, it should be Turkey. We are here, *ground zero*, as you might say, and can make larger strides, more quickly." English was not the man's primary language, but he was able to make his point.

"I'm sure we *all* can appreciate your enthusiasm Gamze, but Turkey is in *no* position to lead this extremely crucial undertaking." Wakefield was stern with the defiant man whom he didn't even think should've been included in this private meeting. "Like you said, your country *is* ground zero, and thus internally infected. This type of operation is going to need to be orchestrated from the outside, by those officials, police and maybe even military whom are not already compromised."

Alan Wakefield spoke and bartered for another forty-five minutes before he was finally able to exit his designated meeting room and close the top to his secure laptop. He had spent his remaining time breaking down numbers and percentages of human and sex trafficking cases and people across countries and continents like a mathematician or data analysts taking over managing a baseball game. Rolling his eyes, he accepted the glass of whiskey that his wife handed to him.

"It sounded like a few of them were onboard already." Teresa Wakefield spoke encouragingly, knowing how exhausted her husband looked. "Maybe a little one-on-one strong-arming will be able to persuade the others."

"Possibly." He conceded. She was usually right. "We must move forward with this. They *have* to see the importance of installing me is to this position. *Our* time is now." Wakefield addressing his wife once again as she sat on the corner of his desk.

"At least Marc and Liam aren't politicking to take control." She referenced the two Prime Ministers.

"No, but the Canadians and Brits still don't trust this office." A sly eye towards his wife. "MY, er, *our* plans are being hindered by the failures of an incompetent administration years ago." Wakefield was increasingly frustrated.

"They'll come around." The First Lady portrayed resolve instead of being passive towards her husband. "Once we get the significant members of NATO to back you on this, the others will fall in line. God bless John Paxton for having a pretty little blonde granddaughter that the American people fell in love with." A slight cackle followed the cynicism.

"It was your genius my dear wife." Standing, Wakefield grabbed her around the waist and pulled her from the edge and into his body. "Turning what was quickly becoming a political nightmare into an opportunity. *The* opportunity that we have been waiting for." He kissed her.

"Taking over NATO from within the wombs of children." Teresa Wakefield returned the embrace. "It will the greatest coup of all time, and nobody will ever know it happened." Another menacing sneer and laugh. "The devil's greatest trick will be replaced." This time the sentiment was shared between the lovers as they toasted one another and pecked again.

"Call the Prime Ministers tomorrow, individually. Persuade them that you *need* to be the one leading NATO," Pausing to casually sip her own drink. ", and if they don't want to agree, then maybe we'll find a different way to *make* them see things our way." Teresa Wakefield returned her own shrewd smile. "I'm sure we can be creative in finding a solution that benefits *all* of us." The woman was beautiful and shrewd. Cunning, callous and coldblooded. The Wakefields were truly a power couple made for one another. Both thrived on power, were resilient and scariest of all, both were ruthless to no end. Lucifer and Lilith sat atop Olympus.

Chapter FOURTEEN

Hot and humid. For the second straight day in Istanbul, Turkey, the temperatures soared between the high eighties and low nineties. Cloudless skies and a penetrating sun covered the transcontinental country like a beacon for travelers escaping their own seasonal changes. August and September were the height of the tourist season in the peninsula where southeast Europe meets Asia, and the entrance to the Middle Eastern factions.

Rachel watched the man, her target, enter his apartment complex that overlooked the Bosporus Strait in the Beşiktaş district. He would push the button for the fourth floor, greet his wife and daughter before they left for the young girl's seven o'clock private swimming lesson. She knew this from the reminder memo that was pasted on the refrigerator in the kitchen when she searched the vacant residence earlier that afternoon.

Checking the screen of the new phone she purchased earlier that day, Rachel closed her eyes and listened to the waves softly crash into one another against the cement walkway. The mother and daughter would leave in approximately ten minutes to walk to the aquatic center.

It had been nearly three days since her escape from New York. She could still feel a slight pain in her right leg from the hard parachute landing, but it was minimal and her hands no longer ached. Technically, she had touchdown in New Jersey, thought about heading for Newark Liberty Airport, but decided that it would probably be the first place that Cross would sent his agents next. Instead, she bought a train ticket, paid cash, and was at the international airport in Philadelphia a couple hours later.

Her backpack contained four different certified passports that were not registered aliases with the American government. Using an American one, Rachel took a one-way flight to Toronto, switched to a Canadian identity and bought two separate round trip tickets, one to London, England and the other to Frankfurt, Germany. After initially boarding the flight to London, she feigned an illness, was able to deboard without too much fuss and quickly ran to the German flight that was leaving within the same time window. Exhaustion had set in once settling into her seat, and she barely remembered the plane leaving the runway.

Arriving early in the morning in Frankfurt, Rachel was able to find a train to Amsterdam before catching an evening flight to Istanbul. Her process was long and tedious, but the constant switching would certainly make her impossible to track. She did not waste her down time either. The train ride to the Netherlands allowed her over five hours to search and read online articles about the human trafficking industry around the world, but specifically she focused on the major market in Turkey.

Through her research, one name kept appearing, Ömer Semiz, a journalist from Istanbul who seemed determined to bring notice to the world about the large scale problems that human trafficking was exploding into. Just over a year ago, Semiz helped Interpol dismantle the largest sex trafficking ring in the Marmara Region of Turkey, Greece and Bulgaria.

There were ultimately too many articles to read and Rachel began skimming through them looking for highlights of something that would lead her in the direction to find the men, or group that she was hunting, but instead, she only found herself developing a headache. She needed a break and searched the name Derian Haynes.

Maybe it was because he helped her in Madison, or that he told her that he too was a journalist, but Rachel really wasn't quite sure why his name had popped back into her mind. The search yielded interesting results. Headlining the computer page were articles written about him from only a few days ago. It claimed he verbally assaulted the President of the United States and was arrested, but not charged for willful disruption of state processes. There was a link that opened a video file, she clicked it.

Rachel smirked to herself. The audio wasn't the strongest, but she could hear enough of the *assault*, and knew it was nothing more than a reporter asking questions to a politician who didn't like the answers he would've had to give. She'd seen it before, but the detention was only something that ever happened in Communist or Authoritarian nations.

Scrolling further down the page, another set of articles, first by the man, then another praising him for his courage. They were dated years ago, but Rachel still was intrigued. As she quickly read over his postings about his time in the Syria, she smiled once again and felt that was why he helped her. He had no ulterior journalistic motives, he was genuinely a good guy. Rachel was impressed.

Her eyes snapped open. Stackwell's internal clock chimed and it was time to make her move. Approaching the apartment's front entrance, Rachel withdrew a small stainless steel cylinder, pushed a small release and carefully looked around. A miniature key appeared from one end, was inserted and two delicate turns later, the handle jerked free. Avoiding the lobby camera, she would use the stairs and make her way to the fourth floor, where her professional device would get her into Semiz's home.

Silently closing the door behind herself, Rachel could hear her target singing to himself around the corner. He was in the kitchen. The front door opened onto a small foyer for shoes and outerwear, then led into a sitting room flanked by an open space where a large dining room table sat. The hallway to the right of these rooms led to three bedrooms and a bathroom, but to the left was the kitchen, another bathroom and an extra area that the man had turned into some kind of office. Rachel had run through her mind the apartment's layout multiple times, knew it, but couldn't think of a way to approach her target without startling him. Shaking her head to herself, she just stepped out.

Chelsea Williamson rubbed her face. She had slept maybe five hours over the past three days and all on the scratchy leather couch in Derrick Cross's office. Hunger pains were creeping back, her head hurt, and eyes ached from staring at her computer for so long, but it was worth it. She had found her target, she had tracked the former asset *Cardinal*, Sophia Warner.

Her current boss, Virginia Bennett, the Deputy Director of CIA Operations was not overly enthusiastic about loaning her back to Cross's Black Ops department, especially after the man's debacle in shutting down Newark's International Airport for what turned into no reason. The delays and cancellations were still being sorted out and all without any true answers.

The only convincing argument that Chelsea was able to make was that with her there, something like that would not happen again. She also promised to report to Bennett first, once she found anything concrete, and then turn it over to her anxious former boss. She did not mention anything about the activation of two more assets, or that the orders were simply for a kill mission. Williamson understood the inner workings of this clandestine department much better than the Deputy Director who was seemingly playing politics with an area of expertise that she had just recently learned about.

She called Derrick at home. The man finally left, but would come straight back in after ending the call with her. She probably had fifteen, maybe twenty minutes before he arrived. It would've been enough time to report in, but instead, Chelsea went to the small office refrigerator to scarf down some cold pizza and a bottle of water. She wanted to be fresh for action when the operations started again.

"You know where she is? This very minute?" Two rapid questions overlapping one another as Derrick Cross burst through the magnetic locking door.

"Yes, and no." Responding steadily to encourage him to do so as well. "After Newark was a bust," She added a look of, *I told you so.* ", I started working the bus terminals and train stations to see if I could find her."

"And you did? Where'd she go?" The tone was much more relaxed, but Cross also knew that wasn't how Chelsea liked to work. "Sorry, please continue. " Nodding and biting his tongue.

"She did try to get out of the area as quickly as possible, but she used the train instead." Chelsea clicked on a couple tabs she already had open on the computer. "Paying cash, she boarded a train at Newark Penn Station and went directly to Philadelphia." Another set of distorted images appeared. "Using an identification that we knew nothing about, she was able to purchase a ticket to Toronto." Closing those tabs and opening two more brought more images, much cleaner and focused this time. "From there, she was taking a flight to London where I lost her because she never got off the plane at Heathrow."

"How is that possible?" The images of Sophia parachuting from a passenger plane were forced across his mind, but even he didn't believe she would be that brazen.

"I wasn't sure, so I went back to Toronto, where I found this." One more click brought a clear video of their target exiting the boarding ramp and then running in a different direction. "She purchased two flights that were leaving at the same time." Chelsea's smile was partly in admiration, but mainly for her own abilities of digital tracking. "This flight here, went to Frankfurt."

"So she's in Germany?" Cross cursed again, this time aloud, but followed it with another apology.

"You know, we definitely need to put more surveillance up in our cities like they do in Europe. It is so much easier tracking people when you can just hack into a city's grid and look through whatever you want." It was a jovial tone like a child playing with dolls. Cross loved the woman's brilliance and capabilities. A giddy little laugh followed the overtired woman. "Alright, here, she's in Istanbul. I won't bore you all her train and plane swapping details any longer.

"Do you know where in Istanbul?" Derrick was already heading towards another technician.

"No. I'm still working on that part." Williamson had a layer of annoyance to her not being completely finished.

"Good enough Chels." Cross was already speed talking to the operator handling the active assets. "Give them both Istanbul. They'll find her from there."

"*iyi akşamlar Ömer.*" Rachel's Turkish was rusty.

"*Allah kahretsin!*" Semiz yelled as he was startled. "*Aman Tanrım!*" Surprise and fear took the man as he lunged for a cutting knife on the counter.

"I am not here to hurt you." Rachel soothed as she held her hands out, palms up, but also was ready to defend herself if need be.

"Who? Who are you?" Semiz trembled as his eyes frantically searched the room. He was hunting for his cellular phone.

"I am only here to ask you some questions Ömer." Stackwell spotted the device first and stepped into the pathway towards it. "I need information."

"You are from the government!" The man wailed. "You are here to arrest me!"

"No, no I'm not Ömer." She continued to use his name to soften the temperature of the room. "I want to *help* you. I want to help you end human trafficking." Rachel tried another tactic that the journalist was passionate about.

"What?" It seemed to work. Confusion had taken the place of hysterics. "How can you help me?" Curiosity now crept into the confusion and Semiz's mind ran rampant over itself.

"I *can* help you Ömer, but first we need to talk." Inching closer. "You need to put that knife down, and tell me what you know." Closer still.

"What I know?" The Turkish man's face tightened as acuities blended together. "Everything I know—" Air was sucked from the man's chest as Stackwell jabbed her left hand into his solar plexus, just below his ribcage, grabbing and twisting his wrist with her free right hand. Semiz doubled over as Rachel ripped the knife from his hand.

"You'll be alright." Once again her soothing voice returned. "Just breathe, deep breaths. In and out. The feeling will go away in a second or two."

"Please. Don't." Each word held a gasp between them. "My wife. And daughter. Will be home soon."

"Your wife took your daughter to her seven o'clock swim lesson. " Rachel continued fluidly. "Her lesson is an hour long, and they will probably take another fifteen minutes to walk home." She smiled at the man as he was regaining his composure. "We have plenty of time to talk." Fear was back in his eyes.

"Who are you?" He repeated again.

"I am nobody Ömer. I just need information from you about the local gangs trafficking women, especially young girls, and those who operate outside of Turkey." Rachel placed the cutting blade back into its slot on the knife block. "I am telling you the truth. I can help you."

"You are American." It was not a question. Semiz switched to speaking English with his simple statement and he smiled at the now perplexed woman across from him in his kitchen. "We will speak English, your Turkish is terrible. I will get my laptop."

Rachel found herself smiling at the remark, but also uneasy. Languages came natural for her, but if she lost the native tongue, then it would be hard to pass as a local when she needed to, she would have to practice.

The journalist was still edgy, wary of the woman's every movement, but he also did not believe she was there to hurt or arrest him. Ömer Semiz was in his late thirties, young and passionate about writing, and considered well known throughout the country by media standards, but that would not stop the government from having him detained if he wrote articles like many of his colleagues did years ago. Whether it was about internal coup attempts, military structures or attempting to spread knowledge to the people about a worldly disease. Instead, he focused on something much more dearly to his heart.

"Why do you want to know about these criminal rings?" The question was posed cautiously. Believing the intruder not to be associated with the government was one thing, but then believing whom she did belong was another.

"I'm not here to help *them* either." Rachel could feel the concerns that the man had seeping out of his pores. "I'm looking for a particular group." She met his eyes and tried to be as reassuring as possible with fire coursing inside her. "It's personal."

"You are looking for someone? A sister, niece, or family friend maybe?" Semiz prodded as he tapped the keys to open his work station.

"No," Stackwell was firm, but also kind. ", nothing like that."

"Then you lost someone." Glancing up from his screen to the woman hovering over him. "I am sorry."

"Not that either. I—" Rachel stopped herself as she could see genuine remorse in Ömer's eyes, but there was something else, sorrow. This was *personal* for him too, but in a more tragic way. "They will be well funded and have access to above average technology." She decided not to pursue and to focus back on the directive.

"*Affet beni.*" Semiz returned to his computer. "It depends on what type of human trafficking you believe this group is doing. Organ harvesting, forced labor and general people smuggling probably doesn't meet the criteria for any of gangs or groups in and around Turkey. You are looking more Africa and Asia, but since you mentioned women, you're looking for sex traffickers most likely." The man began rambling. "Our government has begun to work hard on actually processing arrested traffickers. Last year one hundred and twelve of the hundred and sixty-four detained were convicted. It doesn't sound great, but better than the less than fifty percent from the year before." He only stopped for a short breath. "Turkish women are mainly trafficked to the neighboring countries and there's are brought in, but with our huge Syrian refugee population, the southern provinces of Turkey are what I consider high, or red-zone areas."

Rachel's eyes drifted towards the clock on the wall as Semiz continued rattling of stats and numbers that he had collected. The journalist definitely was committed. He had maps and charts which he himself had put together and collected data from various sources and investigative reporting. No wonder Interpol had chosen to work with him instead of the local police who at-best were doing enough to appear concerned on a global level. "Ömer." Stackwell called his name sharply to change his focus. "The men I'm after work outside of Turkey, in Europe, and are *very* well organized and funded." She had replayed the takedown in Prague over and over in her head, it was tactically designed and the fact that they found her in America means they had some serious capabilities.

"Can you be sure that they are even Turks?" Semiz again spun away from his screen. "Human and sex trafficking is a *global* problem. I mean even look at the United Nations and what happened with peacekeepers over twenty years ago. That *still* goes on in some eastern European countries, but nobody reports it anymore because nothing happened to the offenders back then."

"Ömer!" The agitated man was rambling again about reports and rumors he's heard in places like Serbia, Kosovo and Bulgaria. "Tattoos. They all have the same tattoos on their right hand. A star and a crescent moon." Pointing on her own hand where they should be located.

"Many men have tattoos, scars and markings here, especially those from the outside provinces, away from Istanbul or Ankara."

"I know that." Another interrupted retort from Rachel as they were running out of time before Semiz's wife and daughter returned. There was no time to waste on her understanding of tribal and organizational tattoos from the Middle Eastern part of the world. "But each region or group has different markings or placements." Recomposing herself, Stackwell continued. "The men, the *group* I want have those tattoos here and here, speak Circassian and have access to money, lots of it."

The journalist furrowed his brow, but it was not from confusion, he was thinking. The balled fist moved from his mouth and fingers began to once again furiously skim across the laptop's touchpad. "Wait, wait, wait." It was his turn to interrupt as he quickly held up his left index finger before returning back to his computer. "You said Circassian. I have notes about that somewhere." He was speaking to himself. "Yes! Here!" Directing the American woman's eyes to the monitor, Semiz pointed.

"What is this?" It was Rachel's turn to be confused as she was looking at a photo of an Interpol memo.

"That language is unique, even for around here, but I knew that I had seen it before." Semiz scrolled down the virtual page a little bit. "This notice was sent to the office in Ankara. The group you are looking for are very well known to international police, but they have not been able to locate them. They move quickly in and out of countries all over Europe, possibly the world, I don't have all the information about them, but the dialect, Circassian is a trademark because of its rarity." The journalist was extremely intrigued now with this woman's interests. "How did you know about the language?"

"I recognized it." Rachel casually spoke, but was still reading the page on the screen.

"You? Recognized it?" Amazement met confusion as Ömer thought. Even he didn't understand the rare dialect. This woman was becoming more and more interesting to his investigative side.

"Sorry. What?" Stackwell replied. "Yes. Do you have any more information about this group? Where I can find them, or who is a part of it?"

"I don't," Semiz was beginning to trust her a little bit. ", but I know somebody who might."

"Who?" Rachel was eager.

"An officer here in Istanbul. He is my contact with Interpol and the police for the human trafficking and smuggling stories." Semiz's own enthusiasm was growing inside. "I could set up a meeting for you two, privately of course. He is a *specialized* inspector I guess you could say."

"Call him, don't message him, and no names." Rachel was direct again as she saw the man reaching get up and head over to his handheld phone. Semiz only nodded in response as he was already dialing.

The call was quick. Ömer told his colleague that he had a contact that wanted to meet. They had information that the police detective would be interested in regards to another sex trafficking operation in the city. The man agreed and the meet was set up for tomorrow morning at a small café within the Kadıköy Market of the city.

As Semiz was ending his call, the front door of the apartment was opened and Rachel could hear the voices of an excited young girl and her mother. Ömer heard them too and bolted to intercept before they exited the front foyer. A brief wave of panic swept over him as fear of what might happen to them overtook any trust that he had built up for his uninvited guest.

At the appearance of her father, the girl jumped up into his arms hugging him tightly and animatedly recalling her swimming lesson. The mother smiling and now laughing brushed past Semiz when he tried to prohibit her from stepping further.

Spinning his daughter to the ground behind his wife, Semiz leapt in front to block any danger the intruder might have subjected. Nothing came. His kitchen and dining room were empty. Annoyed and confused, Ömer's wife again stepped around her dumbfounded husband, shook her head and asked why he had the balcony door open. His eyes flickered towards it instantly.

Stuttering, he mumbled something about being warm while he was working and agreed to close it. Carefully peering onto the thin platform, relief replaced anxiety as the fresh air washed his daughter's chlorine scented hair from his nostrils. The balcony was empty. The American woman was gone.

Chapter FIFTEEN

Mid-morning in Istanbul brought about another day where temperatures were sure to sail over the country's traditionally recorded ones, but that did not stop Hakan Köseman from wearing one of his full suits. The special police inspector was notorious for his collection, always dressing professionally like his American television and movie idols from which he based his look.

The fifty-three year old *detective* deliberately paced himself through the narrow alleys and walkways of the Tuesdays and Fridays Market, the Kadıköy Çarşısı located on Istanbul's Asian side. He had already patrolled through the garment areas of the chaotic market and was now on his second lap back around and heading towards the small café where he was supposed to me Semiz's contact.

The reason for his deliberate tactics was twice he believed that he was being followed. The first time by a woman, blue jeans, black blouse, with a yellow and burnt orange designed headscarf. She was already in the popular bazaar, looking at clothing, but glanced up at him when he passed and he believed the stare lasted too long. Doubling back, he found her once again going through women's undergarments, but heed him no attention this time.

The second time was a younger man, a teenager likely, beard not as kempt as his own, but he too seemed to stare a fraction longer than normal before darting away and towards a fruits and vegetables cluster of stands. That boy was wearing a grey sweatshirt with a common sports company logo across the front and sleeves bunched up to his elbows. Trying to move directly towards him, Köseman was accidently cut off by two elderly locals buzzing through. When he tried to regain his ground, the boy was gone. Maybe it was nothing, but an active imagination.

Completing his last wave, the policeman now felt more at ease. Changing direction multiple times, circling around and even stopping at numerous stands allowed him multiple vantage points and surely would've pointed out if he was truly being followed. Now, Hakan was able to enjoy the atmosphere, scents and aromas that Kadıköy had to offer. Freshly ground coffee and baked bread dominated the air around him, but he could also make out the zesty pepper spice of the generational pickle shop down the alley to his left. He planned to definitely stop there after the meeting he was about to take. Checking the old wristwatch on his arm as he sat down, he was still a few minutes early and motioned for coffee.

Rachel hadn't been waiting long when she spotted the man in the suit approaching from the most populous entry point through the throngs of stands and platforms that composed one of the busiest marketplaces in the world. He had a full head of salt-and-pepper hair, a kempt neckbeard and strode upright and confidently. He wore the dark suit with pride and she knew he must be the police inspector that was Semiz's contact. Rachel even snickered to herself, thinking he must be basing his look after the detectives in the old Hollywood movies.

She had arrived over an hour before their determined meeting time, wanting to scout in advance and get a visual layout for herself instead of whatever she found on the internet. Rachel honestly had no idea how long it would take her to get to Kadıköy from where she was staying across the straight separating Istanbul. One of the city's twenty thousand yellow taxis took her to the ferry docks of Eminönü where she departed, boarding a passenger ferry that timed its pace to just over thirty-five minutes to port at the dockyard in Kadıköy. A short walk found her at what she considered the focal point and she began to familiarize herself with the narrow streets and alleyways.

Sleep had eluded her as well that night. Her instincts were telling her that something was wrong, and she wasn't about to ignore those senses again.

Caution was Rachel's mindset for today. She could feel her training and skills coming back, they truly never left, but with repressing her feelings and loss, she was also curbing her abilities. They were still there though, she could feel them at times, like back in New York. Her escape was fueled by intuition and reactions. The detective made another change in direction.

The quick alteration was caught by Stackwell's peripheral vision causing her instantly look up. Did the detective believe he was being followed? Had he seen her? No, she was not the reason for his shift, it was the man in the grey sweatshirt. A local youth who scampered away when the two men made eye contact briefly. The policeman started after the youth, but was held up and stopped. Rachel assumed the teen was afraid of being caught stealing, but it seemed to concern her target more. He wandered two more times around the *çarşi* before seating himself at the café they were supposed to meet. He was still early, and Rachel knew that the man planned it that way.

Waiting a couple more minutes, Stackwell was content that he was alone. Nobody had followed him, and she didn't see any other police waiting. An employee with a stained white apron approached the table with a still steaming cup of coffee. "*Çay alabilir miyim lütfen. Açık.*" Ordering a tea as she approached, Rachel sat across the table from the detective and readjusted her yellow and orange headscarf.

The teen ran north as fast as he could and did not look back. He had completed his mission. After his initial fear of being chased by some man in a suit, he circled back and was able to continue following the woman in the colorful headgear. He removed his grey sweatshirt, stole a plain black baseball cap from a busy vendor's display and slipped in behind a group of European tourists on a walking tour.

As the perspiration was building on his forehead and arms, he did not stop until he reached the wall surrounding the reconstructed Armenian church. Finding the gate and pushing it open, he hurried into the temple, climbing the archaic wooden stairs two at a time until he reached the bell tower. It was an open platform, no bell hanging, but instead a man, American, tanned and wearing a linen buttoned shirt while eating a fresh orange colored apricot. Trying to speak while panting for breath only resulted in a jumbled sentence and the man held up his hand for him to be silent.

"This really is the best place in the world for these." Holding up another fruit for the boy to take he continued in a perfect Turkish dialect. "Take a breath. You know where the woman is." It was not a question. The boy nodded. "Now exhale and tell me." A long stretch of air came from within the boy's lungs as he released the air he had been holding. His words were no longer muddled as he reported the name of the café that she sat with the man in the suit.

When he tried to give the directions, the tall American only glared two hard eyes at him. He stopped speaking once again. The bigger man now handed him five folded Turkish notes and the boy's eyes bulged. They were each one hundred Lira. Forcing his eyes from his prize, the teen tried to thank his benefactor, but the man was already gone.

Tossing his fruit's pit aside in the courtyard, the asset designated as Crimson raised his sunglasses to his face, adjusted the silenced Glock at his waist, and confidently strode out into busy streets of Kadıköy.

The lively Irish pub in Arlington, Virginia was brimming with excitement. Two tables in the back of the classic tavern were occupied by couples dining, but most of the customers were paying attention to the emcee as the weekly trivia night was in full affect. Boisterous laughing and shouting poured out into the street as the thoroughfare filled with late night traffic. Derian sat at the counter, smiling to himself with the activity, before downing the last mouthful of his beer then ordered a second when the barman looked his way. The day seemingly dragged without ending, but still he waited for another of his potential sources.

He watched the President's press conference live and then twice more, each time taking notes on what the man said, didn't say, and what his own opinions might be. One phone call was all he needed to privately meet with an opposing Congressman, but nothing came from it.

Two more off-the-record consultations later, and he was still nowhere, but this source had prospective. Haynes had used the man before, a janitor in the actual White House, an elderly black man that nobody seemed to ever notice when he was around. The man had worked there for nearly thirty-five years, had seen powerful men come-and-go, but had never seen one as personally motivated as the current Commander-in-Chief.

A change in the atmosphere octave caused Derian to look towards the door. Another couple of men stepped through and joined friends at one of the quiz tables. It had nearly been an hour since their predetermined meeting time, but the journalist decided to continue waiting. It was unlikely that the man would show now, but it was still soothing to feel the blissful energy of the pub. Derian found it comforting and uplifting compared to his recent failures. Taking a fresh sip, he allowed himself to drift from his current thoughts and eyes focus on the replay of the most recent Manchester United football match.

Another hour passed and still no contact. Paying his tab, Derian thanked the bartender and decided to head home. His bike was still at the Washington Post, so he needed to take a cab back there first. More explosive laughing echoed as he stepped back into warm night air. It had cooled considerably from earlier that day, but still was an enjoyable evening. Maybe it was the two large pints of Irish beer, but Haynes felt relaxed. He walked south, passing a tortilla restaurant. He didn't know the area well, but knew that in two blocks he could cross over from his one way street and be near a local university and police station. A much easier place to find a taxi.

A loud crash behind him spun his attention. Glass shattering on the cement. One of the patrons of the patio seating had raised abruptly, crashing into the pub's waitress and knocked the heavy tumblers from her tray. The man did not apologize immediately, instead his eyes were locked with Derian's.

An odd feeling washed over Haynes. The set stare had determination behind them. The man was purposely watching him. The journalist sped up, constantly looking back to see what the outcome was. Panic replaced peace. The man ignored the calamity he set in place and was beginning to come after him. Derian ran.

The light was red. Cars intersected his way and Haynes turned right. Cutting around a trimmed shrub and through a planted set of red canna lilies, Derian ran faster. Three Brownstone office buildings filled the darkness ahead. A few lights one in the floors above, but none would be open at this late of an hour. Checking over his shoulder, he saw the outline of the man round the same corner he did.

Sprinting down a single lane road, Haynes was heading towards a parking lot. A dead end. The gates were locked to enter the garage, he needed another way out. The man was gaining from his indecision.

He spotted a railing across the lot. A small set of cement stairs let into a compound of two-story apartment complexes. The Colonial buildings were shrouded in darkness as only a few dull lamps cornered the circular pathway separating them.

Derian was fit from his constant cycling, but the running was tiring him out. Slowing to blend in with the shadows and stillness, he carefully kept an eye on the steps he had just came from. There was no follower. His pursuer hadn't seen the hidden path. Haynes breathed deeply, trying to get as much air in as he could.

Reaching the sidewalk entrance, Derian paused. Going right would head back towards his pursuer, and maybe more, but also back to the lights of the city, other people and a way out. Going left was a street of houses, quiet and covered in darkness. A potential to disappear for hours, but surely he'd be on his own. He doubted anybody in this neighborhood would be answering their door and welcoming a young, black man in just before midnight.

The deliberation was a momentary distraction, and he nearly missed the warning. Footfalls on cement were nearing fast. Hayes spun. The silhouette of the man was back and only meters away. Haynes took off to the right.

Fear pushed Derian to reach his peak speed and he once again gained ground. Sidewalks, crosswalks and intersections all blurred together on the quiet streets. The buildings began to look all the same again, dark red, maybe brown and beige brick.

Three or four story tall, and all closed. Offices with lobbies, cafés, and a yoga studio flashed by as he raced towards the lights. The man was still behind, but his pace was slowing. Derian still had something left inside. Fear always gave the hunted more desire.

This time Haynes ran through the red light, into traffic and dashed towards the gas station diagonally across from him. It was open. A safe haven found. Feeling the sweat on his chest and back growing, then wiping his brow and head, Derian reached the lit up lot. Gasping for air, he tried to control his breathing. He wasn't really dressed to be a jogger out for a nightly run. Air was his friend.

Crossing the lot, there were two other cars parked near the entrance, but a third whipped around the corner, seemingly out of nowhere. The black Town Car slammed on its brakes right in front of him, nearly running over his toes in the process. Haynes jumped.

The driver, pouncing from his seat, immediately stood facing him, hands gripping a standard G17 Glock. The black pistol was pointed directly at him. Derian froze. "Get in the car Mr. Haynes." The voice was firm, deep and offered no suggestions. Derian's mind ravaged for an escape. Would the driver actually shoot him down right there if he made another run for it? Panting and wheezing resonated behind him as his pursuer finally caught up. He too held a weapon. "I said, *get* in the car." It was another order, but this time spoken through gritted teeth. "Senator Paxton would like to have a word with you."

"Ömer says that you are looking for someone, and that I can help you?" Köseman poised his question between sips of coffee. He smiled to himself when he saw the same face and same headscarf that he had noticed earlier.

"I am looking for men who speak Circassian and have distinguishing marks on their right hands." Rachel was direct as well. "Here a crescent moon, and here a star." Indicating on her own hand where the tattoos would be, she continued in a more hushed tone. "They operate at least in Prague, but certainly across Eastern Europe and are very well funded and connected." She recognized a dilation in the police inspector's eyes and a flare in his nostrils. "You *do* know whom I am after."

"Yes," Hakan sipped carefully this time. ", but also no." He too studied the face of the woman across from him. Identifying her own facial tells, but also churning over his head as to her true motives. "Why is it that you are looking for *these* men?"

Rachel became uneasy with his tone. "It's, personal." Hesitating between words, her eyes narrowed while trying to figure out if the police man was hiding his information because he didn't trust her, or because he was protecting them.

"Personal can mean so many things. A loss of a loved one." Pausing, the detective saw fire flash in her eyes briefly. "A sister, relative, or dear family friend." Another sip. "But, personal, can also lend itself towards a much more *sinister* of meanings depending on one's motives, no?"

The man was prodding and Rachel knew it. "Let's just say that I have, *unfinished* business with them, and would like to conclude our dealings." Stackwell felt that she couldn't be any clearer with the police inspector without actually stating out loud her true intentions.

"Yes," He recognized the fire turn into determination. ", and I believe that to be true." It was Hakan's turn to sit up and lean in. Glancing around quickly, he began. This time his voice was in a much more hushed decibel. "I do know of the men you seek, but first I need to know for whom you are working? I will not allow a war in my city. We have had enough terror and blood run through our streets in my lifetime."

Rachel saw a stern attitude on the man's face. He was willing to give her information, but he also truly didn't want the people of Turkey caught in a crossfire. "I am alone." She decided to tell him the truth. "Vengeance takes many forms, and whether it is avenging or revenging, it is still the same." The truth to a degree at least. "There will be no warring in your streets. I *will* also promise bloodshed, but it shall only flow from the men who are my targets."

Köseman breathed slowly. Studying the woman's face across from him, he believed her, and deep down was even happy to have taken this meeting. "The men you seek are *not* true Turkish men. They are from border towns near Georgia and Armenia, some even from the ports of Trabzon and Rize along the Black Sea." A hint of disgust behind his voice as he spoke about his countrymen. "Interpol believes that they are funded out of Russia, but these men are *not* to be taken for granted." It was a true stern warning.

Pausing as the aproned worker passed, Hakan continued. "Those from the group that have been identified all have Red Notices issued by Interpol, but the members change frequently so it is hard to keep up to date."

"So they do operate across Europe?" Stackwell asked.

"Europe?" It was almost held as a scoff. "They operate all over the world." Stopping, Köseman allowed his statement to sink in to the woman. He was purposely amplifying their feats to see if it would bring defeat to her face. He saw none. Instead, he remembered the grainy appearance from the reported videos of the person that had thwarted this same group, in Prague. The recognition brought hope. Maybe *she* could do what the international police could not. "Lucas Viale, *Hayalet*."

"The Ghost?" Rachel tested when the detective stopped again.

"*Evet*. We know he exists, but nobody knows who he is." Continuing. "Lucas Viale, *Zafar* to his followers, is the leader of these men, rumored to be anything from Russian to Australian, appears and disappears just as quickly, but he is said to be the man in charge.

"Then how do you know he actually exists?" Stackwell was curious.

"Although there has been no collected photograph of the man, he *has* been seen, and even owns a large property here in Istanbul." Köseman knew that that would pique the interest of his new friend and even laughed gingerly as he said it. "He is never there, but a few others always are."

"Where is it?" Rachel focused on the man. Her expression was stern and her voice low, terse and determined. The inspector did not answer as he only sipped again, while meeting her eyes directly. He carefully nodded and seemed genuinely pleased as he found his pen and began writing numbers on a paper serviette.

The unexpected throttle of a delivery motorbike spun Stackwell's head to her right. The driver tried to navigate around an approaching crowd, was cut off and was forced to spin towards the café. It was a last minute maneuver and unforeseeable. The bike shook, driver thrown, then chaos ensued.

Hakan Köseman was rocked from his chair as the high powered bullet ricocheted off the front fender and drove him back into the seated couple behind them. The woman screamed at the body and the blood. Stackwell did not hesitate. Flipping the table onto its side, she used it as a shield when the next two shots landed hard. Wood chunks exploded into the air from the thick slab. She did not know where they were coming from, but could not stay there.

A quick glance towards the police detective and he had not moved. Another bullet whizzed beside the overturned table, shattering glass and hitting the aproned man. More cries rang out.

The second group of screaming brought panic and the crowd began to flee in all directions. She could use it as a distraction. Finding the inked napkin, Rachel set herself, launching forward and within a step hurdling the faux fence acting like the café's barrier. One final bullet. The shooter's anticipation had been marginally off while missing her and killing another man standing, a millisecond behind where she originally leapt.

Sprinting through the narrow channels of the market, Rachel tossed her headscarf and did not look back. She needed to focus on creating separation. As she ran, she shoved through many slow and meandering locals, tourists and merchants. Hostile voices yelled back, but she did not answer.

A right turn, left and a second right kept her on a zigzag pattern as she continued crashing past a local Balık restaurant, luggage and mobile store and a vegetable stand. The latter ended up with an upturned front table while carrots, tomatoes and radishes spilled onto the road below. Another string of curses directed towards her.

The crowded streets of Kadıköy were a blessing and a curse. Slowing as she rounded another corner, Rachel looked back first, then down the other three alleyways from her position. They all looked the same. As the day neared noon, the crowds grew and the advancing sun played peek-a-boo with the amassing shadows between the buildings and their canvass awnings.

She could use the multitudes to her advantage. They could help hide her, or as cover, but whom she was running from. Was she even the target? She couldn't believe that the CIA had found her already, but couldn't rule it out. Mind racing. Had the detective actually been followed that she missed? Did Ömer set them up? It was agonizing to think about, and she could not right now. Another aggravating string of cursing flared from where she came. Spinning her head, she did not see the aggressor, but the crowd was parting. Somebody was rushing through them. Rachel ran again.

Purposely swinging to an intersecting street with every break, Stackwell was spanning her lead until she stepped right, foot landing on a drainage grate and sliding just enough to disrupt her balance. The misstep led her turn to not being tight against the buildings, and a food delivery driver sideswiping her with his motorbike. Rachel's body was twirled by the man's handlebars while sending the bike spiraling into a shocked plaza.

Collecting herself, Rachel looked up to see another man rushing her. He was thick, muscular and even through his sunglasses, she knew his eyes were focused on her. Gritting his teeth, he lunged towards his prey still on the ground.

The attack was wild, disorderly and allowed Stackwell a brief opening for her training. Sliding on the stone roadway, she got under his pawing hands before sweeping his dominant foot out from under, sending him crashing hard onto the street. His cream colored linen shirt was stained and a button popped off.

Kicking out first with her right foot, the man blocked it. Then left. Blocked again. Planting herself, she spun and tried a backside kick towards the grounded attacker, but he ducked that too. He had specialized training as well.

The crowd in the courtyard had frozen. Some used their phones to record the fight, and others stood shocked or were simply calling for the *polis*. Stunned, they gaped as the woman continued to lead the assault.

After both kicking attacks were thwarted, Rachel pushed forward, launching off her front foot and tucking her feet. The man in the linen shirt was set to protect from another kick, but instead had to respond to the double knee attack. He was late in reacting.

Blocking one side of the innovative move was not enough and Stackwell felt her left knee make solid contact above her victim's cheekbone and drive him hard into the stone road. His sunglasses were shattered instantly, cutting the skin around his eye and orbital bone, while the forceful bouncing of the back of the man's head initiated a small pool a blood under them both.

Rachel cautiously stood. The downed man was unsteady, but alive. Sirens were echoing in the distance, but growing stronger as each second held her in a trance. Noticing the emerging crowd for the first time, she saw the phones held outward and recording the whole thing. She could not wait around for the local police to detain and question her. Undoubtedly it would be proven that she was only defending herself, but certainly she would end up connected to the dead police detective at the café, and that would bring even more questions that she did not want to answer. There was no time. Scampering back in the direction she came, Rachel disappeared into the labyrinth of the Kadıköy Çarşi.

The journey back to her hotel had been made warily. Once Rachel felt that she put enough distance between herself and the attack in the plaza, she slowed her pace, bought another headscarf, change of clothes and covered almost all of her face this time. She debated the use of the unhurried ferries against the faster pace trains from Haydarpaşa Station, but ultimately decided on the deliberate pace of the ferry boat because it would calm her, allow her time to think and regroup her thoughts.

Instead of returning to the same harbor side ports of Eminönü, Rachel chose the opposite side of the Fatih district. From there, she walked from the Yenikapı Pier to Sultan Ahmed Mosque, the Blue Mosque. Passing her hotel twice on the way, she was extremely wary of its surroundings. With the second pass, she believed it to be safe, but feigned like a lost tourist and asked directions to the famous domed attraction.

Following the unneeded directions, the next two hours were dedicated to circling the grounds, dropping in and out of the multiple walking tours visiting the courtyard for its beauty and historical dusk photo opportunities. Even when she found an opening to speak with another *visitor*, she kept her eyes focused on the surrounding people. Nobody stood out. Nobody was there that shouldn't have been.

Finally completely satisfied, Stackwell headed back to her hotel, but not before stopping to eat at a trendy kebab and grill. Asking for a table inside, she was allowed to choose an open one in the back corner, facing the door and had only walls behind her. Relaxed, safe and calm, Rachel was able to eat and drink.

With that peace. She also remembered the paper napkin still tucked away into a new pocket of these clothes. Retrieving it, she stared at the collection of numbers. It was not an address, they were coordinates. Punching them into the map application on her phone, the spot came up immediately. It was outside the urban provinces of Istanbul, near a small city that was estimated to be close to two hours away. Rachel would look closer at it back in her room.

One last tour around the base of her hotel and she was satisfied, she hadn't been followed, and nobody knew where she was. Entering, she was greeted by the concierge and used the stairs to the third floor. Swiping the key card brought a click and Rachel entered. Relieved, she inserted the thin plastic card into the electricity slot and the lights that she left on sprang to life.

Rachel's eyes flared, a small gasp escaped, but it was her only reaction. "Good evening Cardinal." The man sat in a chair directly across from her, legs crossed and a long barreled gun pointed directly at her. He was older, dark-skinned, in his late fifties and purposely shaven bald. She recognized him instantly. It was Cordovan, she remembered him from Red Shimmer, the CIA program.

Chapter SIXTEEN

The lights of the city had disappeared nearly forty minutes ago, instead, replaced by the ones expansively set along Interstate 95. The traffic was thinning on both sides of the freeway as they headed south towards Richmond and away from Washington D.C.

The ride had been done in silence. Twice Derian had asked where he was being taken, and both times received no answer. Anxiety began to creep over him when the Lincoln Town Car exited right, merged onto a side highway, and then began a process of turns with each finding a new, smaller road becoming less and less paved. Haynes began to feel this was going to be the end for him. He needed a plan for escape.

Closing his eyes, Derian calmly breathed. Reminding himself that he had been in situations like this before. The expedition to interview the rebel leader in Syria had been similar, but at that time, he was also forced to wear a dirty linen hood and couldn't see where he was going. With these thoughts, his fear was dissipating and he could feel the car slowing. His time to act was coming. Derian mentally pictured the three of them in the car. The driver to his left and the shadow that had chased him, perched directly behind. Once the car stopped, the rear passenger would probably open the door for him and that's when he would strike. It would undoubtedly be remote, secluded from watchful eyes, and dark.

He might've been outnumbered, but really only had to incapacitate the man behind him. The driver would be caught off guard, causing him to hesitate for a second. That brief opening would be all Derian would need to then flee in the darkness. It wasn't much of a plan, but it was his only one. Opening his eyes, he prepared himself for the escape.

Instead of the obscurity of nightfall, Haynes was partially blinded by the activation of a bright light on a motion detector sitting atop a large house. Drawing nearer, the outline of the two-story building became clearer and the details of the walls recognizable in the car's headlights. It was a wooden cabin. Huge, and certainly expensive. The momentary fixation on the unexpected view confused Derian and paused his escape plan. The man seated behind him had already opened the door and was waiting for him to get out.

"The Senator is inside." The driver spoke without turning off the engine. "He is expecting you." Still baffled, Haynes cautiously stepped out, spun around to keep himself facing the man who pursued him earlier, but he did not react. Once Derian was clear, the man climbed into the passenger seat and the black car slowly backed away.

The motion light shut off. Derian stood stationary, uncertain how to proceed. "I wouldn't stand out there too long." The voice of John Paxton called out to him. "We are known to have black bears out at this time of year." Haynes turned and the blinding light popped on and he was able to make out the silhouette of the Senator heading from the porch back into the cabin.

Caution kept him wary, but Derian accepted the drink offered to him by his new host. Sitting again in silence, Haynes sipped the bronze liquor. It was strong, held a long after taste and was both fruity and smoky at the same time.

"Not a whiskey drinker Mr. Haynes?" The Senator cackled to himself when Derian's face crinkled at the liqueur.

"No. No sir," The journalist responded as he could still feel the aromas in his mouth. ", but I also wasn't expecting such bold flavors." His second sip drained his glass.

"A hint of mango mixed with chestnut and toffee. It's one of the best I've ever tasted." The Texan leaned over and poured a taller glass for Derian this time. "Twenty-seven year old Irish whiskey." Again, the man casually chuckled. "Only a hundred bottles ever made, but I guess at nearly seven thousand dollars, it better be good." Another laugh, but this time it caused Derian to pause at the price of the half empty crystal decanter on the small table between them.

Haynes's eyes fluttered about the open sitting room. It was dark and represented a general feeling coziness. The large stone fireplace offered the most light, but there were two dull, orange wall mounted circular lights, and another small table lamp to his right. The glowing embers heated the room, probably too much for late summer, but it was also much cooler overnight and Derian doubted there was an interior heating option currently operating.

He could make out a small kitchen in the shadows over the Senator's shoulders and a wide staircase to the second level next to it. It was simple, limited in décor, and other than the oversized steer horns above the fireplace mantel, Derian wouldn't have thought this place was owned by Paxton. The man always seemed much more flamboyant. "I hope my men weren't rough with you." The man spoke again. "I know that sometimes they can be a little too exuberant in their work." This time his chuckle seemed genuine and as an icebreaking setup to something more.

"Rough? No. They never touched me," Haynes returned the sincerity. ", but their guns didn't really offer me any other options." He added with sass.

"No, I guess they probably didn't." The Senator laughed harder this time, than drank again. "Well I'm sure you are wondering why I *invited* you out to meet me here tonight, at such a late hour." The laugh was forced and the journalist could feel the grief filling the room.

"After our last interaction, I have a few assumptions, but this wasn't one of them." Derian continued before his host could finish his drink. "Firstly sir, I want to express my condolences to you and your family, and assure you that myself, and the Post will not be pressing any deeper into the story that I attacked you with the other day."

"The hell you won't!" Senator Paxton roared at the man across from him this time. "I will not allow myself to be *that* man's scapegoat." Finishing, the burst of anger was gone and replaced by a much more melancholy tone.

"I'm sorry?" Haynes was confused. "I thought you brought me here to get me to kill the story. I mean, after what happened with the President in Madison and then your granddaughter."

"Don't put them in the same sentence." Paxton spat back venom. An uneasy silence filled the void between the two men, before the elder set his glass down to refill and spoke calmly, almost whimsicality. "Have you seen that *press conference* from the other day Mr. Haynes?"

"Yes sir." Derian was uncertain where this was going. "I've actually watched it three times."

"Have you? Have you *actually* watched it? I mean dug into the gist of every word and syllable that he says after setting me aside?" The Senator had purpose to his train of thought. "The President's call-to-arms, action plan, whatever bullshit he wants to make it, consisted of him speaking for forty-three minutes and twenty-eight seconds, exactly." Focus and intent were behind the man's eyes now. "And in that time, do you know how many times he says *I*, *me*, or *my administration*? Thirty-three. Thirty-three times he refers to himself."

Haynes could feel the heat in the room growing, but it wasn't from the dying fire. Anger was bleeding from Paxton's every fiber. "I never realized that sir, no, I'll have to watch it again." Sincerity and confusion were muddled together. "I am sorry Senator, but I still don't understand what this has to do with me."

"You're a smart man Mr. Haynes." Paxton sat forward. "I know you've searched this room with your eyes, scouring it for information, good and bad, but I know you've also noticed the key things on this table, yet you haven't even acknowledged them." An open palm referencing a fresh yellow legal pad, two pens, two pencils, and a small USB drive. Paxton only waited for recognition with a look upon them. "They are for you. If!" Stopping again to hold up his index finger and meet the journalist's stare with a firm, determined one of his own. "If, you are willing to do something for me first."

Derian's mind raced. "I'm not sure exactly what you mean Mr. Senator."

"I will give you the story you want, the *whole* story about Polygon, APC Oil, and *more*." Paxton saw the journalist's eyes flare at the indication of further indiscretions." Oh yes Mr. Haynes, there are plenty of others that the President and his administration have side and secret deals with. I will give you access to all of it, with proof of course, but I want you to expose a much bigger story first."

"Are you willing to go on record Mr. Senator?" Derian was hesitant. He could feel the signs of a trap. This could easily be a setup to further destroy his credibility. "Secret sources and unproven theories don't exactly fly too far in Washington these days."

"You have every right to be skeptical, but I will do you one better. You can use me as your source, no hidden agendas, and I will give you this." Paxton scooped up the USB drive and held it towards the reporter. "All emails and communications that incriminate every person or persons involved. Financial records, payment transfers and receipts, all documented. It'll take time organizing, but it's all there." When Derian reached out to take the small device, Paxton pulled it back, palming the computer drive. "First, I want your word, as a man Mr. Haynes. I believe in honoring one's word. I will help you follow the money, but first you will investigate and expose the monsters for who they truly are."

"Monsters?" Derian was trying to figure out if the Senator was genuine or drunk.

"Alan and Teresa Wakefield. The President and the First Lady."

Quietly opening the door to the bedroom in the southwest corner on the second floor of the White House, the President was surprised to see a brass lamp still on next to their bed. His wife was reading, she was waiting for him to return. "So? How did Liam react?" She was eager to hear about the latest phone call between her husband and the British Prime Minister.

"He was reluctant." Wakefield started dower, anticipating a frown or curse from his wife. It came. "Reluctant *until* I was able to persuade him otherwise." He smiled gloatingly.

"Excellent." The scowl turned to jubilance. "And Marc? Did he bend as well?" Using her best French accent to accentuate the Canadian Prime Minister's name.

"Not yet," Alan Wakefield laughed at his wife's awful pronunciation attempt. ", but only because I haven't had a chance to speak with him again. Apparently he's been in Parliament all day today and wasn't available."

"Bullshit." Teresa cursed at the excuse. "More like he's afraid to call you back because he knows he's a weak man on his own." The President laughed again as he entered the oversized room closet connected to the master bedroom. "I was able to get you some *persuading* material if he doesn't want to conform."

"That's why you're the best wife ever." Reappearing, the President grinned slyly. "You always know how to brighten the mood in the bedroom."

Teresa Wakefield pushed back the satin sheets to welcome her husband. "If the Prime Minister won't agree to make you commander-in-chief on this particular project, then we may have to endorse his main opponent from out west. The man is a complete blathering idiot and a jackass, but *if* the President of the United States agreed with some of his platform, then his fellow idiots might make things tougher for the current Canadian leader to win back those Western provinces that he did in the last election."

Wakefield slid next to his wife and kissed her shoulder while removing the strap that held her nightgown. "Your people could arrange that?" He kissed her again.

"You know that they can." Tittering at the excitement of creating disorder and anarchy in another country, she lowered the silk material to expose her bare chest. "Will you then be able to bring Sergei into the fold?" She inquired about their friend, the current Russian President.

"Not immediately." Wakefield spoke between kisses on her naked body. "Once we get the task force running," Kissing again. ", then we use the Russians as our featured intelligence," His wife squirmed this time as he found an erogenous zone. ", and make them into heroes as we officially take down the largest trafficking outlet in Europe."

"Cullen's friend?" Teresa questioned, gently pushing her husband away momentarily.

"The Russian President will need an undeniably major win to allow me to be able to bring them back up into the conversation admittance into NATO, the UN and the G8." The pause between the couple allowed him move back closer. "Cullen will be fine, he'll have to be. Once the initial shock period blows over, I'll even get him started with a new supplier. It's just a means to an end." He found his wife's body once again. "An end we both know is coming once I get Sergei back into the world's good graces."

"And then, once you get him in, the two of you take over NATO?" She was excited again. "The two most *powerful* countries in the world working together."

"But he'll *owe* me." Alan interrupted his wife coolly. "The Russians will all owe me, *owe us!*"

"Yes." An amorous shriek of arousal came from the First Lady as she rolled over and mounted her husband. "We'll have all the *power*. We'll be able to run the world!"

It had been hours. Derian wasn't sure exactly how many, but the crystal decanter was empty and three times Paxton added more wood to the fireplace.

He had scribbled notes, shorthand, lines and arrows to connect the Senator's stories and facts with thoughts of his own as he neared the bottom of the fifth page of the large yellow legal pad.

Corruption ran deep in the current President's administration and John Paxton was in the middle of it. He was a trusted ally and knew the intricacies of all the illicit dealings. The relationship with Polygon and APC Oil was just the tip of the claims that Paxton detailed for Derian. Large sums of monies, in the multi-millions were paid to ensure the government kept the industry blossoming, and particularly their companies. Lax regulations on their drilling practices, certain land titles pushed through and the purposeful delays of shipments to increase demand and price per barrel.

During one of the Senator's more passionate notions, he explained that the major price war from two years ago, was truly brought on because of civil war in the Middle East, but also implicated that the with the help of private military contractors, that the unrest was purposely caused by the oil companies. When asked how he was certain of quite a claim, Paxton only responded to the question with another question of his own. *Who do you think put the oil companies in bed with former General running the PMCs over there?*

The man was willing to be an open book, even when it came to family. The appointment of his brother-in-law, Mason Williams, to be Secretary of Energy was simply because he was loyal to the

President, easily influenced by the powerful man and eager to do whatever was needed to keep Wakefield happy. Paxton joked about the initial bad press that was given to such an unqualified candidate, but only mused, *what were you, the media or everyday citizens going to do about it. Nothing.* He laughed heartily at the thought.

With Williams as the President's lapdog in that sector, once again the big money from the oil industry could control their competition. The fight and desire for cleaner and more efficient solar power or electricity was always a losing battle. A *greener* and safer form of energy was never going to happen with Wakefield in power. Paxton said the man spoke well at functions, showed promise to those industries for potential, but it was all for show, and those who really knew the inner workings, understood the true possibilities were never a reality.

Those were just the beginning to Paxton's revelations. The Senator queried the journalist as well, but they were merely to set up his next trail of explosive information. Highlighting the dollar signs, Paxton revealed the real money wasn't in oil, but to no shock, was from the gun companies. *People will never get rid of guns Mr. Haynes, there's too much money in it for everybody, and I do mean everybody. Both sides of the aisle are getting their pockets lined with cash from the NRA.*

After exposing his insights to guns and money, the Texan moved into the media, specifically online and social media. Controlling the narrative was the

President's biggest aspiration. He knew that if he regulated what was said, then he could manipulate the general public into believing anything.

"People can think for themselves." Haynes retorted back.

"Can they?" Paxton posed sincerely. "Can they really?" The man rested his empty glass on the table and leaned in towards his guest. "Politics changed years ago. At one time it was simply Democrats versus Republicans and people debated topics, made speeches and neighbors argued over talking points. It was simple." The man casually shook his head. "But then it became a game of zealots. To win in the court of the public opinion, all you needed to do was pit people against one another. Find out what they are afraid of, and push a knife into that wound."

"So how do you control that?" The journalist compared this thought process to how wars were started in countries like Yemen, Libya and the initial paths of World War II.

"You give the people with the biggest personalities a platform, and pay them large amounts of money to spew your rhetoric." He laughed casually again. "Whether they believe it or not, they enjoy the money, fame, notoriety, whatever. Hell, I can pay actors, sports figures, or even *you* a shitload of money to say that the sky is red. Blue doesn't exist and that we're being lied to about the primary of colors. I do that enough and eventually it'll catch on. As that bullshit grows, so does the following of simpleton believers, who then regurgitate it and get followers of their own. They then enjoy the notoriety of their fame and then spread it for free for me."

"But most of these people you are talking about are made fun of by the rest of the general public." Derian pressed as he remembered seeing everything the Senator was laying out happen on social media.

"Who cares." A scoffed comment. "Good or bad, it's out there that the sky is red and your opponent is lying to you. The inkling that they may be lying is the point, not about what, just that it's there.

"Why are you telling me all of this?" Haynes had wanted to ask the question since this all started, but also didn't want the man to stop. "Why now? Less than a week ago, you, and then the President, pretty much threatened to have me *disappear* was the word alluded." Haynes wanted to connect the Senator's granddaughter into the conversation, but held back. "You *are* still part of Alan Wakefield's inner sanctum. Why would you want to help me bring it all down around you?"

"That is the real question isn't?" Paxton gingerly laughed again. "Unfortunately I can't offer you any grander a motivation than the truth. I want revenge."

"In your own words, you stated that the President and First Lady are *monsters*?" Derian believed the simple reason was probably the truth.

"Do you know who Cullen Verger is Mr. Haynes?"

"The billionaire financier and hotel mogul?" The journalist started taking notes again.

"Paxton laughed loudly this time. "Yes, *him*." Shaking his head, he continued. "Although you may want to redefine your concept of who he truly is. You called him a financier and mogul, only half of that is true. Sure he *now* owns and operates a hotel chain in major international cities, but his money did not come from any investments, advising or crypto currency windfalls. I can assure you, it came from blackmail and money laundering on an international scale that nobody could even write about in the movies." When Haynes offered no rebuke, the Texan continued. "Cullen Verger is a personal friend of the President, hell, many Presidents, Prime Ministers and other world leaders, politicians, celebrities, and anybody else either famous or has money. Friends is probably too generous a term as the man is absolute scum."

Haynes looked up from his notes and saw his host sit back into the brown leather chair, relishing in his claim. There had always been rumors about Verger's wealth and lifestyle, but those same types of rumors could be said about any professional athlete or doctor in the public spotlight.

"I can see your mind going over everything that you might have heard in the past. Some of it is certainly true, but this is *why* you are here tonight Mr. Haynes, I want you to expose Cullen Verger for whom is truly is, what he does and everybody that benefits or participates in knowing him."

"What exactly would you like me to find out?" Confusion was once again in the forefront. "The man is pretty reclusive, but when is out, it's a pretty big spectacle."

"What I want, *need*, you to expose, will be the first crashing blow of a tidal wave of consequences felt across the world." Paxton's way with words caught Derian's attention immediately. "The man is certainly a mogul, but he is a blackmail mogul. He specializes in sexual fetishes and trafficking discreetly." The accusation caused Haynes to quickly look up and stop his notetaking.

"Excuse me. Can you elaborate on that?"

"Human and sex trafficking Mr. Haynes." Paxton's strong demeanor seemed slightly lessened as he spoke the words. "He uses his hotels as rendezvous meets. Transports whatever you may want, drugs, women, men, boys, girls, *children*." Pausing and swallowing hard before continuing. "He can get you whatever you want and nothing is off the table. He then records it all, either on video or in his famous ledgers. You are forced to sign, a *transaction report* as he calls it, and then he has everything he needs on you."

"Why would you, er, anybody sign such a thing?" Haynes reacted.

"There is no choice. The first time, you don't know, until after. At that point, he already has what he needs." A disheartened Paxton answered the question coolly.

Derian didn't know what to say, or how to react. "Why not just go to the authorities. The FBI or the CIA if it's this big? How am I supposed to expose this kind of story?" Haynes finally spoke.

Paxton chuckled at the younger man's naiveté. "I don't think you quite understand how many powerful men and women he has, *information* on. If Verger wanted, he could probably control how world leaders acted and start wars. Blackmail is the most powerful weapon in the world, and he has the deadliest form of it, sexual desires. Many acts would publicly shame some of the most rich and influential, but many are also illegal, border on, or are straight up crimes against humanity."

"Can you prove all of this as well? Is it on the flash drive too?"

"No. That is where you come in Mr. Haynes." The reporter sat silent. Shocked, but also unsure of how to even begin. "I can see your internal debate. An uncertainty as to even believe me or how to begin your research, but don't worry, I am going to tell you how to get the information that you need."

Another look of astonishment fell over Derian. "And, what if I decide not to pursue this particular angle of the story, or can't?"

"I can only trust that you will Mr. Haynes. It's the reason that I chose you." Moving to replace two smaller logs on the fire and retrieve a new bottle of goldish brown liquor, Paxton spoke evenly, even heroically towards his guest. "After you ambushed me on Capitol Hill, I'll admit, I was pissed, but also impressed." Pouring himself and Derian a glass. "You didn't back down from me. So I did some further digging into who you were and your career. There wasn't much after you returned from Yemen." A gentle chuckle this time. "Yet, the Post kept you around, Kim Rawlings believed, *believes* in you, and that must mean something. She's a major pain in the ass you know, but I respect the hell out of her."

"So do I Senator." Haynes interrupted briefly.

"I also admired your mother when she was in Washington." Derian's eyes flared as he sipped the crisp brandy and didn't react right away. Paxton smiled. "You didn't know that I knew her did you?" A rhetorical question. "She was tough, determined, but was honest as hell. Things were simpler back then, conversations were actually civil and over dinner or drinks, regardless of what political *color* you supported." Paxton sipped again while gingerly remembering a past life. "You remind me of her, and that's why I believe that you will honor my proposal and go after the truth here first."

A moment of silence between the two men. Neither looked at each other. Paxton enjoying the glowing flames and Derian switching his gaze back-and-forth from the glass in his hands to his notes on the yellow pad in front of him. "You said that you were going to tell me where I can find this information?" Smiling up at the Texan.

Paxton's own smile grew wide, he knew the journalist was in. "The ledgers. Everything is in his ledgers, and I know where they are." Haynes was again scribbling his shorthand notes. "Out of Verger's many properties and resorts, there is only one that he actually calls home. The Maldives. It has no extradition. He has a private island there, mainly the setting for a string of three of his resorts, but the other half is his. That's where the proof can be found."

Haynes looked up with concern. "So you expect me to what, find a way onto this private island and then break into his house, undoubtedly secure, and what, find these documents?" The reporter's voice was full of criticism.

"I will get you onto the island Mr. Haynes, the rest will yes be up to you. How you go about it is your choice." It was clear that Paxton hadn't clearly thought a plan through.

Insanity. It was all Derian could think. He downed the remainder of his drink. "How are you able to get me onto the island?"

Senator John Paxton sat alone in the cabin as the glowing embers began to fade. His men had returned to escort Haynes back to Washington after the initial stages of a plan had been set. He had called and booked a stay at one of Verger's resorts in the Maldives under the journalist's name, airfare and given him cash in case he needed it. The seeds were planted and he hoped the man would go through with the strategy. He purposely left out the fact that he knew his granddaughter was being held there as well. Sighing, Paxton finished the last mouthful from another bottle. He was drunk. The Senator was also relaxed, he knew that he had made his deal with the devil many years ago, but now he was backing out of it. It did not matter, nothing mattered as long as Haynes was successful. If he could expose the truths to the world, then it didn't matter, hell could burn itself down.

Chapter *SEVENTEEN*

"Did you really think that I wouldn't find you?" The bald man spoke smoothly, calm and almost soothing, but the barrel of the suppressed Ruger did not waver.

"*They* sent you to kill me." Rachel's mind raced as she searched for a way out. Cordovan had set up his ambush with the calculating poise of a leopard on the plains of Africa. Perching himself at a perfect distance to allow her to enter the room, close the door behind, but also just far enough away that her surprise would keep her at bay. Rachel's only alternative to the flash of a muzzle, was to her left, the bathroom. Diving in there crossed her mind, closing and locking the door, but she disregarded that foolish maneuver, it would only buy seconds to her life as there was nowhere to go from there. "A contract for one of their own."

"Are you though?" It was poised rhetorically more to himself. Uncrossing, then re-crossing his legs, the asset leaned forward when his target changed the weight balance of her feet. He did not fire, but was ready. "You know, I was actually glad, even happy, to see your face appear on my screen, *again*."

With the pause, the smug fifty year old black man saw a level of piqued interest on his target's face. "This allows me to right a previous wrong."

"A previous wrong?" More confusion and interest as Rachel sensed her killer's willingness to continue talking before he finished his task. Switching her balance again between her feet kept her knees and toes alert, but each time she did it, Cordovan's eyes and nostrils flared in acknowledgement, he was paying attention.

"Oh yes, the only blemish on my career." Another haughty comment. With this slower pace of speech, the man's Southern accent was underlying his tone. "I hate to admit this, but it is not the first time that the, *Company*, has sent me after you." He was enjoying listening to himself talk. "The first was over nine years ago, three thousand three hundred and eighty-seven days ago to be precise." A smile as the assassin thought about fulfilling an outstanding undertaking.

"Russia." Stackwell added. Would she have enough time to lunge towards him before he fired the gun? She doubted it, but the options running through her head for escape were quickly disappearing just as fast as they were coming to her.

"Yes," A slight hiss and head nod. ", in Russia. You know, I do understand why you did what you did in Moscow." It was true empathy in the trained assassin's voice. "I probably would've even did the same if somebody had killed my wife or daughters."

"But that's not enough to allow me penance?" An attempt to form a bond with the man that she barely even knew.

"For vengeance? Completely justified." He laughed. "But from completing my assignment? No." Cordovan's tone firmed and Rachel knew he was reaching the end of his allowable discussion.

"Daughters? As in plural? Two or three at least I'm guessing." Another option came to Rachel's mind in an attempt to gain her freedom. "You were able to track me down here, and I'm sure you know why I'm here."

"You of all people know that's not how it works. We get a contract and a location." The first sign of a crack in the man's demeanor.

"Yes, but your local man already failed when I met the detective, so you know that I'm after those who kidnap and traffic women, *young girls* primarily." Rachel thought she was getting through to the asset as a brief look of uncertainty crossed his face. "I know where they are, *here* in Istanbul, just outside the city, and I plan on making sure that they cannot do that to *any*body's children, *daughters*, again."

"Local man?" His facial expression seemed more like skepticism now. "Please don't say anything else Cardinal, you are beginning to sound like a mark, and I don't want to remember you that way."

Derision or exhaustion was his tenor, but she couldn't tell, regardless it wasn't working.

Rachel lunged. During her last weight shifting, she also slide her right leg back ever so slightly and was in an abbreviated starter's stance. There were no good ideas, so only the bad ones were left to takeover. She knew he was going to kill her now anyways, so a frontal attack of her own was her last resort. Rachel was content to know she would die fighting at least.

Pushing off her back foot, Stackwell sprang into the air, corkscrewing her body to distort a clear firing path. Two suppressed shots responded immediately from the shiny gun's muzzle. Rachel could feel a searing pain, but was also alive as she crashed into the seated killer.

The chair toppled over backwards, sending both CIA assassins sprawling to the ground, but neither stayed down. Cordovan's grip still firmly around his Ruger. Rachel didn't hesitate. A forward kick to his chest and then to the wrist holding the gun. He still did not relinquish.

The asset spun, stepping frontward and firing. He missed his mark. Stackwell sliding right, then drawing in closer and pushing away the man's gun hand. Twisting the arms backwards forced a release and she now controlled the silenced weapon. Swinging it wildly once onto Cordovan's opposing shoulder before he blocked the second attack, glided away and slapped her hard with his free hand.

Rachel staggered and the gun fell to the ground. Stumbling into the hotel room's wood desk, she grabbed the cheap brass lamp at its base, striking forwards while crashing at the now bleeding Cordovan. With the second blast, the lamp exploded into pieces and Rachel tossed it aside.

Circling one another, hands up, both assassins were prepared to strike and waiting for the other to move first. The elder did so. Punching with his dominant right, Stackwell ducked under, grabbing his palm, again rotating and twisting his arm backwards and pulling tight into his body. A free elbow finding and cracking a rib.

Cordovan wheezed, snatching a handful of the woman's hair, yanking it back hard and raising her from the ground before driving her hard into wall. The painted drywall disintegrated under the force. She reared, and he slammed her even harder, face first this time. More dust and blood flared at the battle. Rachel countered. Rocking her weight forward, dipping low and flinging the taller man over her back. He released his grip on her head, she yanked on his arm that made a snapping sound with the maneuver.

The CIA asset bent at the waist, howling with a dislocation. Rachel pounced. A backspin was unprotected, she landed her flat, open hand directly into the man's temple, disorienting him further. Red crimson dripped from her face. Another front kick into the asset's chest brought a loud popping in the ribcage. Following with a rotating attack, in the reverse direction, allowed Rachel to chop down hard on his carotid artery.

The killer dropped to a knee, head spinning and gasping for any air he could find. Stackwell didn't let up. Three long, powerful downward punches landing one after another. Blood spurted from around his broken orbital bone.

Desperation set in and Cordovan's adrenaline crested. Berserk, and still without air, his hands clawed for his target's throat, but found only the black spots his distorted vision was creating.

Cardinal wrapped herself around asset's back, her legs clutching his own tightly to his body, and arms squeezing his head and neck. Pressure and pulling were massed together as she wrenched with all her strength. She was again the apex predator. Her prey's arms were the first to go limp, but she yanked one more time. Finding the final cracking sound she wanted. She released Cordovan's lifeless body after snapping the assassin's neck, he was dead.

Heart beating rapidly, Stackwell tried to slow her breathing and control her thoughts. She was wild, but also found solace in her actions. The searing sensation was back and for the first time had realized that one of her killer's bullets had actually found its mark. Only grazing her, but still opening a long cut across her stomach and side. The burning of torn flesh was not her only injury, but none was enough to damage her further, she was still alive.

Marking, cleaning, and stitching her wounds brought gritted teeth and desires to scream aloud, but she held back the cries. Matching her dosing of vodka with a swig of her own helped. There was no time to waste or get drunk to kill the pain. *They* knew where she was and would only send another asset after her. Collecting the dead man's Ruger, extra cartridges and phone, Rachel closed the hotel room door and headed for the back stairwell.

Finishing her mission was the priority. Punching the memorized coordinates into her new phone, she set the map to plot directions. She needed to eliminate her targets before the CIA succeeded in killing her.

The late morning sun was playing peek-a-boo with a developing cloud cover, but Derian's hoodie and sunglasses were not worn for weather purposes. He could feel the beads of sweat on his chest and back forming while he sat motionless, spying the woman enter Smithsonian National Zoo.

Watching her constantly look to her phone, combined with pace and stride, he knew that Kim Rawlings was annoyed. She had already been put off by his request to meet him away from the Washington Post, but then became even more irritated when he changed what should have been a quick ten minute drive into an hour of taxi swapping through D.C., and a twenty minute walk from the Washington National Cathedral.

Entering through the visitor center on Connecticut Avenue, Rawlings passed him as she turned right and headed towards the Giant Panda house on the Asia Trail. Haynes waited, intent to see if she had been followed. When he was satisfied that none of the other visitors to the park were there for her, he descended down the path.

The silenced buzzing of his new cellular phone jolted Derian from his exhausted slumber like a blaring alarm clock. He wasn't actually sleeping though, he was still at his computer, upright in his chair and hands still on the keyboard and mouse. Arriving home close to four o'clock in the morning, Paxton's men had escorted him. Again the ride had been made in silence except for a brief phone call in which Haynes was informed that the Senator had arranged a flight and week-long stay for him at one of the resorts on Cullen Verger's island.

Excitement and fear swarmed him as the reality of what Paxton had requested of him was setting in, but first anticipation. Gripping the small USB device tightly the entire trip home, Derian raced to his computer and immediately plugged it into an open drive. He scanned it, but it was clean of tracking or phishing viruses. Two folders appeared, neither had names. He opened the first one. It was full of documents. PDF files, JPG photos and one page with a string of interlinking webpages. There was easily over a hundred in total, probably more. It was the concrete evidence that he needed to write his story.

The second folder had one file in it only. A recorded movie clip. Derian watched it, three times. It was short, just under five minutes, but in it Senator John Paxton spoke somberly. Apologizing to the

American people for weakness. He spoke about his time in office, his dedication to the state of Texas, and that he was proud for what he had accomplished over the years. He spoke highly about colleagues and begged for harmony, unity against corruption and finished by decreeing a commitment to the words of Derian Haynes. The Senator wanted this to be made public when the time was right, it was the only way to truly authenticate any claims against the President and his administration, but it was the final sentence that hit Derian the hardest. *I am doing this for you, my dear Ginny.* It was the last thing on the clip before shutting off.

The black phone buzzed again. Haynes looked at the screen, he had one missed call and five messages from Reggie. Something didn't feel right. It wasn't even seven yet, why would his friend be so anxious to talk to him this early. It had to be something with his boss, Senator John Paxton.

"Where the hell are you?" Reggie's voice was frazzled.

"I'm at home." Derian was becoming concerned. "Where else would I be at this hour. What's up man?" He tried to play it cool.

"Something awful has happened, put on your TV." The voice still panicked.

"Shit! What's happening?" Images of the Twin Towers and Oklahoma City flashed through Derian's mind. "What? When did this happen?" He was awestruck as the headline scrolled across the bottom of the television screen.

"We don't know. He had been missing for the past day, but everybody assumed he was with family." Reggie seemed rushed. "Listen. I'll call you later. I gotta go." Derian didn't even get a chance to answer when the call was ended. His eyes still staring at the news story, Senator John Paxton had been found dead at his cabin in rural Virginia. Police were saying no foul play and that he had committed suicide.

Rawlings jumped when he approached her from behind. The brief squeal caught the attention of the other panda house visitors, but was quickly ignored when it was obviously nothing concerning. "Shit! You scared me." The Brit swatted at Haynes. "What the hell is all this cloak and dagger bullshit about, and why shouldn't I fire you right now." Her agitation had returned.

"You saw the story this morning." Carefully Derian looked around to ensure nobody else was listening. He lowered his voice. "About Paxton."

"Oh bullocks!" The Washington Post executive editor could always sense when one of her journalists were pushing for an angle. "Nope. We're off that story. *You're* off that story. I'm not gonna let you circle back around to Paxton now."

"I've got the story Kim." Haynes was blunt, but also leery.

"What do you mean? Nope, I don't care. We're not going after a dead man." Rawlings corrected herself mid-thought. "I can't believe you dragged me out here, through all that spy shit for this." Turning away, the Brit muddled to herself.

"Kim! Wait!" Haynes's voice rose, then he returned to a whisper as they exited the bear enclosure. "I was there. Last night. With Paxton. Before." Rawlings stopped. Spinning on her heel, her mouth was slightly agape, but her eyes fully open.

Derian lead Rawlings to a bench as a group of children were led past by two young adults. He explained his night and left nothing out. Starting with waiting for a source at the pub, being chased and being take to see Paxton. He showed her his folded up yellow pad papers full of notes from their conversation and told her about the USB, and the video.

"So he wants us to run the story." It was a claim. Rawlings was itching for a mainstream story.

"Yes, but not yet." Derian stifled her thoughts.

"We have to, it's the perfect time." She returned to a more tender tone. "I mean we'll run it as an honorarium, not a hit piece. A dying man's last wishes type angle. It'll play well and even be accepted by readers positively.

"No, I mean we can't, just not *yet*. I have a bigger story." Haynes was insistent.

"Bigger than a corruption story against the President of the United States?"

"Yes. It's a global conspiracy." His initial enthusiasm waned. "I mean potentially. I still have to investigate it."

"What is that?" Rawlings questioned. "You either have the story or you don't. I need to run the one we have, right bloody now. You know we are in the business of selling media right?" He knew she was right, but needed to convince her.

"We can't. I promised to look into this other story first before I went ahead with the previous one. I can't, I won't go back on my word, especially now." Haynes focused on his word. "Give me a week to put it together."

Rawlings's face furrowed as she looked at Derian. Finally speaking. "You have three days," She held up her finger. ", but then I want something from you or I get somebody else to write it."

"I need a week." He was insistent. "I leave in two days and then it'll take me a couple more to figure out how to proceed."

"You're *leaving*?" The editor was shocked. "Where are you going?"

Derian had been debating how much he actually wanted to divulge. Paxton had said that the people involved were rich, famous, and most importantly, powerful. Part of him wanted to protect Rawlings and his employer, but also part of him didn't know whom he could truly trust. "I can't say." He continued. "Just trust me. Give me a week. I'll either have something by then or I won't."

Rawlings sat next to him silently. Internally debating how to proceed. "Fine. You have seven days, but not a second longer than that."

"I do need one more thing. Well, hopefully I won't, but I need to ask anyway." A grim request as he handed her the yellow papers and small computer drive. "I need you to take these. Keep them safe for me and promise me you won't do anything with them until you hear from me."

"Rubbish." Concern filled Rawlings face this time as she saw resolve in Derian's. "You keep your own notes. I don't want your jumbled nonsense." She was trying to be funny.

"Please Kim." He was serious. "If something, happens, and I don't make it back." Pausing. "You need to run the story without me. Paxton would want that I think." Haynes winked at his boss to try to re-enlighten the mood. "Just not until you know I'm dead though."

Rawlings reluctantly accepted the evidence. The look on her face had turned ashen as she spoke gravely. "What the hell are you into Haynes?"

Checking the time on his phone, Cross cursed again. It was approaching noon, and that meant he had just over an hour before he needed to update the Director of National Intelligence, Garner Housley. He felt the former Congressman was a pompous ass, but also was pleased that he agreed they should leave Virginia Bennett out of any further communications. It was the one thing that the two men had in common, they both believed in the various Black Ops programs that the United States was prolifically involved. They both understood the value that these clandestine services had, and could not allow some of the more intimate details to find their way to politically motivated bleeding hearts that would air on the side of diplomacy before action.

A red light flashed on his desk phone, one of his technicians was contacting him. "Sir, um, we have a problem." The concerned voice was from the man in charge of monitoring the assets. *Shit*. Cross cursed to himself again.

His operations room was often called a *crisis suite* by Generals and Admirals in the Pentagon, but right now it felt exactly like one. Normal daily missions were being supervised and examined by his staff, while the large screen at the front of the room had returned to multiple smaller ones monitoring different regions of the world and their *hot zones*. It was a well-oiled machine balancing that desired diplomacy and his antagonistic way of chaos.

"What do you mean the signal is *gone*?" There was a reserved calmness to the head of the Black Ops division, but a heavy emphasis on *gone*.

"Here." Pointing, the man continued. "The first asset's bloodwork isn't responding to the technology any longer. Asset two's is fine." The technician brought up another screen to show a consistent flow chart, much like on a hospital's monitor. "Both were working earlier today, then it just spiked rapidly, slowed and disappeared." The Tech graduate from Stanford University was certain his computers were malfunctioning. "I've already got a systems check started. I'll run the data against—"

"Don't bother." Cross had already assessed his problem. "The program is working fine. Continue to monitor the asset Crimson."

"But what happened to the other." Trailing off, the naivety of the technician has set in as his voice trailed off

"He's dead." Cross patted him on the shoulder to tell him to continue working. "She killed him."

"Should I activate another asset? One of our European operatives?" Somber and cool, the man was ready to keep going.

"No." Cross pausing as he spoke. He had a different trail of thought. "I've got a better idea." Without another word, he returned to his office. Locating a handheld phone from a hidden drawer, he dialed a number he hoped was still in service.

"*Da!*" The hard Russian voice answered on the fourth ring.

"Vladimir?" Derrick asked.

"*Amerikanets? Kto ty?*" The voice returned the question with another of his own.

"Yes, but I'm looking for Vladimir." Cross's Russian was terrible and he knew it, but he also knew that this was not the voice of the man he was looking for.

"Vladimir Mironov is dead. This is Yegor Vinogradov." Cross recognized the speaker's name immediately. A former member of the KGB and still a presumed senior advisor to the current government.

The American was about to disconnect the call, remove the memory card and destroy the phone, but was caught by the harsh voice once again. "If you have this number, then we must be able to *help* each other."

"Sophia Warner." Cross carefully stated the name. Testing the voice to see what his answer might be.

"*Da*. I know that name." The Russian changed to a firm English tone. "She is yours."

"Indeed she *was*." Desperation was sinking in as he once again checked the digital clock on his personal cellular phone. "I know where she is." Another fishing expedition to see if his counterpart would bite.

"And what might this information *cost* me, American?" There was genuine interest.

"My name is Derrick Cross, I am the—"

"I know who you are Mr. Cross." It was not a threat. "I am now curious though as to why the head of your CIA's Black Ops department is calling the number of a dead Russian agent."

"Let's just say that we were able to *help* one another in the past." He was hoping that they could do so again.

"In what manner, Mr. Cross?" Vinogradov was playing his hand coolly, anticipating a poker's bluff from his opponent.

"I can tell you where the woman who assassinated former President Pavel Taratukhin's son is right now. I know your government is still searching for her."

"Possibly." Another shaded answer. "And what might you be looking for in return for this highly valuable information?"

"I want you to kill her." Cross was blunt.

Chapter EIGHTEEN

The sun was setting into the horizon over Rachel's left shoulder as she waited patiently for the final remnants of the day's light to disappear. She had been studying the massive villa for most of the day, while monitoring the activities and movements of the men that currently inhabited the mansion and their tendencies.

Semiz's source, the police detective's coordinates were accurate, these were the men that she was hunting. After her battle with the Agency's asset, Cordovan, Stackwell knew she had earned some valuable time, but also that they would certainly not be finished with her. They would send another, or maybe an entire team this time. There was no time to conceal the dead man though, so after searching him, she left her room, set the laminated *Do Not Disturb* sign on the doorknob and left the hotel. It would probably buy her a day before the local police would be called upon after the discovery of the

American's body in her room. A day would be all she needed.

It took her less than twenty minutes to track down Cordovan's rental car three streets from the hotel and used the indicating fob to access and start it up. A short drive later and Rachel was in Taksim Square. The famed tourist district was buzzing with life, even so late at night. Spotlights highlighting Aya Triada, the domed church and the Monument of the Republic were ablaze, while vintage trams chimed local music blending with the deep bass thumping of the popular bars and clubs in the area. The absorbing energy in the plaza's atmosphere was electric, but it was not Stackwell's objective, and she headed northeast on foot.

The beats were fading into deafening silence and the aromas of celebrated street foods into decay as the darkness of the battered streets grew stronger. There were not very many lights in the dissolute neighborhood of Tarlabaşi, and most of the ones that did work at one time, were now broken. Rachel's instincts honed while feeling eyes watching her from the shadows. Dangling above the constricted street, clothing and linens were hung on lining threaded between crumbling buildings, reinforcing the feeling of the slum district closing in around her. Passing a hollow doorway, a stray cay hissed, followed by the yowl from another. Rachel wasn't sure if the ominous calls were meant for her or the three-legged dog that ran out with a feeble whimper, regardless, her existence was known.

A young boy stepped out from a narrow alleyway that melded into the darkness. He was no more than eleven or twelve, cursed her in some primitive street level of Turkish and spun a knife in his hand. With his obscenities came a second, then third. All nearby and surrounding her, yet still hiding in the obscurity of the deteriorating building walls. The local youths were playing with her, toying with their prey as they viewed her as either a naïve resident or a lost traveler. Either way, they only saw her as a *woman*, a detestable and retainable item. They would learn a lesson tonight.

Exactly thirty-eight minutes later, Rachel climbed back into the stolen rental car with two Sarsilmaz CM9s and an Akdal Mini 03. All three guns were Turkish made and undoubtedly purchased or stolen off the streets originally. Testing the slides and mechanics, Rachel knew that they needed cleaning before she dared use them in a gun battle. That would come later, first, she needed to find where she was going and see whom was there. She drove with a content smirk.

The first boy cussing her was the third to actually intervene. Initially attacked from another veiled alley, that youth was quickly dealt with before the second tried from behind. Again, the local child was overpowered, weapon availed and tossed away, but these failures did not stop the boy with the knife. He charged.

He had no training. Whirling to her backside, Stackwell spun away from the attack, grabbing the youth's arm and disabling him from the blade at the same time. When the entire pirouette dance had finished, she was holding the knife in her right hand while pressing it firmly against the adolescent's throat. Fear had replaced intimidation and the other two comrades ran off.

Stackwell spoke slowly to ensure the destitute understood her Turkish as his was much more primitive. He did, and led her to his home less than two blocks away. He lived there with his father, who stumbled, cursing loudly at both of them, then tried to fight once he saw a woman in his home. The man was drunk on bootleg Rakı, but eyes grew wide when the *Kadın* chopped and stomped him back to the floor face first. Another attempt to get up was met by a knee dropped into his shoulder blades and head slammed onto the filthy tiling.

A basic string of curses came from the boy in what appeared to be him begging her to stop. Stackwell obliged, then ordered him to fulfill their agreement. The child disappeared momentarily before returning less than a minute later with three black guns. It would have to be enough. Snatching the weapons from the youth, Rachel found the Lira note she promised in return and flicked it onto the floor next to the bleeding father, and left.

Driving through the night had allowed Rachel the opportunity to not only put distance between herself and the Istanbul police, but also whomever

Cross would send after her next. If her former boss was still the man operating the division, then he did not take losing well, and she knew that he would become desperate with his attempts to clear what she imagined he beheld as a black mark on his career. None of it would matter as long as she was successful today.

It was early morning when she cruised into the coastal city of Silivri, still dark and streets quiet. The coordinates projected her another fifteen minutes northwest, away from the urban core of holiday homes and hosts of civilization. Rachel could not approach now. She did not know the terrain and dared not lose her advantage if a solo vehicle was spotted approaching in the middle of the night. Instead, Rachel found a small parking lot overlooking a beach. Parking, she released the windows an inch for the fresh air. Facing east, Rachel closed her eyes and listened to the gentle crashing of the waves from the Sea of Marmara onto the sandy shore. Peace was settling in as she waited for the morning sun to break her slumber.

The jovial barking of a dog caught Rachel's attention as it ran next to a couple on the beach. A slice of daybreak threatened along the waters in the distance, bobbing back and forth between revealing itself and waiting for every precious second below the horizon. As she stretched her confined muscles, the inevitable ball appeared, signaling the birth of another day.

Finding a small café open, Rachel rejuvenated herself with juice, fruit, and a Laz böreği, a locally made pastry with custard filling and sprinkled with powdered sugar. Once her energy had returned, she finished her trek to the spot the coordinates guided her.

Nearing the designated area past the outskirts, and further inland from the seaside city, the roads turned to dirt, sand and rock, still Rachel grew increasingly surprised. The relatively flat, countryside that looked like many US states in the Great Plains instantly changed to a massive acreage of elevated land with an enormous mansion standing atop. Thick clusters of trees lined constructed stone walls easily eight feet high. There was one gate at the base of a long driveway, protected by a heavy steel and cedar stained door which was only accessible from inside the compound.

The villa resting above it all was stone as well and built to resemble a castle. Security was a priority of the estate's residents, but the fortress was not impenetrable. Rachel walked the outer wall for what seemed like hours, but could not find a way around. Seemingly unending, she found the densest cluster of trees and climbed. There were no visible cameras or defensive countermeasures, which was bringing a feeling of doubt about whom might actually be living here. This would all be a waste of time if it was simply a wealthy recluse.

It had not been a waste of time. The final slice of daylight disappeared and nighttime had arrived. Darkness and shadows were her favorite implements. Stackwell's only concern was the change in numbers of the men. On her initial sweep through the villa's grounds, she counted five men, mostly relaxing, enjoying the large swimming pool and patio while topless girls served them drinks and danced. It looked more like a sorority or frat party, but as she drew closer she noticed the look of despair on the young girl's faces and the tattoos on the men's hands. She was in the right place.

The plan was to take them out one-by-one, gaining as much information as she could from each man before killing him, but the roaring of a jet engine changed that. The sound came out of nowhere and surprised Rachel, but then she saw the low flying private jet cross overhead, make a wide banking turn and disappear on the far side of the mansion's grounds. *Holy shit!* Stackwell spoke aloud as she hurried across the estate and watched the aircraft slow to a stop. *They have their own damn airstrip.* Another five men exited the plane and were welcomed by two of the others. Ten now in total, plus the girls whom she didn't know if they would be helpful or a hindrance. Her strategy would have to change.

It was time. Out of the darkness, Rachel sprinted out of the manicured bushes ten meters from the front of the large house. Most of the men were still situated in the rear, drinking and laughing, so a frontal assault seemed wisest. The luxury home was set in stone, detailed with large windows and trimmed in cherry stained wood shutters and canopies. Eight large stone steps led up the wide staircase to the main entrance and were anchored by a smooth cement banister. Rachel used the flat surface as a ramp, three strides before launching herself, one more step in a wall run and she grabbed onto a slat that was pieced together to form a wooden awning. Pulling herself up, skirting along the boards and finally hurling herself horizontally towards an upper floor window. Her first hand slipped past the smooth stones, but her back one grasped hold. Dangling high above the ground by one hand, Rachel tightened her grip, but did not panic as she calmly looked down. Finding the ledge with her free hand, she swung her legs up, kicking open the cherry shutters and pulling her body over and upwards into an empty bedroom on the penthouse floor.

The elegant room was massive, possibly a master bedroom, but with the enormity of the mansion, they all may have looked like this. The bed fittings were tight and room held the aroma of cleaning solution amalgamating into crispness, it had not been used in a while, maybe never. Hunkering in silence, Rachel listened for movement. She heard nothing. Carefully closing the wooden shutters, she headed towards the hallway.

Peering out the doorway, she confirmed the status of this particular bedroom. A thin clear walkway separated it from the rest of the villa, but was also the main vantage point to the rest of the contemporary estate below. From this acrylic skyway, she could see a main seating area and across into the large open kitchen. Music hummed and voices echoed as the sounds were funneled up towards the tinted dome skylight above her. A quick look back towards the great bedroom and she understood that it was soundproof.

Rachel counted three men playing video games on a huge television, shouting and cursing at one another, two girls dancing and pouring drinks, plus another man, tanned, with light brown hair simply standing aback, watching it all. The man answered his private phone and disappeared below. Watching his assertive stride as he walked, Rachel knew he was the one in charge.

A soft whirring to her left prompted a bout of panic. An elevator had been arriving to the penthouse floor, the tanned man was coming up. There was nowhere to hide. A gunshot would echo throughout the house and attract the others. Rachel spotted a large hanging tapestry. Dashing across the walkway, she hurdled the bannister on the platform across the way and jumped against the wall protecting the elevator shaft. Clutching onto the soft fabric of the colorful carpet, she momentarily swung out over the open rooms below before returning like a pendulum. Releasing her grip, a calculated barrel roll landing her on the second floor of the castle villa. The tapestry bounced and folded while rustling and untangling itself. Immediately Rachel looked upwards to the clear catwalk, but the man had not seen the disruption. Her dramatic escape was instantly blocked. Two girls, a brunette and a redhead stood motionless across from her.

Rachel slowly placed her index finger to her slips asking for silence. It was genuine fear that kept the two lingerie clad women quiet. Both wide-eyed, it was the brunette who was about to scream first. Stackwell noticed and sprung from her crouch. A quick punch to the gut of the brown haired girl cut off her air, keeping her from calling out. The redhead tried to run, but was caught by her long hair, spun back towards her friend and sent crashing into one another. Smashing the girl's heads together wobbled them both, allowing Stackwell the valuable second she needed to chop down hard on their carotid arteries, knocking them out. Rachel dragged them over to a rust colored barrel chair and intertwined them.

The commotion had not been detected elsewhere as she heard the men shout again at their video game, but Rachel also now had to assume that the girls here would not be willing to help. Time was now of the essence and she quickly scampered down the stairs to her left.

Descending onto the main floor, the grand staircase opened into the villa's front foyer. Marble floors extended throughout with another front room and a closed door before the hallway led to the rest of the house. The room was dark and Rachel checked the door. A large half bathroom with a standalone sink and toilet. Another bout of rowdy cheers and cursing as she neared the open room where the men were still playing.

"*Orospu! neden giyindin.*" The rough voice called to her from behind. He had been in the unlit room and Rachel cursed herself for not being more thorough. Repeating himself in a sterner tone, he obviously believed her to be one of the girls and was wondering why she was wearing clothes. Her long sleeved black compression shirt and charcoal stretchy jeans were quite a distinct look compared to the flashy bikinis or lingerie worn by the women upstairs or dancing girls. Stackwell slowly turned, kept her head down and simply bowed towards the Turkish man.

He stepped closer. Confused, he reached out for the underarm shoulder bag she wore on the left side. Rachel had found the bag in town and originally designed as a traveler's antitheft alternative, she was able to find it useful for carrying the weapons she obtained earlier that day. When the man's hand grabbed the harness, Stackwell reacted. Stepping backwards extended the Turk's arm and she hammered a palm strike into his inner wrist. Stunned by the momentary pain, Stackwell leapt into his body, her assaulting leg crossing his waist while her back one wrapped behind his front knee. Her hand down for balance and jerking upwards, she drove his body hard to the floor while using the power in her legs to scissor him. A brief yelped echoed when she broke his ankle, but tightening her grip on his stomach silenced him. Spinning on her spine, Stackwell mounted the injured man from behind and using her hands torqued his jaw and ripped it up and back in the other direction. The fierce momentum snapping his neck and his dead body went limp.

"*Timur? İyi misin?*" Another voice called out from the gamers. *Shit!* Scrambling to her feet, Rachel grabbed the dead man and dragged him to the bathroom. She could see the shadow of another man coming to investigate the commotion. "*Timur? Orada mısın?*" The voice asked as he knocked on the bathroom door. He had seen it close.

Bracing herself behind the door, Rachel allowed the searcher to enter. Reaching for the light switch caused him to be partially into the private room, but it was enough. Using the inside wall for leverage, Stackwell drove herself into the door, catching the man between it and the doorframe. Another crash, another cry of surprised pain. The back of the man's head broke open when it made contact with the frame. Stackwell did not relent. Grabbing the staggered man on both sides of his face, she dropped to her knees, smashing his face into the rectangular ceramic sink basin. It did not budge. Blood and teeth flew as the man's face shattered under the momentum of the attack.

This time her assault had become much louder and the others were beginning to notice. Rachel knew her stealth mission was no longer a viable strategy. Dumping the hemorrhaging man onto his associate's corpse, she knew he would bleed out in minutes. Two down. Removing one of the Sarsilmaz CM9s from her pouch, she placed the Akdal Mini into her ribbed side pants pocket and took a deep breath. The heavy flavors of ammonia and iron filled the private room, the combination of sweat and blood were almost intoxicating.

Exhaling as she sprinted, she headed directly into the luxurious seating room, still hoping to catch the others off-guard. A momentary victory. Two more members of the household were carefully waiting for a response to the uproar, but unprepared for an assault.

Bursting into the room, Stackwell fired four times. All four finding their mark and felling both men. The closest to her receiving both to his head while the further took one to the shoulder before the second found his heart. Screaming, the two dancing girls dove to the lush rug then began to cry. Her attention drawn away for a second and Rachel was nearly blindsided. Across the lounge was a wall of doors opening onto a wooden terrace and then the swimming pool. One of the men was always armed. Burak Demir returned fire.

Diving to her right, Stackwell scrambled away from the barrage as the bullets tore through the Italian made fabrics of the oversized sectional. Upending a gray Crema Cielo marble coffee table, she used it as a shield to protect herself against the next volley from the bearded man. She returned fire wildly over his head, forcing him to take cover, but also at the lighting. The darkness slowed his advance and allowed her the opportunity to crawl behind a large leather loveseat. Another shot, this time into the television cast Stackwell's half of the lounge into a subtle darkness.

The man shouted out directions to others. He demanded her dead. Using the shattered wall-mounted television's dim screen as an improvised mirror, Stackwell saw another man approaching. Spinning from her hiding spot, she fired three more times, each catching the advancer flush in the chest. Tossing the empty black steel alloy gun aside, she grabbed the second of the pistols from her chest pouch, but knew that this one did not have the full fifteen round cartridge. Movement to her left caught her attention in her peripherals.

A figure scampered from shadow to shadow. Peering around a corner, she was able to make out the bearded man speaking with him. Another spray of bullets were fired into the wall behind her hiding place causing her to cover her head as dust and insulated plasterboard exploded and fell all around. Stackwell could not make out what the men were saying, but as the carnage ceased, she was able to hear one word, *Zafar*, she knew it was the tanned man, the one that the police detective had claimed to be in charge. Her remaining bullets would have to be enough, he was her only target now.

Annoyed, Lucas Viale had heard the first few gunshots and had assumed his men where firing at an animal on the grounds or testing each other, but when a second and third barrage had followed, he knew something was wrong. Collecting his own Sig Sauer and using a hidden staircase, he ran towards the battle.

Ducking and weaving through the shadows, he wasn't sure who the attacker was, but he found Demir leading his men against them in the rear of the house. "What the hell is going on Burak? *Polis*?"

"No." Demir was sharp in his response, the man was fuming. "It is *her*." Turning back to the men, he pointed at another to circle around the outside of the doors and approach from the far end. "You have nowhere to go, *orospu*!" Now yelling towards the woman he wanted dead. "You are outnumbered and outgunned. Make it easy on yourself and just take a bullet to the head." His English was fluent at best, but even less while shouting with rage.

The whimpering of the two girls still laying on the ground in fear and heavy breathing from the men were the only sounds breaking complete silence. One gunshot echoed and Demir's head whipped towards the direction he instructed his man to go. He was just in time to see the advancer's head snap back from a perfectly placed bullet center forehead. "One less." The American woman smugly called back to him.

Viale smiled at the sass. "Tell the men to back out." His orders were firm, but spoken with composure.

"But Zafar, it is her. It is the woman from Prague." Demir plead back.

"Yes, it appears to be." He was still impressed.

"She needs to be *dead*." The second in command was fuming. "You should have killed her then."

"And *your* men should've gotten the job done in America!" The poise he had just displayed immediately vanished while barking back at his disciple. "Now leave!" This time Viale was yelling. "Take the men and get the pilots on the plane. I will take care of the woman and meet you there."

A slight hesitation was Burak's only initial response. He gritted his teeth and gripped his weapon tightly to release his frustration. He knew he had to follow the order. "What do you want done with the girls?" Finally, he asked with disdain.

Viale's expression was solely focused towards where the woman was hiding. "Kill them and wait for me at the plane." This time there was no indecision in Demir's reaction. Standing, he fired two bullets into the girls laying on the floor and walked away.

The men were arguing. Rachel could hear elevated voices, but then silence. Two gunshots alerted her, but neither were directed at her. Then another scream and two more quick explosions. Then nothing. An eerie silence had filled the villa, before she heard the tanned man's voice. He was alone.

"I have sent my men away." He began slowly and spoke like a police hostage negotiator. "It is just you and me now." Rachel saw him as a reflection. The man had stepped out, exposing himself. His hands were in front of him, open, and empty. Carefully, she stood, fingers wrapped around the Sarsilmaz CM9, trigger ready to fire.

"I could have killed you back in Prague." Continuing, Viale sidestepped laterally into the shadows.

"Why didn't you?" Stackwell hissed her return as she saw that the dancing girls were now quiet because of the red pools forming around them.

"Because I was impressed." Arrogance mixed with adulation.

"Then you shouldn't have come after me." She did not lower the gun at all while she spoke.

"In hindsight, maybe you are right," One more step and he would be out of the shadows. ", but then, what would my men have thought about me." A callous rhetorical question.

"Not my concern. At least they'd know you were still alive." Stackwell returned the cold-hearted statement with a half-smile of her own as she readied to pull the trigger.

"But how do you kill a dead man?" His tone turned confidently arrogant, but it didn't matter. He was stepping out from the shadows, it was all she wanted, to see *Zafar's* eyes when she released the bullet.

Deliberately striding gradually, Viale stepped into a sliver of light. A staunch combination emitting from the kitchen's overhead track and the moonlight entering through the wall of open doors. Stackwell was primed, but couldn't fire. She wanted to force herself to pull the trigger, but instead was frozen with grief once again.

"Hello Sophia." She had been met by a face from her past. He spoke adoringly, but she couldn't see past his striking blue eyes.

"Sean?" The question barely seeped out. Rachel's knees felt like they were going to give out and her brain instantly sent feelings of numbness across her body, but it all emanated from the cavernous aching sensation in her heart.

"Yes, *my love*." Her former fiancé continued softly. "I couldn't believe that you were there either." His tone changed back into one of conceit.

"But...Why...How?" Each word was a question of their own, and all broken apart by the growing lump in her throat.

"You shouldn't have been there." Viale kept his distance as he watched Sophia's trembling hands lower. "You shouldn't have interfered with *my* business." Reaching around his back, he produced his Sig Sauer.

Rachel could see his lips moving, but heard no sound. She was back on the bridge in Prague. Catatonic with rubble crashing down all around her. She didn't even try to fight the welling of tears in her eyes.

Lucas Viale heard the engines on the private jet roar to life and he raised the handgun. Craning his neck just a degree, he could a single tear creeping down Sophia's right cheek. She was still beautiful he thought, but he had also told her the truth. Sean Trevelyan was dead. He pulled the trigger.

ROBERT USHY

PART III

Chapter NINETEEN

Pulling his shivering body from the Vltava River, Sean Trevelyan was met by two more men, each offering the open side of a large warm jacket. The traditional Sherpa coat was designed for harsher winter nights, but he was definitely thankful for the heavier weight right now. He was on the banks of the Malá Strana, *Lesser Town* side of the river separating Prague. The small sandy shoreline of Park Cihelná quickly disappeared under a canopy of trees, thinning as the winter season approached, but still pleasant enough during the sunny afternoons. The sun plunged entirely behind Petrin Hill, disappearing and taking the remaining natural light of the day. Night had settled in, and so did any chance of seeing him emerge from the water.

The plan had been portrayed to precision. Once his accomplice ran up to him and Sophia, he reacted. Dropping the engagement ring and allowing a small concealed transmitter to slide from his sleeve into the palm of his waiting hand, he needed only to time it perfectly with tackling the man over the predesigned section of Charles Bridge. It was. The challenge was clearing his fall from the detonators that had been previously placed underneath the historic *Karlův Most*.

Rocking and disorienting him momentarily, the eruption was successful in maintaining the image of an explosion from the terrorist's body vest. The man wearing the fake suicide bomb was struck on the head by a large section of the crumbling bridge when they landed in the water, killing him instantly, but his body would wash away and eventually be found downstream somewhere. One less payed mouth to worry about speaking to the wrong people was the only thought Sean had.

Looking back towards the carnage on the bridge, he couldn't see her anymore. Police sirens and rescue lights flared from Old Town as a plume of smoke billowed from where the explosions erupted. There was always the chance that Sophia could be killed in the blast, and Sean did even accept that it might be for the best, but always found himself hoping that she would survive the attack. He did love her, he still loved her, but he would never have an opportunity like the one offered to him again.

"It's time to go." An old voice croaked from behind as he watched the final remnants of their strategic violence simmer into an eerie silence. "We need to get far away from here before the authorities start canvassing the river." The man spoke slowly, taking breaths every couple of words from the mask connected to a small oxygen tank. He was seventy-eight, bound to a wheelchair and had a failing heart that worsened with every day. The man would not make his next birthday. Sean believed that every time he saw his benefactor lately, the man was shrinking more and more into his mobile chair, yet his mind was as sharp as ever. Without hesitation, Trevelyan clutched the coat tighter around his wet body and turned away from Charles Bridge. There would be no need for one last look. "Yes *Signore* Viale."

"*Zafar!*" Demir's voice was agitated when addressing his master. "The pilots need to know where they should be going. They want to file a flight plan to avoid other aircraft." The lieutenant was still high strung and stressed from the battle with the woman from Prague.

"Tell them Maldives." A sigh of his own as the man now known as Lucas Viale opened his eyes.

"Is the American dead?" Demir blurted out his question. He had been dying to ask ever since his master had climbed aboard the private jet at the villa, but the look on his face kept the bearded man muted. "Did you kill *her*?"

It was a simple question, but one that took him by surprise somehow. His stomach muscles tensed, fists balled and toes curled in his shoes, but those nerves and bouts of anger were being directed inwards, towards himself. He hated this feeling.

Sean remembered the day that he and his previous mentor, Signore Lucas Viale had met. It was in a quiet tea terrace in Tangier, Morocco, six months before Prague. A warm day, barely summer in the important seaport city, but windy. He was sent back to Tangier by the United States government because of the years he had spent in the country previous, and was looking forward to returning, but preferred the warmer summer months. The intelligence community received information from a source about a possible terrorist plot in country, towards the embassy and needed somebody to vet the source. The decision had been made to use a former member of the consulate instead of any current ones as the source claimed that it was an internal coup which included some locals and Americans.

There was no plot. There was no imminent attack. When Trevelyan arrived at the café, he was met instead by an old man in a wheelchair and his well-dressed brawny bodyguard. The *source* was instead, looking to recruit him. "I know exactly who *you* are Mr. Trevelyan. An extremely bright, underappreciated and misused member of Ambassador Clark's staff." The senior Viale detailed Sean's past, highlights of graduating from Stanford, hand selected by the ambassador himself for his position, and even his grand slam winning home run when he was in high school.

The recruitment also included a few more humbling moments from his past as well. He knew about two failed attempts at positions within the White House and Sean's aspirations to rise out of the aide position that he currently held. Trevelyan almost laughed when the old man covered his past romances, mentioning in detail the name of the girl who turned him down for prom. It was over the top, but Sean also understood it was to prove how thorough and sincere Signore Viale was with his explorations.

"What is it exactly that you are *headhunting* me for?" Sean finally asked. He didn't need to hear more about his past. "I can tell that you're not from any foreign regime, so I'm guessing private sector, but may I ask what company? It seems pretty risky to lay false claims to the American government about terrorism, sabotage or whatever extreme measures you used to get them to listen to you enough."

The elderly Viale laughed and coughed at the same time. "Private sector? Yes you could say that, but you will not find my company on any trading sheets or bank ledgers." Inhaling from the mask attached to a small oxygen tank, he continued. "Fearful of whom? The Americans? I certainly think not." He laughed again, but this time slightly more boisterously and it caused a coughing fit, alerting his larger bodyguard. Composing himself and staring down the steady, bigger man, he continued. "What I am offering you Mr. Trevelyan, is a once in a lifetime opportunity. An opportunity to run the most profitable *business* in the world. Mine."

Pausing this time to breathe in the forced air deliberately, but also to allow his statements to fester. "I am dying Mr. Trevelyan, and there is no amount of money in the world that can stop that from happening. Trust me, I've tried." Anger mixed with a subtle laugh. "So it is my responsibility to find the next Lucas Viale to take over the mantle, shall we say."

"You want me to be, you?" A truthfully confused question. "How can I? We're not related, are we?"

"No, but that doesn't matter. I am Lucas Viale, now, but I didn't have this name my entire life. The name, the man, the repute, they are all characters, shadows to be dreaded. Lucas Viale is a legendary figure that has existed for decades. Passed on to the next chosen one to take over the *business*."

"If I may ask, Signore, what exactly is this *business* that you keep referring?" Sean's interests were genuinely piqued at the mystery of it all.

"That is the ultimate question isn't it?" The old man was contrite and smug now. "Although to answer that question, you first must answer mine. Yes or no?" A deep breath this time. "Although, your answer is one that you need to think about right now Mr. Trevelyan," He held his rigid finger up to note his next point. ", but there are also dire consequences for being flippant with your decision."

"Okay." Sean was even more intrigued and drew out his one word answer as a typical Westerner has accustomed themselves to do.

"If your answer is no, then I say thank you, finish my tea and leave. You will remain until I am gone and we shall never see one another again. If your answer is yes, then it gets, *interesting*." Another broad, self-righteous smile. "Yes means that I accept you as the heir apparent, explain to you what the business is and we begin our process to introduce you as the next Lucas Viale. You will begin your journey to becoming one of the richest and most powerful men in the world, but known to few. You will be revered by Presidents and Kings, all while having access to any desires that you wish. I can see you are attracted to these potentials."

"Of course I am, who wouldn't be," Sean responded when the old man stopped, he was waiting for a response. ", yet I'm sensing there's more to this dream *job* than simply becoming fairly reclusive."

"It depends on your morals Mr. Trevelyan. Some would say that my *business* is built around having none," His true arrogance was showing. ", but my *customers* seem to be always happy and pay handsomely."

"What six figure salary these days doesn't involve shaping your morals to fit a certain guideline or fundamental basis." Sean laughed. It was his attempt to show his flexibility.

"We are well past six figures, believe me." The old man's eyes bore into Sean. He was trying to sense if the American was truly the right choice after all. He continued. "If your answer is yes, we will begin on making plans for your old self to, *disappear*, shall we say." Another pause, and this time he noticed Sean's throat flare, swallowing only the realism of thinking about losing everybody who knew him.

"Here is the part that makes choosing yes so difficult." Removing the oxygen mask, Viale leaned a little closer with a full sneer. "If you say yes, you agree to this becoming your new life, but if you say yes, there is no saying *no* afterwards." The brawny bodyguard standing behind the man's chair moved for the first time since Sean sat down. The muscular man simply opened one side of his suit jacket and exposed the handle of a black handgun. "This is not negotiable. Once you learn about the *business*, then you are in Mr. Trevelyan. Or else." The final statement was spoken without emotion. It was a simple warning, but one that showed the value carried no remorse in the action.

Sean's palms felt like they were pouring sweat. His heart raced as his thoughts looped through his head. For years he had wanted to become more in his career, but was never allowed to advance. The ambassador had hand selected him because he was good, the best even, but also now brought him everywhere with him. Clark had no plans on letting him leave and never granted him the opportunity to become more than what he was. Sean often debated leaving altogether, going back to the United States permanently and doing something else, anything else, but then he would lose spending time with Sophia as she was constantly travelling throughout Europe and the Middle Eastern countries.

    Cursing himself, he hadn't thought about her yet. Their relationship was the best one he had ever had. She was everything that he could have ever dreamed. He knew he loved her, he meant it every time they said it to one another, but this was truly a *once in a lifetime* opportunity. The chance to shape his own life into one of legendary status, as this recruiter had called it.

    Closing his eyes, he bit carefully on his lower lip and thought about his parents, his father mainly. Both were gone many years ago, but he still could hear the man telling him that he would never amount to anything. When he was accepted into Stanford, the response was that he would fail and wash out. When he graduated Summa cum laude, his father simply referred to the honor as specialized toilet paper, and upon him becoming an American diplomat, his father just claimed him to be another man's *water boy*. That anger to prove him wrong still fueled Sean, and possibly became the deciding factor, he wasn't sure.

    "Yes." Opening his eyes, he gave the one word answer that the old man was hoping to hear. Another smile crept across Viale's face this time, but it was one of genuine pleasure. Looking across the table at the man that would replace him, he knew he had made the right decision. He had feelings of concern while watching the American's internal deliberations. The man was obviously debating about his lover, but something there was also something else, and that ended up being the influence that had made the decision for him. Viale wanted to ask, but decided he would wait for another time. Right now he simply stared into the set of eyes of his protégé. Hard, determined, and resolute. The eyes were always the key to a man's soul he believed and right now he was looking back into a set that matched his own. He had made the right choice in selecting this man.

"Zafar?" Burak Demir placed his hand gently on his master's shoulder. It was a sincere act of friendship. "Is she dead? The woman from Prague." This time he asked calmly. He could see that this woman had some sort of history with his leader. He was able to sense it back in the hotel room when he hesitated momentarily before taking the shot, and then killing his own man instead. Demir understood the reasoning he gave about failure not being accepted, but he also knew there was something else to it.

Lucas Viale, Sean Trevelyan, focused on his bearded associate's face. Realizing that the man had asked him twice already and he hadn't answered. Smiling broadly, he met Demir's eyes. Releasing any of the remaining internal anger and tension he felt, he was at ease with the decisions he had made. There was peace within him once again. He had turned the name Lucas Viale into one that even the Signore could not have dreamt. He had become the most powerful shadow that the world had never known. The legacy was cemented with his ambitions, and he knew that even his resentful father would have to proud of him. "Yes Burak, she is dead." He felt only a sweeping harmony as he looked out the small jet window.

Chapter TWENTY

Rachel tried opening her eyes, but found her lids too heavy. Another attempt resulted in one staying half open for nearly a second before falling shut once again. She changed her focus towards listening to her surroundings, but found her head swimming and unable to concentrate. She knew the feelings were being influenced artificially, some sort of morphine or hydromorphone, but also could sense their affects diminishing. Allowing herself to relax, Rachel exhaled, trying again, but this time controlling her thoughts first.

She kept her eyes closed. Listening, she found herself breathing calmly and in tune with a steady low beeping noise. The soothing rhythm was connected to her heart beat and she believed that she was in a hospital. Another deep breath, and this time she inhaled the odors and tangs of her situation. It was bitter. A combination of antiseptics and synthetic fragrances, but neither were an assault on her senses.

She also smelt the alluring aroma of coffee which immediately reminded her body about how dehydrated she was.

As on cue to her dry mouth spasm and shuddering for the relief of an oasis in the desert, she felt the thin plastic of a bendy straw between her lips. Greedily, Rachel drew in as much water as she could before having to stop for a breath. Another attempt to open her eyes was more successful this time. She was in a hospital bed, room facing northwest as she was able to make out the remaining sunlight setting into the far right side of her wide window.

"Welcome back to us, my friend." The voice was coarse, but was attempting to show empathy. The compassion was not forced, just unpracticed. Rachel squirmed to sit up, but was slowed first by the man holding the water mug, and then secondly by the dull ache in her left shoulder. "No, no, don't move around too much."

Hakan Köseman tried to stop her, but Rachel battled through the throbbing and pushed herself up into a seated position. He smiled at her look of minor surprise. The police detective was wearing a full suit, but currently the jacket was off, neatly folded over a padded chair in the corner and his right arm in a sling. "I didn't get off as lucky as you." He laughed while referring to his own injury. "Mine's broken in two places, but you only have a flesh wound."

"How? Where am I?" Rachel was still groggy, but her memories were returning and thoughts becoming clearer.

"You are safe." Köseman began. "You are at Acıbadem International Hospital. *My* people found you when they arrived at the villa. You had been shot, should have been killed, but Allah must shine highly upon you." As Hakan continued, Rachel was beginning to remember what had happened.

She was ready to pull the trigger and kill the man who was her target's *master*. The bearded man called him Zafar, but Köseman was right decreeing him as *Hayalet*, the ghost. He was a ghost, but he was hers. When the man known as Lucas Viale emerged from the shadows, she saw Sean Trevelyan. The man she had once known as her partner, her best friend and her only true love. She was frozen and couldn't finish pulling the trigger, but he did. He was less than ten feet away, why was she not dead?

Rachel's heart ached, but it was not from the physical wound above it. "The bullet missed your heart by millimeters," Hakan was still explaining to her about how she came to be in the hospital. ", but did no damage. It's unbelievable. A simple gunshot wound." The police specialist was still amazed at her fortune. "The doctors said that they had to clean out a large number of fibers to avoid infection, but the thick strap from the body pouch you were wearing altered the bullet's path just enough to avoid it damaging any vital muscle groups or organs."

Rachel's body shuddered as the memory of Sean's gun's muzzle flashed in front of her. He had shot her with the intent of killing her, it was in his eyes. The piercing blue eyes that filled her world with joy were gone, instead replaced by hollowness and emptiness. She saw he was no longer the man she once loved. She wanted to cry all over again, but those tears would have to wait for another time.

"Are you okay?" Köseman was reacting to her spasm. "Should I get the doctor?"

"No." It was her first words. "I'm okay. Just remembering something, somebody that is, gone." Rachel's tone started out as mumbling, but as she continued to speak, she found the strength in her voice returning. Reaching out for the plastic mug, she drank more water and was regaining her focus entirely. "What happened to you? I thought that you were killed?"

"So did I." Hakan chuckled slightly. "Bullet hit my arm and spun me around. I still can't remember much after that until I awoke under a table and there was panic all around me."

"Sorry about that." Rachel recalled the promise that she had made about blood in the streets.

"That one is not your fault, but your attacker did get away." Köseman reached into his wrinkled pants pocket and withdrew his phone. The sling was cumbersome, but he had begun to get used to moving around with it. Selecting the video he wanted, he tapped the imbedded triangle to play the recording. "You have become quite a sensation with some of the female riot squad officers, the men, are quietly impressed." He shrugged his one good shoulder when referring to his fellow male policemen.

Rachel did not need to see the video, she remembered the fight with the man in the linen shirt. "Have you been able to identify him?"

"Yes, but that is where things, and *you*, becoming interesting to me." The Turk's tone went from being a caring friend to careful questioning of a subject. "We've identified him as arriving at the Istanbul Airport the day prior, but his passport is not on file, *anywhere*. I had my friends at Interpol even run him."

Once again readjusting herself, Rachel grimaced at the discomfort to the area between her chest and clavicle. She thought about the look of uncertainty on the asset Cordovan's face back in her hotel room, believing it was because she was getting through to him on a humane level, but it wasn't. She had told him that *his* local man had already failed, but that wasn't true, there was no aide and that had briefly confused Cordovan. There were two contracts out on her. Cross had sent two assets instead of one.

"You know who he is" The detective's question almost was an answer itself. "I can see the recognition on your face."

"No," It was a truthful answer, Rachel had no idea who the man was. ", but I do know why he's here and who sent him." There was a held silence in the room. Köseman was waiting for a response to her statement. "He is here to kill me."

"I figured that part out myself." Hakan smiled as he gently patted his damaged arm. "What I do need to know is, is this connected to your other *project*?" There was a slight tongue-in-cheek uttering to his latest question. Rachel wanted to smile as the memory of her initial impression of the inspector was that he was from old American detective shows, and now his way of speaking matched that original thought.

"No, he's here because of the past, my past." Another truthful testimony. Rachel would allow the inspector to have some information, but she couldn't divulge it all.

"And the dead man in the hotel room that was issued to you, but is also on a completely different passport than the one you arrived into our country on?" Köseman had been holding that piece of information back so he could judge the context that the woman was speaking. So far, he believed she was being honest.

"Yes."Stackwell grinned this time thinking about the calamity she been part of over the past week. "He is, *was*, also here because of my past. I am quite sure that your friends will not find anything on him either, or me if you haven't already had them check." She continued in a friendly manner. "You can do whatever you will with his body, there will be nobody to claim him or even know that he is missing."

Hakan understood what she meant. "And you? Would that have been the same if my people had found your body yesterday?" There was no response this time, just a half turned smile signifying that it was a confirmed answer. "Then I will claim you, if that is to happen." Köseman barely knew the American woman, but also felt a connection. He never had children, but if he did, he wished for a strong daughter like her. There was a history of violence, probably more than he wanted to ever know, but that did not matter, she had already proven herself to him.

When he was stuck in that hospital bed for a day, he did his own research. During their initial meeting, she claimed that the men she was after operated in *at least in Prague*, so he looked into it and found the reports and videos of the attack. The Czechia police and news outlets didn't know whom she was, but he did. Combining that with the recordings he saw from what happened at the villa, he was certain there was more to her than just her past.

"You don't need to do that." Stackwell spoke sullenly as she had accepted a long time ago what her eventual fate would be one day. "Allah, nor any other gods will be looking down favorably upon me when that time comes."

"That is where you are wrong, my American friend." Hakan hesitated as he wasn't sure what to call the woman in the hospital bed. "Even Allah has malaikah, angels who are sent to help communicate with humans, but sometimes they are needed as protectors." Köseman was attempting to encourage her resolution towards her fate. "Allah is a source of justice and sometimes we do not see the truth that is necessary so Allah must see it for us, thus sending the malaikah to carry out that justice. Maybe that is who you truly are?" Köseman wasn't preaching, but Rachel understood the underlining message he was trying to tell her. In fact, she had heard the same thing years before from a man she relied on early in her *career*, a man who was now an old priest.

"*Böldüğüm için üzgünüm*" Another man entered the room and apologized to Hakan before stepping closer and whispering to him privately. The man was dressed in a hospital gown over his clothes, mask around his neck and looked the part of a residential doctor or nurse, but Rachel believed he wasn't either of those. His shoes were dark, thick soles and designed for more tactical purposes than walking around the floors of a local hospital.

"What's wrong?" Stackwell interrupted the men.

"Nothing." Again Hakan was uncertain what to call her so he abruptly stopped.

"The look on your phony doctor's face says that there is something wrong." Rachel combatted the awkward ending to the detective's simple answer.

"Apparently there is a man and a woman somewhere in the hospital looking for you." He did not want to alarm the injured woman. "My people spoke to them and reassured them that nobody with the description they were searching had been admitted, but lost them when they split up."

Rachel knew she had to move and tried to get out of bed, but was initially stopped by the one good arm of Köseman. It was not enough and she was able to get to her feet. Her head spun and she felt like she was about to throw up and had to sit back down.

"You do not need to go anywhere." This time Hakan was firm and commanding her to stay where she was. "They will not find you here. This floor is currently unavailable and not being used for any patients by the hospital."

"You don't know these people." Stackwell closed her eyes tightly and was forcing the final feelings of nauseam out of her system. "The Americans won't stop until I'm dead."

"They are not American." The younger man who had entered the room interrupted them again.

"What?" Stackwell snapped back as her instincts immediately went back towards the men she had been hunting. Sean knew she survived.

"The man and the woman in the hospital." The young Turkish officer looked to his superior for permission to continue. He received it with a singular nod. "They are not American, they are believed to be Russian."

Rachel's eyes burst open wide. She wanted to speak, but found nothing to say. Russian? She repeated it to herself and couldn't figure out how they could have possibly found her here in Istanbul. She was certain that they would still be interested in her after all these years, but actively searching didn't make sense. "Cross." She said his name the instant it popped into her head.

"What is cross?" Köseman asked.

"He's a person." Stackwell hadn't realized she said his name out loud, but also knew she would need help if she wanted to get out of the hospital. "He is the one who sent the other two men. The one you found in my hotel room and the one responsible for the attack at the café." Gingerly, she signaled the detective's arm in a sling.

"So he sent these two? Russians?" The questions were set to understand the complexity of the situation. There was no panic or confusion in Hakan's tone.

"No." Rachel hesitated as she was thinking it through. "He wouldn't be able to do that." Another pause to concentrate. "His initial operation failed. One asset down and the other killed." Stackwell was speaking to herself, piecing together what could have happened. "The agency would want it cleaned up and no more traces to the government. He would have to pull the remaining asset out, but he wouldn't send others in, that wouldn't make any sense." Looking up, she made eye contact with Hakan and smiled while nodding. "He called the Russians. He told them where they could find me and they sent a team. He's using them to do his dirty work because his men already failed."

"So what do you want to do now?" Köseman was looking for direction from the woman. He knew he wasn't going to be able to keep her in the hospital, it was in her eyes.

Stackwell tested out the mobility in her shoulder. There was an immediate reaction of pain, but she was still able to rotate it, move it carefully up and down, and even more cautiously in and out. "I heard airplanes earlier. We must be close to an airport?"

"Yes. Ataturk International Airport is ten minutes from here, but it is no longer a commercial airport. It is a cargo and freight airport now only." The young officer dressed as a doctor spoke excitedly as he intervened.

"They allow *some* passengers." Köseman added coolly. He was already thinking and had an idea. "State and diplomatic flights are also scheduled through Ataturk now. I will get you an airplane." Without waiting for a response, the senior police inspector once again had his phone in his hand and scrolling through his contacts for the one he needed. "I have a few favors that I can call in." He followed it up with a wink which nearly caused Rachel to laugh. Straight out of American detective shows she thought to herself once again.

Chapter TWENTY-ONE

The deep red light requesting entrance to Derrick Cross's Pentagon situation room simultaneously beaconed above the door and on the small encased bulb on the corner of his desk. He habitually checked the live video feed, but already knew who it was going to be. Virginia Bennett. The woman was on the warpath and had already fired Chelsea earlier this morning for failing to report the operational intelligence to her, and essentially continuing to work with and for him. This was not a fight he was looking for, but he was prepared.

"What the hell do you think that you are doing here Derrick?" The Deputy Director of CIA Operations blasted him before his door was even closed. Cross waited until he heard the click, pushed a button and allowed his office windows to frost before answering.

"My goddamn job!" He returned fire once the room had been declared soundproof. He didn't want his people to hear the heated argument that was coming. "One that we do quite successfully."

"Success? You call a public chase and gunfight in the streets of New York a success?" Cross felt she was over exemplifying the position, but allowed her to continue. "How about shutting down a major American airport for half a day for no reason? More goddamn successes? Now there's a possible international incident with your dead assassin in Istanbul."

"There is no connection with him to us." Cross interrupted her sternly. "He's clean Virginia, and you know that."

"Maybe, but it still isn't stopping the Turkish government from asking *us* about him. They know what kind of bullshit games people like you are playing. Their President is personally looking for answers."

"People like me?" Once again he stormed back with an interruption. "People like me do the job that makes yours, his, hell even our own President's easy. With all due respect Madam Deputy Director, you're wandering out of your pay grade here."

"Let me remind you *Cross* where you sit on the depth chart of this administration. It's below me, which means that *you* report to *me*." Bennett was still agitated.

"Not in this building and not in this room." Derrick was deliberate with his words as he leaned forward resting his hands on his desktop. "In this building we deal with real puddles of shit, this isn't a fucking scene in a movie or chapter in a book, these are *real* world operations, with real world consequences, and if you want in, you better get a big pair of boots." His eyes were steady as he spoke. "Your title might say that you have some authority, but I'm the professional here Virginia, so I know when an operation goes bad, you have to tie it off."

"You don't get to hide behind that veil of national security Cross." Bennett lowered her tone, but it still had a scathing bite to its intention. "If there's something you haven't told me about this operation yet, you *need* to tell me right now before I go to the Oversight Committee."

Cross waited. The two simply were in a stare down. It was her threat, possibly a veiled one, but still one that he could not risk. The Senate Oversight Committee meant investigations into commands and missions that had no business in the public eye. "She's an operation that went bad years ago. Before you were here." Derrick finally spoke. Exhaling his anger, he spoke with an easier tone this time. "We still need to finish that mission."

"Then bring her back in." Bennett too reduced her venom. She had read all the intelligence reports that were on file. "For years, your, *agent*, had disappeared, even started a new life and from what I've seen in Prague, Sophia Warner, or Rachel Stackwell or whomever she really is, was helping others and isn't a threat to us." The wrath had been subdued, but the Deputy Director still spoke as if she was issuing an order.

"*My* dead asset in Istanbul would say it's too late for that, don't you?" Cross spewed his rhetorical question as he felt insulted with her new tone. "You don't have to worry, there won't be any more *international incidents* as you referred to it. That operation has ended."

"Ended?" It was Bennett's turn to feel a distaste for the nature of the conversation. The two were no longer heated, but the resentment was thick in the air. "If she's still such a threat, then why has it ended? Why have we stopped looking for her?"

"All you need to know is that you won't have to worry about it any longer. The United States will not be connected to any more *incidents*, so you can go back to your comfortable office without fear of another Senator calling you for answers." Cross was smug now, and it resulted in another silent moment between the two combatants. "Don't ever second guess my operations from behind your desk chair," Calm and content. ", and if you think that you can dangle *me* out in front of the Oversight Committee, the Senate, or even the President himself, you can go to hell."

Virginia Bennett wanted to respond, but she held her tongue. The backlash between them wasn't getting her anywhere and she knew she wasn't going to get any more information out of Derrick Cross, the man viewed himself as a god controlling other's fates. She turned to leave, but was caught at the door.

"Madam Deputy Director." Cross's voice was calm, he was self-assuring when he spoke this time.

"It's funny how altered things appear depending on where you are standing doesn't it?"

"There just isn't enough trust or good faith built up yet Sergei." Alan Wakefield was trying not to scream into his phone at the Russian President. "You have to have patience and let me get a handle on the NATO situation first." He was lobbying unrelentingly with the world leader while trying to keep him from overreacting or becoming brash. "Yes, it is a forgone conclusion that I *will* be appointed to lead this project. Let's just say that I have *secured* the support that I need from the others." He looked at his wife as he reiterated the last statement.

Both men took the break to laugh at the ominous forewarning. "It will take some time though, probably weeks, maybe a month or two," Wakefield quickly continued before the Russian could interrupt. ", *but* I can ensure you that Russia, and primarily *you* will be seen as the greatest asset with the evidence and intelligence we will provide. It will prove to all the other nation's leaders that Russia has changed, that *you* have changed the culture there and then we can certainly sway the mindset of allowing you into NATO."

Teresa Wakefield moved away from the large window in their bedroom. It was still raining. The thunderstorm started in the early evening and was still going, but the ferocity had diminished. She was exhausted. The day had been spent bouncing from a scheduled appearance to three consultations in a row for the Smithsonian Institution, a local charity and finally the preparation for the state dinner at the end of the month. Still, she found herself listening intently to her husband and falling in love with his leadership, direction and control all over again. He was going to be not only the greatest American President, but also the paramount world leader.

"You will owe me for this Sergei, you know that right?" Wakefield posed the question both with jest and seriousness. Again, both men shared a laugh as he paced back and forth across a direct line at the end of their bed, repeating the plan to his Soviet counterpart one final time before the two congratulated and thanked each other in both national languages.

"Does he understand how much his entire country owes you?" The First Lady was excited and barely waited for her husband to disconnect the call. She had removed her shoes and was rubbing her feet.

"He better." The President was firm. "With everything his predecessors did with cyber terrorism to so many countries, then Crimea and Ukraine, he'll be lucky to ever get one foot in the door of NATO."

"But you will get him in right?" There was a crack of concern in her voice as she looked up from her soreness with the feeling of slight apprehension that the plan would not work out how they planned.

"Of course I can my dear." Wakefield sat next to his wife and was reassuring, but also truly confident. He kissed her on the forehead before snatching the foot that she was massaging and began to knead it for her. "*We* can. You are just as much of this design as I am."

She tittered at his touch. "Do you think that he suspects at all?" The rains began to pick up once more and could be heard against the glass. "Or does he believe that the two of you together will hold command over the others?"

"I doubt he has any idea." Smiling at his beautiful wife while still manipulating the underside of the arch in her left foot, accentuating the pressure from the heel to the ball. "Sergei has become driven with getting his country out of that sanction hell that they've been living under for so many years that he won't even see us coming. He's still a stubborn Russian that believes he's a world superpower because he has nukes, but won't use them. He legitimately wants to make his country great again, and the only way to do that is with us."

"And he's not toying with you like you are him?" The question was valid. Teresa Wakefield lay back with a flirtatious wink while crossing her legs so her husband could continue on her other foot. Both heard the low rumbling of the storm picking up again outside.

"I'm sure he has his own agenda already planned," Laughing at her presumed request, he took her right foot and repeated his actions from earlier with thumbs rubbing in a circular motion. ", but it doesn't matter anyway. I could remove them, remove *him* from our new alliance at any time that I want. We don't actually need him to take down that trafficking syndicate, but we need him to be aligned with us. We need him to *think* that he has some sort of power." Raising her foot, he began kissing her ankle towards the top part of her toes.

Squirming at the touch, Teresa flushed and giggled aloud this time. "Just enough power to impose over the others, but not us." Reaching for her husband, she wrapped her legs around him to draw him tighter and bring his lips up towards hers. "Never us." She kissed him passionately.

Alan Wakefield returned the vigorous caress as his hand dove under her blouse. "Never us." Repeating the words of his wife as their conspiring and conniving brought out the lust in both of them. A heavy pattering on the window increased, followed by another dull echoing roar from the rainstorm taking over Washington below, but none of it broke their furious hunger for each other.

Nearing midnight, Derrick Cross jogged across the Ohio Drive Bridge and turned right onto the walking path leading towards the Franklin Delano Roosevelt Memorial. He had been running for nearly twenty minutes and began to feel the sweat forming under his matching black compression pants and long sleeved shirt. The quick dry spandex material would keep his body consistent when he stopped as another warm day had been replaced by cool late night air.

It was calm after the storm. The trees towering over him did not sway and the waters in the Tidal Basin reservoir were serene. During the day, these walking paths would be crowded with tourists and sight seers clamoring for photos of memorials or the Washington Monument across the man-made waterway, but at this hour of night, it was virtually uninhabited.

Passing a park bench, he was able to make out the form of a man sleeping and wondered if he truly was a vagrant or if the man was actually a member of his contact's security team. A covert meeting at midnight in a vacant monument park in Washington, D.C. was so cliché that even Cross laughed to himself when it was agreed upon, but maybe that was why it was suggested.

Slowing, Derrick inhaled deeply to control his breathing. His heart beat faster with the workout, but it was not pushed too far past a normal rhythm. He kept himself in shape even though he was no longer active in the field, and ran multiple times per week. Another late night runner approached from the opposite direction and he pretended to be checking his vitals on his diagnostic watch, but the man did not even look at him.

As the passing footfalls dissipated, a still silence fell over the area. Cross felt that he must've been earlier than his contact, and that was okay by him. It allowed him the opportunity to quietly take in the honorarium to the thirty-second President. Technically the second of the great man's memorials in Washington, the sculptures and constructed scenes depicted twelve years of Roosevelt's tenure, and was the only one to celebrate the wife of a President.

Cross stepped closer to the bronzed figures of The Bread Line, a statue interpretation of the Great Depression. "Good evening Derrick." Freezing and feeling his heart skip faster again, he nearly swore aloud, but kept it to a stuttering gasp.

"You scared the shit out of me." Responding as he regrouped the fluttering spasms in his stomach. Garner Housley, the Director of National Intelligence did not react to the comment, instead he indicated for Cross to follow him.

The two shadowed figures walked through a slim opening in the stone wall separating the memorials from the open grounds of the West Potomac Sport Field. Five softball diamonds lined in a row were home to tournaments on most weekends in the summer, but currently completely black as they stood in the grass of the outfield on diamond four.

"You mentioned that we might have a problem with Virginia Bennett." Housley started softly as the two men stood alone in the darkness with only the light of the moon highlighting them.

"She came to see me today." Cross answered as his eyes adjusted to the pale lighting from above. "She's becoming a pain in the ass about this Sophia Warner business. Why was she even named as the Deputy Director of Operations if she's such a goddamn boy scout?" He felt his anger surfacing again thinking about the conversation from earlier today.

"She's there because she is such a *boy scout*, as you called her. Virginia Bennett checks a bunch of the right Agency boxes in the eyes of the public." Housley was justifying the choice while still honoring the old men's club mentality. He had been nominated to his position by President Wakefield over two years ago mainly because of his loyalty as a party man. "She has her usefulness and will fall in line if she needs to."

Cross scoffed. He knew Housley was formerly a lawyer and congressman, but still had hoped for a better answer than the same politician's grandiloquence. "Well then somebody better get her back in that line because if she follows through with her threats of the Oversight Committee, then were *all* going to be in deep shit." He purposely paused before finishing his thought. "In the eyes of the public."

"Maybe you can try a different path with Bennett?" Housley pompously suggested. "Give her enough information so she feels like she's in control of things, important enough in the operations that it's in her best interests also, if she stays quiet."

"Don't blow smoke up my ass Garner." Cross could feel the man trying to shift the potential problems to him. "You damn well know there is no different path with these operations. These *missions* are how we win, how America wins. If you want to find or create a new path, one without the consequences, then maybe it's time for you to go back to your cushy seat in the Capitol Building."

"I guess in theory that we are all replaceable." It was another arrogant comment, but Cross did not let the politician continue.

"That better mean *her*." It was a sharp and threatening tone. "I've been doing this a lot longer than you *Director Housley*, so believe me that I most certainly have enough skeletons and get out of jail free cards with the right people over there." Speaking sternly still, he pointed towards the lights of the Washington Monument for affect. "It's why *I* was put into this position. I get the job done without any red tape or deliberating committees. I get the job done so people like the President can go to sleep at night without watching our enemies get away while the pencil pushers over there argue about what color ink they should be using. *You* need somebody like *me* in charge of my division because if you turn it over to the Virginia Bennetts of the world, you might as well tell our enemies that America is closed. That we don't care what happens and whomever wants to take shots at our people, feel free, because we don't give a damn." Cross was hot now.

Housley didn't know how to respond. He certainly wasn't about to allow the United States to seem weaker under Wakefield's reign. "So, what you're saying Derrick, is that if Virginia Bennett goes to the Senate about this one mission, then she is essentially exposing *all* of America's secret operations, and *that* would be a threat of its own to our country."

Somewhere in his congested sentence was a question that Cross knew the answer to. It hurt his intelligence to believe that people actual thought and spoke like a politician at all times. He was extremely thankful to be where he was in his role. "Yes." Cross finally responded as it was the only answer that the Director of National Intelligence wanted to hear.

"That I can sell." He was sure of himself. "Proceed with your missions. Bennett won't be bothering you with this any longer. I can make sure of it."

Chapter TWENTY-TWO

Derian yawned as he waited patiently for his turn to check in to the magnificent resort on one of the southern atolls making up the Maldives islands. Leaving just before ten o'clock at night, which seemed like days ago, Haynes felt exhausted. In reality it had been only a day between, but it had been years for him to spend that much time on an airplane and crossing time zones.

Paxton hadn't selected the most expensive and direct of flights, with him connecting first in London, England, but then a second short layover in Doha, Qatar. The Senator did however book him into first class which Derian was extremely thankful as he was able to use the private pod to begin writing his first article on the revelations that Paxton had made to him. He tried to be impartial, but kept finding himself naturally drifting towards the side of gallantry for Senator Paxton. He was fine with it, the American public were going to choose their side anyway based on their own personal opinion of the President, and if *he* had to pick a martyr in this cause, it might as well be the man who exposed it all.

When the pilot indicated that they were preparing to land, Haynes looked out his window and was awestruck. His work would have to wait. The natural blues and greens of the waters surrounding the atolls. He was landing at Velena International Airport on Hulhulé island and from there was to take a speed boat to his resort. It was an easy process with plenty of locals to help guide, answer questions and give directions. He found another couple asking about the same resort and followed them. In total there were six other pairings with him being the only solo traveler.

Haynes gut churned again while climbing aboard the sleek boat as once again he felt apprehensive about why he was truly there. He had the same feelings on the plane every time he tried to create a plan on how to get to the house that Paxton claimed existed. Now, the feelings of being alone with a group of loving pairs made him feel exposed and that his true intention uncovered. A swell of relief came with the wind whipping against his face and generating a nice contrast to the extreme heat and humidity encompassing the islands at this time of year.

His turn was next. The British honeymooners he met previously were just finishing at the check-in. They waved and smiled at him, had already invited him to join them for dinner later that evening, but at the moment, all he really wanted to do was sleep away his drowsiness. "Good afternoon, Derian Haynes, checking in." He responded to the jovial receptionist when he welcomed him to the *lap of luxury*. It was corny, but the man obviously enjoyed his job.

"Yes. Mr. Haynes. You have arrived." The merry man indicated for another to help his customer with his luggage. "We are so glad you made it. Your wife arrived earlier this morning and has set you up already."

"My. Wife?" Haynes was confused, but also felt a wave of panic overcome him.

"*Aan.*" The man's brief curiosity was expelled. "Ah, there she is." He pointed to the blonde haired woman approaching quickly.

"Darling, you made it!" Running up to him, she wrapped her arms around him tightly while gripping his lips with hers. "I know you weren't expecting me until tomorrow, but I was able to leave the conference and catch an earlier flight."

"That's, wonderful, my dear." There was hesitancy in his tone as Derian was still unsure about what was going on.

"Please follow me sir." Another voice, higher pitched, yet less jolly. A younger man had already scooped up his one bag and wanting to lead the way.

"Come dear, you have to see our lovely beach villa." The woman in the pink and white casual summer dress entwined her arm with his and placed her head on his shoulder.

"What are *you* doing here?" Haynes whispered to the woman pretending to be his wife. He had recognized her face immediately, but last time he saw her, she was covered in dried blood and he was helping her escape a police detective's office in Madison Wisconsin.

Rachel placed her index finger to her lips when she saw the journalist was about to speak again. She threw the shades closed to indicate privacy for themselves, but was making sure the porter had returned to the boardwalk. "Sorry about barging in on your holiday." She was considerate, but practical and unemotional. "Give me until nightfall and I'll be out of your way."

"My what?" Derian was still taken aback by what had just happened. "What are you doing here?" He readjusted his questioning to the relevant.

"Don't worry about that," Her response was again short and curt. ", like I said, I'll be gone by nightfall."

A moment of uneasy silence filled the bungalow as Haynes watched the woman he met in a Wisconsin police station collect the few personal items she had removed from what appeared to be a brand new silver suitcase. "Who are you?" He finally asked the woman that he had not thought about since that night. "You're not an undercover or federal agent, yet you had somebody at the CIA running scared."

The woman stopped and turned her head at the homage. "How do you know that?" Asking with a wry smile of her own.

Haynes chuckled to himself. She too remembered their opening conversation. He continued the exchange. "You speak directly, like you're used to being in control, but not like trained military team guys do. I'm guessing you usually work alone," He had piqued her interest. ", and with your performance in the lobby, I'd say that unless you've performed on Broadway, you have plenty of experience pretending to be different people." This time Haynes smiled broadly and swirled his pointed finger towards her upper body. "Also, by the looks of the blood staining your dress, you've recently been shot in the shoulder."

"Oh shit!" Stackwell exclaimed to herself as she looked down at the bandage that had loosened. She had felt a sting shoot through her arm when she had thrown it around him at the reception, but forced herself to bear the pain and avoid grimacing. "Gold star for Mr. Washington Post." This time it was her turn to laugh as she headed to the bathroom to clean her wound.

Haynes followed, but backed out of sight when she began to lower the dress strap on her injured side. "So is it Sophia Warner or Rachel Stackwell?" He was proud of himself for knowing both names. "The police chief didn't really seem to care which it was, but was awfully pissed at both of them."

"Do you mind grabbing me a t-shirt from my suitcase." It wasn't really a question. "Either the blue or black one." Derian obliged and a couple minutes later she emerged from the bathroom wearing only the oversized black top. Falling just below her back end, he couldn't help but stare at her sleek toned legs. "Both. Neither. I don't really know, but let's go with the latter." She answered his previous question.

"A luxury villa in the Maldives doesn't seem like the type of holiday expense that a war correspondent should be able to afford." Rachel continued while riffling through her recently purchased clothes until she found a pair of shorts, slid them on and strode towards the mini-bar that was fitted inside the long desk and drawers, and below the wall-mounted television. "Especially one that is more active with freelance articles and on social media than mainstream television or newspaper."

"You've been checking up on me?" Derian wasn't sure if he should be flattered or concerned. "Any reason for that, Rachel?"

"I had some time and was curious as to who and why you helped me back in Madison?" She crossed back over to sit on the end of the king-sized bed with two miniature bottles of vodka, offering one to her *husband*. The chic room was long and thin. A small foyer welcomed a main bedroom, connecting bathroom and then another set of glass patio doors opening onto a canopied terrace with table, chairs, and a lounger. The elegance of the entire private bungalow was just past the promenade. A plunge pool that faced a setting sun. It was the pure magic of the Maldives.

"And what did you find?" Haynes declined the drink as he was still probing for a level of trust.

"Somebody who generally does the right thing." Swigging back the small sample, Stackwell was unimpressed. She shouldn't have expected anything more, but the vodka was cheap, defiantly not as good as the silky-smooth flavors provided in the Russian labels. "I watched your video with the President. Do you really have a story, or were you looking for a second kick at your fifteen minutes?"

"I have a story, *the* story," Haynes hesitated. Was this all a setup? Was she sent by the government, maybe even the President himself to find out what information he had, discredit him, or worse? ", and I left it with somebody else for safekeeping. Just in case, you know."

Rachel laughed. "Don't worry Mr. Haynes, I'm not here for you." She uncapped the second bottle before once again offering it to him. "I did read some of your stuff from Syria though. It was good." This time Rachel took small sips of the colorless liquor. "You found a humane side to the people living there, even the ones that wanted to kill you and the American soldiers." She was trying to sound good-humored. "Have you ever been back? I mean when there wasn't a raging war. To just see Damascus, Homs or Aleppo?"

"No." Derian was still cautious, but felt more at ease "I probably saw too many things that would make going back hard to stomach a second time around."

"Fair enough." Rachel added. "Too bad though. It really is a beautiful part of the world."

Another awkward silence between the two as they simply stared at one another as the sun was disappearing into the ocean while only a rhythmic purring of the air conditioning filled the room. Derian was trying to get a read on the woman, Rachel trying to figure out how to get out there without increasing his journalistic interest. "How did you find me?" Finally he broke the hum of the cool air through the vents.

Rachel heard the question, but didn't answer right away. Her thoughts momentarily drifted to her past twenty four hours. Hakan had been a man of his word. His team snuck her out of Acıbadem International Hospital to Ataturk International Airport without incident from the Russians, and through his Interpol connections had arranged a private jet for her. He knew that she was not finished with the monster known as Lucas Viale, and made an arrangement that once she had found the man, she would alert Interpol to make the arrest.

After a slight hesitation, she had agreed to the request, but also could not promise that *when* she found him again, that he would not be dead by the time the authorities arrived. Koseman's contact apparently only laughed and told him that *if* this particular trafficking operation was ended, Interpol would be perfectly fine with a body and the evidence. Stackwell knew she could handle that arrangement.

She chose Cairo has the destination for the private jet. It was close enough for the plane to make a quick turnaround if needed, but also the international airport was a principal hub for many of the major airlines, and she knew she could disappear into the crowded streets for a while first.

Once in the sprawling Egyptian capital, Rachel purchased a new phone and called a number she had committed to memory. She only hoped it was still in service. It was. The voice on the other end answered in Italian, but switched to English once the two women traded the appropriate coded phrases.

"Sophia?" It was a whispered question. "I've heard rumors lately that you might be back."

"Not back Maggie, hunted." She knew that the CIA operative already had seen the orders and also knew it would be futile to lie to her. "I need your help with something." Direct and to the point, she could afford to string her contact along. "I need you to find me an airplane. It left a private runway, Silivri Province, just off the Sea of Marmara, outside of Istanbul, two nights ago, and by private, I mean connected to a mansion, not airfield."

She could hear the woman typing into her computer. Maggie was stationed in Rome, Italy and was the Station Chief in charge of the CIA's unit tracking all flights in and out of Europe, Russia and the Middle East. They had access to all private, military and commercial aircraft that had transponder devices. Calling her was a risk, but it was the only chance Rachel had to finding where *Viale's* plane had gone.

"Got it." Maggie continued to speak softly. "It landed at King Khalid in Riyadh." Rachel was about to thank her friend when she was interrupted. "Hold on." The next ten seconds felt like an eternity and she nearly disconnected the call. Was Maggie actually tracing her call and turning her back over to the agency? "I'm searching for any other flight plans for that particular tail number or transcoding signal."

Maggie was the closest person she had to call a friend within the CIA. They had trained together, but she was transferred into another division when it was determined that she wasn't able to finish the combat drills. Still, they had discreetly kept in contact with one another and even helped each other out from time-to-time in the past. "Yep. Just as I thought. Your plane was only there for a couple of hours, probably refueling. It left Saudi airspace and travelled to the Maldives. A private island though, not one of the major airports." Maggie was also one of the only people who knew about her relationship with Sean, and the only other person she had ever told about the engagement on Charles Bridge before the chaos. She didn't have it in her heart to tell her the truth about him.

"Thanks Maggie, now I owe you one." Rachel was appreciative and spoke honestly.

"Just take it from the list that I owe you." A slight comical jubilance in the voice before changing to one of friendly anxiety. "Are you okay Soph?"

"I'm good Mags." The question took her by surprise for a moment. "Nothing a weekend at that thermal spa in Switzerland couldn't fix though." Returning the upbeat attitude, Rachel recalled a weekend the two spent together years ago.

"We need to do that again." It was a somber response as she too remembered the holiday.

"Definitely Mags." This was probably a lie. "I'll set it up and tell you when." Rachel ended the call without saying goodbye.

"How did you find me?" Derian repeated the question as he could see his *wife* was thinking about something else.

"Sorry." Rachel debated changing the topic once again, but also felt that she needed to give him something or else he could easily complicate her plans. "I hacked the resort's reservation database, was going to book myself a room when I happened to see your name and changed it into a couple. I was actually hoping to be already gone by the time you arrived, but my flight was delayed and I only got here this morning instead." She was being casual with her explanation.

"You hacked into their system?" Haynes wasn't skeptical about the method, but was piecing together for himself as to a reasoning. "Because making your own reservation wasn't an option. This place is pretty big, so I don't think that they are fully booked." He was using his hands to act like he was weighing the possibilities, but also was speaking mockingly. "Who are you really? At least two names, I'm guessing more, but you don't, or *can't* use one of them to book a room, so instead you *pretend* to be my wife." He was sharp. Derian was spelling it out pretty well. "I add that to what happened in Madison with the dead guys and a panicked CIA dude," He paused to see if she would stop him. She did not. ", and being *shot* recently." Another caustic remark. "Adds up to me like your some kind of secret agent or something. So what I *need* to know before I choose what to do, is *who* are you and *whom* do you work for?" Haynes set his feet defensively in case he had to defend himself.

Rachel saw the maneuver and smiled. She was trying to look friendly and not threatening, but also was prepared to subdue him if he tried to run or call out for help. "My name is Rachel—"

She was interrupted by a loud knocking on the villa's door. Stackwell immediately spun, grabbing a black gun from her suitcase and sprinting to the front entrance. Peering out the peephole, she slid the weapon into the back waistband of her shorts and slowly opened the door.

It was the British honeymooners from the reception area. "Good evening darlings." The older woman began. "We're sorry for interrupting, but we saw you two downstairs and were hoping you would still be willing to join us for a spot of tea this evening."

"Oh, hey." Derian joined the threesome in the doorway and was surprised to see the travelers he briefly met earlier. "Um, yeah, sure, I can still head over and join you two." He was trying to be polite and didn't know what to say.

"Oh wonderful love." The woman was genuinely thrilled. "We'd love your pretty wife to join us as well. This place just seems so romantic and it would be nice to learn about you lovebirds."

Derian nearly laughed out loud, but restrained himself. A wide-eyed exchange between the American *husband and wife* solved nothing as neither found the words of deterrence. Rachel finally spoke. "Give us ten minutes please. I'll need to change into something more dinner appropriate. Rolling her eyes, she walked back over to her suitcase while Haynes politely invited them into the private bungalow.

The dinner had turned into drinks afterwards as well, and Rachel was exhausted by the time they were able to return to the villa. Her fatigue was entirely based on the charade of being a married couple. She had not been with anybody else in what felt like forever. Twice she excused herself from the table, panicked by anxiety and was going to leave entirely, but both times she returned. She had one calming thought. Killing Sean was the mission, and this was part of the foreplay.

Once back in the small chalet, she and Derian barely spoke. They took turns in the shower and she cleaned her wound one more time. There was only one bed, he offered to sleep on the undersized sofa, but she declined. It was a huge king-sized bed and could easily give them both room to sleep.

Only the ever present whirring of the air conditioning disturbed the darkness. The moonlight slipped through the hanging curtains of the glass patio doors and Derian, who was completely drained earlier, had found a second life and was bordering on falling asleep and staying awake. He stirred restlessly.

"My name was Sophia Warner when I worked for the CIA." Rachel spoke gently. "I was part of a clandestine unit called Red Shimmer. We were assigned missions all over the world when it was necessary to *help* the American government or its interests." Choosing her words carefully, she also believed that the journalist next to her would understand her true meaning. "After a man I loved very much was killed," This time there was no hesitation in her voice or tears to swell. ", I went after those responsible, and was designated rogue and beyond salvage." This time she paused. "That was over nine years ago, and Madison was the first time the agency had found me since."

Once again silence between the two, but Rachel felt relief. She had deliberated with herself on how much truth she wanted to share with the man she barely knew, but somehow she felt like he could be trusted. She recalled the articles written *about* Derian Haynes, the man who reported truths from Syria and how he stood up against the United States military and government when they demanded his favor. She knew he paid a journalistic career price for that. A second time followed once she saw the video of him confronting the President and ending up arrested for his disobedience. The man was one based on strong morals and she felt it was honorable, but her defining decision came tonight during their evening. He played the part of *husband* to perfection. There was no reluctance or unwillingness. Once again he had protected her.

"Did you get them?" Haynes too spoke sleepily and almost in a hushed whisper. "The men responsible for your lover's death."

"Yes." It was soft, but there was general pleasure to her response. "I got every single one of them."

"Good." A sincere reply before the obstinate silence returned.

"It wasn't the CIA who tracked Rachel Stackwell down in Wisconsin though." She continued her story. "I had moved on from that part of my life, even was able to get a teaching position with the university there," Nearly chuckling to herself about that thought. ", but when I was in Prague for a summit, I saw two young girls being attacked. Maybe it's been my time at the university, but something inside told me that I couldn't ignore it and I stopped the men." Another grin remembering the damage she inflicted on the attackers. "They were apparently part of an international sex trafficking syndicate, found out who I was and came for me." Another self-assured half smile. "I don't think that they were expecting to find out who I *really* was." The internal debate roared again as to tell Derian about Lucas Viale and Sean.

Exhaustion and alcohol had taken over as Rachel heard his breathing turn deeper and was followed by a snort then exhale. "They came for me, so I'm coming for them, *all* of them. That's why I'm really here." She knew he was asleep, but wanted to finish telling him the truth anyways. This time she did laugh as he mumbled something incomprehensible.

Chapter *TWENTY-THREE*

Rachel awoke with a start. Morning had already broken, but she was alone. She had stirred earlier when it was still dark, and had to remind herself that the body next to her was a friend. She couldn't remember the last time she slept in the same bed as another person, but now he was gone. Springing from the massive bed, Stackwell spotted his travel bag and then felt her heart jump when she heard the main door to the villa open, and saw him enter.

"Sorry, jet lag must've hit me and I woke up early this morning." Haynes apologized and was carrying a cup of coffee and orange juice. "It would be like ten o'clock at night back in Washington, so I just felt like I should've been awake." Smiling, he offered her, her choice of beverages. "I hope that I didn't disturb you when I went for a swim."

"No." Rachel couldn't help but return the smile as she accepted the black coffee. "I'll get changed and get out of your way. I had promised to be gone by last night, but I'll make sure not to disturb your holiday any longer."

"I'm coming with you." Stepping in front of her, Derian met her eyes. "Cullen Verger."

"Who is that?" Rachel asked. She stopped. There was no dissuasion or avoidance this time.

"That's why *I'm* here." He continued. "I'm not on any holiday, I'm here for the same reason you are, but with different endgames." A sly look as he fully understood that she was here kill the men, but he only wanted proof. Derian quickly continued before she was able to retort. "Cullen Verger owns this place, hell, he owns the whole damn island and has a house somewhere on it. I *need* to get into that house. There is evidence in it somewhere that will apparently expose a lot of high ranking people around the world."

"Including the President of the United States?" Rachel was questioning his true intentions.

"Yes." Haynes nodded. "He and the First Lady, but it'll be an international rendering."

"So this is personal for you?" She continued to prod.

"Somewhat," He began to plead his case. ", but uncovering a global trafficking reign is so much bigger." Rachel stopped him with her index finger.

"I just wanted to make sure it *was* personal." She smiled at him. "It'll make you more dangerous." She wasn't going to lecture him on being subjective, she was the last person in the world to tell somebody not to take something personally. "You can come," there was always a, but. ", but my mission *is* quite different than yours. Are you okay with exposing crimes of dead men?"

It was Derian's turn to smile at her. "How do we find the house on this island?"

"I have a way." Rachel headed to the bathroom to have a shower. "First, we have to have breakfast, I'm starving.

After breakfast, Rachel and Derian searched the grounds before returning to their private villa. He had wanted to ask her the entire time what the plan was, but instead they continued portraying the roles of a married couple on holiday. Anticipation was growing inside of him. He did explain who Cullen Verger was, and found himself quite surprised to see she wasn't as knowledgeable to many of the man's claims to fame and fortune. Rachel's only response was that she *kinda kept to herself*, and he understood. He had been listening the night before, even if he was half asleep.

The woman whose mystique continued to grow on him headed directly for her suitcase once again and this time retrieved a dark gray block no larger than a bulky Handycam camcorder. As she unfolded the four arms with plastic propellers, Haynes realized it was a lightweight quadcopter drone. "A gun and a drone. How the hell did you get those through security at the airports?"

"The drone is actually just under the travel requirement so I didn't need to claim it." Rachel replied with a smirk. "The gun, well I guess you just need to know how to pack." Following her coy look with a laugh.

Powering up the micro drone, Stackwell motioned for him to follow her out onto the terrace. "The box said that it had forty-six minutes of flight time, so hopefully that'll be enough to find this Verger's residence."

"How high can this thing go?" Haynes asked as he flipped open the handling device that looked like a video game controller with a small screen attached to it.

"Not sure exactly, but we can't go too much and risk it being spotted. We don't know what kind of security that they have here." Rachel assumed that they would be on higher alert after what happened outside of Istanbul. "If this guy is as rich as you say, his place is going to be massive." She was confident. "Trust me, I've been to one of their mansions already."

"Paxton said that it was on the *other half* of the island. We should start past the staff accommodations." Their earlier explorations were highlighted by the rose and orchid gardens, tennis courts and small three-hole golf course. The spa huts were all aligned on the furthest accessible point with a locked gateway leading to where they were told the staff were allocated. As they reached each of the breaching points, they were met by a heavy metal fence, perfectly hidden within the native bushes and shrubbery, but still impassable for guests and staff.

Whirring to life, the quadcopter was sent out over the shallow blue waters and then expanding further into the Indian Ocean. Rachel kept the drone low as she toggled and rotated the joysticks, gaining and reducing speed, and playing with the onboard camera. It took only a couple minutes to understand the dynamics of the family friendly vacation toy. "Let's go hunting." Teeming with anticipation, her mission was just beginning.

"I saw the news video from Prague." Derian interjected as they quietly watched the feed provided by the drone's deluxe camera. "Searched for it this morning actually. That was you, wasn't it?" Asking, but they both knew he understood the truth. Rachel didn't answer. "What you did for those girls. It was amazing. They're all calling you a superhero. Straight out of the movies. There one minute and gone the next." He finally added with a slice of charm.

Pausing the gray quadcopter briefly before continuing to zip around the island outskirts, she muttered under her breath. "I am no hero." Rachel didn't want to think about it any longer and allowed the drone to reach up to forty miles per hour, while taking less than ten more indulgent minutes to spot a collection of white erected structures. They weren't housing, and as Rachel once again increased the vertical range, she was able to make out what it was, airplane hangars.

Rotating the camera to a full tilt allowed their view to expand wider and she quickly checked her phone's timer, nearly twenty minutes had passed, she needed to take the chance and climb higher with their eyes. The drone reversed away from the island as it escalated until they found what they were looking for. "There!" Haynes was the first to see it. Calling out excitedly like a kid playing the Punch Buggy game with a sibling on a car road trip. "That's gotta be it."

"I see it." Rachel responded. Swinging the flying model in for a closer look, but casually keeping her distance. The video camera was the highest caliber, 5.4K. Rachel was happy with the discovery, but now needed to use the final minutes finding a way onto the estate's grounds. Derian's confused objection was ignored when she swiftly flew further away from the main structure and found the lush greenspace between it and the resort grounds. "We can't worry about what *it* actually looks like, we need to find a way through *that*." Using the camera toggle, she focused on a small part of the dense mangrove forest.

"My plan was to steal a boat and go *around* to the other side." Haynes spoke cordially, but was only met with a look of disdain. "No good?"

"No." Rachel added. "They would see us coming the moment that we were in the water." A flashing red light on the screen caught her eye. Cursing quietly to herself, she moved the drone as stealthily as she could before the screen began to spiral and then went black. The power supply had been exhausted.

"Now what?" Haynes felt slightly dejected.

"Now we get ready for tonight." Rachel smiled as she flared both eyebrows. She pointed towards the small screen and began to rewind the live feed before it cut off. "Here. It looks like we can get through a little better." Tracing her finger on the handheld monitor, she drew an arched line from a green cluster to another row of small buildings, the staff lodgings. "We'll go when it gets dark."

The last remnants of the daily sun sunk into the ocean hours ago and nobody had missed the American *couple* as they slipped into the restricted staff area and disappeared under the cover of nightfall. Rachel lead as she used the drone's tracking beacon to guide her through the challenging waterlogged forest.

The mangrove species of plant protect nearly every island or atoll in the Maldives archipelago. They help fight climate change while absorbing carbon dioxide, but at the same time are shrinking with the coastal developments across the region. There was an obvious reason why Cullen Verger didn't construct a much larger fence line between his resorts and estate, the forest was not expected to be crossed, especially by vacationing tourists. The swampy shrubs and halophytic trees looked appealing from above with dense greenery, but underneath that thick luster is a mosaic of twisting vines, branches and roots.

Rachel and Derian's movements went slower than she was expecting, and the smell pungent. She had fallen once and him twice into relatively fresh water as the extensive root system filtered out the nutrients in the saltwater ecosystem. The water was clean, but the hydrogen sulfide produced was intense.

Using the drone's footage, she was able to devise a crude map of an expanse that appeared thicker than some of the other areas. It would be their best chance. Dropping the quadcopter in as close as possible for a detailed route, she allowed the battery to drain, it to crash and begin transmitting its recovery beacon. She would use that as her guide.

The little red dot changed from a single pulse, consistently beckoning once every three seconds to quicker beat and now a double flash every second. They were close. Immediately she froze. Motioning for her partner to do the same. In the distance, she could see a light strobing through the trees. Two beams interrupted by the forest. Flashlights. They were getting closer.

Derian hunkered into the protruding roots as he saw the powerful lighting as well. They had not needed any of their own as the full moon provided enough after they allowed their eyes to adjust to the night's subtle darkness, but these beams were prodding, almost searching for something, or somebody. "Are they looking for us?" He whispered as he crept up beside the woman he followed.

"I don't think so." Stackwell replied. "Probably the drone. It must've been spotted on a security radar earlier and they're tracing the same signal I am." Carefully, she dropped her device into the water, allowing it to sink. She did not know if they were tracking the drone's beacon or possibly the one responding from her. "Slowly and quietly, we need to move towards them." It was a hushed order.

The vines and roots rustled with their movements, but were healthy and did not snap or crack. Derian held his breath as the anticipation grew and his stomach knotted from within. They were with ten feet now. He could hear the men speaking, but did not understand what they were saying.

Rachel raised her fist to signal him to stop. Then opened her hand, flattened it and hoped he knew she wanted him to lower himself. He did as she wanted. Slipping into the waters again, she found her feet touching a firmer footing. Shallow ground, they had crossed onto the other side. She listened to the men, they were speaking Turkish and the devil inside was reincarnated.

"*Neydi o?*" One man spun towards the waters with his flashlight and infantry rifle poised to fire.

"*Bu kadar korkak olma.*" His partner chided him for his concern, but left his weapon slung over his back. "Maybe it is a crocodile?" The man laughed as he shone his light on his companion to see a combination of anxiety and fear. They exchanged cursives before turning away from the noises the first man heard.

"*Bu delilik.* Are we even sure there is anything out here?" A third voice. This man did not shine a light, but there too was slight apprehension in his voice. The first agreed as he continued scouring the grounds without relenting the grip on his weapon.

"Demir says to find the security breach, so we find it." The second man cursed again. He was the one in charge. "The signal has stopped now." Smacking the handheld device, he was trying to see if his own tracker would bring back the red dot he was following.

Rachel slowly pulled herself up out of the water and found the stainless steel folding knife in the side pocket of her black tactical pants. They had been hunting her signal and not the actual drone, which meant that more men may possibly be sent if these three had failed to locate their target. She could not allow that to happen. She tested the ground. It was firm.

Stackwell sprinted towards the three men. Her first target was the man holding his rifle. Taking the group initially by surprise, she plunged her blade deep into the man's backside, but the folding knife was too lightweight to kill. Twisting, it stuck and she released her grip, leaving the man to fall to his knees, howling in both pain and shock.

The other two men were next to one another. The taller one closest and she attacked. A spinning hell kick caught him in the shoulder as his instincts protected him. He still fell to the grass. Rotating back, Rachel pummeled two fists into the final Turk, the man holding the tracking device. He dropped it when the first two punches landed to his abdominal, and a third below his jaw.

The larger man was standing back upright and trying to sling his rifle from around his backside. Rachel growled. Striding twice, launching herself into his body, she rotated in the air to grip his core with her legs and pinning his arms. In one fluid motion, she somersaulted her head between his legs, pulling his upper body down and driving his head into the ground. Spinning back up, Stackwell used the heel of her boot to kick him in the face. Blood spurted as a loud crack echoed from a broken nose.

The tracker, the eldest was regrouping and she redirected her attention back towards him. A forward front kick staggered the man, but as she went in for another, grabbing from behind. The first man, had trouble breathing, but adrenaline gave him strength. Snapping her head back with two fists full of hair jerked Stackwell's body off-balance. The smell of blood and sweat overpowered the sulfide odor as the youngest of the men wrenched her backwards.

The trio's hunter cursed her as he charged. Rachel gave into the young man grasping her and focused instead on the approaching one. Her timing was exquisite. Two steps away, she rolled backwards, lifting her feet and embracing the injured man's body. Using it for leverage, she kicked out with both feet. Stunning and driving the older man with a double stomp to his upper body. The forward motion contrasted the younger's momentum and his weakened body buckled against the pressure.

Crying out again, he released his grip. Rachel sprang at the freedom, launching herself towards the elder again, a side boot landed, another crack with broken ribs and a punch to the temple wobbled her target.

The second patrol roared as blood drained from a broken nose. Grabbing the swaying leader, she spun him around, found the rifle still slung to his back, and twirled him in a circle to gain momentum before releasing his frame. The whirling garnered her enough force to hurl him off the ground and crash bodies against the latest attack.

The first Turk attacked again. Swung his fist, but only caught a glancing blow in the darkness. Rachel responded. Stomping down hard on his right foot froze him for second, allowing her to rotate a straight elbow to his cheekbone. It shattered. Following it with a kick to the inside of his left knee, dropped him to turf for a final time. His stab wound and broken face had caused enough loss of blood for him to pass out. The young man would die in the swampy grass.

Stackwell was not finished. Seething, she stormed towards the remaining two men. There would be no mercy. The men were winded, dazed by the onslaught and once again caught off-guard. A running kick to the face of the one with the already broken nose brought another loud cracking sound and more blood. He snaked and stumbled, had no bearings, but did not fall. An aimless punch with his right hand was simply the body reacting. Gritting her teeth, Rachel chopped one last time to his throat before snatching both sides of his crimson stained jaw, ripping in opposite directions and snapping his neck. The man's limp body crumpled.

Hissing as she took aim for the final man in the hunting party, she found him desperately crawling away in retreat. Landing on his back, she flipped him over, wrapping her legs tightly around his body, while forearm and elbow squeezed his neck muscles. The tracker thrashed for air. She would not allow any to enter his lungs. Clasping and clutching with all of her strength, she felt the man's final spasm and released him.

Rachel gulped in the fresh air, but could feel the dead men's blood and sweat on her face. Whipping her head to the right, a loud rustling and she was ready to fight again. It was Derian. She released her clenched fists and was thankful for the shadows and darkness. The journalist's eyes were wide, he was certainly in shock to what he had just witnessed, but he couldn't quite see the true savage on hers that she was experiencing.

Neither spoke until a crackling broke the silence. It was a radio. A voice on the other end was asking for an update to the search. "Now what?" Haynes asked.

"Shit." Rachel swore as her mind raced. She was still recovering from the ferocious attacks and beginning to feel the aching in her shoulder. "I suppose that you don't speak Turkish?" She tried to smile and lighten the mood, but there needed to be a response. It couldn't come from her, even if she tried to deepen her voice, it would not be enough. "Repeat after me exactly."

When the radio crackled again, they were able to find it on the body of the larger men. Handing it to Derian, they rehearsed a quick phrase, and he spoke while holding the transmitting dial between channels. It added distortion to the feed and would hopefully break up the communication just enough to hide his bad Turkish interpretation.

The voice on the other tried two more times, and both times Haynes applied the same strategy, the man was aggravated. Finally accepting the response, he ordered them back to the house and that they would look again tomorrow. Derian was relieved.

"We won't have much time now." Rachel found him in the moonlight. "You can still wait here?" She was calming again as she posed her question and statement.

"I'm good." He knew what she was referring. He had just seen another side of her, and it was going to happen again. "I've seen worse." It was only a half truth, but he had experienced war before. Looking back at the three dead bodies, we deliberated to himself about just leaving them there and what the one man said to the other. "Are there really crocodiles here?" He wondered aloud.

Rachel only laughed at the basic concern. "No. There are no animals on this island that want us dead," Winking, but probably only for herself. ", only people."

Chapter TWENTY-FOUR

The large white estate's layout was not what Rachel was expecting. Using the three dead men's tracks, she was able to lead them back over the same path until music, voices and lights could be seen and heard. She had imagined tall stone walls, cameras and regular patrols, but instead found none of them.

At first, she left Derian hunkered in the edge of the forest trees to perform a general survey of the grounds. There was a stone wall that matched the house in color, but it was no higher than hip high, and even dipped to knee height periodically. Away from the main house sat six smaller lodges, but all still larger than the villas at the resort. She assumed that was where the men were staying. She was right, but all were currently empty.

Armed with one of the MPT-76 rifles taken from the trackers, Stackwell slithered between buildings, neared the boisterous laughing and loud music, before propping herself up against a wall in the shadows across from the swimming pool. She studied the four men. None were Sean. They were relaxed, drinking and floating on reclining vinyl chairs.

"*Acele et kaltak!*" As the song slowed to change from one current American hip-hop artist to another, a booming voice called towards her. She froze. An apology was mumbled back, but not loud enough for the men to hear. A young blonde woman began to walk away from the canopied building. She wore only a bikini bottom and was carrying a tray of drinks. Rachel's glare strengthened as she watched the woman, no, girl approach two of the bearded men, hand them their drinks while they either grabbed at or slapped her on the back end. She found herself tightening the grip around the rifle, but instead of opening fire and killing all four, she decided on a new tactic. Before slinking her way back to where Derian was hidden, she crawled forward onto the small patio and disconnected a portable one pound propane tank from the side grill of an oversized barbeque.

"You said that you're here to get evidence and expose people, right?" Rachel's whisper was harsh, but not intentionally reprimanding. "Does that include the ones who fund them?" She once again was angry at the thought of the trafficked girls.

"If I can find these ledgers that I was told about, I plan on exposing them all." Haynes's eyes were determined. "Every single person, no matter *whom* they are."

"*Every* one of them." It was bordering on a command. "No matter who they are, you have to report it." Rachel had seen and felt enough. Now understanding that killing everybody here was going to bring closure to herself, but it would not put an end to this business. Somebody else would just take the place, the demand had to end so the supply wouldn't be needed.

"You have my word." Derian felt like she was asking for help without directly asking.

"Then you'll need a distraction to get into that house." She handed him the compact Stoeger STR-9 pistol she found in one of the bungalows. "You know how to use this right?" Haynes didn't answer, he pulled back the top slide to check for ammunition, then clicked the release to snap it into position. Rachel's wide smile was her response. "Set yourself up behind those villas and wait for my signal." Derian wanted to ask what she was going to do, but she had already scurried away.

Stackwell crept around the outer side of the main house and found her distraction. She knew her stealth mission would not give the reporter enough time to search the house for whatever he needed if the men were still inside. There was no telling how many were actually on the premises so she decided to draw them out.

Carefully, she continued to use the shadows until she was flat against the rear of one of the three black Land Rovers parked in the arched driveway. The back door was locked. Creeping to the driver side, she tested the handle. It opened and she punched the button on the automatic lock and found what she was looking for in the back of the vehicle, road flares.

Sliding under each, Rachel took the opportunity to plunge her knife into the gas tanks, allowing the combustible fluid to puddle below as she lit one flare and strapped it to the portable tank before placing it in the rear of the open Land Rover. The second flare, she ignited, tossed it under the second vehicle's pooling fuel and sprinted towards the bushes and shadows as fast as she could.

The leaking puddles were widening before amalgamating into one fiery spectacle against the darkness once the flare lit the gasoline. Rachel steadied her aim and fired the rifle. An alarming burst of gunfire broke the stillness around her and was followed by a deafening explosion.

Her rounds hit the propane tank directly. The flare lit the canister which caused it to erupt into a fireball, buckling the vehicle when it was lifted from the ground and landing hard against its matching partner. Windows smashed and glass crackled during the blast, but also from contact. The fire had been creeping up the side of the second Land Rover causing a second detonation almost immediately after the first. Rachel grinned.

Two men stormed out within seconds, weapons drawn, but Stackwell pulled back on the trigger again, cutting them down immediately. A third froze, diving back into the house when he saw his colleague's heads whip up and dead bodies crumple down the stone steps. A brief moment of chaos was replaced with silence and tranquility before both horns from the burning trucks began to blare.

"What the fuck was that?" Cullen Verger shouted after his heart jumped and he spilled the drink he was holding. He had been relaxing in the front den of the large house, mindlessly watching a massive television while numbing himself with cocaine and Raa, he preferred the local sap fermented to have a sour taste. The first explosion was smaller, stunning and confusing him, but the larger second one brought concern.

Two of Viale's men sprinted past him as he tried to investigate, a third man, Burak Demir, stopped, ordered him to stay away from the doors or windows until they had determined what was going on, then followed his men. Verger didn't listen.

Trailing just behind Demir, he witnessed the execution of both men. Demir dove back into the mansion and nearly knocked him over at the same time. "I told you, stay away." The larger Turkish man barked at him in broken English. The open door and frame splintered as another volley of gunfire erupted from somewhere outside. Two more of Viale's soldiers helped their commander up as he cursed loudly. Verger was now scared.

"What is this?" Lucas Viale appeared, Sig Sauer in hand. "Police? The Maldivian Ministry of Defense?" He received no response from the trembling magnate.

"No. *Some*body else." Demir cynically hissed when he addressed Zafar. The windows in the sitting room next to them exploded as another barrage of gunfire tore into the once immaculate building.

"It's not *her*!" Viale spat back. "I killed her."

"Stay with him." Demir issued his own order this time. "*I* will kill *whom*ever it is myself this time." His sneer was defiant. Two more foot soldiers had joined them from the pool. Both still simply in their bathing trunks and brandishing weapons. He gave them orders and followed them back towards where they had come from.

Viale swore and punched the wall next to him. "Get up." Ordering Verger before dragging the man to his feet as more bullets tore the mansion apart. The billionaire squealed this time while grabbing onto Lucas. "Get off me." Shrugging the man's grip, he led him to the staircase down the hallway. "I need you upstairs and away from everything down here."

"No, we can't stay here." Cullen was whimpering. "It's the Americans. They know *she* is here and have come for her." It turned into blubbering. "They'll kill us all. We can't stop their

SEALs." Verger began to squirm and fight back against the arms pushing him upwards.

"Stop it!" Viale struck him, knocking him to the steps before helping him back up. "It's not the fucking Americans." His benefactor's skin had been broken from the slap and blood trickled gently. "It's not them." He whispered it almost to himself, but could only think one thing. *If it IS her, she will definitely kill us all.*

Derian froze when he heard the first explosion. Was that Rachel's signal? The men in and around the pool stopped too, unsure how to react, but when the second detonation was followed by an echo of gunfire, they charged into the mansion. That *was* her signal.

Sprinting towards the house himself, Derian passed the topless girl who was going in the opposite direction. She screamed, but continued to flee when he paid her no regard. Turning left, he found another door away from where the poolside men had entered. It opened onto a smaller foyer, then a right and left and he found himself in a pantry styled room with a door he assumed led into the main kitchen. It did.

More gunfire was followed by shouting voices, but he couldn't make out anything that they were saying. Haynes carefully peered out the door and held the handgun ready. The room was empty. He stepped out, but immediately dove to the floor behind a dining island in the middle of the room when he saw a group of men, seven in total, through the wide doorway across the room. He listened and hoped they didn't see him.

One man gave orders, but again Derian didn't understand anything said. There was another round of gunfire and the bearded leader pointed in two directions. Derian figured he could take a couple of them out from here, maybe help Rachel as she would certainly be outnumbered. He stopped. That would probably only end up getting himself killed, arguing with himself, he decided to avoid the confrontation. They left.

Haynes had no idea where he was going. He knew the large estate had two floors and figured that the main bedrooms or offices would be on the second level, he needed to find a way up there. Crawling on the floor in the opposite direction of where the men headed, he found an alternative darkened doorway and peered around its corner. Another quiet hallway, but this one was much shorter and narrower.

Rising to a hunched walking position, Derian stayed on his toes to try and avoid creating any shuffling of footfalls on the tiles. He found a secondary staircase. Obviously a lesser used one as it too was dark, did not have any lush carpeting or flooring. It was simple, the tiling continued and a thin wooden bannister. Propping his back against the wall, he ascended as quietly as he could, both hands holding the Stoeger STR-9 in front of him like he was once trained to by an American SEAL team in Syria.

Gunfire erupted somewhere outside. The men he saw earlier must have made their way to wherever Rachel was. He hoped she was able to hold them off. Reaching the top of the stairwell, he peered in both directions, scrutinizing his options on which way to go. It was simply shadows at this point. Lights were brighter whichever way he chose, but the front of the house was to his right. It was the likely of the directions for an office of some sort. He moved.

Hearing voices forced Derian to freeze. Two men were fighting, not really arguing, one was whimpering while the other cussed and shouted at him. Another explosion outside rocked the house, more gunfire, and then a second blast seemed to bring a brief calming to chaos outside. He knew the last two were from hand grenades, he had experienced enough of those kinds of detonations before. More dispute between the voices before a gunshot ended the quarrel. Derian continued slowly.

"*Kimsin*?" A man yelled at him from behind. "*Sen kimsin*?" He repeated it again, but was deliberate in his pronunciations. Haynes couldn't understand the shouted question, but also didn't believe it was the man's native language either.

"I'm with you man." Turning to face the voice, Derian was hoping to play on the man's confusion.

"Who are you?" He asked again with gun pointed directly at Haynes. "You're with Señor Viale? One of his *hombres*?" He did not fire, nor did he lower his gun. The man was edgy with the firefight and explosions which made him uncertain. His eyes darted from side-to-side and his tone of voice hesitated anxiety in the translation.

"Yes." Derian lowered his weapon hoping that the man did so as well. He was dressed well, no matching suit jacket, but dark grey anthracite wool dress pants, impeccable black button up shirt and leather shoulder holster. Derian figured him to be private security. When he saw Haynes lower his weapon, he too followed.

The guard's brief look to secure his gun back into the holster gave Derian his chance. Lunging at the man, he tackled him around the waist and the guns scattered. Both men crashed hard to the floor, rolling over each other as the private security was better trained in combat.

Haynes, now underneath the man, kicked upwards, striking him in the ribcage below his right arm as he was about to throw a punch. The guard was momentarily knocked off balance. In the opening, Derian rolled them again and he was the aggressor as both men were able to find their feet.

Trading punches, the fight had turned in favor of the journalist's style, a simple brawl. Swinging violently at one another, neither initially made contact before both were able to do damage with a fist. Each man landed an opposing left hand, Derian's to the chest, the guard's, a glancing blow to the bottom of the jaw. Staggered, it allowed the trained security to attack again. This time a right fist was accompanied by a side kick. Both landed flush. Haynes tried to block, but was slower and with the alternating onslaughts it unable to protect himself.

Another right busted his lip open as his attacker roared with rage. Still, Derian would not submit. He ducked his head. It was purely instinct, but the man swung wildly. It was an opportunity. Adrenaline flowed and Haynes charged forward. Wrapping his arms around the other man and driving him into the wall behind. The motion allowed him to lift his adversary off the ground before the crash shattered the hallway interior.

It was the American's turn to yell, but his was not rage, it was struggle, pain, and an unwillingness to be put down. A second ramming of the guard's body gutted his oxygen and a third forced him through the wall, whipping the back of his head into firm beam of wood. The man screamed as his head shattered. He fell to floor, bleeding, but still alive.

Derian scrambled as his momentum buckled him as well when the hole in the wall was created. Falling, then crawling on all fours, he found one of the guns, it was the Stoeger and he fired twice. Both bullets found their mark, hitting the injured man in the chest and driving him onto his back. The private security guard was dead. Haynes sat back, gulping in air, but also realizing he needed to keep moving. Prepared to defend himself, he approached the next corner only to find the body of another man, shot in the head with blood and brain matter on the wall next to him. He recognized his face immediately and was now uncertain as to what was happening in all the chaos.

Lucas Viale shoved Cullen Verger up the wide vestibule as the man stumbled twice on his own feet. The marble steps were covered by lush red, green and blue carpeting, almost catholic feeling in the embrace of the main estate's stairwell. More gunfire erupted outside and the tycoon cowered, then shrieked when the explosions followed. "We're under attack." He cried again. "The Americans."

"Shut up." Viale hissed at man he was almost physically dragging at this point.

"Lucas. We have to go." Verger was pleading. "You have to get *me* out of here."

"You'll be fine." He quipped back. Anger was mounting. There was no way that she had found them here, yet alone survived in Turkey. "Stay in your office." They had reached the top of the stairs when another blast rocked the whole house. "You'll be fine there."

"No. We have to go. We have to run. Now!" Verger's cries had turned to outright begging. The man truly was a coward. "We can take the back stairs and get to the plane." Grabbing Viale by the arm, he tugged at his friend which forced them both trip over the top step and fall to the floor.

"Don't fucking touch me!" Viale was irate. From his vantage point now, he could see the firefight through the floor-to-ceiling windows. Two of the Land Rovers were engulfed in flames and the fire had spread into the cluster of bushes in the center of the circle driveway. The reds, oranges and yellows burned brightly, casting deft shadows, but also adding light into the heart of the darkness. He could make out three bodies on the ground, his men, and then a figure dash across the path. There was a gingerly pace to the run and the figure was keeping as much weight off their right leg as possible. They were injured. Although, he couldn't see clearly, he knew the body movement and momentum. It was her. Sophia had found them, found *him*.

"I'll give you anything that you want." Verger continued his begging. "You have to get me to the plane and off this island."

"It won't help." Viale's voice was calm, but his eyes were frenzied. Rage had mixed with passion and fear. He knew there would be no stopping her. There would be nowhere he could run that she wouldn't find him. He had to kill her tonight. "She's here."

Cullen Verger had climbed back to his feet, was still shaking and gasped when he heard another explosion. This time much closer and from inside house. "Who's here?" Uttering his words, he looked at Viale who was blank. The man's face was void of expression. He was going to repeat his question, but couldn't. He felt nothing.

Viale' mind had cleared. There was only one thing that mattered now, his survival. He saw Verger mouth some words, but didn't hear a single one. None of it mattered anyways. Raising his Sig Sauer, he pulled the trigger once and ran back down the lavish stairwell. Cullen Verger's body slapped against the wall before slinking down. Eyes still open, one bullet in his head with blood and brain matter trailing behind as it slid to an upright seated position.

Chapter *TWENTY-FIVE*

Rachel watched the Land Rovers blister from her position across from them and the estate. An occasional flare up of burning oils or interior gave rebirth to the flames and she thought the fire may die out before any more men appeared, but instead the manicured cluster of trees and bushes in the arched center of the driveway became engulfed.

Even from her hiding spot ten feet further down the path, she was beginning to feel the heat of the flames, but then movement caught her eye. She was paying attention to both the front door where two men lay dead, a third had escaped back inwards, and to the sides of the large house. Darting her eyes between all three points of attack was stressful, but necessary.

Currently, four more figures crept along the near wall, trying to use it as protection, but her vantage point only permitted her to see the black masses against white wall reflecting the oranges and yellows from the roaring fire. Steadying herself, she pulled back on the rifle's trigger. The fully automatic MPT-76 surged to life with deadly accuracy. Stackwell controlled the smooth firing rifle's recoil and dropped the first two men before the others could even react.

Bullets tore into the house's stone siding as chips and chunks exploded into dust fragments. The two remaining dove to the ground once they realized their peril. Readjusting her vision, Stackwell left the selector lever on automatic and emptied the rest of her cartridge before replacing it with another twenty round polymer magazine. She only had two left.

Hearing another scream shatter through the crackling flames meant she had hit a third man, but only injuring him. Switching the rifle to a controlled setting, Rachel chose to use the targeting sightlines for more pinpoint accuracy. She found shadow on shadow movement. Rounded. A man's head. She fired. The spherical obscurity whipped backwards. Three of the four were dead.

The sanctuary of her own treeline erupted all around her and Rachel flung herself to the grass and dirt. The gunfire came from the other direction. She cursed herself for becoming fixated on the group of men and forgetting about the far side of the estate. Another barrage of gunfire kept her pinned down to the ground. They knew the general vicinity of her whereabouts, but the wide arc sprayed meant her attackers were uncertain to her exact location.

As a third volley came, Stackwell rolled over, was about to crawl deeper into her bushel, but caught glimpse of the fourth man from the initial group sprinting towards her hiding spot. The others were laying cover for him. If she waited, he would be on top of her within seconds, but if she fired, the others would have her exact position. Swearing again, Rachel fired. The advancing man fell instantly as the three bullet combination squared him perfectly in the chest.

There was no moment of hesitation from the onslaught. This time the assaulters knew where to aim and they immediately replied. Scrambling to her feet, Stackwell took two steps before launching herself horizontally. Landing on the grass re-aggravated the ache in her shoulder, but when she began crawling on her belly, a searing pain in her right leg was prominent. She had been hit. Upper thigh, but on the outside. A simple tearing of the pants and flesh. She would need to cover it, but she would survive.

A deep voice echoed in the night. One man was issuing orders. Rachel closed her eyes and listened. Allowing her senses to separate the clatters and uproars of the night from one another, she was able to determine three more voices or tones to their voices. All three were speaking Turkish, but the one of the responders answered first with a Circassian intonation.

These three would spread out to cover more ground. They were unsure if she was still alive or not. Rachel crawled towards the flaming circle on the middle of the driveway. Retreating further away would be what they would expect her to do, but also leave her in the open, vulnerable and her injuries would certainly slow her down. Instead, the fire could protect her, give her refuge by sheer surprise. It was defiantly a risk as the flickering lights would also expose her.

Staying level with ground, she found the outer ridge where the pavement met the bushes and waited. The heat seared her face and she had gotten as close she could to the flames without burning. A body appeared to her left. He was younger and was using one hand to shield himself from the brightness and heat of the fire. Stackwell smiled. Firing once, the bullet tore through the young man's hand and into his head. He fell face first onto the driveway.

The blast and thudding of the dead man's body were immediately met by another return of automatic gunfire. Rachel tightened her grip on the scorching steel, but none of the bullets were fired in her direction. They didn't know where she was. One further off to her left, but the second volley from immediately behind. Rolling out from her fiery preserve, she found the man next to one of the burnt out Land Rovers. Rapidly pulling at the trigger, she fired wildly twice, hit him once in the leg and as he was buckling, spotted three more bullets into his upper body.

The pavement around her was instantly chewed at by a return attack. The final gunman had her exact location. Clamoring to her feet, she ran. The adrenaline allowed her wounded body to combat the aching sensation. A zigzag pattern kept the remaining shooter at bay momentarily as his shots continued to miss, now ripping apart the turf around her. Stackwell spun, reversed her direction and sprinted towards the attack. There was an abrupt hesitation, the man was replacing his magazine. She fired her own weapon at the outline of the body she saw, but also missed.

She drew nearer with each footfall, but suddenly the rifle exploded from her hands. Her attacker had tossed his automatic gun aside, switched to a hand gun and began firing. One bullet hit her MPT-76, sending it flying from hands and with the force, her crashing to the ground.

"I should not have ever seen you again, *orospu*." The deep demanding voice called down to her as he approached and stood over his enemy. "Zafar should have killed you twice already," Rachel recognized the bearded man from the villa outside Istanbul. ", but now that I see it is you here, I am glad he didn't."

The fire still roared through the bushes while casting shadows on half of the large man's body, but Rachel was still able to see the man's broken smile. "This will be pleasure to me." Demir laughed when he noticed her blood soaked leg. "I will not make it quick."

Stackwell kicked back with her left leg as he leaned over him, catching the big man flush under his chin, but not toppling him. "Your friends thought the same thing in America." Rachel spat back at the man in Turkish. "Where are they now?" She needed time, she needed him to attack her and not simply pull a trigger.

The larger Turk roared at the scathing woman. "Those men were my blood. They were my family." This time he kicked back. Driving his foot purposely into her wounded leg before lusting for more of her agonizing screams. A second boot was followed by a stomp. Stackwell writhed, but was timing the next attack. It came. Repeating the same motions, Demir kicked her right thigh and stamped again, but this time when he landed, Stackwell lunged at his planted foot.

During Demir's latest jolt she grabbed the folding knife from her pocket while predicting another stomping would follow. It did. The man's weight was now entirely on his planted foot and using her upper body strength, Stackwell drove the blade into the back of his ankle, slicing the Achilles tendon and climbing on top of him.

Burak Demir howled at the excruciating pain. His body crashed to the ground without the strength in his leg to hold him upright any longer. Shrieking and crying, he had no time react to American woman who fell him. The pain disappeared as numbness replaced all feelings momentarily. Stackwell drove her blade twice into the man's stomach before his chest and finally into his throat, severing the jugular vein. The bearded man would be dead in seconds.

Wiping the blood from his face and lip, Derian passed by Verger's body and continued to search the second floor of the estate. More gunshots rang out. Then voices. A man's followed by a woman's. He could not make out what their raised shouts were saying, but the tones were certainly hostile. It had to be Rachel he thought to himself. She was still alive. He smiled.

Around another corner was a similar looking hallway and Haynes was beginning to think he was in some sort of labyrinth. A maze that would eventually lead nowhere, but it did. When he tried the door knob, it was open and carefully peering in, he determined this had to be the magnate's main office. The art on one of the three walls was equally as gaudy as the rest of the mansion. Derian only recognized a couple names and could only guess what the price range was for them. The other two walls across from him were starch opposites of one another. The outer one was essentially an entire window. Running from floor to ceiling, it had separations of thin wood slats to form patterns and breaks, but was also protected by blinds and shades. All were mechanically controlled from the desk sitting in front of them. Derian presumed during the day, the views could be both mystical and intimidating.

Next to the oversized oak, marble and steel desk was a matching bar, complimented with wines glasses and too many expensive bottles of liquor. In the center of the room sat a chocolate brown microfiber and leather wraparound lounger. Four pieces in total and all adorned with matching cowhide throw pillows. Facing away from the desk and towards the remaining direction, a large screen television was mounted on the wall, faux cabinets and drawers lining below and a wall-hanging above. The tapestry swirled in browns, but artistic gold intertwined forming a traditionally laid out map of the world.

The moonlight cast in through the top of the windows offered enough light for Derian to find a lamp on the table next to the lounger. He figured that the ledgers would have to be in this room, if they even existed at all. He made his way to the desk, sat in the soft leather chair and pondered to himself where would they be hidden. The computer was state-of-the-art. A full, virtual keyboard and touchpad were built into the desk's marble top and as he barely touched it, the collection of four monitors to his right all turned on at once. He began to doubt the existence of hand-written records with this type of technology.

The screen setup looked much like one that avid video gamers or streamers might use. All four connected, layered on top of one another, but when he retouched the flat screen under his fingers, one of them, the largest, became a main hub while the others switched to live security feeds from inside the house. Rotating between who knew how many, Derian became drawn into one as it converted to a picture of two people fighting. He recognized Rachel immediately. Frozen and uncertain if he should go help her, he had been distracted, but his senses became alert when he felt another presence and saw movement out of his peripheral vision. It was too late.

"Who are you?" A stunning blonde woman had entered the office and was pointing a black handgun directly at him. "You are not one of Mr. Lucas's men." The green-eyed beauty spoke English as a second language, but it was clean. She inched closer, but was also shielding another with her body.

"No, I am not." Haynes immediately looked towards his Stoeger on the desktop and then back at the woman. The gun was too far away, and he too inaccurate a shot to attempt a grab and fire. "I am only—"

"You kill Master Verger?" Her question interrupting him as she stepped closer, gun steady in her hand. She definitely knew how to use it. "He is dead. I saw him in the hall." Her cries continued.

"I didn't." Derian exclaimed. He wanted to continue his protest, but froze again when the shielded figure peeked around the Russian woman's fit figure. "Paxton you son of a bitch." He whispered to himself instead.

Closing his eyes, Haynes cursed again as he saw the face of young Virginia Paxton. The Senator knew exactly what he was doing when he made his deal with Derian. The man knew that his granddaughter was here, on the island, and he had wanted Haynes to go rescue her. A combination of pride and betrayal swelled in Derian. Cursing himself a third time, he now fully believed that ledgers were a myth. A tale that Paxton weaved for him, knowing that it was exactly what the reporter would want to hear.

"What?" The woman shouted again as she didn't understand his mumblings.

Haynes held his hands up to show he meant them no harm. "My name is Derian. I am an American," Pausing before adding why he now understood his true mission. ", and I am here to get her and bring her home." He pointed to the girl hiding behind the armed woman.

"American? You are soldier?" Her tone had lowered, but she did not relent the weapon while forcing the girl back behind her legs.

"No, I'm a journalist." He spoke slower to make sure she understood. "A newspaper, a writer," Pointing again at the young teen. ", but her grandfather sent *me* to find *her*. Virginia Paxton. Ginny." This time he was speaking at the girl, hoping she would intervene.

"Ye..ah." The girl poked herself around again. "Tha..t's me. You..know..papa?" She was obviously under the influence of some sort of medicine or drugs.

"Is she okay?" Haynes quipped as he was instantly concerned.

"Yes." Alyona was trying to be reassuring. "The drugs are not harmful. They just keep her happy until she is without them." She was speaking from experience. "I look after her to make sure she is safe." She slowly was lowering her gun, but Derian didn't want to reach for his yet.

"Then you have done a great job, but it's now my turn to make sure she gets home." He honestly had no idea how he was going to do that. His eyes wandered back to the monitors, but none of them currently featured Rachel or anybody else. He could feel the bruises under his face forming and swelling.

Ginny tugged at her protector's dress, spoke quietly and stumbled briefly. "Is woman with you?" The Russian queried. It was not a threatening question and almost posed with admiration. "She is also American?"

"Yes. She *is* the reason that I am here." Haynes was careful again. Unsure exactly how they knew about Rachel. "Ginny's grandfather helped get us onto the island so we could take her home." Derian repeated that fact so the adolescent could hear about her family, even if she wasn't fully able to comprehend everything.

"We watch her." Alyona spoke with reflection. "When we hide. We were still able to see her outside. She was very brave against Mr. Lucas's men." It was an act of admiration.

"Don't tell her that." Derian laughed gently to himself. "C'mon let's get her out of here." Getting up from the chair, he reached out for his gun, but stopped once again as the blonde woman immediately raised hers. "Whoa. Whoa. Hold on." Stepping back. "I'm here to help. I just want that in case we run into any more, unfriendlies." Pausing, he waited for her reaction. "Okay?" She lowered the black gun. Scooping up the Stoeger and placing it in his back pocket, he slowly nodded towards the door. "Let's go, quietly."

"You were looking for something?" Alyona asked without moving. "In Master Verger's computer?"

"Something that doesn't exist." Haynes sighed back. He was frustrated at himself for falling for the Senator's ruse. "Don't worry about it. We need to get you two out of here."

"Master Verger's special files." The Russian woman held Ginny back and held their place. "The ones he writes in and has guest sign?"

It was a probing statement, but immediately triggered Derian's desires. "They exist?" His head shot around towards her. "The ledgers are real?"

"Что?" Alyona didn't understand what he was talking about.

"The ledgers, er, the *files* as you called them." Haynes was fumbling, trying to help her understand what it was that he was referring, and if it was the same as she. "Folders, um, papers, contracts that prove what the, *guests*," He used her word. ", as you said. They signed about what actually goes on here?" He knew he was possibly overreaching. The Russian woman obviously knew what the truth, but how involved was she really.

"Yes. Papers. Master Verger has everybody sign once they select their pleasures." She understood the value that these files possessed. "They are in safe under the bar." She pointed across the room. "A secret button will open floor and safe will be there."

Derian was motionless. Eyes wide and almost frozen in time. They did exist. "How? Where is the button?" Running to the marble slab, his questions ran into one another. She answered and he found the control. Tapping it created a hushed whisking sound as part of the flooring did reveal an electronic panel, keypad and door latch. Six solid red lines indicated that a code was required. "Shit." Derian swore aloud. So close, but without the code it would be useless. Looking at the woman, his gaze fell upon the young Paxton girl instead and he cursed himself again. He'd have to come back later to search for the code. He needed to get the girl out of here first.

"Take me with you." Alyona saddled next to him. "With Ginny. Take me to America and give me asylum." There was almost a pleading to her tone. "I will open that for you."

His head whipped back towards her and their eyes met. Derian searched hers, believed many men probably would get lost in the emerald green, but right now there was pain behind them. She truly was desperate to leave. "Okay." He agreed with her appeal. "I'll get you both out of here, to the United States, but I can't promise you anything else." He was being honest. "Ginny's family is very powerful, connected to other people in our government, and I can make sure that they know how helpful you were to me, but especially Ginny." It was the offer he could make.

"*Ладно*." There was hesitation and a shade of uncertainty in her voice, but Alyona agreed. Still keeping one eye on the young girl, the Russian squatted and entered a six digit combination into the keypad. A gentle click immediately followed and she stood back up.

Slowly yanking on the heavy door, Derian smiled broadly when he saw stacks of brown leather file folders. He was euphoric and felt like Indiana Jones opening an undiscovered tomb or pyramid. Paxton was telling truth. Haynes quickly scanned the room, he wanted to sit down and start reading through them right then, but knew escape was now the most important thing. "Aright, let's get you *both* the hell out of here."

Grimacing, Rachel rested in the shadows against the side of the far side of the large house. The aching sensation in her shoulder had escalated into an agonizing throbbing that was relentless There was no doubt in her mind that the wounds had been torn open as her fingertips tingled in her left hand with general numbness and lack of feeling rotating through. Taking a deep breath, she actually smiled to herself. The gunshot to her thigh was nothing compared to this anymore. That pain was still noticeable, but it had become bearable after using the bearded man's belt to tie around the gash and slow the bleeding.

Inching her way to the rear of the estate, she found an already partially opened door. One hinge ripped off by what she assumed was the men rushing in from the pool area. She slipped in with the dead man's black Girsan handgun level. The night had turned quiet. After killing the bearded Turk, no other attackers came. Where was Sean? Rachel limped carefully from one room to the next. Did he escape again? Or was he hiding? She cursed to herself while trying to listen for any signs of movement.

Lucas Viale stood quietly in the shadows. Waiting for his target to enter the house. He had watched her slink around to the side before sprinting down the stairs and towards the possible entry points. She didn't use the first door he purposely unlocked, but was still able to hear her enter through the back. Her breathing was short, had a huskier intake than exhale, and he could tell each one carried feelings of pain. She was injured. He smiled as he stepped out of the darkness once she exited the room they briefly shared.

He was soundless as he intentionally placed each foot slowly down. She was less than ten feet from him, but simply shooting her in the head would not be satisfying any longer. She had completely disrupted his world. It would take time, but he could put it back together.

Watching her legs, Viale could see she was struggling to control the weight under the injured one she protected. The other would be his target. She peered around a corner into an open concept room. He kicked out. Striking her still strong leg behind the knee and sending her crashing to the floor. "Hello Sophia."

Stackwell heard rustling, but it was too late. A driving force hammered into the back of her knee and her body gave way. The hard landing jarred the gun from her hand, but only a few feet. Half crawling, half dragging her damaged body on the carpet, she heard Sean rasp her name as she tried to upturn a glass table for cover, but her right arm wasn't as responsive and she found herself exhausted on her back instead.

"You should not have come here." His voice wasn't as adoring as it was at the villa outside Istanbul. "Why couldn't you just stay away?"

"Why Sean?" She had not answered immediately, but also was not overwhelmed by the past this time. "Why did you—"

"No!" His shout interrupted her. "Sean Trevelyan is dead! He died in Prague nine years ago!" Calming himself from his initial outburst, he continued. "There is only Lucas Viale. There is only one and you should remember that." He pointed the barrel of his gun at her.

"I want to know why?" Rachel yelled back.

"You don't need—"

"You *owe* me that much." Her shouting continued. The fire in her voice was dampened slightly with cracking and sentiment. "You son of a bitch." Pain and emotion had brought tears this time. "I want, *need* to know why." A stream came from each eye.

"Why? You want to know why?" Viale's brief explosion turned into a strict diatribe. "You of all people should have understood. You've seen how governments work. It's all a show for the media and public relations, especially internationally. You've been around ambassadors and diplomats, and all the bullshit. They only care about the fancy parties, titles and six figure salaries, and *I* fucking deserved to be there too." His moment of hesitation was only interrupted by his own capricious rhetoric. "Don't you try to tell me that *my time was coming*, you did that once before," He cut Rachel off before she could even speak. ", and it was bullshit then and bullshit now. Clark was never going to allow me to prove how much more competent I was than him, and he was never going to allow me the opportunity to get to his status, so I took it myself." He hissed the last sentence. "No government in the world dares to touch me now, I am the most powerful man and I don't even need an army to protect me. I have no fake peace deals to worry about. No secondary and tertiary agendas to adhere to, and none of the daily minutia that bogs down progress." Viale's confidence was growing with every word he spoke. "I am simply a business man."

"You trade in people's lives." Stackwell shot back.

"And it's no fucking different than any President, Prime Minister, King," He stamped his foot, shouting and spitting before narrowing his eyes and rasping. ", or *you*." Fire was the returned look, but no words. "Oh yes, Sophia Warner, Rachel Stackwell, or whatever your name is now, I know who you *really* are. An operative for the CIA, a *killer*, so don't pretend your actions aren't the same. You trade the lives of people for whatever some politician tells you is right or just. I at least give these people life, not death. They get the chance to live a cherished life, often times much better than the ones they left behind." It was the credence that his mentor had taught him to believe many years ago.

There was no response from Rachel. Her eyes simply scanned the floor and focused on the Girsan, but Sean, Lucas, also saw what she found. Cocking his head slightly to the side, the confidence had grown to arrogance. "Is this what you're looking for?" Kicking the gun towards her. "Go ahead, pick it up. You couldn't kill me before and you won't now." Without hesitancy, Rachel grabbed the gun and pointed it towards the man she loved. She didn't fire.

"I did love you, you know," Viale boasted. ", and originally thought about bringing you with me. I dreamt about us living the life we used to talk about, no restrictions because of work, or money, we could have been free."

"Then why didn't you?" The gun drooped, shook and was forced back into a level position. "Ask me to go with you." Rachel tightened her eyes to flush the new tears as she remembered the times they spoke about the future.

"You would've said no." Viale's response was simple and heartfelt. "You would've *had* to say no, the Agency couldn't let you go, and then you would know my truth and I would've been forced to kill you." The voice of a scorned lover.

"So instead you made me believe that you were dead?" It was almost a pleading question.

"My only mistake really." Viale's attitude returned to one of nonchalant. "I underestimated the Russians. I really believed that they would've been able to kill you," He simply shook his head. ", but I guess I can now see why they failed. You, my dear Sophia, are truly a hard one to put down."

"You were right." Rachel's eyes swelled again as her words were barely audible. Lucas Viale smiled before leaning in closer. "Sean Trevelyan is truly dead." Pulling the trigger brought the full onslaught of tears again. She dropped the gun and curled back into a ball as the body of her lover first fell to his knees, eyes staring straight ahead, but without sensation, a hole in his forehead turned deep crimson and he landed face first.

Chapter TWENTY-SIX

Derian leaned back into the cushioned chair while taking in his current surroundings. A pretty, young woman wearing an audio headset instructed him that they would be live in five minutes and he nodded to acknowledge that he had heard her. Across from him was a legend in media circles. Brian Faulkner, a semi-retired seventy-two year old news anchor who the national television broadcaster would still hire for special interviews, like the one he was doing tonight.

Haynes was in awe of the man who he had been fond of ever since he was a child. His mother always made it a point to tell him how great a person Faulkner was, and even remembered meeting him once when he was young. The man was speaking with an assistant director or producer, Derian wasn't sure, as a make-up artist was applying their finishing touches in accordance to the lighting reflecting off the glass countertop between them.

It had been a whirlwind week for Derian once he made it back to the United States. Leading Alyona and Ginny through the estate, he followed the voices. A man and a woman, he knew one had to be Rachel's. Their tones and expressions danced between yelling and sweetness, but he panicked when he heard the gunshot. Ringing throughout the house, Haynes raced into the room where it originated, his own weapon drawn and prepared to fire, but instead he found another body. A man, face first in a pool of his own blood and Rachel, arms wrapped herself and sobbing. He helped all three woman outside.

While Alyona and Ginny searched the villas for the remaining girls, he simply held a grieving Rachel. Derian didn't know what to say so he just remained silent. She was the first to speak. A soft explanation that *it* was over. The dead man was the group's leader, her mission was complete. She called him Sean twice and after a moment of confusion, Derian remembered why the name was important. The man she just killed was the same one that she loved and apparently lost years ago. He held her tighter. He understood what she was feeling. The inner turmoil and guilt for being responsible for a loved one's death, he had blamed himself for his mother's.

The woman with the headset called his name and indicated that they were live in as many seconds as her fingers were showing and counting down.

"Good evening ladies and gentlemen and thank you for joining us tonight. My guest is Washington Post journalist Derian Haynes, and Derian, to say the whole world is watching the White House right now is not an overstatement." Faulkner began the special news report with the most recent claim made by him and his employer. "Today, you revealed documents signifying that the President and First Lady were, and are complicit in the now, very public, and very graphic sex trafficking and exploitation investigation into the late billionaire tycoon Cullen Verger." The man spoke directly and elegantly. "Which is also a global blockbuster you uncovered. As of this broadcast, there has been no official response from the White House, but Turner Jarvis, the President's Chief of Staff has claimed that you are simply heading up a smear campaign, and that you are falsifying documents with the help of his opponents to quote, *steal the White House and democracy from the American people.*"

Haynes smiled and couldn't help but laugh a little. "I don't think I'm alone here, but I feel that *stealing* the freedom and innocence of children is an extremely heinous act."

"Let's talk about that." Faulkner began leading his viewers on the journey towards the facts he just presented. "This all started for you only weeks ago, when as we've all now seen by now the recorded, confession, as you termed it, by the late Senator John Paxton in which he supported your claims of governmental collusion and bribery among other things against his former friend, President Alan Wakefield, and stated he was doing it for his granddaughter Virginia Paxton, who it was reported had been kidnapped just prior." The seasoned interviewer's voice pitched and carefully drew his viewer's in for more. "This almost seems like he specifically chose you to be his amplifier."

"In a way, I guess he did." Haynes agreed. "Obviously my confrontation with the President in Wisconsin has been well documented I'm sure," Another slight chuckle. ", and there certainly wasn't a lot of affection for me from him either, but the Senator ended up being a decent man. A good American, who ended up caught up and corrupt with the way politicians have changed the system nowadays. He was a strong family man that understood he needed to right the wrongs that could and sought me out to see if I was able to help him bring Ginny, his granddaughter home."

"Which you heroically did, I might add."

The conversation drifted to the island in the Maldives. As Derian's mind recalled the time, he also purposely left out everything that had to with Rachel Stackwell. After the initial shock diminished, she was ready to leave. "Where are you going?" Haynes objected.

"I'm going to take his body to the airfield. Neither of us can be here when they get here." Rachel limped two more steps before Derian stopped her.

"What? No, you can't do that." Fear and confusion had set in." Who's coming here?"

"A friend of mine." She was sincere. "I called him before we left the resort. He is a Turkish special police detective, Hakan Köseman, and he should be here by morning with Interpol. He'll be able to get you all back to the United States." Her head movement indicated the approaching woman. Alyona had been able to find the two other girls whom had gone into hiding.

"There's going to be questions." Derian was trying to stand his ground with wounded woman that he admired. "Questions that I cannot answer."

"Don't worry, I'm sure he's not expecting to find any live bodies when he arrives. He knows why I came." Rachel's smile was genuine when she spoke. It was also comforting.

"You could come back with us." Haynes blurted it out Rachel hobbled further away. "Let me tell your story. Let *me* tell your truth. What you did in Prague, what you did here, it will show the world how much of a hero you truly are." He caught up to her and grabbed her by the hand.

Rachel turned with another tear in her eye and kissed him on cheek. "I am no hero." Her smile curved into a friendly smirk. "You got what you came for." Pointing and tapping the leather bag he had slung over his shoulder possessing the ledgers. "Use them to do what you do best Mr. Washington Post. Go be the champion for everybody like them." Her head tilted towards Alyona, Ginny and the two girls.

"If you need help, look up a reporter in Istanbul, Ömer Semiz, tell him *every*thing that happened and he'll be able to help you. He's been doing this for years." Derian wanted to stop her again, force her to stay, but instead stood silent as she disappeared back into the large house. When he did finally decide to go after her, she, the body of the man she called Sean, and the third Land Rover were all gone.

"So after your harrowing tale, yourself, Ginny Paxton and three other women are all rescued by the Maldivian police and Interpol, is that correct." Brian Faulkner took his time with the question as he could tell his guest was reliving an experience.

"Uh, yeah, but it was actually one woman and two more *girls*. We all need to make sure exactly what we're dealing with here." Derian corrected the legendary anchor simply because he wanted the viewers to grasp the true tragedy of the situation. "They were all barely teenagers trafficked by Cullen Verger's sexual syndicate." He chose his explicit words deliberately. After a dramatically chosen second of silence, he continued. "Before heading over to the Maldives, I contacted a journalist friend of mine, Ömer Semiz because I wasn't that familiar with the human trafficking trade. With his help, we were able to work with the Istanbul police, a special investigator, Hakan Köseman and Interpol to set up a game plan. Together, with them and the support of the Maldivians, we conducted an interagency operation on the island. Unfortunately, the men on the island decided to fight back and were killed by the authorities, except for Mr. Verger, who chose suicide instead of arrest." Derian was able to retell the story that the three men had concocted together. They all had agreed to keep Rachel out of the fictional account and only stick to the truth about real people affected.

"Alright, let's talk about Ömer Semiz." Faulkner changed focus once again. "A highly respected journalist who has been writing for years about human trafficking, gangs, cartels and syndicates, but this is even bigger than that." The host listed five names that were all known to the general public, three celebrity actors, one sports athlete and one world leader. "You two are not only taking on governments, but the prestige of Hollywood as well." There was a question in the statement somewhere.

"We see it more as exposing pedophiles and sex traffickers actually." There was a righteousness to his tone now. "These are men, and women, who *were* paying Cullen Verger to set up experiences, many of them in a sexual nature, with people. Sometimes *children* who had all already been trafficked. This is not an American problem, or a European gang, or Russian Mafioso, this is global epidemic that happens millions of times per year." Derian could feel himself beginning to rant and stopped. He wanted to remain composed, but added. "Although, those names you stated is also just the start." He found himself a camera. "If you're seeing this and have done this kind of business with Mr. Verger in the past, you *will* be exposed." With the dramatic break, Faulkner allowed time for a commercial.

Following the pause in the interview, Brian Faulkner returned by talking about Derian's past. Praising his time spent in Syria, the stories he told and time he spent on the ground with what at that time was described as the *enemy*. He highlighted Haynes's journalistic integrity and commended his decision to stick to his moral. "I think your mother would've really been proud of that." An uneasy hesitation between the men was ended by Faulkner's quick thinking. "You probably didn't know that I knew her, did you?"

"We actually met once." Derian collected himself and chided back. "When I was kid."

"I guess that makes me an old man." Both laughed this time. "Now, I only bring this up because, in the past, you've been painted as both an antagonist and a protagonist either by the government or other media outlets, but right now, everybody seems to be regarding you as a hero. I can speak from experience that us as journalists and correspondents aren't always seen as honourable." Faulkner spoke with humor, truth and sincerity this time.

"That's not why I'm doing this." Haynes gritted his teeth behind his smile causing almost a pained expression. He had heard that word, *hero*, used so many times in the past few days. He knew who the true hero was, but she would never allow herself to see it that way. "There's so many people trying to help now, I just hope can put an end to it."

"A modest man, but," The interviewer was serious once more. ", but we keep hearing more and more rumors about an American woman on the island?" No response from Derian was offered, he only swallowed. "Alright, no comment from Mr. Haynes. Virginia Paxton has spoken out, almost pleading for her to come forward because her acts of bravery." An open ended question almost.

"I know Miss Paxton was kept under a heavy dosage of narcotics by her captors, so I think she might be misunderstanding some of what she actually saw." Derian lied, but couldn't help his bashful look of reserve.

"And the Russian woman, Alyona Kasparitis, echoed those words in her deposition to American authorities?" Another leading question was trying to get Derian to tip his hand.

He couldn't help himself from laughing out loud this time. "Maybe a member of the Maldivian police force or an agent from Interpol. I'm know we had women there to help with the girls when the time came."

"So no blonde woman, *running through fire to save everybody*?" Faulkner looked down to his sheet of paper in front of him to read the young girl's quote properly.

"Sounds like a superhero to me." Derian still trying to use the humor to help him through the interrogation. "Maybe something from a comic book or a movie."

"Even if I ask you if you've seen the cellular phone footage taken in Prague a few weeks ago about a blonde, American woman saving two girls from being abducted in broad daylight," He held up his finger to show importance. ", and couple it by saying that the men she attacked there had connections with those that were killed by the police in the Maldives?"

Derian was beaming a stoic smile, but did not answer. Finding his glass of water he simply took a sip. He desperately wanted to tell the truth. Explain to everybody who Rachel was and how she *was* the real hero that the public was waning for to be. Instead, he only readjusted himself in his chair. Trying to find even ground and compose his facial expressions, but he couldn't, he knew how much he admired the woman that would never allow herself to be considered as valiant. "Like I said, sounds like a superhero to me."

Chapter TWENTY-SEVEN

The days were becoming shorter as the hours of daylight dwindled with each passing one in late September. There was a distinct possibility that in a month, Moscow would be covered by the first appearance of a new snowfall. Yegor Vinogradov turned off the engine to his reliable Lada Niva and stared at his dark two-story townhouse. He always felt a kinship with the colder weather, but as he aged, so did his disdain for the icier climate. Now, in his early seventies, the winter months made his bones ache.

As a young man, he would spend hours outside in the snowy weather, training to be part of his country's Olympic team one year. He dreamed of participating in the biathlon, cross-country skiing combined with rifle marksmanship, but he was never quite good enough. Shooting a rifle was never a problem, he was far superior to many that actually were chosen for the team, but he could never quite get his ski sprint times to a strong Olympic level.

Instead, he was selected and placed into the Red Banner Institute, the premier espionage academy run by the KGB over fifty years ago. He quickly excelled in their dynamic programs, was sent to the fabled *Coca-Cola City*, a veiled American made town hidden away in the Ukraine, where he fell in love with his enemy's way of life. After a year in Lomonosov Moscow State University, he was enrolled at Stanford University, where he would continue his *studies*, but ultimately be an agent for the Motherland.

Vinogradov's life in California ended up being uneventful, so upon graduation, he was returned back to Moscow and the KGB found more work for him. He had become very aware of the Westernized customs, and was deployed frequently with foreign ministers and ambassadors, always covertly, and to ensure Russia's best interests.

Twice he had foiled the American's attempts to recruit one of their emissaries, and twice he had put a bullet in their head. His reputation had grown because of dedication to even the point that the current regime at the time lead by Mikhail Taratukhin, requested to meet with him. Vinogradov's status was raised even more. He was appointed the position of Seventh Directorate in the KGB, responsible for the surveillance of Soviet Nationals and foreigners. That position was short lived as with his Undergraduate Program degree from Stanford in economics, he was made the Sixth Directorate and put in charge of counter-intelligence of economics and industry.

Vinogradov found the position stale and boring. He missed his days of action. By luck, he found himself reporting directly to President Taratukhin one day and seized his opportunity to showcase his skills. Yegor's boldness payed off and was promoted to Second Dictorate while continuing his counter-intelligence, but now doing it with political control.

In this new role, the one-time Olympic hopeful was now played a key role in the information that the Russian President made decisions upon. Over the years, Yegor and Mikhail Taratukhin became close friends and it was the latter that insisted he continue as a special advisor to Sergei Radulov, the current Russian President. In recent days, the longstanding consultant had spent more time inside the Kremlin walls than in his own home. Rumblings and rumor of a political challenger to Radulov were forming once again. Another reformation looking to spell his current leadership while promoting their own form of freedom or libertarianism. Vinogradov would find a way to end their budding uprising before it gained too much traction.

Using his smartphone, the aging Russian disconnected the alarm and turned on the lights to his main hall and study. Yegor was not part of the aging generation that did not understand or use technology, he embraced it, so much so, that even the junior technicians employed by the KGB's successor, the FSB, Federal Security Service of the Russian Federation, came to him for advice about products and troubleshoots. He attested it to falling in love with gadgets in Coca-Cola City and his time in the United States.

Within ten minutes, Vinogradov had changed out of his military uniform, found his bottle of premium vodka, made his way into his private alcove and sat comfortably across from his electric fireplace. He chose the soft neoclassic silk winged arm chair instead of the one behind his desk, he would not continue working tonight. The house was dark again after extinguishing the immediate lights. Only the flickering orange and yellow of faux flames danced on the cherry wood walls. Shadows hid the numerous photos he had hanging, but it was the tranquility of the atmosphere that gave him somber to the moment. Placing two vintage faceted shot glasses onto the table, he filled each with the cold clear liquid from the vodka bottle. "If you are here to kill me, at least come and drink with me first so I can see your face." He called out to nobody. Silence. No response. No shuffling of feet or exhales of held breath. "I know you are here." Yegor added while calmly sipping his drink.

"Yet you make no move of defense," An equally composed Russian voice was returned. ", and no call for help or distress signal."

"Would it matter?" Vinogradov croaked. "Please, come and join me." He held the other glass out and waited for a face to match the voice. Yegor's nostrils flared in recognition, but he would not allow the intruder to see his mild disbelief.

"You are not surprised to see me." Rachel Stackwell stepped from the darkened hall, walked through the door frame and took the antiquated Soviet glass. "Did you actually think that *your* people could finish the job?" A slight resentment to her tone.

"*Net.*" The old Russian drank again before pouring both of them another short glassful. "I have not heard from them in almost three days." His demeanor was stale. "I had assumed that they had failed, and that you had already killed them."

"You would assume correctly." Stackwell sneered.

"May I at least ask where their bodies are?" He seemed genuinely concerned.

"Why?" Rachel posed. "Do you now care what happens to your assassins?" She was trying to figure out if the he was stalling her, or if in his matured age, had begun to truly care about the agents.

"No." He had no care for them as people. "I only want to ensure that there will be no connection back to *Mother* Russia."

"That I cannot promise you." Rachel's tone turned brash. "They will be found in Athens with an American, one of Cross's people." Another pause before she added. "I'm sure you know who *he* is."

"Yes." Vinogradov did not mince words or feign recognition, but did show his umbrage when uttering the letters. "The CIA's lapdog for its black ops department."

"And the man that *you* and the Russians are apparently working *for*." She almost spat out the last word. "That connection might look bad."

"*Vozmozhno.*" This time he essentially brushed her words aside. "I doubt anybody will even care about three dead unidentified people. The local police will have questions, but will not find any answers, so they will move on. There is no point looking for people that don't exist. You should know that better than anybody." He smiled and was right. Yegor was sure of the results, yet still agitated about her stating that he was working *for* Cross and the Americans. "Although, you are most certainly mistaken if you think that *I* would ever align myself with the United States C, I, A." Once again disdain as he spoke about the agency.

The flames continued to dance, but there was no crackling of wood or hissing of burning air pockets. Both drank in moment of silence. "What is it that you want Ms. Warner?" Vinogradov offered to pour again as he refilled his own. "If you were simply here to kill me, I would already be dead, and you on your way."

He was right again. Rachel could've easily avoided this whole process, but she did want to know something. "I came to tell you, that *I* was wrong." Stopping and humbling herself with her own statements. "Years ago, I concluded that your government, your President," She corrected herself. ",

Mikhail Taratukhin, that he was the one responsible for backing and financing a terrorist attack that killed somebody very dear to me."

"Prague." The elder interrupted with a hollowed whisper."

"*Da.*" She drank. "Recently, I discovered that it didn't happen that way at all." Rachel remembered Sean's enlightenment. "It was orchestrated to make me think that it was done by your government."

"And why would somebody want to do that?" Vinogradov was genuinely interested. He had heard rumors that there was another story other than the one spun by the Americans about her going rogue, but with them openly hunting her as well, it seemed less likely.

"They predicted the fallout." Her eyes narrowed fiercely, but it was for her thoughts of being played by the man she once loved enduringly. "The parties involved also didn't expect me to survive your retaliation."

"Then they underestimated you." It was a sincere statement. "Should we still be worried about any future designs from these *parties*?"

"*Net.*" This time a wry smile followed as she downed the remaining mouthful of vodka. "They're all dead now."

Vinogradov nodded approvingly as he too finished his drink. "And that brings me back to my original question, what is it that *you* want?"

"I need to know if you, or if your government is still hunting me?" This was Rachel's entire reason for coming to see the old KGB man. He was one of the remaining few that would still be associated to her decade's old history. The former President, Mikhail Taratukhin had died from cancer a couple years ago, and most of his senior administration were no longer affiliated, alive, or had formally retired and out of the military and politics altogether.

"You have been honest with me *devushka*," Vinogradov spoke complimentary. ", and I will return the courtesy. If your name is spoken anywhere within the Ministry, most would now have to ask another about it, or search for it, but it *is* still on our interior ministry database." His tone switched to a formal warning. "I might be one of the last to actually understand your *value* to Russia if you were paraded as captured or killed."

"Even with my admission and acceptance of my own mistakes, to *you*." She did not plead, but was searching for a distinct answer. "Would you be willing to live out the rest of your days without ever seeing or hearing my name again?"

Yegor Vinogradov looked at her with soft eyes, almost like a grandfather might look upon his granddaughter, and spoke with the same easy tone. "Mikhail Taratukhin was my greatest friend, and Pavel like a son to me as well." He sat upright and content with his choice of words. "So Ms. Warner, I will certainly ensure that your name and legacy are a responsibility that every generation of Russians know."

Rachel saw the old man's smile and returned one of her own to him. Both understood the consequence of his words and she did not hesitate to prolong the exchange any further. Pocketing the faceted glass, she withdrew an Udav. The Russian made black 9mm handgun had a suppressor attached to the muzzle. She snapped off three shots, twice to Vinogradov's chest and a final one into his forehead.

Derrick Cross was glad to be home and away from the chaos in Washington. The district had turned into a political nightmare with more scandalous bombshells dropping each and every day. It did not directly affect him as his operations were carried out despite whomever was going to be the newest Senator or Congressperson taken down by the damning evidence that that Washington Post journalist was releasing, but the media outlet was taking its time with the proclamations. Some of it was to obviously vet the information, but he was also sure it was to keep the entire country invested in their stories and to make more money selling newspapers and social media clicks. Derrick scoffed to himself. One massive publication would've been sufficient, shit would've hit the fan, but everybody could've moved on by now, it was Washington, there is always going to be some sort of scandal.

Slinking his way across his darkened kitchen, Cross found the ice cold German beer in his refrigerator that he had been saving for the weekend, but after today, decided he wasn't waiting any longer. He was caught in the crossfire between orders. Garner Housley had arrived to his operations suite earlier that day with orders to have him conduct a mission to stop any more information leaks against the President, at *whatever* costs. When he inquired about the full meaning of the request, he was barked at. *You damn well know exactly what He wants you to do.* The order obviously hadn't originated with Housley, but he was giving it out. Cross had refused at first, proclaiming that those weren't the types of missions his division was running. His refusal only spurred Housley further. The Director of National Intelligence wasn't returning to the White House without his cooperation.

Cross found the newspaper he purchased on his way home and flopped into a soft leather chair across from his oversized wall-mounted television, tugged upwards on his wooden handled opener and took a deep gulp of the cold golden liquid in the green bottle. He couldn't remember the last time that he even looked at an actual physical newsprint, years probably, but now he was searching for a particular article. It was the only stimulating part of Housley's visit, he told him to check today's newspaper, page eight.

After the DNI Director's own threats of exposing Derrick's program, he agreed to the operation that the President wanted to be run. Housley stated only one objective, Derian Haynes was to be removed, and it didn't matter how it was done. Cross demanded written approval and was granted his request. Using the computer in his office, Garner Housley typed, printed and signed a formal request for the mission that was, *hereby authorized by the office of the President of the United States, Alan Wakefield*. Cross had his get of jail free card if the Senate Oversight Committee had ever found out about the mission on American soil against one of its own citizens.

Taking another long sip, Derrick allowed his eyes to wander up towards the bright screen as the play-by-play announcer's voice pitched in mild excitement. His beloved Baltimore Orioles had given up another home run. Cross cursed. The team was tragic again this season, but he was a lifelong fan and still wanted to see them win. Flipping through the first three pages, he knew the piece he searched for wasn't going to be front and center on the page.

After accepting the DNI Director's request, the man seemed to actually relax, told him to look at today's newspaper and left Cross's office relieved with their agreement. Derrick filed the directive away safely, but knew he was never going to carry out the command. It was an order from a lame duck President, the man wasn't going to last the month in office, and Derrick certainly wasn't going to allow any connection between himself with that administration. Heads were going to roll across the board from every department from janitorial to the intelligence community. It would be every man and woman for themselves. Instead, he figured that disobeying the order could actually be beneficial to his personal future. The succeeding President would be a staunch dissentient to the current one's reigning, and they might look favorably upon him for adhering to a conscience with the Constitution and Patriot Act.

Cross smirked to himself. Partly for his decision, but mainly because he found the article he was searching. Bottom corner on the back of the eighth page. The underlined headline indicated a car accident claiming the life of a government employee. He found the key information he wanted. *Metropolitan Police Department announced Wednesday the tragic death of CIA Deputy Director Virginia Bennett, who died of injuries suffered in a violent car crash yesterday near the Southeast Anacostia Freeway interchange. Authorities state the cause of the deadly crash is still under investigation, but the fatal crash is the second accident to occur in the area over the past month.*

Once again Cross smiled to himself. This was not his intention when he expressed to Housley that something had to be done about Bennett, but he also didn't feel badly about the outcome. She had threatened to expose clandestine operations that were vital to the country's security. There had to be consequences. It was his justification.

The small black cellular phone next to him vibrated. It was not his personal device, but the one he usually stored hidden away in his office. Until recently he barely used it, but over the past few weeks, he kept it available to him at all times, waiting for it buzz. There was no name displayed on the screen, but he instantly recognized the numbers from where the call was originating. It was a Russian phone number. It was Yegor Vinogradov. "*Da.*" Cross answered. There was no reply and he repeated himself thinking maybe the connection was had been interrupted. "*Privet. Eto ty, Yegor?*"

"*Net. Yegor mertv.*" The voice answered flatly. There was no remorse in telling him that the Russian was dead.

"Sophia?" Cross sat upright, nearly spilling his beer in the process. He began to sweat.

"Hello Derrick." Her tone was calm. "It's been a while." Rachel added.

"Yes, um, we probably have a few things to, um, talk about." There was concern in Cross's voice as he frantically headed for his gun safe.

"You can relax Derrick, I'm still with your *comrade* here in Moscow." She could hear his heavy breathing and knew he was searching for a weapon, checking his doors and windows, or both. "I haven't made my way to you, *yet.*" She purposely paused before adding the last word.

"But you *will* be coming after me?" It was a question, but one he seemingly didn't truly want the answer.

"That depends on you Derrick." Stackwell was direct and truthful. "Are you still looking for me?" She could feel his relief through the phone. He was actually panicked that she was already in his home.

"You had a bad mission, *unsanctioned* and then disappeared. We still have some questions." Cross had grown bolder again once he felt safer, but also kept his Glock ready.

"You already know *all* the answers." She quipped sharply. "I gave you all the information years ago, and you didn't want anything to do with it." Her newest revelations proved her to be wrong, but she couldn't admit that to Cross, not yet anyways.

"It wasn't verified." He was remembering this exact conversation they had once before. "You know I couldn't authorize any action against the Russians. Your intel wasn't good enough. Your sources of where it came from weren't considered reliable by us." He was right, but she had been hell bent on finding an enemy.

"You could've sanctioned anything." Stackwell hissed. She still held the truth, but also not a lie, he did have that authority. Cross didn't answer. She allowed herself to calm before asking anew. "So I am still beyond salvage?"

This time Cross paused before responding. "That depends on you Sophia." Derrick was trying to take back the direction of their exchange. "You were gone, but now you've reappeared. There must be a reason. Maybe you are trying to get your life back?" Another hesitation before confidently adding. "Why don't you come in and we'll talk."

"I had a life again." Stackwell was dismissive. "One that didn't include you or the agency any longer." She took a second to think about her next choice of words. "I was forced back into the open."

"So then *we'll* talk. You and me. Nobody else." Cross believed he was gaining momentum.

"Your Russian friends are dead Derrick, the ones you sent to *kill* me. Cordovan is dead, and tomorrow you'll read about another American found in Greece. I believe he told me his designation was Crimson. It's over. Interpol will have more questions for the American government I'm sure." Rachel spoke with conviction. She had been setting this up for over a week and gave Hakan and Ömer enough information to uncover the United States clandestine operation. "Red Shimmer is going to be exposed to the world and everybody is going to know exactly who you are."

Cross was speechless. "Then they'll expose you as well." He was grasping and didn't know what to say. "Every mission that you were sent out on, every kill that *you* executed will be born all over again too."

"Yes." There was almost pleasure in her tone now. "They'll find out who Sophia Warner is, Cardinal, but she doesn't truly exist anyway, does she Derrick." Rachel was right. Sophia Warner was another legend, they all were just names, and none of them authentic, but his name was. Derrick Cross was a real person. "I vanished once before and you couldn't find me. I *will* disappear again." There was self-confidence in her voice now and she smiled, knowing Cross understood that she was right.

The former Air Force Colonel looked at the weapon in his hand and thought about the turmoil he left behind earlier today. It was going to get worse, and now it *was* going to include him. Thoughts pulsed through his head, but they were interrupted one last time by the woman on the phone. "Don't worry Derrick, I already removed all of the bullets out of your gun."

EPILOGUE

Prague in November was still her favorite time of year. With a slight limp impeding her pace, Rachel crossed through Křižovnické Square, passing under the Old Town Bridge Tower, and onto Charles Bridge. She could once again feel the emotions flooding from within, but she had specifically chosen today as the day to be back where it all began and ended.

She had nearly timed it all down to the minute. It was colder than nine years ago, and the wind held a stronger bite as the afternoon sun was dipping in behind Petrin Hill, ending another late autumn day. Tightening her thick tan cardigan, Rachel noticed that there seemed to be more tourists and locals on the historic bridge than years ago, but the normal array of street artists, musicians and buskers had currently dwindled. Still, a dark-haired woman knelt on a blanket, head down, and hands upwards, holding a white and orange plastic cup.

Her bare hands trembled in the colder temperatures, but her son and dog next to her, were wrapped in a second blanket and warmer clothing. The crowds passed by her without a second look. Even two police officers patrolled without a care when normally beggars were not tolerated by the local authorities. Rachel stopped. Removing her wool mittens, she dropped a small handful of Czech koruna into the cup and placed the handmade gloves on the ground next to her.

The bowed woman muttered a blessing without looking up, but the motion caught the attention of the boy and the dog. Rachel stood and continued towards her target. The statue of St. John of Nepomuk. The only bronze baroque statue on Charles Bridge, and possibly the most famous depending on what legend one chose to believe. Rachel waited as another group touched the bronze plaque and whispered their wishes or dreams to fabled priest.

The sun had set. Yellow and orange lights filled the picturesque Prague Castle as Rachel stepped up to the towering figure on the ledge. Somehow, many years ago it had not been damaged in the explosion that nearly killed her. She would not touch the plaque, firstly because she did not believe the myth, but more importantly she held no dreams or desires. They had already been fulfilled.

Instead, Rachel looked over the stone barrier and reached into her pocket. Withdrawing a small red velvet box, she opened the front of it one last time and looked at the sparkling silver ring. Smiling to herself, she snapped the case shut and flung it into the Vltava River below. The red box bobbed once under the casual ripples, then a second time, but on the third it disappeared into the cold dark waters.

It was done. There would now only be memories, both good and bad, but she was free. She would choose to remember Sean for who he once was and not whom he became. It was something that she was not capable of doing for herself though. *Don't let your past define you of who you could be.* The words Derian spoke came back as she pushed away from the stone railing and turned away. She still refused to believe him referencing her as a hero, but he was also right. Sophia Warner died nine years ago on Charles Bridge in Prague and Rachel Stackwell died a month ago in a house in Madison, Wisconsin, but another was born. That person, she could shape into whomever she wanted, but first she needed to visit the Christmas Market and buy a hot chocolate.

The woman stood and slowly shuffled away as he wanted to thank her, but the boy dared not speak. He had been cursed and spat at before by foreigners when he tried. He saw his mother thankfully put the warm mittens on her hands and he slowly untangled himself from his blanket and pet. The dog grumbled and whined from the motion, but only reset himself by wrapping his tail around his furry body.

Cautiously observing the woman, she spoke silently either to herself or the saint overlooking her. Reaching into her pocket, she deliberately dropped something, watched it momentarily and then walked back towards him. She smiled and winked, but instead of speaking to her, he ran to where she had just been standing. He saw nothing in the cold, dark river.

The woman's pace was fluid, the limp she possessed seemed to have healed and the boy quickly looked up towards the bronze statue that almost appeared to be smiling himself. The boy shook his head. A swift glance towards the foreigner and then refocusing on the effigy. There was no smile, he was seeing things and he immediately looked towards the woman in the tan coat. She was gone. Running past his mother and dog, the boy raced to the bridge's opening. Nobody. Spinning around in all directions and examining every face, but still he could not find her. *Zjevení?* Mouthing to himself, he wondered if she was an apparition. The woman had vanished.

ACKNOWLEDGEMENTS

My first *Thank You*, will always be for my readers, fans and critics. You allow me the opportunity to continue writing and creating.

My parents continue to be my maintenance and support team. Their passion to read my efforts and tell me when I'm just wrong is a welcoming dose of reality when it is sometimes justly needed.

To entertain through story and imagination is the strongest form of flattery I could receive. To know that a person permit me and gave me the responsibility to guide their escape from reality for a period of time is the powerful aphrodisiac one can experience.

Made in the USA
Middletown, DE
23 August 2022